MR. EMERSON'S WIFE

Amy Belding Brown

AMY BELDING BROWN

Mr. Emerson's Wife

ST. MARTIN'S PRESS ⚓ NEW YORK

www.stmartins.com

Library of Congress Cataloging-in-Publication Data

Brown, Amy Belding.
    Mr. Emerson's wife / by Amy Belding Brown.—1st U.S. ed.
        p. cm.
    ISBN 0-312-33637-3
    EAN 978-0312-33637-0
    1. Emerson, Lidian Jackson, 1802–1892—Fiction. 2. Emerson, Ralph Waldo, 1803–1882—Fiction. 3. Authors' spouses—Fiction. 4. Married women—Fiction. 5. Feminist fiction. 6. Domestic fiction. I. Title.
    PS3552.R6839M7 2005
    813'.54—dc22

                                                                                    2004023940

First Edition: May 2005

10 9 8 7 6 5 4 3 2 1

This book is dedicated to the memory of my father,
Robert French Belding,
1921–1969.

He blessed me with
the passion of intellect,
the magic of story,
the felicity of humor,
and the benediction of unconditional love.

She rose to his requirement, dropped
The playthings of her life
To take the honorable work
Of woman and of wife.

If aught she missed in her new day
Of amplitude, or awe,
Or first prospective, or the gold
In using wore away,

It lay unmentioned, as the sea
Develops pearl, and weed,
But only to himself is known
The fathoms they abide.

—EMILY DICKINSON

PART I

January 1835 – April 1839

Lidian

A woman of well-regulated feelings and an active mind may be
very happy in single life—far happier than she could be made
by a marriage of expediency.

—LYDIA MARIA CHILD

1

Manners

Grace, Beauty, and Caprice
Build this golden portal;
Graceful women, chosen men,
Dazzle every mortal.
—RALPH WALDO EMERSON

Had I known how momentous the evening would be, I would not have tarried at my chamber window that afternoon but busied myself in preparation. As it was, three o'clock found me lifting the curtain to watch a red sleigh drawn by two black chargers skim down the hill to the harbor. The morning's clouds had long since streamed out to sea, leaving blue sky and four inches of new, wet snow blanketing all of Plymouth. The horses cast vaporous balloons to the air and flung up their heads as if intoxicated by the change in weather. Of the storm, only an ashen streak remained on the horizon, lying over the water like a bitter dream. That and the combers breaking in chalky ribbons against the wharf pilings. I let the curtain fall and turned in time to see Sophia bolt past my door in her chemise, dark hair flying.

"Sophia!" Fourteen, nearly grown, yet still wild as a colt, my niece was as much a trial to my sister, Lucy, as I'd been to our mother. With her long, sharp nose and gray eyes, she even resembled me. "Sophia, what sort of be-havior is this?" I crossed to the doorway and regarded her with elaborate solemnity, though I had to master a smile to do so.

Sophia stopped beneath the portrait of my father, which had hung in the same spot since it was painted ten years before his death. Her cheeks were a frenzy of red splotches. She dipped her chin and brought her index fingers together at her waist in a posture that she likely hoped I'd perceive as prop-erly demure.

"Aunt Lydia?" She smiled up at me through long lashes. Practicing, no doubt. Before long, some young man would be the recipient of that look.

I glanced at my father's likeness, to derive strength from the stern line of his mouth, his judging gaze. "If you expect to attend Mr. Emerson's lecture this afternoon, you must comport yourself as a lady," I said. "You are not a wild animal."

Sophia bowed her head, yet I caught the pucker of agitation—of mischief even—upon her young brow.

I stepped into the hall and said after her, "Ladies do not run down hall-ways half-dressed. Ladies walk with elegance and grace. Even when they're in a hurry."

"Yes, Aunt Lydia."

"Show me."

Sophia closed her eyes and took four prim steps.

"No, no. That's not it at all. Look." I walked the length of the hall. My hem sighed over the carpet, my arms swung quietly against my skirts. I knew how it looked—it was plain in Sophia's admiring glance—I was gliding rather than walking. It appeared as if my slippers never touched the floor. It was an effect I'd spent years perfecting. I turned and walked back to her.

"Now you. Lengthen your neck—feel it stretch—and let your body hang from your shoulders. Look, imagine it as a bolt of fabric draped across your bones."

"My *bones*?" My niece made a face.

"Your flesh is a kind of fabric, is it not?" I adjusted my sleeves at the wrist, and saw that a thread had come loose and the hem must soon be mended, a task I did not relish. "It ought to be cared for and worn with grace," I said. "Now you show me you've learned what I taught."

Droplets of perspiration had dampened the tiny curls in front of her ears. I touched one and it wound instantly around my finger. "Show me," I said, dropping my hand to her shoulder and turning her so that I could observe her back as she walked obediently to the head of the stairs, where she turned and came back to me.

I nodded. "Much better. You must practice every day. Do you still stand in the dancing stocks?"

"Sometimes."

"Every day, Sophia. For thirty minutes every day."

She nodded again but would not look at me and I knew her habits would not change. The only thing that could make a girl stand in the stocks was a lively and determined will.

"Surely you won't forbid me the lecture?" Her voice was anxious, ready to plummet toward despair should I deny her. "All Plymouth will be there! Everyone I know is going!"

"We do not attend lectures that we might be *seen*, Sophia," I admonished. "We go to *hear*. I've heard Mr. Emerson speak and I know he's a man of wisdom and intellect. His ideas are forward-thinking, and it behooves us to hear and understand them. But it is not a fashion show." My ears caught the scolding tone of my father's voice in mine, and I stopped. Hadn't I sworn that I would never speak to a child that way? Hadn't I cringed every time my father had bridled me with his hard tongue?

Sophia bent her head again in a posture of penitent resignation, yet I saw that her toes were nearly dancing upon the floor, as if she could not control their expectancy.

I instantly relented, for she reminded me so much of myself. "You may attend as long as you behave like a lady," I said. "Now go and get dressed. We must be at the meetinghouse in an hour."

I HAD CHOSEN my gray silk for the occasion, and had already laid it out on the bed. Though Lucy declared it out of fashion, with its pleated bodice and plain collar, it suited my taste as well as my principles. I'd long since abandoned interest in the whims of society, and settled on a simple and comfortable style without corsets or stays. I regarded simplicity as a virtue, one that encouraged clarity of thought and action.

I took the pins from my hair and let it fall in heavy brown waves to my knees. Even at the age of thirty-three, I enjoyed letting it down, for it never failed to make me feel girlish and unencumbered. As I combed my hair, my gaze drifted around the room, lingering on my bookshelf. Goethe was my current favorite; the cover was already worn from the many times I'd read it since summer, when George Bradford gave it to me in appreciation for my contributions to his philosophy class. I had also read extensively in Swedenborg, the French philosopher on whose work Mr. Emerson was scheduled to speak that afternoon. I was eager to hear what he would say. My aunt Priscilla had lately charged me with Swedenborgian leanings, though I'd retorted smartly that I would never fall under the influence of any one philosopher.

When I heard Mr. Emerson in Boston, I knew he was as great a philosopher as any I'd read. Yet it was not merely his thoughts that impressed me, but his mannerisms, which suggested a distinctive refinement education alone could not produce. He did not move his hands and arms in the great sweeping gestures so common to orators, but stood quite still, allowing his clear voice to persuade the audience. On the few occasions when he did lift his hand for emphasis, the effect was startling and forceful.

The clock on the landing struck four and I came to myself, wondering what Mother would think of me, staring at a pile of books when I had so little time to prepare for the lecture. I could hear her voice in my ear, reminding me that punctuality was a courtesy that married trustworthiness to respect. I gathered my hair, rolled it up onto my head, secured it with combs, and studied the effect in the mirror.

The face I saw there was unmistakably sad. My long chin and milky skin, my deep-set eyes, all hinted at some unnamed sorrow. I'd always believed my features too plain to attract notice, but now I considered that the fault might lie more in this melancholy gaze. I resolved to look more cheerful that evening.

I removed my day gown and took my dress from the bed. The skirt swirled around me with a soft, gray hiss, like the sea upon the shore. Mother had insisted I wear such a dress to my first dance lesson when I was seven. It had been a blue silk gown with a white lace collar. I'd relished the sensation of the cool, slippery fabric against my arms and shoulders, though I did not want to attend the lessons. I believed dancing was one more severe restraint imposed on proper adult ladies. I'd been used to climbing trees and swinging on branches. Yet it was Mother's wish that both Lucy and I master all the womanly arts, and so once each week we walked up North Street to the Town Square. This duty soon became a privilege when my French dance master revealed that he was a distant cousin of Napoleon Bonaparte. I was immediately won over, for Napoleon was my hero.

Monsieur Remy was a small man, only a few inches taller than I, with long, slender hands and auburn hair that fell to his shoulders. He favored bright colors and fine embroidery—though worn at the cuffs and collar, his waistcoats were always the latest fashion. Yet he never smiled. He regarded dancing with the same solemnity that my aunts viewed their Calvinist faith.

I adored him.

He taught me to carry myself like a princess. Each Wednesday morning Lucy and I appeared at his door, where we lifted the knocker shyly and waited for his white-haired housekeeper to grant us entrance. She never spoke to us, never once said our names, but smiled as she nodded us in and led us through the smoky kitchen. My heart never failed to race as I stepped into the cold room where Monsieur Remy waited.

Though it was an empty bedchamber, to me it was a hall. The floorboards gleamed from the scouring of slippered feet. There were no drapes covering the room's three windows, so morning light drenched the walls and floor and expanded the empty room to grand proportions.

Monsieur Remy was always there, standing at the window and looking out to sea, hands tucked neatly into the small of his back. On the first day he looked at me and, in an accent that melted the ends of his words, said, "You must submit each day to the discipline of the stocks. As soon as you start to dance, I will know if you've been faithful."

The stocks were a single block of wood with back-to-back slots for the feet, so that when a dancer stood in them, her legs turned out and the backs of her heels touched. Lucy complained, but I stood in them every day for more than an hour. The pain always began slowly, deep inside my hips— from there it slid down to my knees, which began to throb after ten minutes. Then my calves protested and moments later my ankles as well, until I was encased in pain from the waist down. Yet I never avoided them. I bent my will to their iron discipline, for I loved dancing with all my heart.

I practiced my steps for hours, urging my feet into the complex patterns, positioning my body with the regimen of a military officer, heel just so, toe pointing at that particular angle. Exactly as I was taught. I turned and bent and took small, exquisite leaps. I forced my body into positions it did not want to assume, for dancing required pitting myself against the forces of gravity and air. It was a sort of levitation, a defiance of the laws of nature. Though not—I was certain—the laws of God. No matter what my stern aunts told me, no matter how many times they warned me that I was pirouetting directly over the fires of hell, I knew God wanted me to dance. Why else would I feel so like an angel, as if I'd sprouted strong, white wings lifting me toward heaven?

AT FOUR-THIRTY, Sophia and I stepped over the threshold into the crystalline air of late afternoon. For a moment I stood looking down the hill to the harbor. It was a view that always affected me because it so starkly symbolized the convergence of man and nature in the orderly march of buildings along the various wharves and the unbridled tumult of the ocean beyond. At the moment, the sea was calm, but I knew that the merest flick of God's finger could transform it into a tempest. Mrs. Brig's house had lost a shutter in the morning's storm, and the linden tree at the foot of the hill was leaning precipitously across the road. The brief sun of late afternoon had begun to melt the snow along the roadside, and I heard the trickle of water close by.

Behind me loomed the reassuring bulk of Winslow House, like a mother's skirts protecting and enfolding me. It was where I'd been born and raised, where I'd lived most of my life, save the few years after my parents' death when I boarded with my aunt and uncle. A square-built, wooden house, covered in salt-grayed clapboards, it was handsome in its simple elegance, rising two-and-a-half stories at the end of North Street, on the broad promontory overlooking Plymouth Harbor. Its most notable feature was its double chimneys, which could be seen from Burial Hill, the high ridge where the Pilgrim forefathers lay.

Sophia broke my reverie by taking my arm and begging me to hurry, lest we be late. We walked up North Street and beyond, to Town Square, where we found people streaming into the meetinghouse of the First Parish Church. The building, only recently completed, was made of wood and painted gray to resemble stone. Its centerpiece was the great circular stained-glass window that surmounted the doorway. The Gothic style seemed to be all the rage now, yet I wondered at the impulse that prompted this imitation of the cathedrals of Europe. Were we not a new and democratic nation? Should we not invent our own fashions?

The pews were already crowded—the only available seats being the second-rate ones to the far right of the pulpit. I grasped Sophia's arm and pulled her smoothly past the round knees of Thomas Batchelder, then settled myself quickly on the wooden bench. I was relieved to note that Mr. Emerson had not yet entered the pulpit. I smoothed my skirts and straightened my bonnet, then discreetly signaled Sophia to straighten hers.

A ripple of voices at the back of the room drew my attention, and I turned to see Mr. Emerson walk down the aisle. His brown hair glinted in the lamplight, his face serene and composed. He climbed the steps, his arms at his sides. He was a tall man with an unusually long neck and sloping shoulders, a feature of his anatomy that gave him an air of cultivation and congeniality. I noticed that his dark suit betrayed a genteel poverty in the sheen at the elbows and the fraying threads at his cuffs.

I sat at an unfortunate angle to the pulpit and there were three tall men seated in front of me. I could not see properly without stretching sideways and craning my neck. Mr. Emerson took some folded papers from the pocket of his jacket and laid them on the lectern. In profile, his nose was beaklike and reminded me of an eagle, an image that somehow matched the sharp blue of his eyes. He turned and his gaze swept over the audience and I imagined that they rested momentarily on me. The sensation unsettled me, but left in its wake a not-unpleasant tingle at the nape of my neck.

I refolded my hands—when had they separated and clenched the bench?—and pressed them deep into my lap, then glanced at Sophia, who was again playing with her bonnet strings. I had no time to correct her, for at that moment Mr. Emerson began to speak.

As I listened to his words—and not merely his words, but the music of his voice—I felt a strange constriction of my mind and heart. His voice was melodious and oddly calming—its lyric quality made me think of a summer sea. It was as if his tone exerted a physical pressure in my brain, changing its shape and opening it to new ideas.

His lecture lasted nearly two hours, but I was unaware of the passage of time until he stepped back from the lectern. Then I turned to smile at Sophia and the sudden ache in my neck and shoulders informed me that I'd been frozen in a forward lean throughout the event.

Applause filled the meetinghouse. I clapped until my hands were sore. Mr. Emerson bowed and descended the steps. People rose, preparing to leave, some still applauding as they fastened themselves into their cloaks. There was a great sizzle of skirts and shawls. I saw that Mr. Emerson had been detained by a knot of men, all of whom appeared to be addressing him at once. He listened closely, yet his gaze strayed past their shoulders and, for an instant, met mine.

He smiled and my heart fluttered like a curtain at a newly opened window.

Sophia caught my sleeve. "How does it feel to hear your own words from Mr. Emerson's mouth, Aunt Lydia?"

"My own words?" I turned.

"You've spoken those very thoughts a hundred times!"

I stared at her, and for a moment the sounds around me ceased, or seemed to, as if cotton or water had stoppered my ears.

"I have read and admired Swedenborg," I murmured.

"So has Mama, but she doesn't talk the way you do! You and Mr. Emerson are of one mind!"

Suddenly, I was desperate to be outside where I could draw cold air into my lungs, for they were aching with fiery pressure. I turned toward the door and saw Mary Russell pushing her way through the crowd toward us. Mary, with her elegant neck and fluttering hands, wrapped in her black mourning cloak, had been my friend for twenty years.

"You *are* planning to attend Father's reception for Mr. Emerson tonight, aren't you, Lydia?" Mary touched my sleeve, her hand a clutch of bone and nail sheathed in ivory gloves.

"Of course," I said, though I dreaded the small, hot rooms of the Russell home.

"We are so honored to have Mr. Emerson as our guest!" She leaned toward me, so close the brims of our bonnets rustled. "I believe he may be in the market for a wife," she whispered. "You should have seen the longing on his face at breakfast this morning when he spoke of seeing his newborn nephew!"

I had to smile. Mary was always setting her cap for a husband.

"I cannot believe a man like Mr. Emerson would have difficulty finding a wife should he want one. I suspect he is more intrigued by ideas than by female wiles." I patted Mary's arm, detaching her hand from mine. "Get some rest before the reception. You look weary." I pried Sophia's hands once more from her bonnet strings and quickly made my way out.

AT THE RUSSELL HOUSE, gaslight sconces flanked the door and light swirled from the front windows to pool on the snowy lawn fronting Court Square. Mary's mother welcomed me at the door. I was surprised to find her up; she had spent the past month in bed, daily purged and bled by Dr. Roberts. Her pallor had yellowed alarmingly since her illness and her hand on mine was cold as death. She wore black crepe, in mourning for her youngest daughter, Mercy. As I stepped across the threshold, a suffocating wave of heat assaulted me, caused by the fires and close press of people. Ever since Mercy's death, the house had been kept overwarm, as if the scorching temperatures might discourage further dying.

Mr. Emerson sat in the front parlor, surrounded by admirers. I occasionally glimpsed the crown of his head and heard the gentle timbre of his voice, but could not imagine pushing my way through the tight-pressed bodies to meet him. Instead, I moved freely through the downstairs rooms, enjoying the warm sociability of the event. It was nearly ten and I was on the point of retrieving my cloak when George Bradford detached himself from Mr. Emerson's side and approached me.

"Don't leave. Our guest of honor wants to meet you." He held a glass of port in his right hand. "He asked particularly to be introduced."

"To me?" I searched his face to see if he spoke in jest, but his gaze was direct.

"Have you no desire to meet him? Weren't you impressed with his lecture? I thought certainly his words would move you."

"They did. Most assuredly. But I fail to understand why he would ask for me."

"Lydia, your reputation precedes you. I wrote him weeks ago of the woman in Plymouth whose brilliance of mind challenges his own."

"Surely not."

George bowed so that his face came near mine. "He seeks a woman's companionship and conversation. You'd not deny him those simple pleasures, would you?"

"He does not appear to be lacking them." I smiled at the circle of women who sat attendance on Mr. Emerson. "From what I've observed, he's been enjoying those very pleasures all evening."

George drained the last of his port. "He does not like superficiality. He wants substance in his social discourse."

"As do I."

"You make my point." He placed the glass on a nearby table and took my arm. "Come. The hour grows late and Waldo is waiting."

I SAT IN the yellow wing chair that Mercy had embroidered in flowers and butterflies the summer before she died. I must have looked singular in my unfashionable gown. Singular and no doubt apprehensive, for the smile Mr. Emerson directed at me was so warm it seemed to heat my face. Beneath its force, all my thoughts immediately took wing and left my mind as empty as my drained teacup—an effect that intensified when the other guests mysteriously left the room and I found myself alone with Mr. Emerson.

"George has spoken of you with great admiration," Mr. Emerson said. "My determination to meet the woman whose mind is Plymouth's shining light is in part what brought me here."

I was surprised to find myself blushing. It was not my habit to respond to flattery. "George has misled you," I said. "I'm but a student of his. And a poor one at that."

His expression grew solemn and he inclined his shoulders toward me. "You ought not to succumb to false modesty, Miss Jackson. Not when there are so many who follow the habit of false pride." His smile returned. "Tell me. Do you keep a journal?"

"I do." I thought of the small volume in which I'd jotted my thoughts for three years. "I have for some time. At George's suggestion, in fact. He believes one must examine one's life closely if any mental expansion is to be achieved. I've found it a profitable exercise."

"And satisfying as well, I hope?"

I smiled over my teacup. "There is always satisfaction when the mind is stimulated to higher thoughts. Yet we must look beyond ourselves for instruction. It's our duty to admit our deficiencies and seek the help of friends, is it not?"

He was silent for a moment, and I did not know whether he were pondering my thoughts or composing his own. He studied me intently, as if his eyes could penetrate my skull and read my mind.

"I used to think so," he said finally. "I was convinced I needed instructors, but now I'm wary of attaching too much importance to the counsel of friends. The highest wisdom can only be attained by each soul for itself. Don't you agree that the best teacher is solitude?"

I placed my empty cup on the small marble table beside my chair before I answered. "If by solitude, one means reflection and prayer. An empty solitude confers no wisdom but emptiness itself."

"Well said!" He shifted forward in his chair and I felt a responsive clutch at my throat. It was gratifying to be the recipient of Mr. Emerson's close attention. "Contemplation and inspired meditation teaches each soul its own highest wisdom. And 'tis the truest act of piety to do so. You must trust yourself undividedly. Who but God gives you the faculties of reason and intuition?"

I'd never heard such ideas expressed aloud, though I had thought them myself in secret. This convergence of mind with Mr. Emerson seemed of great consequence. I wanted to hear more.

"But when counting God's gifts, one should not omit friendship," I said. "Is it not our friends who give us spiritual aid in times of doubt and confusion?"

"Exactly!" Again he moved forward so that he sat upon the very rim of his seat. "Spiritual aid is the most precious assistance anyone can offer. Yet how many friends settle for a common round of domestic hospitality and meaningless gifts?" He began to tap his knee with his right hand, though I sensed he was unaware of the gesture. "I hope you will not take offense if I tell you that your ability to express my own thoughts is uncanny. It's as if you had been reading my journals." He paused a moment, his head tipped slightly to one side as he studied me.

The effect was disconcerting. Though his words were laudatory, I nonetheless felt that I was being measured against some impossibly high standard. I tried to compose my mind, to think of an appropriate response, yet he spoke again before I had the chance. "I would like you to read them sometime. Would you consider doing me that honor?"

Some adversarial mischief was in me, for instead of acknowledging the elation that coursed through me at his words, I said saucily, "I'm not in the habit of reading men's journals."

His smile disappeared. "I assure you, it's not my custom to share them. I merely thought you might find an interesting association of our thoughts."

Instantly, I regretted my words. "Forgive me. In truth, I cannot think of a greater honor." I touched his hand where it rested on his knee. It was the slightest contact, a mere brushing of the back of his knuckles with my fingertips, yet a shock raced through me—an electrical current that made the skin on my neck prickle. The expression on his face suggested that he, too, had felt it.

I contrived to change the subject. "How long will you remain with us in Plymouth?"

"I'm bound for Boston in the morning. But"—his smile reappeared—"I return here in a fortnight to lecture again. Perhaps you will attend."

"You may be sure of it," I said. "Have you settled on a topic?"

"Not yet. I've considered sharing some thoughts on marriage." He signaled a passing servant for more tea, a discreet raising of his index and second fingers, and before I could protest, my cup was refilled. "What is your philosophy on the subject?"

I nearly dropped my cup into my lap. It rattled noisily on its saucer.

"I've discomfited you," he said. "Forgive me. I long ago abandoned the custom of dissembling."

I picked up my cup. "Marriage is a complex subject, Mr. Emerson. One that should not be discussed lightly."

"I don't ask the question lightly," he assured me. "Swedenborg, as I'm sure you know, addresses the matter in great detail."

I looked straight into his eyes, to discern if he mocked me, but his gaze was direct. "I'm not a Swedenborgian," I said.

"I didn't imagine that you were, Miss Jackson. The truth is, I sense myself to be in the presence of a singular soul. A woman who is not afraid to follow her own mind wherever it leads. I would enjoy accompanying her." His smile had returned and his gaze seemed to concentrate a strange heat that suffused my face. "Please," he said, lowering his voice and leaning toward me once again. "I didn't mean to embarrass you. I'm genuinely eager for your thoughts."

I glanced into my cup, and felt a dim surprise to find it still filled with tea. For want of something to do while I composed my mind, I raised it and took a small sip.

"I believe marriage is most happily rooted in the principle of balance," I began. "The strength of one party should correspond to the weakness of the other. It's God's design that our closest associations should perfect us."

He regarded me with a curious intensity and, though the effect unsettled me, I went on, for I'd embarked on a subject to which I'd given much thought in the wake of my sister's marital misfortune.

"Each soul has its own relation to the universe," I said. "And the task of discovering that relation is the burden of the individual. Yet in the best relations, another person of a dissimilar nature is present for counsel and correction."

I paused, for Mr. Emerson had begun to frown. "I find your argument paradoxical," he said. "Don't such dissimilarities create conflicts in a marriage? How can discord reflect Divine Will?"

"It's not God's fault if a man and wife abuse his blessings. The true purpose of their dissimilarity is to strengthen and perfect each other, and so they must seek a higher law of marital harmony than is common."

"An intriguing theory," Mr. Emerson said. "If I understand correctly, you propose that the marriage of opposites is an ideal condition—one to be embraced rather than opposed."

I nodded. "It's a practical doctrine. It teaches humility, respect, charity, and patience."

"Yet you must surely admit that, while many people marry their opposites, the quality of relation you suggest is rare." He was smiling again and his eyes seemed very bright, despite the low light.

"Many couples are not truly united," I said. "There is as much misery as happiness to be found in marriage. The union will be strong and happy only as long as love is balanced by principle." I took another sip of tea, but it had gone cold. I placed the cup on the table.

"Then you acknowledge the value of affection," Mr. Emerson said. I thought I detected a hint of mischief in his eye, as if he meant to catch me out in some false or foolish doctrine, but I had seen that look before in the glances of men, and was undaunted.

"Of course I do. Affection is wine to the bread of duty. It's our duty to respect the distinctions of our own natures."

His beneficent smile assured me that I was not caught in any trap of his devising and I felt a pang of remorse for imagining that he meant to lay one. Before me sat—I was now convinced—the most direct and earnest of men. He was unlike any man I'd ever met—worlds away from Lucy's husband, Charles Brown, who had so recently deserted her and his two children, Sophia and Frank, leaving them penniless and unsupported.

Mary appeared suddenly at my elbow and offered another cup of tea. I came to myself, appalled at tarrying so long. I rose, scattering biscuit crumbs from my skirts onto the rose-embroidered carpet. "Mr. Emerson, I apologize for the late hour. I have taken too much of your time."

"On the contrary." He had risen with me and was reaching for my hand. "I feel as if we've just begun our conversation."

"Yes!" I took his hand, or rather let him take mine, which felt small and warm when clasped in his long fingers. "Yes, that is exactly my own feeling!" And then—startled by my reckless confession—I left. No, I fled, for there is no better metaphor than flight for the sensation that overwhelmed me as I stepped out the Russells' door and into the sea-charmed night. I felt as weightless and graceful as a bird.

———

SOPHIA WAS WAITING up for me in the parlor. The fire had died to embers, but she was wrapped in a heavy blanket and perched on the sofa with her legs tucked under her, reminding me of the winter nights I'd endured in Uncle Rossiter's house after Mother died. I'd been determined to model myself after Napoleon, who allowed himself only four hours of sleep each night.

"Why aren't you asleep?" I asked, though I knew it was a foolish question—the answer was written in her eager curiosity.

"Tell me what happened! Did you speak with Mr. Emerson?"

"For a considerable length of time. And stayed too late as a consequence." I removed my cloak and laid it over a chair. "I meant to be in bed early so that I would be fresh to greet your mother and brother when they return tomorrow."

"Mama will understand. You must tell me what Mr. Emerson said. Every word!"

I laughed. "Would you deny me the chance to order my thoughts? Go to bed, Sophia, and I'll tell you all my adventures tomorrow."

I took her hand and together we climbed the stairs to our sleeping chambers. I felt as if I were in a dream, one that delighted and surprised me, one from which I did not want to wake. Despite the cold, I found myself lingering at the window after I took down my hair and put on my nightgown. The half-moon hung over the harbor, casting a silver path across the water. I stood there a long time, watching the frost print leafy fronds on the glass. Thinking of Mr. Emerson's smile.

Visions

Beauty is of very small consequence compared with good principles, good feelings, and good understanding.
—LYDIA MARIA CHILD

Just after eleven the next morning, the driver of Lucy's rented carriage reined the horses to a stop at the front door, and I ran down the steps to welcome my sister home. Frank scrambled out of the carriage first and dashed across the snowy lawn before I could catch him. His five-year-old body was as sturdy as his father's and his bristle of brown hair reminded me of my brother's at that age.

Lucy looked weary as she stepped from the carriage and paid the driver. I embraced her, pressing my warm cheek to her cold one, before urging her into the house.

"Was your visit taxing?" I asked, responding to the dullness in her brown eyes. She had spent a week at the home of her in-laws.

"Only to my heart." She removed her bonnet and set it wearily on the table by the door. "I believe poor Mrs. Brown suffers more than I. Not one day went by but she wept. She feels a monstrous guilt on Charles's behalf."

She peeled off her gloves and glanced out the window in time to see Frank dive into the snowbank beneath the eaves. "Will he never obey me?" She sighed heavily. "I told him to come inside immediately."

"I'll send Anna to bring him in." I guided Lucy into the parlor and settled her in the big chair by the fire.

Though Lucy was four years older than I, the death of our parents in 1818 had struck her the harsher blow. I had taken on the role of elder sister to both her and our younger brother, Charles Thomas. When Lucy married Charles Brown just two years later, I rejoiced, though I never cared for the man she chose. He had always seemed a shallow sort to me—boisterous and good-humored in the company of friends, but dour and domineering when at home. From the first I wondered what Lucy saw in him and it was only after his desertion that it occurred to me that perhaps she was simply desperate to escape the iron influence of our aunts. She had accepted the first proposal offered and, though she tried to convince me that she was in love with Charles, I doubted her attachment from the start. Lucy was always more womanly in both her nature and manner than I. Perhaps she did not trust that she could weather the storms of the world without a man's arm to lean on. For myself, I was content with my single state, and wanted nothing more than to continue my life exactly as it was.

I hastened down the hall and into the kitchen, where I found Hitty, our kitchen maid, scrubbing pots at the sink. I asked her to set out a tray of tea and cakes in the parlor, then went to fetch Anna and send her after Frank. Anna was our maid of all work and one of the two servants we now had the means to employ. I'd briefly considered teaching in order to supplement our income, but Lucy refused to allow it. "It's bad enough that my husband was the instrument by which you lost your fortune," she said. "I couldn't bear it if you had to sell yourself as well as the furniture."

"Teaching is not selling myself," I'd replied. "And we've only sold three pieces."

"Still, I'll sell every stick before I see you forced to earning wages like a common laborer."

"Honest work is nothing to be ashamed of."

"Not in the eyes of God, perhaps. But in the eyes of Plymouth, common labor is not something Cottons do with pride."

"But we're Jacksons." I gave her an impish smile. "And Jacksons do what they can for money."

"Our mother was a Cotton," Lucy said solemnly, ignoring my badinage. "You are as familiar with that responsibility as I am."

"John Cotton has been in his grave for generations. He may have been a great man in his day, but we are in a new age." She could not dispute that, nor did she try. The Revolution had changed the very structure of society—titles and class divisions were gone, and so were the overbearing Puritan clerics. What mattered now was an individual's nobility and character, not his name.

I did not seek an immediate position for there was much to do at home. I had housework and gardening to tend to as well as cooking and sitting watch with the sick in our neighborhood. The greatest satisfaction of my week was leading the Bible class of young women who gathered in our parlor each Sunday evening. Yet I did not entirely dismiss the thought of teaching. Experience and observation had taught me that circumstances sometimes forced one to unfamiliar measures.

When I returned to the parlor, Sophia was there, her arms wrapped securely around her mother's neck as she covered Lucy's cheek with kisses.

"Sophia, for goodness' sake!" I cried. "Have you forgotten your manners in one short week?"

"Your aunt is right." Lucy gave her daughter a kiss and detached herself. "Now sit down here and tell me what you've accomplished while I was away. Did you finish the hem on your dress?"

"Almost." Sophia dropped gracelessly to the carpet. "I went to Nelly's party on Wednesday and wrote three letters on Thursday and yesterday I attended Mr. Emerson's lecture." She rose on her knees. "You must make Aunt Lydia tell us of her conversation with him, Mama!" she cried. "She had a private audience with Mr. Emerson!"

Lucy withdrew her gaze from her daughter to focus on me. "Is this true, Liddy?"

"It is." I could not prevent the smile that widened my mouth as I watched astonishment transform her face.

"What great fortune! You must tell me every detail!"

"And me, too!" Sophia cried, bounding again to her feet. "You promised!"

I spent the next hour relating my experience at the Russells' reception. Though it seemed a poor sort of adventure, it rendered Lucy and Sophia silent throughout the telling.

"He comes to lecture again in two weeks," I said. "If there is another reception for him, you must attend, Lucy."

Lucy's eyes sparkled. "If you will promise to introduce me."

"I doubt that he will remember me." I laughed. "I was but one of hundreds of admirers. Most of them female."

"He will not have forgotten you." Lucy was suddenly solemn. "Whether you know it or not, Liddy, you are the most memorable of women."

"Any distinction I possess is due entirely to God's grace and my peculiar baptism." I smiled again, knowing that I had trumped her flattery with the plain truth.

I WAS SIXTEEN on that cold October morning of my baptism. Our mother had been on her deathbed for a week. She lay in her upstairs chamber with its tight-shut windows and heavy green drapes, her face flushed pink with fever, her poor chest and rising and falling as she drew in long clattering breaths and slowly released them.

She had been afflicted for ten years, and I don't know how she comprehended that her release was finally at hand. Yet just after the noon bell tolled, she pushed herself off her blood-flecked pillows and bid me fetch Dr. Kendall.

"I want to join the church," she said, in the voice that had grown so abraded by hemorrhage that it was no longer familiar.

"The church?" At first I thought her fever had spiked again and she was delirious. Mother had never expressed a desire to join the church—she had withstood the relentless badgering of my aunts all her life.

"Mother, lie down." I placed my hands on her thin shoulders and pressed her back into her pillows. "Let me get you some water."

"No!" She pushed me away with unnatural strength. "Send for Dr. Kendall at once!" She stopped as a gurgle surfaced from her ruined lungs. She began to cough and fell back onto the pillows, pressing her handkerchief to her lips. I watched her chest wrench up and down in long spasms. When the paroxysm finally subsided, I took the blood-soaked handkerchief from her and pressed a fresh one into her hand.

"And I want you baptized," she said. "I want you all baptized before I die."

"Mother, you must rest." But she would not listen. An uncommon urgency had overtaken her and she refused to lie still until I fetched the minister.

It was a long, cold walk. A northeast wind bore down on Plymouth, spitting snow. The houses were charcoal in the gray light and they appeared to lean wearily against one another. When I reached the two-story brick parsonage, a maid let me in and showed me to the pastor's study, a dark room even on the brightest day, for he always kept the shutters closed. "Against the distractions of the world," he said. My aunts often commented on the extravagance of this practice, since it required burning a lamp constantly so that he could see to read and write. Yet I sympathized with his attraction to low light. My own eyes were sensitive to brightness, and I shrank from naked sunlight.

The study was lined from floor to ceiling with bookshelves. I stood gazing at them, awed by the concentration of so much wisdom in one place. I longed to take down a volume, but Dr. Kendall had risen from his chair and was glaring at me behind his spectacles. His hair, which he still wore in an unfashionable queue, was disheveled.

"I apologize for disturbing you, but my mother insists on joining the church. I don't know why, now—"

He stopped my words with a shake of his head. The gray queue bounced upon his shoulder. "It is not ours to question the Lord's work. Give me a moment to ready myself, child."

I watched him pack his Bible and communion effects into a small leather bag. Then he pulled on his coat and hurried past me out the door. I had to race to keep up with him. When we reached Winslow House, he strode straight through the front door and up the stairs, directly to my mother's chamber in the southeast corner.

Lucy had combed Mother's hair and tied a fresh cap on her head, but the pillows were freshly stained, and the room bore the too-familiar scent of blood.

Dr. Kendall opened his bag and placed his utensils on the small table by the bed, all the while questioning Mother about her knowledge of Christ. She could barely whisper out her answers, but they seemed to satisfy him, for he soon read the liturgy that united her to the church. He then administered the Lord's Supper with great tenderness—almost as if she were a young child. When she choked on the wine, he bent and wiped her mouth, assuring her that the sacrament was no less efficacious for the weakness of her flesh.

Mother then told him that she wanted us baptized, and so Lucy and Charles and I waited at the foot of her bed while the housemaid went to fetch a pitcher of water. I stood nearest the window, where I could watch the sky darken over the harbor and feel the long spindles of wind slip through the crack beneath the sill. Red and brown leaves rattled on the trees on Cole's Hill—leaves the color of blood.

I became aware of an icy darkness within as Dr. Kendall walked over to me and raised Mother's silver pitcher above my head. I looked up briefly at the curved, bright belly of the pitcher, and before I could say a word, he had tipped it and I felt the cold shock of the water on my crown as he baptized me Lucy Cotton Jackson.

"But I'm Lydia!" My hands flew to my dripping hair.

I heard Mother gasp, though I didn't know if it was reaction to the error or the exhalation of her consumptive lungs.

Dr. Kendall frowned. "You're not the eldest?"

I shook my head and pointed to my sister. "*She's* Lucy."

"I assumed because you were taller—" His frown settled deeper into his stern face. "We must begin again." He turned to Lucy. "In order of age."

And so I was baptized a second time by my own name, Lydia Jackson. I stood with my back to the window, water dribbling from my hair onto the floor in such quantity that it formed a puddle. As I listened to Dr. Kendall intone yet another prayer, I was struck by a thought so disquieting that I clapped my hand over my mouth to avoid crying out.

I was double-bound to Christ.

The next day Mother sank rapidly toward death and by afternoon she had settled into a stupor, from which she roused only to cough up bloody flows or call for water. My aunts came and said their farewells while Lucy and I took turns sitting watch. It had been spitting snow all day with no sign of sun. By nightfall the snow had changed to a freezing rain that lashed the windows. Around nine o'clock, on my watch, Mother began to shiver so violently her teeth chattered. I piled more blankets over her, poked up the fire, and massaged her icy hands, but she did not respond. Again I went to the fire and added more wood, and as I passed the window on my way back to her side, I glanced out at the street below, where the light of a lamp cast a jaundiced glow across the frozen troughs of mud. Rain slatted past the glass in sheets, yet I longed to be outside, free of the confines of the stuffy death chamber.

Mother's groan called me back to the bedside. I lifted her and pressed a cloth to her mouth as she began to cough. The fabric was instantly saturated in blood. I dropped it into the bucket beside the chair and crushed another against her lips. When she finally ceased coughing, I eased her back onto the pillows and wiped her face. I was surprised that the spasm had not woken her—she remained insensible throughout. The rusty odor of her blood filled my nostrils. I sat in the chair and again smoothed her hair away from her cold cheeks. Her face no longer held the chaotic flush that she'd carried for so many years. Her skin had assumed the pallor of snow.

I sat, measuring time by her sodden, labored breaths. Her drowning lungs seemed to me like a great bellows, pumping steadily toward death. Just after midnight, she opened her eyes once and looked at me.

"The Scriptures, Lydia," she whispered, "they've been flowing through me like the sweetest wine."

She spoke no more after that. I offered what comfort I could—a wet towel, a prayer, my hand—but Mother had crossed to a place I could not follow. There was nothing for me to do but stay awake and alert.

I felt no sorrow. All I knew was a great, encompassing fatigue. Dawn began to gray the edges of the windows when I sagged dizzily upon the bed. I thought—*I'll just close my eyes for one minute.*

I woke to the sound of voices and pushed myself upright. It was morning and the room was filled with women, their voices muted but hard. My aunt Joa stood on the other side of the bed, braiding Mother's hair. She looked at me.

"The end came while you slept," she said.

I felt the spear of her condemnation. Guilt, like a great black dog, strode into my heart and took up residence there. Is it any wonder that when I heard Mother's voice on a hot June afternoon in my twenty-third year, I fled directly to Christ? I joined the church in the throes of a religious passion so fierce no human emotion could have offered competition.

MR. EMERSON'S SECOND LECTURE was on a Sunday evening, so there would be no reception. Lucy, Sophia, and I all attended the lecture; for once, I managed to arrive at the appointed hour, and with time to spare.

We sat in the fourth pew back from the front, a situation that afforded an excellent view of Mr. Emerson as he held forth on the Quaker leader, George Fox. He wore the same suit as before, and his hands moved in the same graceful gestures. Though his voice was hoarse and roughened—the effect, I believed, of too much oratory—still his words were filled with barely tamed passion, and I had the sense that he was courting the entire audience. "Love and religion are the remedial forces by which the degeneracy of the human race is hindered," he said. "The Inner Light directed Fox as surely as it addresses us. It is the most republican principle, and it is the source of all modern, democratic ideals."

I was relieved when, midway through the speech, Horace Billington brought forward a pitcher of water and a glass for Mr. Emerson's use.

I found this second lecture as moving as the first, though I'd read nothing by Mr. Fox. Yet Mr. Emerson brought Fox to life by modulating his voice and using his eyes to kindle an ardent light in the audience, the way a focused sunbeam can kindle fire in a pile of leaves. His arms hung easily at his sides throughout, except for three occasions, when he used his hands to great effect. Yet, even when they did not move, I sensed a great vitality and strength in his hands—and I shocked myself by remembering what my own hand had felt like clasped in his.

The heat of the close-pressed bodies and the heat of my mind combined to make me long for fresh air. As soon as the lecture ended, I excused myself, assuring Lucy and Sophia that I would make my own way home. I squeezed through the clots of excited townspeople and left through a side door.

Outside snow had started to fall in large, wet disks. I pulled up my hood and walked behind the meetinghouse, taking great swallows of icy air. On my right loomed Burial Hill, where the remains of the Pilgrims lay entombed. Stones slanted black against the indigo clouds.

I was startled by the sound of footsteps, and turned to see a tall figure approach. I could not make out the features and felt a momentary stab of fear. Though most people in Plymouth were trustworthy, there was the occasional miscreant intent on robbery. The thought flashed through my mind that I should flee, but before I could put my feet in motion, Mr. Emerson's voice cut through the falling snow.

"Miss Jackson? I saw you slip out the door and was afraid you had left. You're not ill, are you?" He came closer. I could see his face—the kind smile, the jutting nose.

"No." I shook my head and smiled back, though I doubted he could see my face beneath my hood. "I just wanted some fresh air. It's so close inside. It muddles my thoughts."

He nodded. "I, too, find that the outdoors helps to focus my mind." His right hand, which had hung at his side, moved in front of him. "You have not forgotten your promise to continue our conversation, I hope?" He extended his hand and took mine before I realized his intent. "I would very much enjoy hearing your thoughts."

"On George Fox?" I looked into his eyes. In the glow from the meeting-house windows they appeared suffused with tender interest.

"On any subject."

For a moment my mind was empty. I stood staring at him like a bewitched schoolgirl while the snow fell around us. I was aware only of the way his hand curled around my fingers, of the faint odor of damp wool emanating from his coat. Then, mercifully, words came to me, spilling into my brain as if God Himself placed them there for my use.

"I have a few questions," I said, finally withdrawing my hand, "on a matter of great concern."

He smiled. "Please ask them."

"I would enjoy hearing your opinion on the abolition of slavery. The Quakers have been advocating it for generations."

Was it my imagination, or had I taken Mr. Emerson by surprise? If so, it lasted no more than a moment. "I'm not a Quaker," he said.

"Yet surely you've considered the question." I was eager to press him on the subject. "Don't you agree it is the great moral challenge of our age?"

He smiled—that warm, attentive smile that I'd dreamed of all week long—and I thought: *I would give a good deal to see that smile each morning.* The notion shocked me and I quickly swept it from my mind, as a maid sweeps dirt from the back steps.

"I agree it's one of many issues we must discuss," he said. "I favor the American Colonization Society approach—one that would gradually emancipate the slaves and send free blacks as colonists to Africa."

"But gradual emancipation requires that we tolerate an intolerable condition!"

"Slavery is the unfortunate result of a flawed economic and social system," he said. "There's no question of that. But emancipation must be efficacious and orderly. The alternative is chaos."

Too agitated to remain standing, I began to walk. Mr. Emerson fell into step beside me. "Slavery is a sin!" I insisted. "One that implicates all Americans! There are no acceptable half-measures!"

"Full measures do little good if they don't effect the desired end."

"True," I said. "But surely you agree that it's an issue of the highest moral concern! One that tests a man's nobility and character."

"All issues test character," he said. "And I believe a high character is the noblest achievement of anyone, male or female."

I turned to look at him, startled by his inclusion of my sex. "Then we are in agreement!" I impulsively put my hand upon his arm. It seemed a natural gesture and he treated it as such, yet I was aware of a tingling sensation at the point of contact, a sensation that spread throughout my body.

"It's our task to discover and pursue the will of God, and to live in accord with the highest principles He reveals." I noticed that we were walking along North Street. I had been unthinkingly leading Mr. Emerson toward Winslow House. Yet I did not want to go in yet, so we passed and continued down the hill to the waterfront. I was exhilarated by the conversation. Despite our disagreement, we were clearly of one mind in our desire to freely share our thoughts with each other.

The sea was pulsing with stiff-chopped waves and the wind came up as we walked along the wharves, at one point whisking off my hood and tearing at my heavy knot of hair. The snow still fell, swirling in elegant braids around our faces, but I don't think either of us noticed. It was the words, the sheer pleasure of the debate, which held our interest.

"You stir my mind, Miss Jackson," Mr. Emerson said, stopping beneath a streetlamp and turning to face me. Beyond his shoulder, the jumbled buildings on the wharves made thick shadows against the night sky. The snowflakes caught the light and for a moment it appeared to me as if a hundred tiny candles flickered over the water. He released my arm and took both my hands in his. "Your words challenge and enchant me. I feel as if I'm in the presence of a sibyl of wisdom."

I wanted to laugh, but my fluttering heart would not permit frivolity. I was acutely aware of the warmth and pressure of his hands through my gloves.

"You are too kind," I said. "Yet surely you've heard thoughtful words from women before tonight. Or are you unaccustomed to hearing women express their opinions?"

"On the contrary. All my life I've been acquainted with women whose brilliance eclipses my own."

"I find that hard to credit."

"You haven't met my aunt Mary," he said. "Miss Jackson—" He stepped closer. "Will you permit me to call you Lydia?"

"If you wish." I wondered if he could hear the thudding of my heart over the sound of the sea. "Though I'm usually called Liddy by my friends."

He frowned—the slightest crease of his forehead, his eyebrows tugging together briefly. "Liddy is a common name for a remarkably uncommon woman."

I withdrew my hands, frightened by the sudden weakness that coursed through my limbs. "I should go home," I said. "My sister will be wondering what has become of me."

He gave a slight bow. "Forgive me. I've ignored the hour. You must be chilled."

Although I didn't contradict him, I was not at all cold. Rather, my entire body was suffused with an unfamiliar heat. Despite my stated concern for my sister, I was reluctant to part from him. Yet I expressed none of these disordered feelings, but allowed him to escort me back up the hill to Winslow House.

My frightened sister met me at the door. She grabbed my shoulders with both hands and pulled me inside as if the snowy night imperiled my life. It was only when I pulled away and turned back to the open doorway to thank Mr. Emerson that she realized I was not alone.

"Mr. Emerson!" she cried, both hands to her face, her eyes gone wide at her own blunder. "Come in! Come in! Please, come in!"

It was nearly midnight and I was certain that he was expected elsewhere. Yet the words of invitation were no sooner out of Lucy's mouth than Mr. Emerson stepped across our threshold and into our parlor. Lucy, of course, did not ply me in his presence with the many questions she longed to ask, but stoked up the fire and sat in her chair while we continued our conversation as easily and naturally as if we had never ceased talking. It was nearly one in the morning when Mr. Emerson took out his pocket watch and marked the lateness of the hour. Still, he took his leave in a leisurely manner, thanking me for the pleasure of our conversation and declaring that he hoped we would soon meet again.

As I closed the door behind him, I leaned my forehead against it.

"Oh, Liddy!" I heard Lucy whisper behind me. "I think he *admires* you!"

"Admires me?" I turned to face her. Her eyes were shining with excitement. "Please—I hope you aren't suggesting he's formed a romantic attachment."

"I know what I witnessed. Here, in our own parlor."

"A conversation, Lucy," I said, moving past her toward the stairs. "You witnessed a conversation. One that has fatigued me. I'm going to bed."

THE SNOW CONTINUED to fall all night and by morning there was a two-foot drift against our front door. I stood at the window and counted the ship masts in the harbor. I wondered if the weather would delay Mr. Emerson's departure, then abruptly dismissed the question. It was none of my concern. And, in any case, it was Monday and there was work to be done.

I spent the morning in a frenzy of housecleaning, rousting dust and cobwebs from the corners of each downstairs room, polishing the fireplace andirons and what remained of Mother's silver, dusting and waxing and buffing until everything shone. Sophia worked by my side, chattering about all manner of things, while Lucy went to market and supervised dinner preparations. I even pressed Frank into service and he was soon loading the wood box and sweeping the ashes from the fireplaces. When we finally gathered around the dining table at one, we were all too weary to enjoy the fish and fresh brown bread.

Despite my morning's labors, I had little appetite. Thoughts of Mr. Emerson continued to fill my mind. After dinner, I ascended the stairs to retire to my chamber where I hoped to better order my thoughts. My mind was full—too full—and wanted purging. This penchant for thinking to the point of exhaustion was a trait I'd inherited from my father, along with an unfortunate tendency to dyspepsia. The only cure I found was solitude and prayer.

As I reached the landing where the looking glass hung, I reflexively started to turn from it—recalling, as I always did, Mother's admonition against preening—when something in the glass caused me to stop in midstep and stare. Though it was my own form I saw there, I was not wearing my brown housedress, but a fashionable white gown with large, puffed sleeves. My hair was twined with flowers. I looked like a bride. The realization stabbed, yet even as I sought to blink it out of existence, I noticed that my form in the mirror was not alone, but was attended by a tall man in formal dress. A man who resembled Mr. Emerson.

"No!" I cried out, dashing my hands against my eyes, for I didn't believe the vision could be mine. Some dark enchantment was at work. I blinked again and saw the image fade. Relieved, I ran to my room and threw myself on my bed.

I was ashamed of the vision. Mr. Emerson was surely everything that was noble and true and good that a woman might seek in a husband, but I had no desire to alter my single state.

Did I? Did the vision indicate that I harbored secrets from my very *self*?

The thought was absurd. I tried to convince myself it was a delirium of fatigue—I'd spent the morning in frantic activity, and had gone late to bed the night before. Yet I did not sleep, but lay staring at the swirls of plaster in the ceiling. I finally sought reassurance in prayer, begging God's guidance. I received no relief from my distress. The vision lay seared in my mind like a brand upon the flesh of a slave.

WHEN I FINALLY SLEPT that night I dreamed of my father. He sat at the head of the table in the dining room, just as he had at every meal until his death. Except there was no food on the table—only the crisp white cloth and one crystal goblet of water. He lifted the glass and took a sip, then slowly set it down and fixed me in his gaze. "It is time you learned to keep a house of your own," he said. "I want you to master the skills of a wife."

I was standing at the far end of the table. "I have no interest," I said. "I'm not well-suited to the role."

He rose, frowning. He seemed to take up all the space in the room. "Lydia, you have a rebellious and difficult nature. You must labor to subdue it."

"I don't want a husband who is not pleased by my nature."

"You have a reckless tongue. It wants harnessing."

I woke suddenly, gasping in the darkness as the dream dissolved into a terrible memory of my fifteenth summer.

It was night and I was in my chamber. I heard a heavy tread outside my door, then a thud and the door sprang open.

"Lydia, I have been betrayed again." My father swayed into the room and sat on my bed.

"Papa, you should not be here." I'd been sitting in my nightshift at the window, but rose when he entered, and stood, pinching my fingers together, while he listed back and forth on the bed.

"Don't cast me off, Daughter." He fell back onto the mattress and closed his eyes.

"You mustn't sleep here." I tried to pull him upright, but he did not respond. "Papa, please! You must go to your own chamber!"

His eyelids fluttered. "*You* understand my nature, Liddy. You and I are the same."

"You must go! Mother's waiting for you."

He waved one hand dismissively. "She's not waiting for me. She's waiting for death." His eyes popped open. He reached up suddenly and, grasping my shoulders, drew me down on top of him.

I tried to rise, but his fingers grew as hard as manacles. Terrified, I began to struggle. He grunted and rolled over, pinning me beneath him.

"I'm a man." His words were gelatinous and garbled, as if a thick wad of wet cotton had jammed in his throat. "With a man's needs. And she's not been a wife to me for eight years now."

I squeezed my eyes shut and put my hands over my ears, but he pulled them away and pinned them beneath my back. A cloud of rum spilled from his mouth and covered me like a shroud.

"Look at me, Liddy. Look at your papa who loves you." His voice had changed to a thin whine and sounded as if he were close to weeping. He shifted, and his hand pressed my breast, then moved down my body to rest on my thigh. Its weight burned through my shift.

I understood in some dim way that his caress was not intended for me, but for my mother. Mother, who was no longer available to him as a wife. Mother—whose illness kept her pure.

I gave a sudden great thrust with my legs, and he rolled off me with a groan. I leaped from the bed, trembling with terror and disgust, but something held me long enough to watch him thrash and clutch himself. He peered at me with rheumy eyes and let out another moan.

"Go to your own bed!" My voice was a hiss I didn't recognize. "I feel no pity for you. Nor ever will."

I fled to Lucy's room then, where I crawled into bed beside her, and for the rest of the night lay restlessly turning. By morning I had a fever and Lucy was easily convinced that I'd left my own bed in search of warmth.

I kept to my chamber for a week, less out of illness than mortification. But when I finally faced Father over Sunday dinner, he displayed his customary dyspepsia and grumbled that I did not look as if I'd been ill enough to shun housework. I realized that he had no memory of the incident between us. His drunkenness had protected him from a proper shame.

When he died of a fever the next August, I could manufacture no tears to mourn his passing. Yet the smell of his breath hibernated in my nostrils for years, stimulated to wakeful anxiety whenever I caught the scent of rum.

I CAUGHT THAT SMELL on the cold Wednesday morning a few days after Mr. Emerson's lecture, as Sophia and I entered the butcher's shop. I took special care to notice that Mr. Fagan properly filled my order and that the mutton and beef cuts I purchased were fairly weighed. As we left the butcher's, Sophia began fretting over her boots, which she claimed had grown too small. I was listening with only half my attention when we encountered Sarah Kendall coming out of the milliner's shop. She wore a green bonnet in a flounced style I had never seen before. Though she was the minister's daughter, she had always been excited by the latest fashion. Before I'd finished complimenting her, she began to talk about Mr. Emerson.

"I hear he considered staying another night in Plymouth," she said. "But the coaches were running and he left in midafternoon. Greatly excited, from what I'm told."

"Excited?" I said. "Where did you hear this?"

"I saw Mary Russell in the dry goods shop just a few moments ago. She was glowing." Sarah reached up to secure a bonnet ribbon that the wind threatened to remove. "I believe Mary has formed an attachment to Mr. Emerson," she said, smiling. "She's convinced he wants to marry, and I believe she hopes he'll settle on her."

"She mentioned this to me after his first lecture," I said. "I hope she won't be disappointed." I spoke the words sincerely, for Mary had been thrown over by a young man from Cambridge just the year before. "I think Mr. Emerson would be a good match for any woman. He has a fine mind and a great career before him."

Sophia hugged herself and began shivering so violently that I excused us and took her to the bakery, where I allowed her to select a loaf of currant bread as reward for her patience.

That week brought its usual round of work and engagements. On Thursday I attended the Anti-Slavery Society meeting and on Saturday, George Bradford's philosophy class. The discussion focused on Mr. Emerson's two lectures, yet I found myself with uncommonly little to say. It was as if my tongue had vanished from my head and I could only listen to what others said. George gave me a quizzical look as I passed him on the way out and was about to speak, when Ann Carter approached and diverted his attention. I was relieved that he had not been afforded the opportunity to question me privately, for I have no doubt that I would have stumbled over my own words.

That evening I experienced another unsettling visitation. I was seated at my desk in my chamber, recording the day's thoughts and events in my journal. The south-facing window was cracked open to relieve the heat from the fireplace and an occasional gust of frigid air disturbed the curtains. It was during one of these gusts that I looked up at the window and saw Mr. Emerson's face. He was smiling and his eyes were tenderly searching me. The effect was disquieting and exciting at the same time. I put down my pen and touched my forehead. The image faded at once, and I felt relieved, though I continued to puzzle over its meaning. But I could make no sense of it at all.

3

Proposals

I please myself with contemplating the felicity
of my present situation—may it last!
—RALPH WALDO EMERSON

On Monday morning Anna brought me a letter. I was in
the dining room, sorting sheets for mending. When she
came into the room, I did not at first pay attention to her.

She coughed. "This just arrived from Concord, Miss Lydia," she said.

"Concord?" I put aside the sheet and took the letter, turning it in my
hand. It was of fine paper, the address written in a strong hand. "I don't
know anyone in Concord."

"I paid the man and gave him coffee. He seemed weary from his
ride."

"That was kind," I smiled at her. "Offer him some pie, as well. And perhaps you'd be so kind as to bring me a cup of tea."

Anna reluctantly retreated as I broke the seal and unfolded the
letter.

Concord 24 January 1835

To Miss Lydia Jackson

I obey my highest impulses in declaring to you the feeling of deep and tender respect with which you have inspired me. I am rejoiced in my Reason as well as in my Understanding by finding an earnest and noble mind whose presence quickens in mine all that is good and shames and repels from me my own weakness. Can I resist the impulse to beseech you to love me?

My hand began to tremble as I turned the paper over and studied the signature at the bottom: Ralph Waldo Emerson. I bit my lip and continued reading.

The strict limits of the intercourse I have enjoyed, have certainly not permitted the manifestation of that tenderness which is the first sentiment in the common kindness between man and woman. But I am not less in love, after a new and higher way.

"Miss Lydia?"

I had neither seen nor heard Anna return but when I looked up, she was standing before me, holding the cup of tea I'd requested. "Is it bad news come from Concord, miss?"

Rather than take the tea and risk spilling it—for my hands still shook—I bade her place it on the side table. "All is well," I said, my voice nearly cracking with agitation. "I need a few moments of solitude. Thank you."

She left, slowly backing her way out the door. I knew her reluctance to leave was out of concern as much as curiosity, yet I experienced a profound impatience as I watched her out of the room. "Please close the door behind you," I said. It was only when I heard the click of the latch that I turned back to the letter.

I have immense desire that you should love me and that I might live with you always. My own assurance of the truth and fitness of the alliance—the union I desire, is so perfect, that it will not admit the thought of hesitation— never of refusal on your part. I could scratch out the word. I am persuaded that I address one so in love with what I love, so conscious with me of the everlasting principles, and seeking the presence of the common Father through means so like, that no remoteness of condition could much separate us, and that an affection founded on such a basis, cannot alter.

I raised my head, for suddenly I felt as if all the air had been sucked from my lungs. Though I'd not finished reading, I could no longer stay seated, but went to the window and swiftly raised it. I leaned out into the frozen afternoon and took long, deep breaths. I tried to recall in detail the thoughts Mr. Emerson and I had shared as we walked along the waterfront the week before. They did not seem extraordinary in themselves, yet there had been something in the exchange that had made my entire body grow alert in a new and unfamiliar way.

I found myself staring blindly at a small branch that had fallen from our linden tree onto the snow. It resembled a scrap of black lace that I suddenly perceived was in the shape of a question mark. I withdrew into the room and closed the window, though I continued to stand there as I finished reading, in case I might require another measure of air.

I will not embarrass this expression of my heart and mind with any second considerations. I am not therefore blind to them. They touch the past and the future—our friends as well as ourselves, & even the Departed. But I see clearly how your consent shall resolve them all.

And think it not strange, as you will not, that I write rather than speak. In the gravest acts of my life I more willingly trust my pen than my tongue. It is as true. And yet had I been master of my time in this moment, I should bring my letter in my own hand. But I had no leave to wait a day after my mind was made up. Say to me therefore anything but NO. Demand any time for conversation, for consideration, and I will come to Plymouth with a joyful heart. And so God bless you, dear and blessed Maiden, and incline you to love your true friend.

Ralph Waldo Emerson.
My address is Concord, Mass.

My palms and fingers had left damp blots upon the paper. There was a cold spot at the base of my spine. Heat flooded my face. I moved away from the window and into the hall and climbed the stairs.

I found Lucy in her chamber by the fire, mending one of Sophie's black woolen stockings. When she saw me, she leaped up, spilling the stocking and spool of thread to the floor.

"What's happened, Liddy? You look like a ghost!"

I pressed one hand to my neck and held out the letter. My voice, when I spoke, was hoarse. "Mr. Emerson has asked me to marry him."

She raised her hand to her mouth and her eyes widened in shock. "Mr. *Emerson?*" she whispered.

I nodded and took a deep breath. "It's very flattering. But I cannot accept."

"Cannot accept!" Lucy's cry reminded me of the mewl of an injured kitten. "What do you mean? Why couldn't you accept a proposal? Especially from someone as remarkable as Mr. Emerson? I can't think of anyone who would suit you better."

"Lucy, I hardly know the man. We've had two conversations. I can't imagine what precipitated his offer. Perhaps he was drunk."

"Drunk! Mr. Emerson?" She tore the page from my hand and examined it. "A drunken man doesn't write such fine words! If only Charles had written such lines to me!"

I turned away at the mention of Charles, for I could not bear her look of mingled loss and love. "You know I have no desire to marry," I said, crossing to the window overlooking my snow-covered garden. "I'm entirely satisfied with my life here in Plymouth." I gazed down at the hummocks of snow. Buried deep beneath the white mounds were my roses, waiting for summer's warmth and sun so they could bloom. I turned back to my sister. "You know better than any how poorly suited I am to marriage. My spirit is too independent. It's why I refused Nathaniel's proposal."

"Nathaniel was not your equal in intellect. But Mr. Emerson *is*! Liddy, imagine what it would be like to spend each day of your life by his side, discussing all manner of philosophies and issues! Meeting and conversing with his famous friends! Why, your home would be the center of philosophy in New England! You would have brilliant soirées every night of the week!"

I could imagine the scene she described all too well. I had imagined it dozens of times since Mr. Emerson's first lecture. I sighed. "I've never been able to submit gracefully to a man's will. Even Father, when he was alive, couldn't make me bend."

"Mr. Emerson isn't asking you to submit! He merely begs you to love him!"

"Yes. Begs me to love him. But what man understands the enormity of that request? Or comprehends the nature of love's dependence?"

"Surely if any man does it is Mr. Emerson."

I stared at her. She was right. Mr. Emerson was unlike any man I'd ever met. He was not afraid of new ideas and new ways nor did he discount his own flaws. Lucy's face was flushed. I wondered if she had feelings for Mr. Emerson herself.

"So what would you have me do? Write back and accept his proposal as if I were a silly girl without a thought in my head?"

"Of course not! I'd never expect that of you! But you could at least welcome his offer to come and discuss the matter."

I looked out the window again, at the snowy drifts that covered my garden and the house roofs beyond descending in gray slate ranks toward the harbor.

"As a courtesy, if nothing else," Lucy said.

"I'm too set in my ways to marry." I slid the letter into my pocket, as if I might put it out of my own mind by hiding it from my sister's view.

"Set ways are a challenge to God." Lucy repeated an aphorism our mother had often recited when we were children. "Perhaps you should pray on it before you respond. Seek God's guidance."

"Of course." I felt the sting of her words, for I had not thought to pray about the matter. "In fact, I will pray this very hour and then I'll write to Mr. Emerson." Yet my words were bolder than my heart, for, as I returned to my chamber there flashed in my mind the image of myself dressed as a bride that I'd seen in the looking glass. What if the vision had come directly from God?

All my life I've been alert to portents and visions, convinced that God speaks as surely through strange occurrences as He does in Scripture. Yet there is always the difficult matter of discernment. Thus, it was not until Lucy's words cautioned me to examine my heart through prayer that I knelt in my chamber to beg God for clarity in the matter of Mr. Emerson's proposal.

Sometimes God does not answer us in full, but merely nudges us in the direction of His choosing. When I rose from my knees an hour later, it was without the clarity I'd sought. God's will was clouded and elusive. And it was in that state of uncertainty that I took up my pen and wrote to Mr. Emerson, inviting him to come to Plymouth and discuss in person his astonishing offer of marriage.

HE CAME on Friday evening in the midst of a thaw, so that when he entered the parlor the first thing he did was apologize for his muddied shoes and splattered coat hem. Anna took his coat and I took his hand. He thanked me for letting him come and then stood looking at me for some time, simply gazing into my eyes, as if he might read the answer to his petition there. But that answer was not yet mine to give.

I invited him into the parlor and offered him tea and cake, both of which he accepted with the eagerness of a boy. He sat on the sofa and I took the chair opposite him, which I had carefully placed some distance away. I sensed that, without care, I would quickly fall under the spell of his gaze and all the questions I'd so carefully prepared would fly from my mind like a flock of startled sparrows.

"I trust you had a pleasant journey," I said, stirring milk into my tea. "Your carriage didn't get mired in the road, I hope?"

"Not even once. Mere mud could not have stopped me in any case. I felt borne on a heavenly chariot." He smiled and I felt myself awash in heat. Looking at him, I could not think how to begin. There seemed to be no graceful way to move to the question at hand. I drew in a deep breath and put down my teacup.

"This is an awkward meeting," I said. "But I must know why you proposed to me. We don't know each other well, and I cannot fathom why you would choose me out of dozens of women—"

"There are not dozens," he said, smiling gently.

"Nonetheless, your letter came to me as a bolt of lightning out of a clear sky. Nothing in our former conversations led me to expect it. And there's much in it I do not understand."

He looked down into his cup, as if studying its dark contents. "I am not an impulsive man, Lydia. But the circumstances of my life have taught me not to postpone an action once I've made up my mind. I'm convinced that we'd make an excellent marriage."

"I'm flattered that you think so," I said. "Yet marriage demands great sacrifices of a woman. It's not an equal yoke."

He lifted his gaze; his eyes were blazing. "It would be up to us to make it one. This is a new age! Our marriage would not be bound by the old conventions. We would be companions—equal partners—in a quest for beauty and truth."

"Your words and thoughts rouse me," I said, smiling. And though it was not intended as a smile of encouragement, I believe he took it as such. "I won't deny that. Yet I fit well into my present pattern of life. I will forsake it only if you can assure me that you love me and need me enough to justify the sacrifice."

"I don't think I'm capable of assuring you more forcefully than I already have. I want you to be my wife. I'll answer any question you ask."

My eyes focused on the tops of his knees, which pressed against his trousers like small mountain peaks under the dark brown cloth. And then, because I could not continue shamelessly staring at his legs and because I knew that looking at him would dazzle and scatter my thoughts, I closed my eyes.

He answered every question with what seemed to be complete candor. He appeared to have the utmost forbearance, and expressed no impatience at my repetitious and long interrogation. When I had finally run out of queries, I opened my eyes.

"The truth is, Mr. Emerson, that I shrink from the labors and cares of managing a home. If you seek a housekeeper, I am not the wife for you."

He laughed. "We'll manage together. A house is of small importance. What we've discovered in one another is a confluence of minds." He paused. "And of hearts as well, I hope."

"Hearts." Heat suffused my body and my shoulders ached the way they did when I had been dancing for hours. I looked at him and smiled carefully. "Still, marriage is a risk for me. What if we don't find ourselves as compatible as you imagine?"

"I do not believe that will happen, but if it does, I assure you I will keep my vows. Ultimately, I must answer to myself and God."

"As must we all," I murmured.

He drained his cup and put it on the low table between us. "Perhaps it will reassure you to know that I've been married before. I don't take marriage lightly."

"Married before? I had not realized."

He stared into his empty cup. "Ellen died of consumption four years ago. She was very young." I thought he was going to say more, but he continued staring down and did not continue.

"I'm sorry." My heart twisted in sympathy, for his face was a well of grief. "Are there—?" I did not know how to ask this gracefully, but I had to know. "Do you have children, Mr. Emerson?"

"No. Unfortunately. Ellen was not strong enough to bear a child." He raised his head—finally—to look at me again. "But I have hope that I might be a father. Should you accept me."

Children. My heart twisted again. My one regret in remaining single was that I'd never know the joy of holding my own child in my arms. I grew suddenly uncomfortable, as if the fire behind me had blazed up and scorched the back of my neck. I shifted forward. "Tell me about Ellen. Do I resemble her?"

"No," he said softly. "Nor would I want you to." He moved, and for a moment I thought he was going to rise, yet he remained seated. "Ellen is dead and in the past, and my life must go on. And I would like you to be my companion on the rest of the journey." He smiled—an infinitely sad smile, rooted in grief.

His sorrow moved me more profoundly than his words. Thus it was not until that moment that I clearly perceived God's hand at work in our association. I rose from my chair and spoke words I had not prepared—had not imagined I would ever say to any man—convinced that in answering Mr. Emerson, I was also answering God.

"Yes," I said. "I will be your wife."

4

Conversations

Connections which are likely to lead a woman into a sphere of life to which she has been unaccustomed, to introduce her to new and arduous duties—and to form a violent contrast to her previous life—should not be entered into, except at a mature age, and with great certainty that affection is strong enough to endure such trials.

—LYDIA MARIA CHILD

He did not kiss me.

I had expected he would, for it is the custom when a couple pledges to marry. Instead, he took my hand and gently squeezed it.

"My Queen." He smiled. "I'm deeply pleased." Then, instead of embracing me, he said, "I have a fancy. Forgive me if I presume too much, but will you allow me to call you Lydian?"

"Lydian?" I thought suddenly of my baptism. Surely he could not know that in giving me a second name, he so vividly reflected that experience. Perhaps it was another sign of God's imprint on our bond. "It has a pleasing sound. But why?"

"The name suits you, with its twin connotations of musical harmony and beautiful ancient cities. It's my notion—a thought that struck me after our first meeting, in fact—that your parents misnamed you. Lydia is a common name, after all. And you are the least common of women."

"Lydian," I said again, testing the sound. There was a peculiar sweetness to it, a softening of the familiar syllables. "Your words are flattering. Yet the fact remains that you wish to take my given name and make it into a modifier."

He laughed. "You'd have me defend even the smallest point, I see. My intellect will soon be the keenest in New England when daily sharpened on your tenacity." He tilted his head. "Would you like it better if we changed the spelling? Thus rendering an adjective into the most melodic of nouns?"

"I might consider it."

He studied my face. "Perhaps the memory of those who named you Lydia is still too tender? I intend no disrespect to your father."

"No." My hand was still in his, but now I was the one who clasped. "I *want* you to call me Lidian."

He kissed my hand before releasing it. "And I'd very much like it if you addressed me as Waldo."

"Waldo?" I tried the word on my tongue, tested it against the back of my teeth, but it felt whimsical and foolish. "No, I'm afraid I cannot."

"Cannot?" He looked bewildered. Clearly he hadn't expected a refusal. "Why not?"

"It lacks respect."

"We're engaged. Surely our respect for each other isn't bound to titles and formalities. *Mr. Emerson* is so formal. It lacks warmth."

"Warmth is no more bound to a name than respect." I smiled, seeing that he perceived my meaning, for he made a hollow sound that I took for a laugh.

I realized, though, that I'd touched a nerve, that my resistance discomfited him. I heard my mother's voice, scolding me for the sin of obstinacy, pressing me to relent to this man's will. But I couldn't make myself say the assenting words and agree to call him Waldo. My tongue behaved as if it had cleaved to my teeth.

After a moment, he said, "Think on it. I won't press you to a hasty decision on such a small matter when you've so recently pleased me with an eventful one. There will be time." His smile then embraced me, if his arms did not.

When he departed, I sat by the parlor fire, watching the mantel candles burn down on their prickets. After a while Lucy came down, her shoes ticking on the stairs. She stood in the doorway and I watched her expectant smile collapse around her mouth when she saw me.

"You refused him, didn't you?" She moved into the room, hands whispering across her dress. "I thought perhaps, since he stayed so long . . ." Her voice slid into the hiss of the guttering candles.

I looked up at her dark brows, so creased with worry. "No," I said. "I accepted his proposal. I told him I'd be honored to be his wife."

"Liddy!" Lucy swept me from my chair, the knob of her right elbow pushing into my side, her long fingers compressing my spine. "How wonderful! I'm so happy!" She let me go and looked into my face. "But why the long face? I'd think you'd be in raptures!"

"I don't know what I feel," I said. "I imagined an engagement would be different."

"Different in what way?" Lucy was doing all she could to tame her excitement, and though her face showed sympathetic concern, she could not keep her eyes from dancing.

"More fervor, perhaps—isn't a passionate abandon customary?"

"Oh, Liddy, you're just frightened!" Lucy's arms surrounded me again, dragging me close. "I never thought I'd see you scared of anything. *I'm* the fearful one! But it's natural—entirely normal—to be anxious about marriage. It will pass, I promise you. It's only temporary. Soon you'll be glowing."

I disengaged myself by turning sideways and stepping out of Lucy's arms. "I'm very tired. I'm going to bed." I moved toward the hall, my feet gliding across the carpet without my willing it, taking me away without a sound.

Yet, at the door, I turned, and whispered, "Lucy, what have I *done?*"

I WOKE AT DAWN from a dream I couldn't remember, but the dream's feeling remained—a sweet relief, an impression of assurance that I had been right to accept Mr. Emerson. My doubts of the night before had evaporated, and I laid them at fatigue's door.

Late that morning a letter came while I was ironing. I recognized Mr. Emerson's writing at once, and hurried to my chamber, where I opened the envelope with trembling fingers. As though he had perceived my confused sense of deprivation, Mr. Emerson began by addressing his failure to demonstrate any sign of passion. He explained that his lack of ardor was actually a sign of the permanence of our relationship. He was convinced that our marriage would be founded on truth and universal love. The rest—the physical and verbal expressions of personal love—would come in due time. He promised that, if his schedule permitted, he would travel to Plymouth on Friday. Then he raised the issue of where we would live. He was resolved, he wrote, to make his home in Concord.

I read the letter three times, focusing on each sentence and its meaning. His devotion to Concord troubled me. I could not imagine living anywhere but Plymouth.

"But think of the influence you will have!" Lucy told me later that afternoon. We were walking back to Winslow House after calling on Mrs. Hedge, who had broken her leg in a fall on the cellar stairs. "To be the partner of a man who has the ear of multitudes! Why, you were made for this, Lydia!"

"I have no desire for influence," I said. "But I admit I'm excited by prospect of the evening conversations we'll have together."

I had not yet mentioned Mr. Emerson's fixation on Concord. Nor his alteration of my name. A great deal remained to be understood.

HE CAME on Friday in the middle of the afternoon. When I met him at the door, he kissed my hand. His lips were soft—they tickled like feathers against my skin. "My dear Lidian," he said, "you look very well."

I yielded to his smile—something at my center went soft and pliant. I wondered if I might be in love. We walked down to the harbor and I pointed out the stony circle embedded in Hedge's Wharf.

"It's the base of the Forefather's Rock. When they moved it to Town Square, it broke in two."

Mr. Emerson studied it, pressing his toe against the rock's edge. "Perhaps that break is a metaphorical truth," he said. "Mr. Webster made a monument of a myth in his oration of 1820. Surely the Pilgrims must have considered such a boulder an encumbrance rather than a stepping-stone."

I looked at him. "Its symbolism is its significance. It's strange that you should mention Daniel Webster. I once had the honor of dancing with him."

He raised his eyebrows slightly. "Indeed. That's quite a triumph. And what sort of dancer did you find him?"

"Adequate."

He laughed. "I'm sure his talents are far superior to mine."

"Do you dance?"

"Alas, no. I've heard of your dancing ability and you'd find my poor talents laughable, I'm sure."

"Perhaps I could teach you." A gust of wind ruffled my bonnet and made the ribbons stream out over my shoulder.

"I'd rather not display my inadequacies until we're better acquainted." His smile graced me again, encouraging mine. I felt washed in it, honored. It was small wonder people acted dazed in his presence.

He took my arm and we continued walking along Water Street, following the curve of the shore. The storehouses and offices rose on both sides of the street, but we left the wharves behind us as we walked north. The sun was beginning to slide behind Burial Hill, throwing long spears of light over the water. A recent thaw had freed the ships from ice and they rocked smoothly at their moorings. I pointed to one with a dark green hull.

"That's the *Columbus.* One of my father's ships. You can't see the figurehead from here, but it's finely wrought." I turned to Mr. Emerson. "The cape billows as if a sea wind were lifting it. I used to think Columbus a very sad man, though. The carver made him look so wistful, as if he were longing for Spain."

"You have an uncommon way of looking at things, Lidian." He was staring at me, the way a man stares at a complex puzzle he cannot cipher.

"If you seek the common attitude in a companion, you ought not to spend time with me." Fear lurked just beneath my bantering tone. Perhaps I had already lost what I'd never sought to gain.

He laughed. "You misunderstand me. I mean that as a compliment. I consider myself most fortunate that you accepted my proposal and I'm earnestly seeking a home in Concord so that we may soon be man and wife."

I felt instantly ill at ease. His gaze made me blush, but his words alarmed me more. I dreaded the thought of leaving my home. I slid my arm from his and walked on, just ahead of him. "You still wish us to live in Concord, then? I had hoped that you might consider Plymouth."

"My dear Lidian."

He had stopped and stood waiting for me to face him. A shaft of sunlight illuminated his somber expression. "I thought I explained in my letter. Concord has cast her spell on me, and I can't leave her if I'm to pursue the scholar's life I desire. Plymouth"—he swept his hand toward Cole's Hill, and I followed his gesture to the twin chimneys of my home—"is lovely, but it's full of shops and streets. I require communion with nature—an expanse of fields and trees."

"But I've lived here all my life," I said. "All my family are here. I can't imagine living anywhere else. Especially not in a remote country village. How will we find like-minded people?"

"They'll come to us!" His eyes flashed. "We'll create a country haven for scholars and philosophers! Our home—think of it Lidian!—will be a center of refinement and transcendent thought!" He reached for me and for a panicked moment I feared he'd forgotten himself and was about to embrace me there on the street. Instead he scooped both of my gloved hands into his. "I have so many plans for us!"

I caught the spark of his excitement and felt a responsive thrill. I pictured myself standing at his side in a doorway, greeting philosophers and scholars. I turned to look at the water, though he had not released my hands. The sun had fully retreated and the sea assumed a gray cast—a sheet of wrinkled pewter.

"I promise I'll woo you to Concord," Mr. Emerson said, pulling me back to face him. "We'll make plans for you to visit as soon as possible. I want you to meet my mother and brother."

"Perhaps in the spring. Winter travel is so chancy."

"Early spring, then. March."

I laughed. "March is hardly spring, Mr. Emerson."

"It will be *our* spring, Lidian. We'll make it so."

IN THE LAST WEEK of March I made my pilgrimage to Concord. Mr. Emerson drove a rented buggy that wobbled because of a loose back wheel, so that our comfort was as precarious as my emotions. The journey lasted nearly eight hours, through rolling fields that became snow-covered as we traveled west. The towns drew farther apart, and the houses shrank in size and charm. Once Plymouth and Boston were behind us Mr. Emerson grew loquacious, and I saw that he drew great ease from natural places.

"What we'll have in Concord, Lidian, is a kingdom of *ideas*. The wind in the trees and the melody of streams will be our concerts. Our shops will be the woods and meadows. Fashion and social conceit will hold no sway in our realm. Thought alone shall reign."

"A pleasant notion," I said. "But Concord's not the only location for such a kingdom. Plymouth isn't all streets and shops. Nor is it without philosophers."

"Indeed it's not." He smiled. "I consider you chief among them. And I intend to keep you by my side." He reached over and touched my hand.

I felt a curious sadness. Mr. Emerson's small attentions both delighted and unsettled me. Though I'd grown fond of the idea of marriage, I was haunted by the loss of my independence, which I deeply cherished. "What puzzles me," I said, "is why you've settled on Concord. You were raised in Boston. Surely you're at home in the city."

"You forget that I used to visit my grandmother every summer and that my grandfather was Concord's first patriot in the War of Independence. My roots are deep in Concord soil."

"Still, that doesn't seem sufficient reason to tear me from *my* roots."

Mr. Emerson's face became suddenly solemn—an expression I found oddly chilling—perhaps because his smile disappeared so completely—the smile that was otherwise always present. "I'm convinced you'll soon be persuaded to my point of view, Lidian. Charles himself will convert you." Charles, Mr. Emerson's youngest brother, was studying law under a Concord judge, and planned to be married to the judge's daughter as soon as he established himself. "Wait until you meet him! You won't want to be separated from him any more than I do!" His smile returned and I felt an astonishing relief. "I've often entertained the thought that we might all live together."

"Together?"

"Charles and Elizabeth, Mother, you, and I."

I stared at him. Did he truly mean to begin our marriage in such a large company? Did he expect me to keep house for so many? "That's a great many to care for," I said. "Especially when I'm used to only one."

"They won't be a *care,* Lidian! They'll be a community of like minds, surrounded by the satisfactions of nature."

"A community doesn't have to live under the same roof. I'm already part of such a community in Plymouth. And I abhor the thought of being parted from my sister."

"Then she must move to Concord," he said cheerfully. "We'll find her a suitable house—it will be our first order of business!"

I looked down and picked at a thread on the back of my right glove. "My sister cannot afford to live anywhere but Plymouth. She has no funds. Nor do I, for that matter." I glanced at him and perceived the effort he made to conceal his surprise—his eyes shifting down, then sideways, his long jaw working.

"I thought, because of the house you lived in—"

"Winslow House came to us through our grandfather. It's in sad need of repair. We'll need to install a new roof before the year's out."

"Still, your father was a shipowner. Surely he left you an inheritance?"

"He did. A comfortable one. But last fall Lucy's husband took it and fled. Where, we do not know." Shame scalded my cheeks, but I forced myself to look at him. "We have a small bequest from our mother, but it barely meets our expenses. Without my help, Lucy cannot properly care for Frank and Sophia."

"I wasn't aware of this."

"Everyone in town knows. I assumed George told you." My mouth went dry. "I intended no deceit, Mr. Emerson. I didn't imagine my marriage portion would be a concern. If you had expectations—"

"I have no expectations." His words were clear, almost hard, as if they crystallized in the air between us as he spoke. "Only that we share that love of the mind which drew me to you. And I won't part you from your sister. Lucy must live with us in Concord. A large house will be our first requirement." He glanced at the sky. "I detest talking of financial matters." He drew a long breath before looking at me. "I'll soon receive an inheritance from my late wife. One which will provide me with the means to pursue my philosophy and support a family as well. As long as we're frugal."

"I'm well acquainted with economy, Mr. Emerson. But have you considered the ministry? There's no nobler profession and it will yield a steady income."

"I've left the pulpit for good." His voice was firm. "I won't return."

"Surely you would if you required the income."

He nodded. "I go where my understanding takes me. I can no longer hold to foolish, outmoded doctrines."

"Foolish? What doctrines do you consider foolish?"

He hesitated a moment before answering. "The divinity of Jesus. The sanctity of the Lord's Supper."

"The Lord's Supper?"

"I don't think it's necessary. It devolves upon the authority of Christ. It's my view that he didn't establish the church—or any of its rites—to glorify himself. Nor did he even intend them to be permanent. Read the Scriptures. He continually pointed to God as the source of creation and redemption. Yet the church persists in making an idol of Christ. Thus—in my view—obscuring God."

As always, when Mr. Emerson shared his thoughts with me, I felt a rush of blood to my temples and a zeal for debate.

"But the Lord's Supper has the power to transform us," I said. "The bread and wine are a window to God's love."

"But that window could be anything, Lidian! The washing of feet, the singing of hymns, even a walk in the woods. It's not the bread and wine that make the experience holy. It's the awareness of intimacy with the divine."

A jay darted from the trees, shrieking, and Mr. Emerson turned his head to follow its flight. We were passing through a forested hollow—dark trees rose on both sides of the road.

"Yet it's surely the clearest window," I said, eager to pursue the conversation. "I cannot believe you left the ministry solely because of this."

He glanced at me, his eyes bright, appreciative. "You're right. There are other reasons." He sighed. "I must tell you about Ellen."

The skin of my face felt suddenly brittle. "Perhaps this is not the time." Though I'd been profoundly curious about his wife, I was not at all sure that I wanted to hear what he wished to tell me.

"I fear there will be no better. I've known for weeks that I must speak of her. I must employ what occasion I can."

I carefully rearranged my hands in my lap. "Then I'm ready to hear."

He stared ahead at the road, and I saw his fingers tighten again on the reins, though our chestnut mare hadn't broken her gait. "I met her in New Hampshire when I was fresh out of divinity school, traveling from pulpit to pulpit, earning what I could. In New Concord, I stayed at the home of Deacon Kent—Ellen's stepfather—a good man. When I rode up to the house she was standing on the steps. It was a warm day and she was dressed in a blue gown, simply standing there, smiling—as if she were waiting for me." He paused. "From the moment I saw her, I was under her spell." He paused again, and seemed to be waiting for me to speak.

"She must have been lovely," I said.

"She was. I wish you'd known her, Lidian. You would have been as charmed as I. She was a child of seventeen, yet she had the face and form of an angel, and the character of a saint."

I could not bear to watch his face as he spoke. I directed my gaze to the woods beyond. The air beneath the trees was dark, impenetrable.

"I courted Ellen with total abandon," Mr. Emerson said. "I couldn't wait to make her mine. But there was a cruel darkness overshadowing my joy. She suffered from consumption even then, and though she rallied from time to time, she was often desperately ill. She hoped"—he paused and sighed again—"*we* hoped she'd recover—that a day would come when she'd have children. That we'd grow old together. But she died eighteen months after our wedding."

"Oh no!" I murmured.

He nodded, still without looking at me. "She was a saint, Lidian. She died ministering to me. I knew she was in pain—terrible pain. And her attacks—so much blood—covering her head and chest! You'd not think a body could hold so much."

"I know." I recalled Mother's copious flows of blood clotted with scraps of her lungs. And there was the awful smell too—the rotting stench of death, which had so permeated Mother's chamber that I could still smell it six months after she died. "My mother died of consumption."

He did not appear to have heard me. "Yet she sustained cheerful spirits throughout her ordeal. She was the picture of Christian resignation. An angel! A saint!" He took a deep breath. "She spent the last of her strength reassuring *me*!" His voice caught and he fell silent. The mare's hooves made sucking sounds in the muddy road.

"She's at peace now," I said. "You must believe that."

He glanced at me and his haunted expression told me plainly that he would never cease loving her. If I wanted to love Mr. Emerson, I must also love Ellen Tucker. I turned my face from him and bowed my head. My fingers clutched at my cape, as if they might wring some strength from it. I'd always been a woman of strong feeling. I didn't know if I had sufficient humility to weave Ellen into the fabric of our marriage. But I knew that I must try.

WE ENTERED CONCORD at dusk. The houses looked small and dreary, squatting in flat, open fields or pressed against the backs of hills. A few blighted trees stood like lonely sentries in the dooryards. Once a black dog crossed the road directly in front of our buggy, so close the chestnut mare shied into the ditch. Mr. Emerson tried to urge her awkwardly back onto the road with sharp, impatient snaps of the reins and much unhappy pleading. The horse obviously discomfited him. I laughed and told him that she wouldn't bite.

"I fear you've found me out." He gave me an abashed smile. "I'm not familiar with animals." Yet when I offered to drive, he would not let me, though it would have been a simple matter for me to encourage the mare by gentle words and a light flick of the reins. Instead, we sat in the ditch while Mr. Emerson continued to plead. It was some time before the mare decided to continue the journey.

We came at last to the Manse, where Mr. Emerson and his mother boarded. The house was a plain gray box of a building, set well back from the road on the bank of the Concord River. We followed the drive between a double row of chestnut trees and drew up before the front door. Immediately a white-haired man threw open the door. He was stooped with age, yet he nimbly descended the steps and welcomed us with a smile and outstretched hands.

"Mr. Ripley, may I present my fiancée, Miss Lidian Jackson?" Mr. Emerson climbed down from the shaking buggy, and extended his hand to steady me as I followed. "Lidian, this is Reverend Ezra Ripley, my late grandmother's second husband."

"I've heard you speak, sir," I said, as the minister clasped my hand, "when you came to Plymouth last summer. It was a great pleasure."

He smiled and tightened his grasp. "The lady certainly knows how to warm an old man's heart, Waldo."

Mr. Emerson laughed. "Give her a chance and I warrant she'll warm your mind, as well, sir. Lidian bows to no man in conversational skill."

Reverend Ripley laughed and finally released my hand, for which I was grateful, since it had begun to ache. He turned and clapped Mr. Emerson on the shoulder.

"Congratulations, Waldo!" He looked again at me. "I know what a blessing to our town you'll be, Miss Jackson. Your reputation for good works precedes you." His face was kind, his eyes bright with intelligence. He gestured to the broad field beside the house and said that it was the very battleground where American patriots had first demoralized the British regulars. The field that evening was a white sheet spread beneath the black sky.

The entryway was sparsely furnished—wide plank floorboards, a row of three wall pegs, pale green wallpaper. The hall ran straight to the back of the house, interrupted only by a narrow stairway on the left.

"My dear," Mr. Ripley said, addressing me, "you must be overcome with fatigue. I'll show you to your room, where you can refresh yourself before tea."

I followed him up the creaking stairs to a small chamber at the back of the house, where he bid me make myself comfortable. "Rest while I gather the family. They're eager to meet you, but they can wait an hour more. In the meantime, I'll assure them that their hopes will not be disappointed."

When he closed the door, I sank onto the bed and pressed my hands to my eyes. Despite the good minister's words, I despaired of impressing Mr. Emerson's family. If they were all as brilliant and articulate as he, I'd quickly find myself tongue-tied. I went to the window and stared out at the night, tracing frost on one of the small panes. There was nothing to see out there—no lights, no houses or shops. The silence was staggering. It pressed against my ears, invaded my skull, and filled me with a dreadful unease. When Mr. Emerson knocked only fifteen minutes later, my discomfiture had become so oppressive that I eagerly joined him. Downstairs, we stepped into the parlor, where white candles burned in iron sconces between the long windows. The light blue carpet matched the drapes and the wallpaper of blue medallions. On the wall to my left hung a framed Bible etching showing Jonah cast up by the whale on a deserted beach. The sky was filled with forbidding clouds, but a single ray of sunlight slanted through them to touch Jonah's head. I was well-acquainted with that touch of grace. And the terror of those clouds.

The family sat on straight wooden chairs. My first impression was that I had set foot in an alien land. I knew that country people had different customs, ones I did not understand. I felt like a broodmare at an auction. Mr. Emerson's mother sat in the darkest corner of the room. Her hand, when I took it, was dry and cold, stippled with brown age spots. She spoke little, beyond inquiring about the discomforts of my journey, but I was aware of her scrutiny throughout the evening. Her eyes were the color of tarnished pewter and seemed to harbor a smoldering and inexplicable anger.

"And this is Charles," Mr. Emerson said, turning me toward a smiling young man. He had thick, fair hair—his nose was not as prominent as Mr. Emerson's, but was classically Roman. "Be on your guard. His charm hides a dangerous wit."

Charles laughed. "Welcome to Concord, Miss Jackson. You must feel as if you've been exiled to the wilderness."

"Not at all. Concord's a lovely village." But I wondered that he had so quickly discerned my private sentiment and didn't hesitate to name it.

"A town is lovely insofar as its inhabitants make it so by their inner attractiveness," Mr. Emerson said. "I believe Lidian will find it an amenable community."

"It's certainly pleasant to the eye," I said.

"I'm glad that—despite his many shortcomings—my brother is able to interest a woman of quality." Charles sent a grin in Mr. Emerson's direction and then turned his full attention on me. "You've done us all a favor, Miss Jackson. Waldo's demeanor is greatly improved in the presence of a lady."

Laughing, Mr. Emerson clapped him on the back. "She'll learn my shortcomings soon enough, Charles. Let her enjoy the fantasy that she's caught the choicest fish in the sea."

"But you cannot be the choicest, Waldo," said a sweet-faced woman who approached us from the far side of the room. "That position is already taken." She was nearly my height and her hair was a deep brown, but her most striking feature was her dark, luminous eyes.

"Elizabeth," Charles said, and took her arm in a gesture that was both casual and possessive. "You'll make me blush." I knew this must be his fiancée, Miss Hoar, whose intellect and charm Mr. Emerson had already mentioned.

"I don't think it's possible for you to blush," Elizabeth said, smiling. "You're much too shameless."

"Miss Jackson, I'm sure you'll forgive her romantic sparring," Charles said. "From what Waldo tells me, the two of you do your own share." He gave me a mock bow.

Charles and Elizabeth charmed me as Mr. Emerson had promised. Charles's sense of humor put me immediately at ease and his manner was even more captivating than his looks. He was clearly the family jester, always on hand with a witty remark whenever the conversation flagged. Even the dour Mrs. Emerson smiled at his comments. He had a particular way of looking at people that made one feel as if he were entirely amused at every word spoken.

Elizabeth was as gentle as he was boisterous. Her dark, understanding eyes and sweet expression won me over at once. Warmth and generosity seemed to flow from her as naturally as clear water from a spring.

Reverend Ripley retired soon after we finished our tea, but the rest of the company remained in the parlor, engaged in what soon became a conversation on marriage.

"It's a woman's institution," said Charles, and I perceived from his grin that he was once again teasing Elizabeth. "Her principal agency for civilizing the brutish male."

"Then you agree that men need civilizing?" Elizabeth regarded him with a pure, innocent expression, which caused a general laughter.

"Yet surely the purpose of marriage is as solemn as it is agreeable," Mr. Emerson said. "It's a light affection which first binds a man and a woman, but if they're wise they will build a deeper one on the truth of each other." He looked at me. Tenderly, I thought.

"Marriage is God's chief means of perfecting us," I declared.

"How Swedenborgian," Charles said.

"It is my own thought. I've observed that couples are drawn together by a magnetism of weakness to strength."

"Including you and Waldo?" Charles asked.

"I believe so, yes."

"Lidian and I have discussed this before," Mr. Emerson said. "But I've not yet had the courage to ask who's the weaker and who the stronger."

Charles and Elizabeth laughed.

I turned to my fiancé. "We each have strengths that balance the other's weakness."

He smiled. "And all this time I believed myself drawn to you by an affinity of intellect and opinion. I'm yet blind to your dissimilarities."

"You're teasing me, Mr. Emerson."

"Not at all! I simply don't see this matter from your perspective."

"But from an opposite one," I said triumphantly. "Which exactly proves my point."

Charles laughed out loud. "You've certainly found your match, Waldo!"

Mrs. Emerson spoke from the shadows. "It's a match, perhaps, but a Petruchio one, from the look of it."

"Mother!" Charles looked as if he'd been the one stung, but I found myself smiling.

"I don't consider myself a shrew, but if I'm to play the role of Kate, I'll do my best to play it vigorously." I glanced at my husband-to-be. "I believe a man of Mr. Emerson's intellect and renown can only profit by some dissent from his wife."

Whereupon even Mrs. Emerson joined in the general laughter.

Throughout the evening there were many references to Ellen Tucker—in particular to her beauty and loving spirit. The family spoke of her as if she were still alive, gone on some extended and mysterious journey. I sensed that, despite the attempt to receive me warmly, I was being compared unfavorably to her.

Elizabeth was the exception. She had not known Ellen, had only met her on one occasion, and confided later that she recalled a sickly and giddy young woman who'd seemed so unlike Mr. Emerson in temperament and disposition that she had difficulty crediting that he proposed. From that day, Elizabeth's understanding sustained me. We became instant and fast friends.

That first evening, after Mrs. Emerson retired, Charles and Elizabeth withdrew to one corner of the parlor, while I sat with Mr. Emerson by the fire. It was then that he showed me his miniature of Ellen. He took the small portrait from his coat pocket and put it into my hands as reverently as if it were a sacred relic. I studied the rosebud mouth, the dark hair parted in the middle, the thick curls framing the oval face, the pale, slender shoulders, the luminous eyes. They were astonishing eyes, pale blue and brimming with an intoxicating mixture of innocence and wisdom. They were so striking in paint that I was not surprised they'd captivated those who saw her in the flesh.

"She was very beautiful," I said.

"Yes," he whispered, closing his eyes as if I'd just spoken a prayer.

ON THE LAST MORNING of my visit to Concord, Mr. Emerson suggested a quiet walk beside the river. The air was unseasonably warm, and the snow was melting, flowing in streamlets down the muddy banks and into the water. The ice had broken into irregular slabs and floated freely on the black water. Mr. Emerson put his arm around my waist. Instantly I felt myself softening inwardly; the sensation was one of dissolving and melting into a warm liquid, not unlike the snow beneath the warm rays of the sun.

"Tell me, are the residents as unfriendly and backward as you imagined?" His voice was a smile.

"Elizabeth is a delight," I said, carefully shaping my reply, for I knew his intention and that he would soon press me again to agree to establish our home in Concord. "As good a friend already as many I have known since childhood. And Charles—how could anyone not love him?"

"You have yet to mention my mother." He was smiling and I was gratified that he was not offended by my diffidence.

I stopped and turned so that I blocked his path. "I'm determined to win her love," I said. "She's your mother, and warrants reverence on that account alone."

He lifted my hand and kissed it. "I don't deserve such devotion."

In that instant I discovered the secret to pleasing Mr. Emerson. He required a discerning admiration. He loved me not for my nobility or intellect, but for the man he saw reflected in my eyes.

5

Encounters

Hail to the quiet fields of my fathers.
—RALPH WALDO EMERSON

On a warm June afternoon as we strolled down to the harbor, I capitulated to Mr. Emerson's desire to live in Concord. Ships rocked gently at their anchors, their masts black against the bright blue sky; behind us, the narrow streets of Plymouth climbed toward Burial Hill under graceful linden trees. Mr. Emerson held my hand and assured me that he'd begin at once to look for a house in Concord that I would like. I kept my eyes on his face, so sad at the thought of leaving my beloved town that I couldn't bear to look elsewhere.

When she heard the news, Lucy was as distressed as I, but hid her concern behind enthusiasm for my wedding preparations.

"You must have a new gown, Liddy. Something which doesn't emphasize your pallor. Gold perhaps, or light rose. Let's go to Boston and look at the new fabrics."

"We can't afford such extravagance," I said. "I'll wear what I already have."

"But everything is gray or slate-blue! Your wedding should be a festive occasion."

"I could wear the lilac silk Betsey loaned me."

"You've already worn it. Think of your station! You're not marrying a farmer."

"Sometimes I wonder," I murmured, for Lucy's comment made me think of Concord's wide and lonely fields.

It was Sophia who suggested that, with some small modifications, my white muslin gown would make a fine wedding dress.

"Set in some puffed sleeves, and it will be in the height of fashion," she said. Her proposal delighted me and satisfied Lucy, who volunteered to do the handiwork herself.

One of my duties before wearing the gown as Mr. Emerson's bride was to receive his aunt. I'd heard Mary Moody Emerson whispered of in Boston circles for years. Famous for her peculiarities, she was a brilliant woman, though blunt to the point of rudeness, with a tenacity that intimidated all but the most stouthearted. Mr. Emerson was eager that we know each other.

"She came to live with us after my father died," he told me one evening as we walked in the garden behind Winslow House. My pink damask roses were in full bloom and their heavy scent sweetened the air. "I owe my education to her as well as my interest in philosophy. She was, in her way, as singular an influence as my mother."

"And what of your father?" I asked. "Was he not an able influence? It puzzles me that you never speak of him." I was instantly sorry, for the look of hollow pain he turned upon me immediately raised the memory of my own father's debasement.

"He died when I was eight," Mr. Emerson said quietly. "My only memories of him are"—he paused—"unfortunate."

I sighed—a sound that seemed to mingle my memories with his. "My own father was a complex and difficult man."

"I hope he wasn't cruel." He studied my face in such a way that I felt both protected and understood.

"He was not always kind," I admitted. "He grew worse after an accident in which he fell into a hold while inspecting one of his ships. It took him months to recover, and he was never the same after. He became a disagreeable and angry man."

He took my hand. "There are more correspondences between us than I dreamed, Lidian. But let's not allow unpleasant thoughts to compromise our happiness." And to my great surprise, he kissed me. His mouth was soft and warm. I tasted his breath—it was musky and sweet—and I drew it into my lungs, savoring it, as if it were a honeyed confection. A tide of desire swept through me—so forcefully my knees began to shake. When he released me I felt the need to grip his arm for support.

"Your aunt," I said, when I had regained a measure of poise. "Tell me more of her."

"What would you know?" He put his hand over mine, binding it to his coat sleeve.

"I worry that she may not find me congenial. What if she doesn't approve of me?" I pulled away and bent to pluck a dead bloom from its stem.

He smiled. "She'll approve. How can she not? You two are as alike as twins."

"Alike?" I rose and turned to him. This was the first I'd heard that I reminded him of anyone. "I'm flattered, since you admire her so much."

"As I admire you." He leaned as if to kiss me again, but I turned to examine another blossom.

"I'll happily invite her to visit. Perhaps if she's convinced that Plymouth will suit you, you'll listen to her."

"Fortunately that matter has already been decided," he said.

The blossom suddenly came away from its stem and fell into my hand.

"In any case," he went on, "I doubt you'll be able to convince Aunt Mary of anything. More likely she'll convince you." He laughed, a rare sound I had already come to love. It reminded me of the music of the sea, with its deep and complex undertones.

I RECALLED his laugh two weeks later as I stood at the window watching Miss Emerson light from her carriage. She was the smallest woman I'd ever seen, as small as a child, and the way she darted up the walk to the door made me think of an excited bird. She held her head high and her blunt nose so resembled a beak that I had to suppress a laugh.

The bird image remained with me even after she crossed the threshold, for

Miss Emerson seemed to flutter and flap about in her worn cape until I relieved her of it. Her cap was too small to contain her hair. Or perhaps her hair was as wiry as her wit, and refused to be constrained by a fragment of linen.

"I'm poverty-struck," she chirped, "else I would have brought you a gift. But if Waldo tells me true, then you'll cherish no gift more than a vigorous conversation. Which I mean to grant you." She smiled up at me, her eyes shiny as black beads in her lively face. I detected a mischievous note in her voice, and was surprised by her uncommon candor and high sense of humor—a combination of qualities that first charmed and later embarrassed me.

In the parlor she perched on the lip of her chair, her hands dancing across the black froth of her skirt, shoulders twitching, eyes blinking, gray wisps of hair escaping her cap. She spoke quickly, the words rushing from her as if there were not time enough left in the world to say all that needed to be said. I found it difficult to keep up with her sudden shifts in subject. It was not really a conversation at all, but a combination of interrogation and sermon. One moment she was lecturing me on the necessity for wives to zealously advance moral reform and the abolition of slavery, and the next she was asking my thoughts on the doctrine of the Trinity.

Lucy and Sophia were also present, Lucy knitting a finely clocked stocking, glancing up every now and again to smile, while Sophia poured tea. She demurely handed a cup and spoon to Miss Emerson.

"A handsome spoon," Miss Emerson declared, examining the silver handle closely. "Such elaborately etched leaves! A testimony to your taste, Miss Jackson."

"It was my mother's," I said. "One of the few remaining."

"Oh, dear." Miss Emerson placed the spoon daintily on her saucer. She looked as if I'd just announced the death of a favorite cat. "Why few? What has happened to the rest?"

"I melted them down," I said.

Miss Emerson looked at me sharply. "In a moment of violent grief, no doubt."

I let her think what she would. "It is an act I've come to regret."

"I should think so." She tapped her tiny feet on the carpet and changed the subject. "I've heard you are admired as a woman of Christian nobility. But marriage demands humility, you know. And marriage to Waldo"—she paused and rattled her teacup—deliberately, I thought—"will require courage."

Courage? I wondered at her meaning. "I'm certain that God will provide what strength is needed. He's never failed me."

Miss Emerson's eyebrows vaulted toward the tangle of gray curls above her forehead. "Perhaps He has not tested you."

My shoulders tightened and I found it necessary to measure each word before I spoke. "I assure you, I've been tested many times. I've never sought a comfortable life."

"Yet it appears to be comfortable nonetheless." She glanced meaningfully at the parlor drapes, as if she might find on them my spending ledger.

"Appearances can deceive," I said.

"And reveal." Her eyes narrowed. "Tell me, my dear Lidian, what does Waldo see in you? You're not a great beauty."

It took me a moment to recover from this new assault, but I managed a smile. "You'd have to ask him, Miss Emerson. It's as much a mystery to me as to you."

"Ah, but mysteries always have their reasons."

"Indeed. And what is more mysterious—or more reasonable—than God's will?"

Miss Emerson's eyes narrowed and she rattled her cup again. "You dare suggest that God is the architect of this union?"

"He's the architect of all our lives. Is it even possible for us to escape His desire?"

The tiniest of smiles tipped the corners of Miss Emerson's mouth. I saw that I'd passed a small test.

ON MONDAY AFTERNOON, Dr. Kendall came to pay his respects. As I served tea, Miss Emerson questioned him vigorously on his Sunday sermon, attacking it with a ferocity and determination that shocked me.

"Theology ought to be open to every student of nature." She spoke rapidly, stressing each word, as if all were of equal importance. "A mind can detect the infinite wisdom in the laws by which the humblest shrub grows and flourishes. If the weed, sprouting from rock, can seek the sunlight and be rooted in the earth, then how infinite may be the relations of man!" She inched forward in her chair as she spoke, propelled by small jerks of her hips, so that I feared she'd soon launch herself off the chair completely. Her feet twitched beneath her skirts. The movements became more pronounced as she continued to expound, and I could not take my eyes off her rhythmically bouncing hem and the periodic emergence of a black-slippered toe.

"But my dear lady," Dr. Kendall finally said, "man cannot use nature to deduce moral principles! Morality comes from God and He alone—"

"Nonsense!" Miss Emerson sputtered. "He's arranged the universe precisely so His laws *can* be deduced!"

Dr. Kendall tried again to speak, and once more, Miss Emerson cut him off, this time before any word had emerged from his lips.

"What one requires is *imagination*!" Miss Emerson half-rose from her chair, as if the urgency of her discourse were so great she couldn't remain seated.

"Dr. Kendall hardly lacks imagination," I said sharply. "If you'd permit him to complete his thoughts, you'd discover it for yourself."

"By all means," Miss Emerson said. "I delight in discoveries!" And her eyes sparkled as brightly as a young girl's.

My stomach ached, and a painful ball had formed within my chest—a horror at the realization that this caustic old woman would soon be my relative. What sort of family was I marrying into that harbored harshness under the guise of honesty?

Dr. Kendall quietly embarked on a lengthy explanation of his orthodoxy. Three minutes into it, Miss Emerson suddenly, and without apology, rose and left the room. I tried not to reveal my astonishment, but rearranged myself in my chair and encouraged him to continue. When he looked too bewildered to do so, I asked after his wife, and inquired into the health of Anne Miller, a widow who was chronically at death's door. Moments later, I was startled to see Miss Emerson appear in the doorway behind Dr. Kendall's chair, urgently beckoning.

Frowning, I excused myself. When I stepped into the hallway, she rose on her toes and whispered, "Lidian, dear, I'm desperate for fresh air. Please come and take a walk with me."

"Now? But we have a guest!"

"Oh, leave him!" Miss Emerson waved her tiny hand. "He's a stuffy old man. I've worn out my patience with his antiquated notions. Come." She patted my arm. "We have more stimulating conversations to share."

"I can't leave Dr. Kendall!"

"Of course you can! Men are forever leaving women to sit alone in their parlors. It's time the tables were turned."

I tried to get my bearings. "I'm sorry, Miss Emerson, but I won't walk with you now."

"Very well, then. I'll walk as I always do—alone." Miss Emerson's eyes flashed, but whether with anger or mischief, I could not tell.

WHEN MR. EMERSON CAME two days later to take his aunt back to Concord, I greeted him joyfully, delighted to be in his presence again, and relieved that my time with Miss Emerson had drawn to a close. As we walked down to the harbor, he told me of the enthusiastic reception of his lecture series before turning his attention to my week. He asked if I'd enjoyed his aunt's visit.

"I hope she did not try your patience," he said.

"She has a fine imagination. And I appreciate her candor."

He smiled in a way that showed me he understood what I was not saying. "Please assure me that she hasn't altered your disposition to become an Emerson."

"She has not," I said, "though I admit she gave me pause." I smiled, but the truth was that I was increasingly excited by my new future. I believed that, as the wife of Mr. Emerson, I would be a woman of consequence whose words and deeds would be noted and admired. "Of our marriage, I have a pretty conceit." I smiled into his eyes. "I picture the two of us sitting before the fire on a January evening, discussing the great works of Plato or Goethe late into the night."

"And then to bed?" he said in a low voice, touching the back of my neck very lightly. I shivered and glanced at him and the look he gave back to me was a challenge.

"I also look forward to that," I said boldly, returning his warm smile with my own. I'd never spoken so openly, yet I rejoiced in the growing candor between us. I believed our marriage would be a union of true minds, unlike any the world had ever seen.

At dinner, I noticed Mr. Emerson's unceasing deference to his aunt. I watched him rise, smiling, when she entered the room. I watched him listen raptly to every word she uttered. Even when he argued with her, he did so with the utmost respect.

When he left the next morning to take her back to Concord, I stood in the doorway and waved him out of sight. I noticed a curtain move in the front window of the house next door and couldn't resist the urge to wave once in that direction before closing the door.

6

Transformations

That her hand may be given with dignity,
she must be able to stand alone.

—MARGARET FULLER

We set our wedding for the fourteenth of September. That morning, I rose from a fitful sleep and stood some time at the window looking out into a steady, cold rain. The weather seemed an evil portent, combined with the events of the evening before, when my entire Bible class came to bid me farewell in a manner that felt more funereal than celebratory. I'd been deeply shaken when Alice Temple burst into tears and confessed between sobs that I reminded her of the vestal virgin who let her lamp go out.

"You look as if you've prepared yourself for a living burial," she lamented. Her words chilled and frightened me. And now morning had finally come, gray and cheerless and powerless to banish the apprehension of the night before.

The possibility that I was about to embark on a disastrous union was not one I dared contemplate. My foot was set on the path, and I could not turn back. Yet I was unable to eat a morsel of breakfast, and told Lucy that I feared such a gloomy beginning to my wedding day was a bad omen.

"What nonsense!" Lucy slapped butter onto her bread as if it were a dis-obedient child. "Who are you to translate God's favor into weather?"

Though I recognized the truth of her words, they failed to pacify me.

Mr. Emerson was due at noon, but by two o'clock he had not yet arrived. It was another unfavorable sign. I stood at the parlor window for nearly an hour, distraught as I watched the long darts of rain score the glass. The road was muddy and dark. I prayed that only weather conditions kept him.

When he finally arrived shortly after four, my anxiety evaporated and I greeted him with joyous relief. His coat was flecked with mud and he looked appallingly weary, yet I led him into the parlor and made him sit near the fire and drink a cup of tea before the ceremony. I took his hands, which were cold as icicles, and chafed them briskly between mine. He was gratifyingly appreciative as he described the long, wet ride from Concord. In his presence I always felt as if I had all the time in the world. So we sat, warming ourselves with the hot tea, and talked of his recent speech in Concord, on the occasion of the two hundredth anniversary of the town's founding.

"There were ten veterans of the Revolution," he said, "seated right in front of me at the foot of the podium, and I was aware of them throughout—though I've always focused on someone in the back row, as that naturally ele-vates the voice so all can hear."

"I cannot imagine anyone having difficulty hearing you," I said. "Your voice is always clear and commanding."

He bowed his head modestly, but I knew my words pleased him.

"Tell me what you said. I would know my new home better."

As he spoke of Concord's history, I became so engrossed that I didn't mark the passage of time, and it fell to Lucy to interrupt us with the news that our wedding guests were beginning to arrive.

I flew up the stairs to my chamber, where Sophia helped me into my gown. The soft muslin caught on one of my combs, yanking it and spilling my hair down my back and shoulders like a shawl. It seemed yet another ill omen and I frowned into the mirror over the dresser. My face in the mirror looked unfamiliar, as if a tragic pasteboard mask had been fixed to it.

"Are you frightened?" Sophia asked.

"Yes," I said. "I believe I am. A little."

Lucy entered then, her face flushed. "You look like an angel, Liddy!"

I didn't turn from the mirror, though I managed to say, "Mr. Emerson is the angel."

"You're clearly meant for each other!" She lifted my hair and caught it in my silver combs. "Everyone says so. Just yesterday, Lavinia White declared that you and Mr. Emerson had two of the finest minds in New England."

"How kind," I murmured, securing my hair with yet another comb.

At that moment a shaft of light escaped the heavy clouds and splashed into my chamber, washing it in a wave of gold. I looked out the window where, from a long horizontal gash between the clouds and the horizon, sunlight flashed across the roofs of Plymouth. Gold turned to lavender and finally to violet, while I stood mesmerized, my hands still raised to my hair.

"Liddy?" Lucy's voice seemed to come from a great distance—I wasn't sure I heard her—it might have been Mother's voice against my ear. "Mr. Emerson's waiting." Her words woke me from my enchantment and I perceived how late it was—the ceremony should have been long over. Where had I been? I fixed my final comb securely in my hair and left my chamber in a confusion of white muslin.

As I started down the stairs, I saw Mr. Emerson ascending. And so we met on the landing, he took my arm, and we walked down together. Just as my vision in the mirror had foretold.

Dr. Kendall performed the ceremony, as he had performed all the ceremonies of my life. Mr. Emerson and I faced him as he stood with his back to the fireplace and addressed the room of gathered friends and relatives. I found myself staring at the mantel, which Sophia had decorated that morning with evergreen boughs and a blue vase holding the last of my summer roses.

Then—very suddenly, it seemed—Dr. Kendall pronounced us man and wife. I stared at the thin mouth out of which the momentous words had come. Though the ceremony was over, I did not move—*could* not move—for I was rooted to that single place, knowing beyond doubt that it was the fulcrum of my life. All that ever happened—both past and future—was hinged forever to this place and moment.

It's my nature to take such experiences seriously, to mine them for purpose and direction. I do not casually dismiss feelings. Thus I would have stood and puzzled for some time on the moment's significance, had it not

been for the flood of guests who swept down on Mr. Emerson and me, circling us in their excitement and good cheer. I was embraced again and again,
given countless congratulatory kisses. Small gifts were pressed on me—flowers
and handkerchiefs, a pewter sugar bowl and a painted green vase.

Mr. Emerson was ever at my side, greeting people with his usual charm,
blessing all with his smile. George Bradford, who had stood up for him during the ceremony, toasted us with a glass of claret, and teased Mr. Emerson
for such undeserved good fortune.

FOUR HOURS LATER, as I climbed into my four-poster bed beside Mr.
Emerson, a spiderweb of fear enclosed my body and stopped my tongue. Perhaps every bride feels the same. I knew something of what to expect, but I
could not imagine how the experience would be in any way pleasant. What
filled my mind was the memory of Father's hand upon my breast and thigh
and his rum-drenched mouth covering my own. I had heard that some men
were brutal and some timid and that the size of a man's organ would determine how much a woman suffered. Yet I knew I had to open myself to my
husband in order to seal our marriage and conceive a child. Thus I lay silently
waiting for what was to come.

"Lidian." Mr. Emerson rolled on his side to face me. "I have something I
must tell you." He touched my waist with his hand. His fingers rested there,
just above my navel. I felt them as small circles of warmth through my
nightgown.

I did not move. My heart was racing. I reminded myself—*this is what God
has ordained*—and sent up a small prayer of preparation.

"Lidian," he said again, and I realized with surprise that he was searching
for words. "Like most men, I've had some experience in these intimate matters. But there's something I must confess." He paused and I could hear him
swallow. "Ellen and I never consummated our marriage. She was too ill—we
were both afraid that the exertion would weaken her. And we wanted no risk
of childbearing."

I felt a burst of relief. My hand covered his. He slid his free arm beneath
my shoulder and drew me to him. And then he began to kiss me—gently,
tenderly, the way I had dreamed it.

What I recall most clearly from that night was how he tried so hard to be gentle, how he stroked my hair away from my forehead and whispered, "Lidian, my wife." And how, when he was finished, he displayed such astounding gratitude, as if what I had given him was not my body, but a miracle.

WHEN I WOKE the next morning, Mr. Emerson was seated in the armchair by the window, staring out to sea. His face was unreadable, his skin shining in the morning light.

I reached down with my hand. The place between my thighs was moist and sore. It seemed a strange sign and seal of love—this confusing mixture of discomfort and desire.

"The sky is clear," Mr. Emerson said, as if nothing had happened between us. "It's going to be a fine day."

I watched him. He seemed so calm. I couldn't detect any trace of the bliss I felt. Had not his sensibilities been transformed by the night's events as mine had? I sat up. "A fine day?" I thought of what lay ahead—my departure from Plymouth, the long journey to Concord.

"Come and see for yourself."

I rose and went to him. He settled his arm around my waist.

"Look, the sun is shining. The world gleams after yesterday's rain." He smiled up at me. "Are you eager to see this new house that you are now mistress of?"

"Of course." I had yet to see the house where we would live; it was the custom that a bride not set eyes on her new home until she was safely wed. It was a practice I did not care for, but had conformed to it nonetheless, eager to avoid anything that might jinx our future happiness or call down the contempt of Mr. Emerson's family. "You make me sound like a queen with my own realm awaiting me," I said, laughing.

"As indeed you are." He rose and took me into his arms and kissed me. "A Lidian Queen."

Lucy had overseen the preparation of a sumptuous wedding breakfast. Tea and coffee were served with apple pie and strips of ham, sweet potatoes in a warm orange sauce, oatmeal and hasty pudding, biscuits and johnnycake and applesauce. I sat across the table from my husband and throughout the meal was aware of his gaze resting on me, ardent as his nighttime kisses.

We did not break our fast in peace. A constant stream of visitors came to

say their farewells. My aunts and uncles who had attended the wedding returned to embrace me once again, as if to reassure themselves that I was finally and truly wed.

Mr. Emerson and I set out on our journey in midmorning. Most of my
furniture had been sent ahead, packed in two great carts, but we carried my
trunk of clothes and a few other personal things in the chaise. Mr. Emerson
held my hand as we rode, the pressure of his fingers quickening my palm.

We reached Concord late in the afternoon. The sun was low and the air,
which had been warm all day, turned cool and crystalline beneath the still-
blue sky. Tiers of saffron light lay across the fields, broken by the long shadows of trees that grew beside slanting rail fences. We passed an orchard on
our right—red fruit winked brightly among the darkening leaves. Clouds
clotted the western horizon, their edges silvered by the sun. The trees on the
hills were already shrouded in darkness.

We passed houses I recognized from my first visit: a small brown hut with
a listing chimney; a two-story brick home set well back from the road; the
charred posts and beams of a burned barn. Mr. Emerson, who had been
telling me of his delight in Montaigne's essays, said, "We're almost there,"
and I felt my stomach twist in a flutter of goosey anticipation.

We rounded a narrow curve and the road grew level and straight, running
between two wide fields bounded by woodlots. Ahead, on the left, I glimpsed
a white house between the trees. I pressed the heels of my hands hard into my
waist in a vain attempt to quiet my rebellious insides. Mr. Emerson had promised that I would like the house, and I'd believed him—had felt obliged to believe him—but I was suddenly overwhelmed with doubt. What if he hadn't
noticed crooked-set windows, or overlooked a missing pantry? What if the
dining room wasn't large enough to hold my mahogany table? Or the bedchamber too small to contain my four-poster? What if the stair balustrades
were broken or wobbly?

Suddenly the trees opened and the house came into full view. Mr. Emerson slowed the horse. We turned beneath a row of horse chestnuts, went
through a gate into a grassy yard, and drew up in front of a small portico. He
slipped the reins and settled back in his seat.

"Welcome home," he said.

My stomach clamped down hard. *My home is Plymouth.* I thought, the
words beating in my mind with the fervor of drums, but I did not say it, for
at that moment I couldn't speak. I stared at the house, at the long white

clapboards and twin chimneys. I knew from Mr. Emerson's letters that the building was L-shaped, but from my angle in the buggy seat, it looked like a two-story box. It was neither as elegant nor as large as I'd expected.

Beyond the fence to my left lay an unkempt field, and behind the house the land dipped, then rose again to a low ridge occupied by a large brick house that, even at a distance, I could see was sadly in need of repair. I caught the bright glint of a stream twisting through the field. A few young birch trees grew at the water's edge. The landscape looked raw and barren—the low hills a drab brown in the dwindling light.

"You're unnaturally quiet," Mr. Emerson said. "I hope you're not disappointed."

I managed to find my voice. "It's a handsome house. How could I be disappointed? Is the inside plaster and lathe still exposed?"

He laughed and assured me it was not. As he helped me down from the chaise, the front door swung open and Charles appeared.

"Waldo!" He leapt down the steps and embraced his brother, as if he hadn't seen him in months. "Congratulations on your new life! To both of you!" He turned and clasped me in such a hearty embrace that my bonnet twisted off and fell to the ground. At that moment, Mr. Emerson turned to secure a box from the chaise and accidentally trod upon the gray satin brim.

"I see marriage hasn't relieved you of any clumsiness, Waldo." Charles stooped to retrieve my crushed hat. "I had hopes that this union might reform you." He straightened and grinned at me. "I apologize for my brother. I fear he'll remain forever unredeemed in this matter of gracefulness. Which will, no doubt, be a severe trial to you." He bowed and handed me the bonnet.

I couldn't help laughing, despite my ruined hat. "Bonnets are of no account in the theater of marriage," I said. "Nor is grace a requirement for love."

"You see, Charles?" Mr. Emerson said. "Her manners and elegance should relieve all your anxiety. She may even reform your mischievous ways."

Charles's reply was cut off as a horrifying shriek filled the air. He winced and Mr. Emerson's smile disappeared in an annoyed frown.

"That's Sarah Sales." Charles gestured to the building on the ridge. "Chief resident of the poor farm. It's on the other side of Mill Brook but it might as well be in your yard for the all the protection the brook offers. Sarah's lived there for sixteen years, demented after the birth of a stillborn son. Some days she screams for hours on end, and yet there are days when she won't utter a sound."

I must have looked distressed for Mr. Emerson quickly laid his hand on my arm. "Don't fret. I plan to set a screen of trees along the stream that will soon block both sight and sound."

"No," I said, for pity had filled my bosom. "I won't have it obscured. Better that it should serve as a constant reminder of Christ's words to attend to the least of these."

"Or perhaps as an inducement to ingenuity, since I doubt that God wishes my studies to be so distracted." Mr. Emerson had assumed a cheerful tone. "We'll discuss the matter at another time. I've waited three months to learn if this place merits your approval. I can't wait a moment longer. You must see the inside."

He led me around the house to the front door, opened it and stood aside as I entered. I found myself in a wide hall amidst a jumble of chairs and small tables facing a bare wooden stairway. My eyes instantly began gauging and measuring. Good quality carpeting would be costly, but it was a necessity in a home whose chief occupant was devoted to study. Mr. Emerson should not have to endure the clattering of shoes up and down stairs all day. Likewise, something would have to be done about the entry. Despite its width, it seemed cramped and unwelcoming.

"This will be my study," Mr. Emerson said, guiding me through an open doorway to my right. The last of the day's light slipped through two west-facing windows and lay in yellow spears on the wooden floor. There were six windows in all, two each facing west, north, and south. I was glad that someone had thought to clean the panes. The walls were papered in frescoed India ink—a vigorous pattern of houses and barns and trees. A square center table was flanked by two straight chairs. It was a large room—too large for a study. And, with so many windows, it was certain to be cold in winter, despite the odd-looking coal stove that sat in the corner.

I crossed the room and swung one of the shutters back over the window. It closed securely and seemed tight enough, but its true worth would not be known until colder weather arrived.

"We'll remove those two windows," Mr. Emerson said, as if able to read my thoughts, "and build a chimney, with two fireplaces. Charles's and Elizabeth's parlor will be on the other side of the wall. And here"—he indicated the blank wall to my left—"I'll have bookshelves from floor to ceiling. The shelves will be separate units, with handles, so they can be easily rearranged. Or removed from the house entirely in case of fire."

"How clever!" I said, marveling at the scope of my husband's genius. I had not, until then, seen him exhibit any interest in things of a practical nature apart from finances and was pleased that his love of philosophy might be balanced by a pragmatic efficiency. "Will you build them yourself?"

He shook his head. "No. Nor are they my design. Reverend Ripley's study is arranged that way and I've admired it since I was a boy. I fear I have no more talent with the saw and hammer than I do with animals. Any effort I made in that regard would distress us both. But there are many skilled carpenters about who are ready to turn out a fine shelf for a small fee."

I saw the wisdom of his plan, yet a stab of disappointment lingered, regret that he was not well-versed in these male arts. I recalled my father fixing the hinges on the half door that led from our kitchen to the garden. It was through that same door that our milk cow, Buffalo, used to put her head, seeking the food scraps I slipped to her. When I was four, I'd discovered that by wrapping my arms around her neck, I could swing in and out of the door without opening it. I'd spent a warm spring afternoon practicing my new skill, until my delighted squeals summoned Father, and he put an end to it.

"Lidian." The gentle pressure of Mr. Emerson's hand at my elbow brought me back to the present. I found him smiling at me. "It seems you are forever slipping away from me to commune with unseen spirits. Let me show you your parlor. It's right across the hall."

The parlor was a mirror of the study, except that it had four windows instead of six, and held more furniture, most of which I recognized as my own—a small mahogany desk, a narrow sofa, and a Queen Anne chair covered in gray watered silk. A fireplace claimed the south wall.

"Mrs. Emerson?" A tall woman appeared in the doorway to the left of the fireplace. Her round, pink face was set off by black hair, braided into a great twist at her crown. She wore no cap. "Tea's nearly ready, ma'am, but I haven't been able to find the china. There's no plates."

I must have stared at her oddly, for I was not yet accustomed to being addressed as Mrs. Emerson. I tried to imagine serving tea without plates.

"This is Nancy Colesworthy," Mr. Emerson said. "My mother sent her to help ease our labors as we adjust to our new situation. I believe I wrote you that she's been a cook in our family for many years."

"Yes." At last I began to come round. "It's very kind of your mother." I'd retained one of our Winslow House servants and arranged for another recommended by my aunt—they were both to come to Concord within the week—Hitty to keep house and Louisa to cook—but it would be several days before their arrival.

I was grateful that my mother-in-law had declared her wish to remain at the Manse until I furnished the house. I was not eager to have her move in with us, for I sensed that our natures would often be in conflict, and it would be necessary for me to frequently hold my tongue. Though I regarded the coming trial as part of God's plan to perfect me, I did not relish it.

"I took the liberty of using saucers, ma'am," Nancy said. "I hope that suits you."

I smiled. "An excellent idea. Let me help you set things out."

"Oh, no, ma'am! That won't be necessary at all. I've taken care of everything. Just wanted to check about the saucers." I detected a hard scrape of disapproval behind Nancy's tight smile.

"We'll have our tea as soon as Mr. Emerson has finished showing me the house," I said firmly. Whereupon I linked my arm through my husband's, praying that he would quickly proceed.

We followed Nancy through a second entryway and into the dining room. Its lively red wallpaper wearied my eyes, yet the fireplace looked in good condition. I found myself picturing pale green walls and the green-and-white carpet from my Plymouth bedroom covering the bare plank floor. The kitchen beyond was plainly furnished with cupboards and a long counter, but it was spacious and well-lit. I was pleased to see that a range companioned the fireplace and that a large pantry was easily accessible.

We then went back through the rooms to the front entry, for Mr. Emerson insisted that my first ascent to the second floor should be by the front stairs. At the landing, the stairs turned, and I mounted the last few steps to find myself at the second-floor hall window overlooking the street. I counted nine horse chestnut trees along the fence, none yet old enough to have grown as tall as the house, but their long flat leaves were already beginning to turn yellow. A farmer in an ox-drawn wagon passed slowly on the road beyond the fence. The clatter of his iron-rimmed wheels shook the windowpanes and raised a trail of dust.

Behind me, Mr. Emerson said, "It's closer to the road than I would like, but we'll set out more trees and soon we'll feel as if we're on a remote country lane."

I did not tell him that I experienced that remoteness already, and it was not a pleasant feeling. Instead I again took his arm and together we inspected the upstairs rooms. We allotted them with little discussion, for the choices were obvious. Mrs. Emerson would occupy the room over my husband's study, while the chamber above the parlor would be the master bedroom. The room over the kitchen would go to Charles, who had already installed his bachelor bedstead there. The remaining chamber we assigned to Lucy. Frank and Sophia and the servants would sleep in the garret.

Though some of my furniture had already arrived from Plymouth, my bed, in which we had slept on our wedding night, was not due until the next day.

"We'll just have to make do, and sleep in my old bed." Mr. Emerson kissed my cheek. "We're in the country now and must adopt country ways." And he gave me such a frankly ardent smile that I glanced away, blushing.

We went back downstairs to the dining room. The candles had been lit and cast a yellow light over the linen-covered table. I saw with relief that my silver tea set had been unpacked and waited on the sideboard. Our wedding cake dominated the center of the table, emanating its strong, fruity perfume. A platter was heaped with slabs of cold mutton. Thick slices of bread sat beside a bowl of strawberry preserves. Nancy filled our glasses from a bottle of claret as we took our places, and then we bowed our heads as Mr. Emerson prayed that God's blessing would rest always on this house and the bright enterprise of our marriage.

"Well, Lidian." Charles raised his head and aimed his smile past Mr. Emerson to me. "What are you going to do to this place?" He swept the room with a large gesture of his hand. "To make it sufficiently transcendental for my brother's needs, that is?"

I smiled back at him, my heart singing. "Since peaceful surroundings are the first requirement for transcendence, I must change these hideous red walls."

He laughed, as did Mr. Emerson, in a short burst. "I didn't expect you would find everything to your satisfaction," my husband said. "But don't burden yourself with so much transformation that you injure your health." He lifted the platter of mutton and passed it to me. "I'm convinced that the country air will agree with you, Lidian. Starting with the improvement of your appetite."

"I'm sure of it. As long as it's well mixed with conversation and marital concord," I said.

Once again, we all laughed.

That night, I prepared for bed by the light of a single candle, while

Mr. Emerson and Charles talked in the parlor below. I could hear their voices rising and falling, and the occasional eruption of Charles's laughter.

I laid my nightgown on the bed. Its blue satin ribbons gleamed. The night air had turned cold and the buttons on my bodice were knots of ice beneath my fingers. I drew my arms from the sleeves, loosened the hooks at my waist and let the dress fall. I unlaced my petticoats, pulled my chemise over my head, and stood shivering in my pantaloons and shift as I removed the comb, false curls, and pins from my hair. I placed them on my bureau, as was my habit, though with a sharp awareness that the furniture was no longer mine. Mr. Emerson owned it now, as he owned everything that belonged to me—as he owned even me, in my own flesh and person.

I turned and quickly scooped my nightgown over my head. It spilled around me in soft, cool folds. Impulsively, I pressed my face into the cloth at my left elbow, to catch the scent of Plymouth in the fabric. A wave of home-sickness swept through me, so intense that I clenched my hands to the sides of my face.

After a moment I opened the windows and blew out the candle, then climbed into bed, pulling the heavy wool blanket over me. The cornhusk mattress crackled pleasantly beneath me. I wondered how much longer Mr. Emerson would remain downstairs talking with his brother. The bed was not uncomfortable, though it sagged alarmingly in the middle and was set too low to the floor to take advantage of the warmer air in the upper part of the room. I lay in the darkness, listening to the wind in the field below my window.

It was some time before I heard Mr. Emerson's footsteps on the stairs. He put his candle on the nightstand, then removed his collar and placed it care-fully on the bureau beside my comb. He was humming a tune I didn't recog-nize. I watched him through half-shut eyes as he took off his clothes and stood naked a moment before putting on his nightshirt. The light from the candle flickered across his thighs and stomach. I felt a stab of excitement. I couldn't see his face, but I knew that he was smiling. How I loved his smile! Especially when it was directed at me. As he got into bed, I rolled to face him, suddenly eager for his touch, as I had not been the night before. Suddenly and desperately in love.

I DEVOTED most of the next day to wrestling the parlor carpet into place. Nancy and Mr. Emerson tried to help me as they were able, but neither had

the patience to stay with the task, so it fell to me. At three, a load of my furniture came from Plymouth, and we hurriedly pushed most of it into Mrs.
Emerson's room. The four-poster was set up in our bedchamber and I piled it
festively high with pillows and blankets, before going back to the carpet. The
rough matting edges scraped and cut my fingers so that by the day's end they
were torn and bleeding, yet I was satisfied with the outcome, and relieved that
the task was finished.

Hitty, my Plymouth chambermaid, arrived on the evening coach, and her
presence revived me. That evening, as I sat at the dining-room table writing
my first letter as a married woman to Lucy, I reflected on how everything
pointed so clearly toward the perfection of my union with Mr. Emerson. I
was certain that we were on the threshold of a new age when harmony of
thought and conduct would rule us all.

LUCY ARRIVED a week later, on a day that was to prove the most trying of
my young marriage. I was in the kitchen coring apples for a bird's nest pudding, when I heard a carriage pull up to our east entrance. I went to the window and watched a strange man and woman step out of an ornate vehicle.
He was tall, with thick brown hair that curled down over a long forehead.
The woman was shorter, and round as an apple. I called for Nancy to greet
them, which she did, though not without a sidelong glance of reproach, a
look to which I was already growing accustomed.

"They're here to see Mr. Emerson," Nancy announced when she returned.
"I put them in the parlor."

"Thank you." Apple juice stained my hands and apron but I had no time
to change into a presentable dress. All I could do was remove my apron and
hastily wipe my hands on a towel.

Mr. Emerson introduced the couple as Benjamin and Martha Rodman,
friends from New Bedford. "You must stay the night," he told them. "We've
so much to discuss. And here we are"—he gestured with pride to his surroundings—"rattling around in this big house. We must put it to good use."

"You're an excellent friend, Waldo," Benjamin said, "but we cannot im-
pose so soon after your wedding."

"Nonsense! Good friends are never an imposition. Are they, Lidian?"

I had no choice but to smile and echo my husband's words and hurry off
to make arrangements. There was no place for the Rodmans to sleep except

Mrs. Emerson's room, which was jammed so tightly with furniture it could not be entered. I sent Hitty and Nancy to start moving what pieces they could into the hallway.

I was nearly frantic with worry. Lucy and her children were due at any moment. I'd worked all morning to prepare my sister a warm welcome. Now my plans were thrown into disarray by my husband's largesse. I could not, of course, display my displeasure in front of the Rodmans, but I intended to make my feelings plain to Mr. Emerson before we slept that night.

When Lucy arrived just after three o'clock, I perceived her exhaustion at once. Her trip had been complicated by the presence of a loutish man who insisted on smoking cigars. I whisked Lucy up to her room, while Frank and Sophia trailed wearily behind. Lucy stepped over the threshold and burst into tears.

I made her sit down as I untied her bonnet and unhooked her cloak. The children stood in the doorway, silent as stones.

"Go down to the kitchen," I told them. "Ask Nancy to bring up some tea and cake for your mother." They left obediently, but I noted the reluctant set of their small shoulders.

It took me some time to persuade Lucy to reveal the source of her dismay. Finally, in halting sobs, she told me that, while she would be forever indebted to my hospitality, she was devastated that she would no longer be mistress of her own home, or mother of her own children.

I tried to console her, to assure her that we would share the management of the house, and that certainly she'd never cease being the mother of her children. But she would not listen. She sobbed on and on. How desperately I wanted to stay with her, to confess my own doubt at my ability to serve as Mr. Emerson's wife! But there was too much work to be done. I left her to unpack and joined Hitty in Mrs. Emerson's chamber. Together we moved as many pieces as we were able into the hallway before Nancy summoned us to the table.

She had prepared a simple but substantial supper, and I saw by Mr. Emerson's expression that the sight of so many at his table charmed him. He led the conversation from the pleasures of reading to the properties of acorns, and successfully engaged the interest of all parties, even Sophia and little Frank.

After the table was cleared and Mr. Emerson had taken the Rodmans off on a long walk, I took Hitty and Nancy upstairs, where we finished making the bedchamber suitable for our guests. It was half past ten at night when I was finally able to invite the Rodmans upstairs. It was then that Mrs. Rodman confessed in her soft voice that she had neither nightclothes nor brushes with her. Did I have some that she might borrow? And so I handed over my silver brushes and my best nightgown with the ribbons and silk insets.

When I finally retired that evening it was nearly midnight. Mr. Emerson was already in bed, though not yet asleep. I undressed, put on my old yellowed nightgown and took my hair down, then sat in the chair by the fireplace to plait it.

"There's something we must discuss," I said, reciting the speech I'd been silently preparing all evening. "I hope in the future you'll consult me before you invite unexpected guests to stay the night. It puts a great burden—"

Mr. Emerson spoke before I had finished and I wondered later if he, too, had prepared what he would say. "Surely the true worth of a hostess is measured by her ability to respond generously on the instant, making the comfort and pleasure of her guests her chief concern." He propped himself on his elbows. "And Lidian, you were magnificent! More gracious than I could have hoped for."

I dropped my braid as he rose from the bed and crossed the room to me. He took my hands and drew me from the chair. "Don't you see, my Queen? It's already begun! Our country home has become a temple of friendship and hospitality! And only days after your arrival! I could not have dreamed so swift and perfect a beginning to our enterprise!"

His enthusiasm and approval stayed the complaint in my throat. His smile lit my heart. And soon his kisses turned all thoughts of recrimination to joy.

7

Associations

The true economy of housekeeping is simply the art of gathering up all the fragments, so that nothing be lost.

— LYDIA MARIA CHILD

Mr. Emerson quickly established the routine he kept for the rest of his life—he rose at six, pulled on his blue wool robe, visited the privy, washed his hands, splashed a few drops of cold water onto his face, dressed, and was seated at the dining-room table by seven, awaiting his breakfast. He rarely wanted much to eat—a thin slice of pie and a cup of coffee sustained him through his morning labors. Sometimes he took a second cup with him into his study, always closing the door firmly behind him. I learned to resent the click of the falling latch, for it meant I would not see him again until one, when he emerged for dinner. In the afternoons, he spent an hour or two writing letters, then went out for a long walk. I sometimes accompanied him, though he had a penchant for woodland paths and fields where brambles caught at my hems and burrs stuck to my petticoats. After his walk, he retired again to his study until the lamps were lit and tea was served. In the evenings, we entertained. Guests came so frequently I began to wonder if I'd ever have the opportunity to speak with him alone again.

Lucy's presence and companionship was a pleasant compensation. I consulted her on all manner of things and once, during the privacy of a walk home from the butcher's, I questioned her on the matter of pregnancy. It troubled me that I'd not yet conceived, for Mr. Emerson's attentions had been constant and vigorous. I told her this without looking directly at her, focusing my gaze instead on a tree in front of the First Parish Church.

"I recall that you were quite ill with Frank," I said. "But my digestion is so often disrupted that I don't know how I'll distinguish one condition from the other. I may be expecting a child unaware."

"You'll know well enough when the time comes," she assured me. "Your menses will cease and you'll feel fatigued and sore in your bosom." She stopped and shifted her market basket to her left arm. "Didn't Mother tell you any of this?"

I shook my head, and at last found the mettle to face her. "I worry that age has robbed me of fertility. I'm three years past thirty. And I don't think I could bear it if I were unable to give Mr. Emerson the child he longs for!"

Lucy's smile disappeared. I watched something close in her face and knew she was thinking of Charles. "Men are always eager to replicate themselves. But remember, they have no understanding of the rigors of childbearing. Or child rearing, for that matter. I've sometimes thought that the barren woman has the best of it."

"Lucy! You can't mean that!" I put my hand over my open basket, as if there were a babe lying inside who required my protection. "How could you imagine living without Sophia and Frank?"

"I love them dearly, Liddy, but you have no idea—you *can't* have any idea until you have your own—what they cost me."

"I'm astounded to hear such thoughts from you." We'd stopped walking and I moved to face her, blocking her way. "God gives us children to increase our love. I thought you of all people, took delight in motherhood. It's one of the reasons I want my own child."

I thought she'd hang her head but instead she looked me straight in the eye. "A child will disturb every belief you ever held, Liddy."

I wanted to smile, to make *her* smile; I tried to think of something light and amusing to say, but her hard gaze emptied my mind. I was relieved when the sound of an approaching wagon required us to move to the side of the road.

FOR THE FIRST MONTH of my marriage I was entirely caught up in the flurry of decorating. I was so busy I scarcely had time to miss Plymouth. In the parlor I installed cream, watered-satin wallpaper and a carpet in vibrant shades of red. My rosewood cabinet and center table, the red moreen-covered sofa with its elegantly carved legs—all went into that room. The brass andirons I'd polished as a young girl gleamed from the fireplace. In the dining room, I installed my old green-and-white carpet beneath Lucy's mahogany table.

I distributed and redistributed the other furniture, convinced that there was a proper place for each piece. I set Mr. Emerson's favorite rocking chair in the study and added his bachelor bedstead to Charles's room. The green rocking chair, which had belonged to his first wife, matched the dining-room carpet, so I placed it in a corner of that room, though I soon questioned my wisdom in doing so. Sometimes when we were eating, Mr. Emerson's gaze rested there, and a certain look came into his face that made me feel forsaken.

Every day presented countless chores—sweeping floors, dusting furniture, airing chambers, making beds, cleaning and refilling lamps. I spent long hours in the kitchen, preparing meals and supervising Louisa and Nancy. I made caraway cakes seasoned with rosewater, and Indian cake of meal and molasses, adding stewed pumpkin to enrich the batter. I made pies daily, varying them so that Mr. Emerson would not find his diet tedious—apple, cranberry, rhubarb, custard, and huckleberry. I made hasty puddings and cranberry puddings from recipes Aunt Joa gave me. My favorite was bird's nest pudding, which filled the kitchen with the scent of baking apples.

All day I moved like a dancer across the scratched wooden floors, responding to the changes of sunlight as it climbed the wall behind the pie safe. By the time Mr. Emerson emerged from his study for dinner, the house was filled with the perfume of domesticity.

WHEN BRONSON ALCOTT FIRST APPEARED on our front doorstep in his worn and unfashionable clothes, I thought him a vagrant and was about to ask him to go to the kitchen door, when Mr. Emerson came out of his study. Greeting Bronson with a hearty handclasp, he introduced him to me as the most interesting teacher in New England, and led him into the parlor, where Charles was sitting by the fire. Soon the four of us fell to discussing philosophy and education. Our guest had a beatific smile, a serene disposition, and a voice that made me think of sun-warmed seas. Before an hour had passed, I'd invited him to dine and offered him accommodation should he wish to stay the night. His manner was so congenial and his attentions to me so generous that when he accepted I felt he'd bestowed a favor.

Over dinner, Bronson explained at length his use of Socratic dialogue as a tool to unlock the minds of the young. "I've recently been discussing Luke's description of the birth of Christ with my students. My method is to first ensure that they know the meanings of the words. Let me demonstrate. If one of you would play the role of student—" He turned to me. "Would you be willing, Mrs. Emerson?"

"I'd be honored." I wondered where Bronson intended to lead me. I felt vaguely wary, as if I needed to be on the alert for the possibility of both pain and pleasure.

"What is the meaning of the word 'conceive'?" he asked.

"To be with child." I glanced at my husband, but his face registered nothing but a cheerful curiosity.

"And how do you think a mother feels knowing she is with child?"

"Happy, of course. She rejoices in her good fortune." I thought of Lucy, how joyfully she had announced her pregnancies to me. She had been afraid, as well; I had not missed the dread behind her smile.

"Precisely!" Bronson pushed back his chair, and extended his long legs, digging his heels into my carpet. He rubbed his hands together as if they were cold. "Yet what is women's experience of childbirth?"

I felt as if I were reciting a catechism. "Pain and suffering."

"And if that is true, how can a woman rejoice when she is with child?"

"Because she knows she will bring a new life into the world."

Bronson beamed, but I saw that Mr. Emerson was frowning.

"Are you actually teaching such lessons to children, Bronson?"

"I am!" Bronson turned his radiance upon my husband. "And the children prove Plato's thesis, that all knowledge resides within the mind at birth, and merely needs the right instruction to draw it forth."

"Has no parent objected to your introducing such intimate matters to schoolchildren?" Charles asked.

Bronson shrugged. "A few. But I cannot be controlled by narrow opinions. These children are vessels of wisdom! They must be allowed expression!"

"You must pay some attention to your public, Bronson," Mr. Emerson said. "They are not so wise as you."

"It's a matter of witnessing the truth," Bronson said.

"Indeed it is," I said. "Throughout history the man of greatness has had to stand against the crowd."

My husband was still frowning. "That may be. I must say that your disregard for the opinions of others fascinates me."

"I advise no course of action that I'm not willing to take myself." Bronson straightened in his chair and raised his hands. "I've applied this teaching method to my own daughters with excellent results."

"You have children then?" I smiled at Bronson, whose face seemed to shine with a sacred glory.

"Three." He folded his long fingers across the tops of his knees. The brown fabric of his trousers had the faded look that comes with frequent washing. "Elizabeth was born last June. Anna is four and Louisa is two, as different in nature and appearance as two girls can be. Yet both have benefited by early training and observation." He smiled. Like an angel, I thought. "I've discovered in each of them my own affections incarnate."

"We hope for children soon," I said. "I believe the innocent of this world are the greatest teachers."

"Yes! It's been my experience, precisely, Mrs. Emerson! Every child is a revelation!"

I smiled. "I would go farther. I include the animal kingdom among those innocents."

"But so do I, my dear lady! I *do*!" He could no longer confine himself to his chair but rose to his feet and began to pace in a small circle. "The treatment of dumb beasts is an *abomination*! No less than *slavery*!" He stopped and faced me. "I trust you have an abolitionist's soul?"

"And heart!" I said vehemently.

Bronson returned to his chair, his face flushed. "I cannot express the extent of my good fortune in meeting you. I believe I've at last found my paradise—in this unexpected corner of creation."

Mr. Emerson leaned forward. "You must consider living in Concord, Bronson. I mean to gather a community of philosophers and lovers of nature here, and you ought to be part of it."

This was the first I'd heard that my husband planned to assemble a group of like-minded people to live nearby. I would come to be astonished at the lengths to which he would go for that purpose, but then—in those early days—I was as enthusiastic as he, for Bronson utterly inspired me with his words and his serene countenance.

I HAD, by this time, received several letters from Aunt Mary, who, once I was unequivocally bound to her nephew, had replaced her hostility with a forceful assault on my affections. She was convinced that I could have an exemplary effect on Mr. Emerson and lectured me on methods by which I might divert his pursuit of spiritual beauty to the fight for abolition. She praised me for my devotion to the Cause and insisted that she'd found in me someone so like herself in temperament and thought that it could only be a miracle of God's grace.

She soon took it upon herself to invite to my house two abolitionists she'd heard speak near Boston. Not for an evening of conversation in our parlor, but to breakfast. When I pointed out the inconvenience this caused me, she replied in her blunt way that the full schedule of the men prohibited another arrangement. She clearly was used to having family members cater to her whims and expected me to do the same.

I was equal to any conflict and was determined to stand my ground, until Mother Emerson intervened on Mary's behalf.

"It would go a long way toward smoothing the waters if you'd accommodate Mary in this case," she said when I called on her at the Manse. "What harm can it do, after all, to expose Waldo to these ideas? If it's a matter of food preparation, I'll come to the house and help you."

Her manner carried an unspoken criticism. Yet in those days I was still so eager to please that I extended the requested invitation without consulting my husband.

Miss Emerson arrived with George Thompson and Samuel May just after seven o'clock in the morning and they were already settled at the dining-room table when my husband came down for his morning coffee. Although he handled the situation with grace, their presence postponed his habitual retreat to his study, which set him in a bad mood. Yet he sat patiently through an emotional and heated discourse by Mr. Thompson, then put down his fork and fixed him closely with his gaze.

"Your feelings are noble," he said. "Yet a cause so sacred as the abolition of slavery requires facts and principles above personal feelings."

The abolitionist hesitated in his response, which gave Miss Emerson an opportunity to leap into the conversation, reanimating Mr. Thompson and his friend.

Though I noted some pointed barbs in my husband's remarks, neither man appeared to take offense. They departed with Aunt Mary in high spirits, apparently convinced that they'd converted Mr. Emerson to the Cause, while he enjoyed a hearty laugh at their expense.

Later that evening, when we were alone in our chamber, he raised the subject again. "I'll always admire your loyalty to principle and truth," he said, "but I beg you, do not invite guests to our breakfast table again if you wish me to be civil. I require the solitude of my study and the companionship of my books before facing such dunderheads."

"*Dunderheads?*" I cried. "They're men of principle and compassion!"

"They're fools who do no benefit to their Cause. Mr. Thompson is vanity-stricken and won't allow the words of any other to make the slightest impression on him. Where did you find him?"

"Aunt Mary asked that I invite them."

"I should have known."

"I'm entirely in agreement with their thoughts," I said, as calmly as I was able. I did not like his condescension. "And I think your aunt has done us a great favor in her suggestion."

"Lidian." He took my face between his hands. "You must not let her bully you. She would soon rule the nation if women could vote."

"Can you doubt that would be an improvement?" I asked.

He didn't answer, but kissed me, chuckling. It occurred to me as I smiled back at him that he had his own sort of bullying, which was just as effective as his aunt's.

SHORTLY AFTER the abolitionists' visit, I joined the Female Anti-Slavery Society. At my first meeting there were not many in attendance—a handful of women headed by Mrs. Mary Brooks gathered in the dimly lit yellow parlor of the Thoreau boardinghouse on the Mill Dam. We discussed the ethics of secession. Many believed that Massachusetts should withdraw from the Union, for the slaveholding states had cast their spell too completely over

Congress. We also complained of the corruption of the churches, the passiv-
ity of the clergy, and the depravity of those who justified slavery by quoting
Bible verses. As we turned from the issues and began to address ways we might
increase our membership, several loud thumps sounded directly over our
heads.

We all looked up, startled, and Cynthia Thoreau apologized. Her boarders, she said, were not always considerate of other guests. There was also her
own family, including two active sons. She gestured widely as she spoke, and
something in her motions suggested to me a couple of gangly schoolboys
wrestling on the floor above our heads. I was thus surprised at the end of the
meeting to discover that John and Henry Thoreau were not boys at all, but
full-grown men—John a teacher and Henry a student enrolled at Harvard
College. John was both charming and cheerful and exchanged pleasantries
with the ladies, while Henry hung back in the doorway's shadows, apparently
too shy to mingle. I did not take any particular notice of him that evening,
except to observe the depth of his gaze. His eyes were unusually large—or at
least gave that impression—and seemed to regard the world with an ageless
curiosity.

Despite our small number, the meeting was lively, and we ended the evening debating whether or not to engage a speaker knowledgeable about the
southern plantation system. We argued back and forth for nearly an hour
without reaching a satisfactory conclusion. I suggested we might wish to discover who was available for such a lecture before dissipating more energy in
speculation. They all regarded me for a moment of chilling silence. Then
Cynthia spoke.

"I'm sure you're right, Mrs. Emerson. We are going at this thing back-
wards. We must first find our speaker, then raise our funds. Who shall it be,
ladies?"

The women all began to talk at once. Frederick Douglass was mentioned,
as was William Lloyd Garrison and Samuel May. Each had a different
suggestion—all of them men.

"Why not invite a woman?" I said.

"A *woman*?" Their faces registered no less shock than their voices.

"We're a female society. What better group to engage a female speaker?"

"We'd subject ourselves to ridicule," one woman said.

"No man will attend," said another.

I smoothed my leather gloves on my lap. They were warm under my hand, satiny as newborn pups. "My husband will attend," I said. "Mr. Emerson is as interested in the thoughts of females as of his fellow men."

Perhaps it was the incredulity of the women's faces that caused me to doubt my bold assertion. For, while it was true that my husband had expressed his belief that women were the intellectual equals of men, he had not yet asserted that women should speak in public.

"Do we have your word on that?" Mary Brooks asked.

"You do."

"But can he persuade others to attend?" Cynthia moved restlessly on her chair, rocking from side to side so that her cap ruffles fluttered. She was a tall, sturdy woman, outspoken in manner, and renowned throughout the village for her love of controversy.

"I cannot speak to his success. But I believe he will try."

I returned home that evening filled with enthusiasm, for the women had tentatively adopted my plan. My husband listened patiently and then commented with a smile that it appeared I had taken Concord by storm. I protested that I had done no such thing, and then insisted he must help me by promising to attend our lecture.

"I can't promise my presence for an unknown date. You know my own lecture schedule often takes me out of town."

"But I will tell you the date as soon as I know it myself!"

He unwrapped my long wool muffler—in my excitement I'd neglected to remove it—and then proceeded to change the subject by kissing my neck and leading me upstairs to our bed.

THAT FALL, Aunt Mary converted Charles to the Cause, and he began to lecture for abolition. Though he was a less eloquent speaker than my husband, he made up for it in zeal. He faced great hostility as a consequence of these lectures, and I once overheard Mr. Emerson cautioning him that, if he did not take care, he might face a violent attack similar to that suffered by Mr. Garrison in Boston. Charles retorted that the threat of violence by a group of slavery-sympathizing thugs was precisely the reason he was compelled to speak out.

"You should lend your own voice to the Cause," he said, pressing a long finger into my husband's chest. "And soon. History will not look kindly on those who bury their heads in dusty old books while people lie in chains."

Mr. Emerson smiled gently. "I have no desire to be remembered by historians," he said. "I merely want to be left in peace."

The two brothers loved each other dearly, but they did not approach life in the same way. Mr. Emerson always played the role of the older, wiser brother, who weighed each action carefully before taking it. Charles was passionate and impetuous, with a zealous mind and a great heart, and I often found myself siding with him over my husband.

Aunt Mary came and went as if she were part owner of our home, always complaining about her lack of a permanent residence. Though Mr. Emerson offered to acquire her a house in Concord, she was like a restless chickadee, unable to alight in one place for long, forever moving to what she regarded as a more auspicious situation.

I enjoyed her company, despite her penchant for cutting remarks, so often at my expense. Perhaps she liked to see what my retort would be, for I always had one ready. And it was clear from her reaction that my own comments sometimes cut her more deeply than she cared to admit. Often we argued for more than an hour, our voices rising in angry octaves, before someone stepped in to call a truce. I knew that Aunt Mary relished these bouts as much as I did. Her eyes sparkled like small, bright jewels as she spit out her noxious words, and her mouth twisted in odd shapes that told me she was very near laughing.

One afternoon late in November, as the entire household sat over dinner, our repartee got out of hand, creating a rift that chance and circumstance abraded beyond repair. We were in the midst of a discussion of economy, a subject dear to Mr. Emerson's heart. He spoke at length on the distinction between a principled thrift and a miserly one. Aunt Mary joined in heartily, inserting her points often, calling to my imagination a small child dancing around a cookie jar and reaching in to pilfer one sweet after another.

Suddenly the conversation turned bitter.

"Take, for example, the extravagance I witnessed on a recent visit to Plymouth," Aunt Mary said. "Society governed the tiniest detail, from the drape of a curtain to the arrangement of spoons on a table." She picked up her own spoon and turned it slowly in her hand.

I frowned at Mr. Emerson, but he was watching his aunt with his usual warm regard. I was beginning to resent his mask of affability.

"I did not realize you had an objection to my tastes, Miss Emerson," I said. "But you are wrong to believe that I follow the dictates of others on any matter. I have always—*will* always—follow my own principles."

Aunt Mary regarded me with mock astonishment. "But you must admit, Lidian, that you often indulge your taste for luxury. Look at the way you've decorated my nephew's house."

"I think it's lovely," Lucy said, in an uncharacteristically firm tone.

Charles put down his fork. "What's wrong with it? I happen to *like* Lidian's taste. Beauty eases the digestion."

"Not mine." Aunt Mary lifted her small chin. "I find such excess distinctly unappetizing."

"Excess?" I cried, and would have said more, had not Mr. Emerson interrupted.

"Aunt Mary, kindly move us on to a more pleasurable topic."

"Pleasure is it, now? Is that all you seek in life, Waldo? Has the Jackson extravagance seduced you so completely that you've abandoned principle?"

I would have risen to leave the room, had not Charles spoken. "You go too far, Aunt Mary. Lidian is a woman of character and nobility."

"I've never hidden my thoughts in hypocrisy, Charles, and I'm too far advanced in years to begin now. If I'm sometimes more outspoken than you like, at least you can be assured I speak the truth as I perceive it."

"You perceive wrongly in this case!" Charles rose. His face had reddened dramatically. Mr. Emerson signaled him to sit down, but Charles ignored his brother. "And I think you must apologize—to Lidian and to all of us."

"Charles—" Mrs. Emerson interjected in a warning tone, but he did not look at her.

"Apologize?" Aunt Mary looked at me. Her eyes reminded me of sparks from a crackling fire. "You don't require an apology, do you, Lidian? Surely this is *one* home where I'm not required to apologize for the truth!"

I said nothing, for my feelings had been sorely tried, and I knew that silence is sometimes the most effective retort of all.

"It is *not* the truth!" Charles roared. "Waldo, why on earth don't you *say* something to this woman?"

"*This woman?* Now I'm *this woman* in my nephew's house?" Aunt Mary pushed back her chair and got to her feet. "It's plain I'm no longer welcome!"

My husband was finally stirred to action. He rose and went to her. Mrs. Emerson, Lucy, and I were the only ones still seated. "Please calm yourself, Aunt Mary. Nothing has been said that cannot be unsaid."

"Indeed there has!" She shot a deadly glance at Charles. "When my own nephew refers to me with such contempt!" She gathered her skirts and marched to the doorway, where she turned and faced us. "If I am ever in this house again, it will be because I've been carried here on a litter!" And she left in a bustle of wool and cambric.

I believe we were all stunned silent, for it was several minutes before Mr. Emerson thought to follow her, and by then it was too late. She'd taken a vow that she could not undo. More than apologies would be required to mend the broken tie.

8

Nettles

It is so universal with all classes to avoid me
that I blame nobody.
— MARY MOODY EMERSON

Charles paced back and forth between the dining room and parlor, shoe heels cracking on the hallway floor, hands clamped hard at the small of his back, his fair hair leaping about his forehead. "Inexcusable!" he raged. "There was no call for such incivility!" After several circuits, he stopped before me, where I still sat at the table. "I apologize on my aunt's behalf. It embarrasses me to admit it, but today I'm ashamed of my family."

"Charles!" His mother pressed her napkin to her chin for a moment and then dropped it beside her plate. I noticed with dismay that the plate's white rim was chipped. "You know how volatile Mary is! Why did you provoke her?"

"I didn't provoke her, Mother! She provoked me by criticizing Lidian!" He flung his arms out in frustration and knocked askew one of my botanical rose prints, which hung above the sideboard. As he turned to straighten it, Mr. Emerson came back into the room.

"She's gone." He sat slowly in his chair and raised his hands to his face. "I fear it will be months before she returns. Charles—"

"Don't take me to task for defending your wife!" Charles spun to face his brother. "Aunt Mary was clearly in the wrong! She's forever pitting one person against another, and I won't tolerate her doing so within the family! One must draw the line somewhere!"

Mr. Emerson looked at him sadly and let his hands drop. "You're usually the first to laugh at her barbs, Charles. You understand her better than anyone. And you know how dear you are to her."

I saw the flash of tears in Charles's eyes. He turned back to the print and tried again to straighten it. "I understand she has wronged your wife, Waldo." The words lay in the air like stones in a field. My husband's gaze shifted to me.

"Do you feel wronged, Lidian?"

"Of course she does!" Lucy blurted, and I turned to her in surprise, for it was not like Lucy to forget her manners. "How could she not? Liddy has never been interested in luxury and fashion!"

"It's all right, Lucy." My hands, which had been resting in my lap, rose to clutch the hem of the tablecloth, seeking the coolness of the smooth, starched linen. "I hold no rancor toward Aunt Mary. I try to be tolerant of eccentricities since I've been deemed peculiar myself." I intended my remark to elicit a laugh, but there was no response.

It was Mrs. Emerson who spoke into the silence. "Perhaps you men should indulge yourselves in a long walk this afternoon. It would do you both a great deal of good, I'm sure."

The meal was over. No one except Frank had any appetite for the bowls of bread pudding that Nancy carried in from the kitchen. I asked her to save the leftovers for tea. I rose and I looked at my husband. "I hope you and Charles enjoy your walk." I was not able to keep the bitterness from my voice.

"Lidian." Mrs. Emerson's voice forestalled my exit. "I'd like to speak with you a few moments. In private, if that is possible."

As I turned to face her, I caught Lucy's alarmed expression. "Of course, ma'am," I said, though I longed to climb the stairs to my chamber and spend the next hour in solitude. I helped her from her chair, took her arm, and led her into the parlor, where I settled her close by the fire and called Hitty to add more wood. I stood a moment at the window, studying the shape of the black tree limbs against the sky. The sunlight of the morning had disappeared behind heavy clouds and the light that came through the windows was pearl-gray and watery.

"It's been a most unfortunate day." Mrs. Emerson's voice sounded like the scrape of an iron skillet across a range.

"Indeed it has." I turned from the window and gave her a sad smile. "I join you in hoping that Miss Emerson will soon return."

"She won't." She flicked her fingers across her skirts. "When Mary makes a vow she doesn't break it. She's been a second mother to my son."

"Yes, I'm aware of her influence. Mr. Emerson speaks of her with great reverence."

Hitty came in then, her apron full of wood, and dropped to her knees before the fire. I studied her narrow back, the coarse black curls that clustered at the nape of her neck, curls that were forever escaping her cap. She leaned into the fire, dropped a small log on the jumbled coals, and rocked back.

Mrs. Emerson glared at her.

"Thank you, Hitty," I said. "You may go. I'll take care of the rest."

Hitty bounced to her feet and scurried from the room. It was plain she was as discomfited as I by the tension in the room. I went to the fire, stirred the coals, and set two more logs on the fire before sitting opposite Mrs. Emerson on the couch.

"I'm sorry to be the focus of family discord, Mrs. Emerson. You must agree, however, that I did nothing to contribute to it."

She turned her glare, which had not lessened with Hitty's departure, on me. "I believe that, as hostess, you should have endeavored with more vigor to bring harmony to the meal."

"You blame *me* for what happened?"

"One word from you could easily have diverted the conversation to a happier course." Her eyes narrowed and she leaned forward. I wondered how clearly she could see. Her voice chafed in her throat. "We women have great power when we exercise it prudently."

"But her remarks were not at all justified! In fact, they were injurious and unfounded. I'm *proud* of Charles for rising to my defense!"

"Pride goeth before a fall," she said. "You cannot allow conceit to overwhelm your responsibilities. You're a wife now."

"Conceit!" I rose, for my outrage no longer permitted me to remain still. "I'm well aware of my responsibilities!" My fingers clasped and unclasped the folds of my skirt. "Mr. Emerson did not choose me because he believed I would be like other wives. Nor has he indicated disappointment."

"I hope things will not progress to the point where he feels the need." Her mouth clamped shut.

I gazed at the lines puckering the skin above her lips. My rule of courtesy was suddenly overwhelmed by my desire to have the last word. "Please don't forget that it was *my* virtue that was questioned today, Mrs. Emerson." I left the parlor and went directly to my chamber, knowing even as I climbed the stairs that I would suffer the consequences of my rudeness, for every wife knows she cannot expect to gain her husband's sympathy in a contest with his mother.

I paced back and forth in front of the north windows, pulling at the sleeves of my gown, pinching the cloth circling my wrists and emitting great sighs, before I could bear it no longer and sought out Lucy for sisterly comfort. I found her reading in her chamber but I knew from how quickly she closed her book that she had not been able to concentrate.

"Tell me," she said, dropping the book into her brown serge-covered lap, "what did Mrs. Emerson want of you?"

I made a mocking face. "To admonish me for my indiscretions at dinner. To remind me that it was my responsibility to turn the discussion toward harmonious conversation."

Lucy laughed. "Well, you have uncommon skill in conversation. And I couldn't help noticing that you remained uncharacteristically silent through dinner."

"So you're siding with Mrs. Emerson?"

"Of course not!" Lucy batted my arm. "But why didn't you defend yourself? It's not like you to sit silent while your honor is attacked."

"I'm married now. I can't continue to act the part of the obstinate spinster."

"Of course you can! Nothing's changed but your title. You're still Liddy Jackson. And always will be."

But my sister was wrong. I was not the same. In marrying Mr. Emerson, I'd changed in ways that even I didn't understand.

CHARLES AND MR. EMERSON returned from their walk just as I was lighting the evening lamps. Charles was in high spirits, having persuaded my husband to join him in paying a call on Elizabeth. She had played her pianoforte for them and sang a very pleasant tune. Mr. Emerson invited her to join us for tea, but she'd declined. I was genuinely sorry to hear this, for my spirits would have benefited from her presence.

Lucy did not come down to tea and Frank and Sophia were unusually subdued. But the walk and Charles's company had evidently done my husband good, for he made no reference to the scene at dinner, except to inquire quietly after my mood. When I assured him I'd spent the afternoon in the excellent company of Mrs. Child's novel, he laughed good-naturedly. We drank our cider and passed a platter of cold mutton and cheese while Charles and Mr. Emerson discussed the writings of Burke and Webster. Then the conversation turned to the value of reading in general.

"A man ought to make the woods and fields his books," Mr. Emerson said, firmly putting down his knife.

Charles laughed.

"No, I am quite serious. If a man invested thus in experience, at the moment of passion his thoughts would spontaneously infuse themselves with natural imagery."

I was about to comment when Charles rocked back in his chair, and laced his hands behind his head, his grin widening yet further. "Art is it now? For how long have you concealed your feelings for that noble lady? You hide your passions well, Waldo."

Mr. Emerson, who could no longer contain his own good humor, put back his fine head and laughed.

IN NOVEMBER, Mr. Emerson received a call to supply the pulpit of the church in East Lexington. He told me offhandedly as we undressed for bed, mentioning the offer as if his decision was of no consequence. I stopped brushing my hair in midstroke and demanded that he tell me every detail. He explained that he was reluctant to accept, citing his unpopular views on the Trinity and the Lord's Supper. I urged him to reconsider, for I had secretly nurtured the dream of sitting in the front pew beneath a pulpit of some church, listening to my husband preach.

In the morning, as we sat over a breakfast of coffee and squash pie, I took up the crusade again. "You must accept this call as the blessing it is!" I wore my gray calico housedress and my husband his blue wool robe. "Think how many minds you influence from a pulpit!" I stabbed at my pie, caught a prong of crust on my fork tine, and popped it into my mouth. "You'd no longer have to seek out your audiences! They'd be waiting for you each Sunday morning. It would be a life of privilege compared to the uncertainty which burdens you now."

He smiled affectionately. "Lidian, you have things backward. You flatter my pride when a reprimand to my hubris is required. Remember, I'm no stranger to the pulpit. I'm as well acquainted with its pitfalls and discomforts as its privileges. It's not the pleasure you presume."

"Still, I'd like you to accept it. At least for a while. It would bring us a more reliable income than your lectures, and you wouldn't have to journey far."

He was silent for some time, staring into his coffee, as if he might find guidance written on its black surface. Finally, he spoke. "All right." He put down his fork and wiped his mouth with his napkin. "I'll accept their offer. For a few months you'll be able to watch your husband play the minister's part. On the condition that when I leave that pulpit you'll not browbeat me into taking another."

"Browbeat! I haven't beaten your brow nor any other part of you!" I declared.

"Call it what you will. You haven't let the matter rest." He smiled again—his generous, blessing smile that instantly swept my furies away. "You have the persistence of a terrier, my dear."

"It's a trait that serves us both, Mr. Emerson."

His smile disappeared and he looked uncharacteristically chagrined. "I'd not change you, Lidian. But you must not try to change me, either. Promise you'll not press me to return permanently to the ministry. I'm convinced that God has called me to another service."

I could not argue with God, and so I promised, though not happily. It struck me that the most demanding and onerous task required by marriage was the silencing of my tongue.

Yet my happiness was greater than my vexation. When Mr. Emerson retired to his study a few moments later, I flew up the stairs to roust Lucy out of bed and tell her the good news.

TWO WEEKS LATER, on my first Sunday as a minister's wife, I wore my bridal dress under a gray velvet cape with a matching bonnet decked in white ribbons. The sky was overcast, as gray as my bonnet, and I tasted snow in the air.

The church building was only a few years old and very similar in style and size to Concord's First Parish Church—a stately white building with a two-tiered steeple facing the road. We climbed granite steps and entered a wide front door, then ascended more steps to the assembly room. The pews were already filled. I glanced at him; he smiled and took my arm, and together we walked up the long aisle to the front pew, where I settled myself while he mounted the steps to the pulpit.

Oh, it was heaven to hear God's word from my husband's mouth! I sat in a trance of admiration, gazing up at him, silently thanking God that He had brought us together.

After the service, we proceeded to the home of a deacon, where over a meal of cold beef and turkey we discussed English literature. Mr. Emerson was about to begin a series of lectures on that subject at the Masonic Temple in Boston. He was particularly taken with Shakespeare's wisdom and articulate grace and for that reason had recently read *Romeo and Juliet* and *Hamlet*. He was fond of quoting particular lines that were not commonly known. Despite my own delight in the conversation, I quickly realized that the deacon and his wife were not familiar with Shakespeare, and out of charity I managed to steer the conversation in the direction of the new book of Watts's hymns, which better pleased the entire assembly.

On the way home, Mr. Emerson complimented me. "Your manners are unusual in the country, yet they serve us well." He surprised both Lucy and me by leaning over and kissing my cheek.

THAT WINTER he began to complain. First about my habit of opening windows to freshen the air, which he said chilled him and exposed him to lung ailments. Hadn't he told me that he had a weakness of his air passages and joints? I argued that cold, clean air was the best cure for such debility. It had kept me from consumption—I was certain of it.

Next he complained that I fretted too much over the arrangement of furniture and the color of the drapes and carpet. These things were of no consequence, he declared. They distracted the mind from lofty concerns. I contended that an attractive and graceful home was necessary to put the mind at ease. How could one concentrate on philosophy if an unsightly carpet or a dilapidated chair offended the eye? He had chosen me to manage his house, had he not? Did he now doubt my skills?

He retreated before my arguments, but did not stop complaining. When I sent him to the village for hooks and insisted that he repair a broken hinge on a cupboard door, he protested that my demands were interfering with the writing of his book.

"Surely you can wait a month while we get our home in order," I said. "You were the one who envisioned a spa for philosophers here in Concord. It was you who required a particular environment for the cultivation of your muse. Do you now believe the opposite? Does place no longer matter to you? Do you think that all one needs is a bush to sit beneath?"

"A bush." He stroked his forehead. "Strident as they are, your words always give me pause, Lidian. Perhaps we ought to call our home *Bush.*" I thought it a foolish name for a home, but it stuck and our house on the Cambridge Turnpike came to be known everywhere by that curious appellation.

"It's not my words which are strident, Mr. Emerson," I said. "It's my heart." Yet I admit that my voice sometimes grew shrill, and that I rarely submitted to his will without first vehemently asserting my own. I had believed from the first that Mr. Emerson and I had formed a new sort of union, where the wife was equal in influence and intellect to her husband. What I had not anticipated was the degree to which other people were made uncomfortable by our arrangement. I even began to wonder if Mr. Emerson himself found it awkward.

Despite our disagreements, Mr. Emerson and I remained physically passionate. He sought me nightly, and my initial disinclination for the marriage act soon turned to unexpected satisfaction. I began to respond to his caresses with unfeigned pleasure. I welcomed the feathery stroke of his tongue on my neck and mouth, the silken insistence of his hand on my thigh. Our embraces, which had at first been swift and urgent, grew less hurried as my pleasure increased.

Far from regretting the marriage, in those early days I thrived on it. My body and my mind had finally achieved a balance I had not dreamed possible. Best of all were our conversations. Mr. Emerson and I had glorious debates on every imaginable subject—the nature of men and women, the philosophy of freedom, inspiration and imagination, and the importance of social reform.

———

ONE EVENING Mr. Emerson told me that he wanted to follow the country practice of having only one table at dinner. "The servants should partake with us," he said. "They live under our roof just as Charles and Lucy and the children do."

I confessed that I'd never heard of such a custom. Yet the nobility of the idea appealed to me. "I'll speak to them tomorrow," I said.

The next morning I found Nancy, Louisa, and Hitty in the kitchen, peeling potatoes into a white ceramic bowl. When I explained Mr. Emerson's plan, Nancy and Louisa agreed, but Hitty shook her head. "I'll stay in the kitchen, ma'am," she said firmly. "It's unnatural to eat with my betters." She held a large, half-peeled potato in her left hand and she tipped it back and forth as she spoke.

"But we're not your betters," I told her. "We're your family while you reside with us."

"I'm sorry, ma'am, but I wasn't brought up to consider such notions. I was raised proper." She turned away, flicked her knife against her potato and a long strip of brown skin fell into the bowl.

Only Nancy sat with us at dinner that afternoon. Louisa had complained of a headache and taken to her bed. When Mr. Emerson tried to converse with Nancy, kindly inquiring after her family, Nancy answered, but sullenly, and pushed her food around her plate as if she had no appetite. The next day, she refused to sit with us, firmly telling us she'd changed her mind.

"I'll stay out here with Louisa and Hitty, ma'am. Where I'm comfortable."

Two months later, Hitty left us and returned to Plymouth where, she said, "People know their place and know enough to keep it."

I began to understand that the link between noble ideas and social improvement was not a simple one. Familiarity and habit were formidable opponents.

IN JANUARY, Mrs. Emerson took up residence in the room above my husband's study. I was determined to make her feel welcome, but I dreaded her long silences and Sunday soliloquies. Was this because my own mother had not sufficient health and time to teach me the ways of mothers? I'd observed the tender way Mrs. Emerson conferred with my husband and found myself longing for an older woman to look upon me with similar devotion. Yet it was impossible not to read disapproval in her scowling glances and the tart condescension in her tone of voice.

"You have a fine eye for decoration, Lidian," she told me on a Tuesday morning a week after she moved in. We were in the parlor, where I was busily removing dust from the claw-foot legs of the petticoat table. Mrs. Emerson sat on the couch, knitting stockings. Though I was turned away and couldn't see her face, I perceived she did not intend her remark as a compliment. I knew she'd lived very plainly since the death of her husband, twenty-five years before. What had begun as a necessary economy had become a beloved habit, rather like the favorite dress that a woman wears long after it grows threadbare.

"I seek bargains, madam," I said. "I'm careful with my money." I rolled the cloth tightly around my finger and pressed it deep into the mahogany grooves.

"Mr. *Emerson's* money."

I stood and busied myself with the drapery folds at the east windows. "He's never objected to my purchases."

"He has a gracious soul."

I flushed. "He appreciates beauty, madam! The philosophical mind requires pleasant surroundings, and I consider it my duty to provide him with objects harmonious to the eye."

"Please do not continue addressing me as *madam*," she said. The steady cadence of her clicking needles did not slow. "I am neither a guest nor some old woman invited to one of your soirées. I would prefer that you call me *Mother*."

I turned to look at her. She had her eyes on her knitting and the frilled brim of her white cap shaded her forehead so that I couldn't read her expression. "If that's what you prefer, then of course I'll honor your request." I folded my dust cloth and dropped it into my apron pocket. "Now you must excuse me for I have to go out and buy meat for dinner."

I don't know why I consented so readily to her request when I'd never surrendered to my husband's desire to be called Waldo. *Mother* seemed too intimate an appellation and forced me to recall each time I used it that I had no mother of my own. As I took off my apron and prepared to leave, I wondered if this were the true reason behind her request.

9

Portents

Always the soul says to us all: Cherish your best
hopes as a faith, and abide by them in action.
—MARGARET FULLER

The air in Concord was drier than in Plymouth, more extreme in temperature, and less congenial to activity. I found myself reflecting on how closely the people mirrored their climate. Concord was mud and dust and uncouth manners—all sharp edges and unhemmed fringes. It was the butcher and the judge at the same soirée. It was field dirt packed under ragged fingernails. It was the odor of pigs and cattle lying close upon the air all day, without the relief of a cleansing breeze from the sea.

I was dismayed that I was not yet with child, and wondered if I had been cursed with barrenness. My husband's physical attentions had been both constant and tender, and it seemed strange that God had not yet granted our mutual desire. I turned to the Scriptures for solace, where the cries of lamentation were countered by reminders of God's faithfulness and love. I made it a point to count my blessings, and yet Concord itself often moved me to mourn my removal from Plymouth.

I was thinking such thoughts one winter morning as I walked to the village with my market basket on my arm. I'd invited Lucy to accompany me, but she complained of a sick headache and retired to her chamber as soon as Frank went off to school. I wished she had not sent Sophia to boarding school in Boston the month before, for the girl's presence refreshed me.

The roadside mud had frozen into hard, gray ridges that made walking treacherous. Clouds the color of oyster shells loomed overhead and darker clouds crowded the western horizon. A damp cast to the air promised snow. Three large crows perched on a branch of the chestnut tree in front of First Parish Church and took flight as I passed. I stopped to look up at the tree. Its branches made an intricate black lace. The stark beauty enchanted me.

As I stood in the road, gazing upward, my mind aflame with wonder, I heard a voice at some distance call out, "Ah! A kindred spirit!" Startled at having been so boldly addressed, I turned to see a lone man advancing toward me. Despite the cold, he wore no hat and his jacket looked uncomfortably thin. His gait was a rhythmic lope that was oddly graceful. Intrigued, I watched him approach, and was suddenly reminded of my childhood dance master— for this man carried his body in the same way, and seemed to possess a similar focused intensity. As he drew near, I recognized him as one of Cynthia Thoreau's sons.

"Good morning," I said pleasantly. "Mr. Thoreau, isn't it?"

He nodded and moved to let me pass at the same moment I moved to proceed, and we found ourselves face-to-face. It was an awkward impasse, which I attempted to redeem with a sidestep, only to find that he, too, had decided to move sideways.

I smiled. "It appears we're destined to oppose each other. Perhaps one of us should wait while the other passes."

"It's less opposition than encounter," he said. "And now that we're so well met, I remember where I saw you—you attended my mother's antislavery meeting a few weeks back. You're Mr. Emerson's new wife."

"I am." I was struck by the luster in his gaze. Although he was in no way handsome, this was the second time I'd noticed his eyes, which had a penetrating quality that was both intriguing and unnerving. I was also aware of his youth. He retained a boy's innocent manner and persuasive intensity.

He glanced up at the tree. "You must tell me what message you've received from this venerable chestnut. I've often heard her speak to me, but thought it was a singular gift. She's more genial than I realized."

Again I laughed, charmed by his notion that the tree had a secret social life. "I confess she told me little, Mr. Thoreau—"

"Please call me Henry."

"Henry. Only that she wonders what you're doing in Concord. She thought you were a college student."

"Even newcomers promptly learn everyone's business in this town." He barked out a cheerful laugh. "Yet the tree is right, Mrs. Emerson, as trees so often are. The truth is I'm on my way to catch the coach to Cambridge."

"Godspeed," I said, and went on my way, more cheered than I had been yet that day. I wondered if I might after all accustom myself to Concord's country ways and come to regard them with affection.

IN MID-FEBRUARY, my monthly flow ceased. Since it had happened before when I was ill, I was afraid to hope what it might mean this time. Yet my breasts were tender and I woke in the mornings filled with an enervating nausea that grew stronger each day. At the end of the month I went to Lucy and told her my symptoms. She confessed that she'd already suspected I was with child.

"I couldn't help but notice that you haven't been eating normally. How wonderful, Liddy! What a blessing!" She gave me such a robust embrace I nearly toppled over. "You must make certain you eat properly now," she admonished. "No more picking at your food!"

My protests only provoked her to more vehemence in her prescriptions. "I'll make sure you take daily infusions of peppermint. We must take extra precautions that your dyspepsia not plague you—I know how susceptible you are to stomach complaints. And the child will rearrange your internal organs without the slightest regard for your comfort." She smiled and clasped me to her yet again. "Tell me, what did Mr. Emerson say when you told him the news?"

"He doesn't know," I said. "I wasn't sure myself, so I came to you first."

"But surely he's guessed! When I conceived Sophia, Charles knew before I did. Or suspected, at any rate. He was always observant of my monthly phases." She blushed suddenly. I tried to think how I might frame a reply that would not embarrass either of us.

"Mr. Emerson is always solicitous of my wishes in intimate matters," I said. "He leaves it to me to watch the calendar."

"So he has no idea?" Lucy smiled a woman's smile—secret and knowing. "Yet you think he'll be pleased?"

"I'm sure of it. We both want children. I think he's dispirited that I didn't conceive immediately after we were wed."

"Then you must plan your announcement!" Lucy was glowing, fairly dancing about the room in her excitement. I knew her love for all the small rituals of family life, yet this was different, more zealous. As I studied her flushed cheeks and bright eyes, I was forcefully struck by her resemblance to our mother. Though I had rarely known my mother in good health, still there had been a womanly vigor beneath her frailty, a reservoir of strength, like a spring of sweet water hidden beneath gray, forbidding stones. "You must set a moment aside from the rest of your day so that you will always remember the look on his face when you tell him. Take him a glass of claret at bedtime. Or wake him early to greet the dawn with your tidings."

"What tidings are these?" Mr. Emerson appeared in the open doorway. His hand was braced against the doorframe and his smile was so full of innocent expectation that I could not keep from blurting out my news on the spot.

"I'm carrying our child," I said.

His hand dropped to his side and he stared at me as if I'd just told him some rude gossip. I did not look at Lucy, but I could feel her holding her breath, just as I held mine.

"So," he said, "I'm to be a father."

"It would seem so." I smiled through a sudden wave of nausea.

"Well." He seemed to be struggling for words, an adversity I had not thought him subject to. "Very good then, Lidian. Well done." He stepped into the room and reached out to me. Thinking he meant to take my hand, I extended my own, but he ignored my gesture and placed his hand on my waist.

"Welcome, my child," he said, in a voice as reverent as a prayer. I saw then the wonder and fear in his eyes, and knew it was a moment of utmost solemnity. Yet some inner mischief made me laugh out loud.

Both Lucy and Mr. Emerson looked at me as if I'd suddenly gone mad.

I ANNOUNCED my news to the rest of the family the following Sunday at dinner. Elizabeth Hoar was there, having attended worship services with Charles and unwilling to be parted from him for the remainder of the day.

Mother Emerson sat stolid and forbidding at my husband's side. Before I finished speaking, Charles leaped from his chair and raised his glass in a toast. Elizabeth rose to embrace me.

"What wonderful news!" she cried. "I promise to be a devoted aunt!" But it was Mother Emerson I watched, waiting for some sign of approval. She didn't raise her eyes from her plate, but continued cutting and chewing her slice of lamb, behaving for all the world as if she hadn't heard a word.

I WAS DETERMINED to perform the task of childbearing properly and well. The infant I carried was no ordinary babe, but the child of Mr. Emerson— and certain to be an extraordinary being. Yet pregnancy was not the instinctive process I'd hoped or that my husband chose to imagine. From the beginning, I felt invaded and beleaguered. As Lucy predicted, dyspepsia plagued me and for many weeks I could tolerate no food but mild custards and broths. My appetite, never robust, diminished to nothing. Weeks before the child quickened, I felt its presence within, draining my vigor and altering my flesh. My skin coarsened and darkened beneath my eyes. My hands grew dry and freckled with brown spots. I craved sleep and cold air. I often threw open my chamber window and leaned out. How like a captive bird I felt! A bird trapped in an overheated cage, desperate to fly, yet unable to find my way between the imprisoning bars.

My husband grew more devoted, daily asking after my health, urging me to sleep late into the mornings, discouraging me from taxing work. He no longer objected to my airing the close winter rooms. He insisted I must do nothing to harm the child, by either act or disposition. Calmness and clarity of mind were of the utmost importance. Lucy remarked at his tenderness.

"He treats you like a piece of fine china," she said, as we rolled out pies one morning in the kitchen. "You must disabuse him of the notion of female frailty or he'll suffer terribly when he hears you in labor."

"But I enjoy his attentions." I lifted a circle of dough carefully into its pan. It was perfect, save for one small wedge that had broken off. I sighed, bunched the dough back into a ball, and started again. "I feel that things between us have assumed their proper arrangement."

Lucy straightened to massage the small of her back. "Were they not satisfactory before?"

I frowned as I rolled out yet another circle of dough. "Satisfactory, yes.

But I aim for higher goals. Improvement is always desirable." When she did not respond, I looked up at her. "Don't you agree?"

She looked at me sadly. "Perfection is not a goal that can be reached, Liddy. Not when it comes to marriage."

I put down my rolling pin. "But if two people are high-minded and devoted to truth, surely they'll achieve a measure of it."

"It can't be done." She spoke with an ill-humored certitude that reminded me of Father. "It's never happened in the history of the world."

I picked up my rolling pin and slapped it back down on my circle of dough. "Well, the world has not yet had Mr. Emerson in it," I snapped. "It's a new age and the old assumptions are valid no longer." I bent over the table, and ruthlessly attacked the dough, not glancing her way again for fear I would find either hurt or amusement written on her face.

EARLY IN MARCH, carpenters came with their saws and hammers and measures to add the two new rooms that Charles and Elizabeth would occupy after their wedding. Their parlor would be located behind Mr. Emerson's study, and their bedchamber situated directly over it. Charles was filled with excitement and good cheer. Each morning he woke early to greet the carpenters, two muscular and taciturn brothers who carried the scent of fresh-cut wood on their clothes and skin like some strange cologne. They worked without speaking, laboring steadfastly inside the noise of their saws and hammers.

Elizabeth came daily to watch the downstairs room take shape. The prospect of living under the same roof with her became even more attractive to me, for she radiated such serenity and happiness that I was always uplifted in her presence. Her gentle gaze calmed whatever anxiety I was feeling and I found myself confiding in her with increasing frequency.

Elizabeth wanted the parlor done in blue. She chose dark blue serge for the drapes and a blue-and-rose carpet. She had her couch upholstered in blue velveteen. Her wallpaper was blue fleur-de-lis on a pale blue-green background. I praised her choices, though for decorating I preferred plain creamy colors that did not distract a visitor's eye from the room's occupants.

Though Mr. Emerson was eager for Charles and Elizabeth to be married and installed as a couple under his roof, the racket necessitated by the addition distracted him from his studies. By the end of the month he was protesting that it was taking too long, that the addition should already be completed. He could not think clearly enough to put two sentences together, he said. Reading was nearly impossible under the cacophony of hammers.

He increased the length of his walks in the afternoons and was sometimes out for three and four hours at a time. He looked forward to his out-of-town lectures, especially those that required him to visit a city. Upon his return, he would inspect the new construction and complain that more progress had not been made. It disturbed me to see this petulant and despondent side of my husband, for I'd failed to imagine that he might be in any way like my father.

Spring was slow in coming. For as late as April that year, a rough and crystalline snow stood ankle-deep on the ground. In the hollow behind the house, it had melted into miniature gullies; rivulets of melt water ran beneath the snow. I could sometimes hear it in the short silences between passing wagons and thudding hammers.

Each morning I walked to the Mill Dam to shop for meat and such vegetables as were available. Lucy or Nancy sometimes accompanied me, but more often I went alone. In this way, I came to know the immediate environs of Bush—the long, empty fields; the poorhouse; the gray bulk of the Hosmer farmhouse that reminded me of a woman dressed in half-mourning; the small village houses on Lexington Road; and the unpainted wooden schoolhouse, not three hundred yards from our house. I delighted in the sounds of children at play during their recess hour and found myself recalling my own school adventures, such as the time I'd challenged all the girls to climb a bank of snow and fling themselves from it—an exercise that resulted in my sitting through the rest of the day in wet wool stockings and petticoats. I passed the First Parish Church, where I often saw Reverend Ripley's buggy parked in the stables behind the building. Close to the Mill Dam stood the tavern and the shops, and on the sloping hillside to the right, the burial ground with its canted stones, each telling its own brief tale. I often took a few moments to walk there and read the stones, just as I had done in Plymouth. Mr. Emerson's great-grandfather, the Reverend Daniel Bliss, was buried there with his wife, Phebe. He had been a New Light during the Great Awakening, whose visions had distressed so many in his congregation that he was dismissed. But what, I wondered now, had Phebe believed? I took off my gloves and traced the carved letters of her name with my fingers, studied the symbols of eternity and hope cut into the dark slate. Her solemn visage stared back at me from the smooth surface. Had she privately disagreed with her husband? Had his public shame shamed her as well? How many friends had she lost when the church voted to dismiss her husband?

I straightened and looked at the sky, which was streaked gray with clouds. The bare branches of a maple stretched above me. I was reminded of my encounter with young Henry Thoreau in front of the church and the memory made me smile. He was embroiled in his studies at Harvard now, perhaps struggling at that very moment to memorize a page of Greek or Latin. I tried to picture him bent over his books in a great library but, oddly, my imagination was only able to place him beneath an open sky.

THAT SPRING a bitter wind swept down daily from the western hills and blew through the cracks of the windows and doors. My husband complained constantly of the cold. He would have liked summer to last all year-round. He told me he'd heard wonderful tales of Florida, and suggested it was his fondest dream to move there.

For my part, I spent my afternoons walking back and forth behind the house, planning my garden. There the land sloped steadily down to the brook, where Charles had supervised the planting of a screen of trees shortly after my arrival. As soon as the ground thawed, I would have the soil turned and send for my Plymouth rosebushes, now in the care of my aunts.

Near the end of March, Charles became suddenly and gravely ill. A winter chill had settled deep in his lungs, spawning a noxious fever. His cough could be heard throughout the house, and it followed me from room to room, reminding me of my mother's cough.

"It's just carpenters' dust," he said, but after two weeks Mr. Emerson sent for Dr. Bartlett, a large and gentle man, with a head too big even for his massive shoulders. He had thoughtful eyes and a voice that sprang from deep inside his chest and inspired a rare confidence. He was still young, a few years older than I, yet wonderfully skilled in medicine and the healing arts. After nursing Charles for two weeks without improvement, he declared that the only cure would be for him to go south, to free himself from the damp New England climate.

We were gathered in Charles's room that afternoon—my husband, Mother Emerson, and I seated in chairs near the window, while Elizabeth sat by Charles's bed with his hand clasped between hers.

"They say it's lovely and warm in Puerto Rico this time of year," I offered.

Charles shook his head. "Not there." His breath raked the air in the over-warm room.

"Edward died in Puerto Rico a year and a half ago," Mr. Emerson said gently. "Perhaps some other place."

"Forgive me." I knew little about my husband's next younger brother, except that he'd battled consumption for many years.

"Europe, I think," Elizabeth said. "Italy has an agreeable climate. A few months in the sun will bring you to health, Charles. And we can still be married in September, as we planned."

"No," Charles said, between spasms. "I won't leave Concord."

"But you must!" Elizabeth stroked his hand. "You must do it for both our sakes."

"No. I cannot." He gazed up at her. "I refuse to be parted from you."

Mr. Emerson sighed and dropped his head into his hands.

I heard a tap at the window and looked up to see a chickadee sitting on the sill. "You have a visitor." I gestured, hoping to distract us all from our sorrow and turn the conversation to pleasant matters. "It's a happy omen," I said. But before the others could turn to look, the bird had flitted away.

"Omen of what?" Mother Emerson's tone was bitter.

"That Charles will soon be well," I said cheerfully.

Yet his illness continued. One April morning, when he came downstairs to survey the progress of his parlor, he was so weak he had to be helped back to his room. Elizabeth turned pale overnight; her skin assumed a waxy, gray cast. She fretted about the progress of the building and stood over the carpenters, urging them to hurry. She displayed an excessive animation, as if not only her mind, but her body as well, would not experience a moment's peace until Charles recovered.

ONE AFTERNOON, Elizabeth and I measured between the two windows, only to find that the space was three inches too narrow to accommodate her beloved piano. Dismayed, we stretched the string repeatedly along the new plaster wall, but to no avail. After the sixth try, poor Elizabeth sighed and threw down the string. "It's *hopeless*," she cried. "What a futile endeavor!" Her face had reddened and her hands were clamped into fists. She looked like a small, peevish child.

"That's nonsense," I said, my heart melting for her as if she were my sister. "We'll make the piano fit. If the carpenters have to redo their work, then so be it."

"It's not that," Elizabeth moaned. "It's everything! This whole endeavor." Her right arm swept out. I followed her gesture and looked around the room—its gracious lines, the late afternoon light falling through the windows, the curled wood shavings on the floor.

"There's no need to worry," I said. "The carpenters are on schedule. It'll all be finished in another month."

But Elizabeth continued to shake her head so violently that her hair came loose from her cap and dropped in heavy loops onto her shoulders. "It's a dream that won't come right." Suddenly she began to sob.

I embraced her. "Of course it will!" I stroked her disordered hair. "I know your future with Charles seems too good to be true, but rest assured it will come to pass."

She gulped air and drew away to look at me directly. "Did you feel this way before you married? That it would never happen?" There was such longing, such raw desire in her sweet face that I could not hold her gaze, but glanced away.

"I think all brides feel it," I said. "It's a consequence of our imperfection— our human sin. That knowledge of our incompleteness is God's way of fulfilling His purpose."

She looked at me blankly through her tears. The rims of her eyes were the pink of fresh salmon. Her fine skin was blotched red.

I had given her no comfort at all. She was so utterly lost in her love for Charles there was no room in her mind or heart for the grand principles that had propelled me toward union with Mr. Emerson. Elizabeth's view of marriage was molded wholly by her relation to Charles.

I longed to comfort her, but knew my thoughts and feelings were sorely inadequate. Nonetheless, I tried. I led her into my parlor and murmured all the wise adages that I could remember. Yet it was not until we heard the sound of Charles's slow footsteps on the stairs that she wiped her tears away and regained her composure.

10

Affliction

I have felt in him the inimitable advantage, when
God allows it, of finding a brother and a friend in
one.

—RALPH WALDO EMERSON

I prayed daily for Charles's recovery, yet as April advanced and the days gradually became longer and warmer, he grew weaker and his fevers grew stronger. He lay in bed for days at a time, filling the house with the sound of his terrible cough.

When Charles had his first lung hemorrhage, I was there to spread a doubled towel across his chest and press another to his mouth, to wipe the blood from his hands and arms and replace the soiled blanket with a clean one. His countenance was as white as the bleached pillow casings. I found a clean nightshirt in his bureau and helped him strip off the old one, for he was too exhausted to do so himself.

"I'm sending for Dr. Bartlett," I said, gathering up the stained towels and blanket.

Charles nodded, not yet able to speak. I knew from his melancholy gaze that he feared the worst and was too weak to oppose me. He closed his eyes as a triangle of sunlight fell across his face. I was struck by how sunken and dark his eyes were—an effect normally eclipsed by the liveliness of his gaze. His chest slowly rose and fell and I supposed he had fallen asleep. I recalled how deeply my mother had slept after her attacks—as if God took intermittent pity on her, granting a few hours of oblivion.

I was about to tiptoe out of the room when Charles spoke my name. "Stay with me a moment longer. Please."

"Of course." I hurried to his side. "What would comfort you? A prayer? A favorite Scripture?"

His eyes were still closed but his hand emerged from beneath the blanket. I took it in mine and began a prayer.

"Do you believe in heaven, Lidian?" His words interrupted my supplication.

"Of course I do."

"There's no idea that's so certain it can't be questioned. I mean are you— in true sincerity—assured of the fact of eternal life?"

I found myself sinking into the chair next to the bed. I thought of my mother and father. I had often tried to picture their spirits meeting in an ethereal realm of clouds and sunlight, my father's caustic disposition dissipated in the beautiful surroundings. "Christ has promised us heaven. That should be assurance enough."

"Perhaps," he said.

"Aren't you a believer, Charles?"

He did not appear to have heard me. "I was so young when Father died that I scarcely recall him. Yet I remember little Mary Caroline well. She was born a few months before his death. Such an angel—all smiles and yellow curls—a family pet and special consolation to Mother." He smiled and I noticed a smear of blood across his teeth. "She was three when she died. I remember standing by her coffin in the parlor, waiting for her to wake up. I must have been five or six. I like to think of her in paradise, but I'm not sure if she survives anywhere but my memory."

A dark image of my infant brother laid out in his coffin rose in my mind. I saw my mother weeping and Father sitting alone in the darkened parlor near the head of the coffin, his head bowed forward on his chest. The odor of flowers was wet and ropy.

"You must not allow yourself to think morbidly, Charles. You need to conserve your strength." I was speaking to myself as well as my brother-in-law, for I was aware of the harm such thoughts could do to the child I carried.

"I've spent years fighting these melancholy thoughts. Did you know that for a time I wanted to follow my father and Waldo into the ministry? As a bulwark against despair, I suppose. But my mind wasn't made for the mysteries of faith. I'm much too practical." He paused to briefly raise his free hand to his mouth and I feared that he was about to hemorrhage again, but his thin white fingers soon fell upon the bed. He gave me a sad smile. "Yet even Waldo could not preserve his faith when Ellen died."

I frowned. "What do you mean? Waldo leads our family prayers every morning and evening."

Charles shook his head. "When Ellen died his hope and confidence in God disappeared. He's more seeker than believer now."

"His faith will return in time," I said.

He gazed up at me. "You are too innocent for us Emersons, you know. A lamb among wolves."

"Innocent?" I released his hand. "I'm far from innocent, Charles."

"Compared to your husband, you are. I love Waldo dearly, but he'll never be able to love you as he ought." He took a breath, let it out. Fresh blood blossomed at the corner of his mouth. "His heart is not free."

I took up another towel and gently wiped his mouth. "I know that," I said. "I'm not as innocent as you suppose. Nor am I without my own resources." I rose and smoothed my skirts. "In any case, I have confidence that time will loosen those bonds."

He gave me a sorrowful look, but I didn't allow him the opportunity to continue his low thoughts. "You must rest now. And I must fetch Dr. Bartlett."

I left the room then, carried the bloodied towels down to the kitchen and pushed them into the wash barrel behind the door. Nancy was at the table, cutting apples for a pie.

"Where's Lucy?" I asked.

"Gone for a walk." Nancy didn't look up at me. The apple slices slipped off her knife in slick, white crescents.

"If Mr. Emerson comes out of his study," I said, "please tell him I've gone to fetch the doctor."

Nancy dropped her knife and looked up at me. Her dark eyebrows were raised in two perfect arches. "You're not going out in your condition?"

"My condition should not be an embarrassment," I said. "It is, after all, the most natural of circumstances."

I left the house and walked to the Mill Dam, paying no heed to the budding trees and new calls of the spring birds, for my mind was in a state of
great agitation. I had not realized that Charles so clearly perceived the complex nature of my union with Mr. Emerson. It troubled me that he'd noticed
it. I'd cherished the superstition that silence protected me, that things that
had not been spoken aloud did not fully exist. I had not yet confessed to anyone else—not even Lucy—that I hoped to change Mr. Emerson's heart. It had
been a furtive, secret hope, well hidden beneath the pleasure I expressed in
my marriage, a hope I examined and nurtured in private. Yet Charles had not
been fooled; he'd discerned the truth of it. And I was both ashamed and
relieved to know that the understanding was no longer mine alone.

Dr. Bartlett was not at home, but his housemaid assured me she would
send him word that he was needed immediately at the Emerson home. I
thanked her, refused the cup of tea she urged on me, and continued down
Main Street to Judge Hoar's, where I found Elizabeth sewing in her chamber.
Her look of alarm when I told her of Charles's attack was heightened by concern for my condition as we waited for the Hoar family buggy to be brought
to the door. I reassured her that the exercise had been beneficial to both me
and the child and she seemed to draw strength from my reassurance.

Dr. Bartlett's familiar horse and buggy was standing at the east entrance
when Elizabeth and I arrived. We found him in the parlor, solemnly confer-
ring with my husband.

Mr. Emerson turned when we entered. "Elizabeth! Lidian!" He crossed
the room to us, extending his hands to offer a necessary comfort. Elizabeth,
who was naturally ardent of feeling, turned away and burst into tears.

"Go to Charles," I said, though it was plain she did not need my urging,
for she was already running up the stairs.

"It's good that you brought her." Mr. Emerson passed a hand over his
eyes. "She's his chief comfort now."

Mother Emerson sat in the corner chair, her knitting lying untouched in
her lap. I sat slowly upon the red claw-foot settee, removed my bonnet, and
silently laid it in my lap. When Dr. Bartlett began to speak, I found that I was
stroking it for solace, as if it were one of my beloved cats.

"He must go south at once," the doctor said. "His situation is very grave.
Only sun and warm air will save him. I'd recommend Puerto Rico."

My husband drew in a sharp breath but said nothing.

"I'd like your assurance that such a long journey would be efficacious,"

Mother Emerson said. "It would do Charles little good to wear himself out in travel."

Dr. Bartlett nodded gravely. "I wish I could give you my warranty, Mrs. Emerson. All I can promise is that Puerto Rico is his only hope."

"Then it's decided." Mother Emerson picked up her yarn, as though she intended to begin knitting, though in fact her needles remained still. "Charles shall go to Puerto Rico. I'll take him there myself."

ON THE FIRST DAY of May, to accommodate Charles's weakness, the morning coach to Boston pulled up in front of our east entrance, and Charles and Mother Emerson slowly descended the steps and walked across the short strip of grass between the house and the coach. Elizabeth was present, struggling to manifest a cheerful countenance despite her sorrow, while my husband held a last-minute conference with the drivers, informing them of their passenger's grave condition.

Mother Emerson insisted that she had long been planning a trip to visit her son William and his family and that Charles's journey offered a perfect excuse. She planned to stay at least three weeks, and would oversee Charles's recovery from the trip and his subsequent departure for Puerto Rico. I experienced an unworthy gratification as I watched her settle into her seat. For nearly a month I would be able to manage my own house without her scrutiny.

As Charles boarded the coach he looked like the ghost of a man, barely able to smile. He clung to Elizabeth's hand through the open door until the coachman came to close it.

"We'll be married as soon as you return!" Elizabeth called as the door was firmly shut. She stood waving until the coach was out of sight. Only then did she tearfully collapse on my husband's supporting arm.

Mr. Emerson drove Elizabeth back to her home in our buggy while I retired to the kitchen to oversee dinner preparations. The cracks and thuds of the carpenter's hammers were oddly comforting—they seemed to signal a matter-of-factness to the day, as if to reassure all within hearing that Charles's illness was not a matter of great significance, but only one small incident in a long and interesting lifetime.

On the fourth morning after their departure a letter arrived in Mother Emerson's hand. Since Mr. Emerson was lecturing in Salem that afternoon and would not be back until dusk, I opened it at once. Its contents and brevity alarmed me—it insisted that my husband hasten at once to Staten Island. The trip had proved too much for Charles, seriously weakening his already frail health. William's doctor had purged and bled him and insisted on complete bed rest. It was clear he could not sail until he regained some measure of strength.

All day I was beside myself with worry, distracted from every task, unable to think of anything but Charles's affliction. I dispatched a messenger to Mr. Emerson, telling him to cancel his lecture and come home at once, but when he arrived, late that afternoon, his composed expression told me instantly he hadn't received my communication. He was still seated in the buggy when I drew his mother's letter from my apron pocket and handed it to him without speaking. His face blanched, as if he already knew its contents. He read the letter and looked down at me, and I noticed an odd thing—the blue had gone out of his eyes and they were only smudged shadows in his face.

"Where's Elizabeth?" he said in a voice that tore my heart.

ELIZABETH AND MY HUSBAND left for Staten Island just after daybreak on May ninth. Had it not been for Lucy, I might have traveled with them, but she'd taken to her bed with a fever the day after the letter arrived. And so I stayed to nurse her and wait for word of Charles.

For three days I waited in suspense, with no knowledge of what had transpired. On the fourth day, a public coach pulled up in front of the house and Mr. Emerson stepped out. He did not look at me as he helped first his mother and then Elizabeth down the wobbly steps.

Only when they had entered the house did he face me. "Charles is gone," he said.

I put my hand to my throat. "No!" I whispered.

My husband turned away and followed the two women inside. By the time I entered the house, he'd already retired to his study, and I was left to comfort Elizabeth and Mother Emerson as best I could.

Aunt Mary Moody attended the burial, which took place on an unseasonably cold day. Clouds the color of an old bruise threatened rain. The new leaves looked gray and pearly in the wan light. Mary leaned on the arm of Sarah Ripley and stared down into the grave with such a fierce expression on her face that my gaze instinctively leaped away. After the ceremony,

Mr. Emerson invited her to return to our home for the collation, but she shook her small head so violently that her bonnet strings snapped.

"I keep my vows," she said.

Despite her stubborn words, I detected a terrible regret in her eyes, which looked as dull and tarnished as a winter's sky.

In the days following Charles's death, Mr. Emerson spoke little except to voice his concern for Elizabeth. When I tried to comfort him by reminding him that Charles was no longer sick and in pain—that he had surely found in heaven the joy and peace he'd given so often to others—Mr. Emerson turned away, declaring that he did not care to speak of a heaven in which he had no hope.

A week after his return he told me that he wanted Elizabeth to come and live with us at Bush. I could not imagine why she would want to leave her own family in her time of sorrow, but I gladly extended the invitation. She accepted immediately.

"My dear Lidian," Elizabeth said the day she moved in, clasping both my hands with grateful fervor, "it's so generous of you to take me in. I know that I'll find Charles's spirit in residence! You still feel his presence, don't you?" And she looked at me with such earnest hope in her lovely face that I could not confess to her that I'd felt only Charles's absence since his death. Or that I was shocked to discover how thoroughly the atmosphere at Bush had been charged with his charm and good cheer. For there was a darkness about the place now, a pervasive melancholy that was not created by grief alone. It was as though the house itself mourned his passing. I decided that, should our child be a boy, I would name him Charles.

At Elizabeth's insistence, we moved our parlor furniture into the new room behind Mr. Emerson's study. "It will accommodate more guests for your conversations," she said. We turned the old parlor into a guest room, and it was quickly designated the Red Room, in honor of its crimson carpet.

Elizabeth was installed in Charles's room, where she stayed for three weeks. During that time, my husband turned to her often for comfort in his grief. Some days they were nearly inseparable. He brushed off my attempts to console him and retreated to her companionship or the fortress of his study. My skills as a wife seemed very meager.

As I watched Elizabeth and Mr. Emerson, I saw that she was able to offer him a solace I knew nothing of. A bond had formed between them that replaced Mr. Emerson's affection for his brother. I tried to convince myself that this was a good thing. But it pained me, nonetheless. I was his wife, the woman he should turn to in his grief.

But the dead are formidable adversaries. To challenge them is a profitless endeavor.

AFTER CHARLES'S DEATH, Lucy's growing discontent became clear to me. She spent most of her time alone. She took long walks, often visiting the graveyard to brood over stones, as if to extract counsel from the ancient Puritan verses. She no longer confided in me, or shared Sophia's letters, but retreated into extended silences from which I was unable to draw her. One day she came to me and announced that she wished to leave Bush and return to Plymouth and board with Aunt Joa.

"You've been a gracious hostess," she said. "But a hostess after all, and I require my own home."

I would have protested more vigorously had my pregnancy absorbed me less. I spent my days marveling at the rapidity with which my body changed, at its peculiar combination of strength and delicacy. During my cold-water bath each morning, I examined my breasts, marveling at their tenderness and the prominence of new veins—like undiscovered rivers crossing desert sand. I puzzled over the increased intensity of my moods. I struggled with nausea, nibbling dry salt biscuits in bed after waking, avoiding the kitchen until afternoon. I took long naps. I woke late in the afternoons when the sun was already low in the sky, making long shadows on the roads and fields. Despite all the sleep, I felt wrung out, weary, the way an aged cat is weary, one who can barely drag itself from one sunny window to another. And so, when I embraced Lucy the morning she left, my sorrow was mixed with a blessed relief.

On a Sunday in late May, as I sat alone in the dining room writing a letter to Sophia, something soft fluttered deep in my lap, a peculiar and unfamiliar sensation that made me think of moths trapped within a lantern. It was late afternoon; Mr. Emerson was out for his daily constitutional and for some minutes I did not move, but simply sat puzzled and wondering. Quite suddenly I understood what it was and put down my pen. In awe, and with a nearly giddy excitement, I rose and went to the window, hoping to see my husband returning from his saunter, for I was thrilled and impatient to announce that my child had quickened.

In the distance, I saw a figure advance toward the house across a neighboring field. Thinking it must be Mr. Emerson, I ran outside without my shawl, my skirts and apron in disarray, my cap sliding halfway off my head. It was only when I reached the gate that I perceived that the man's stride was too limber to be my husband's. Nor was he sufficiently tall. Yet there was a buoyant grace about him that was familiar, a lightness of step that seemed to echo the joy in my own heart. As he came closer, the sun fell on his shoulders and face and, though he was nearly the length of the field away, I recognized Henry Thoreau.

I stood grasping the top rail of the gate, wondering if I ought to greet this man I had foolishly mistaken for my husband—for I was certain he had seen me—or if I could return to the house without giving offense. I felt the flutter again, a fretful twist at my center that made me mindful of my disordered state. I looked down at my waist, as if there might be some visible manifestation of my experience, but there was, of course, no sign. When I looked up, Henry had crossed the road and disappeared into the scrim of trees beyond.

11

Experience

True wisdom lies in finding out all the advantages of a situation in which we are placed, instead of imagining the enjoyments of one in which we are not placed.

—LYDIA MARIA CHILD

My first labor pains came on me late in the morning on the thirtieth day of October in 1836. I was kneading bread dough in the kitchen, when my lower back convulsed. The pain curled around my hips and pressed hard into my abdomen.

I stood still. I tried to think of what I must do. Lucy was in Plymouth and Nancy had gone to the Mill Dam. I sank into a chair, where Mother Emerson happened upon me a few minutes later. She knew at once that I was in labor and helped me to bed before sending Louisa to fetch the midwife, Eliza Wilson, who lived over the butcher's shop. My husband, roused from his studies by the sound of his mother's sharp commands, came and stood helplessly by the bed until Eliza arrived. She immediately set about putting things in order, after firmly closing the chamber door on my bewildered husband.

I'd attended deliveries before, had wiped away the sweat and heard the moans, held women's desperate, clutching hands, had even held the legs of one of my cousins while the midwife pulled out her dead son. I knew that la-bor was aptly named, that pain and struggle lay at its heart. But what I expe-rienced in my own labor was a new frontier, beyond the realm of suffering.

I had no control. I, who'd always prided myself on my deportment and ability to govern my body, was ambushed by labor. The sheer wildness over-whelmed me. I was no longer myself, but another person, writhing on the bed, moaning and slapping away Eliza's hands in fury. I screamed and wept and tore at the sheet with my teeth. My husband, who was grudgingly granted entrance once during my ordeal, retreated in horror.

The nature of childbirth is eternal—a woman in labor feels as if it will never end. I was pinned liked an insect to a specimen board, nailed like Christ to His cross. I knew, even as these thoughts darted through my mind like scuttling mice, that I was blaspheming God. That the birth of this child was part of His will and purpose for my life and, in resisting it, I was resisting Him. Yet I was no more in charge of my thoughts than of my body. I moaned and raged at heaven, but no relief arrived. Eliza repeatedly wiped my face with a cold towel. Mother Emerson held my hand and prayed aloud.

In the evening, the wind picked up. Trees tossed their naked limbs against the sky and the house shook as one gust after another broke against the north-east wall. My groans were buried in the gale's howls. Just before ten, every-thing went suddenly still. The pains ceased and the wind died. An hour later, my son slid from my body, slick as butter, his head molded to a lopsided cone, his face streaked with mucus and blood. Yet it was the most beautiful face I had ever seen.

When I put him to breast a few moments later, he suckled with the skill and mastery of a veteran. The midwife opened the door and permitted my husband to enter. He said nothing at first—it appeared that words had en-tirely deserted him. Then he took my hand and kissed it.

"We have a son," he whispered. "My Queen." His eyes were shining with tears.

ELIZABETH HOAR CAME the next day, bearing gifts—a box of fresh pears for me and a silver rattle with a mother-of-pearl handle for the baby. She bent over the cradle, cooing, "What a beautiful baby! My little Charles!"

"His head's not right," I said, for my son's ill-shapen skull worried me, though Eliza had assured me that it would come right within two weeks.

"His name is Waldo." My husband spoke from the doorway.

Elizabeth straightened and turned to look at Mr. Emerson, then at me. "I thought it was understood. If it's a boy, his name would be Charles."

"The first son is always named for the father," Mr. Emerson said.

I was astounded. We had not yet discussed a name. "But I assumed, like Elizabeth, the name would be Charles," I said.

Elizabeth gave my husband a look that sliced open my heart. It was a look of both intimacy and outrage, a look of abject betrayal.

"Elizabeth?" I said, to the woman who'd been my only friend since I arrived in Concord. But her gaze was locked on Mr. Emerson's.

"His name is Waldo," he said again, and turned away.

I stared at the space where my husband had been, trying to grasp what had just happened. What was most disturbing was that I was given no say in this matter, that the name of my child was not in my custody. The dispute lay between my husband and Elizabeth.

"I was certain he'd be Charles," Elizabeth whispered. Suddenly, shockingly, she threw the rattle on the floor and ran from the room in a flurry of gray satin.

I rose from my bed and lifted my son from his cradle. "Waldo," I said, testing the name against his small, sleeping face. "Waldo, my beautiful son." How could anyone not care for such a beautiful child? What did it matter what he was called? No name on earth could signify his splendor.

MY WORLD GREW very small. At its center was my son—his cycles of sleep and hunger and his small body with its amazing, silken skin. I couldn't bear to be separated from him for more than an hour at a time. Everything about him charmed and fascinated me. He woke before dawn, and I nursed him in the dark, warm bed. I heard the birds wake and sing and knew they were begging me to feed them from the window, but I could not pull my gaze from my son's small face. The sounds he made as he suckled mingled with the cooing doves, creating an entrancing music.

At times, when I fed him in my husband's presence, I detected an odd jealousy in Mr. Emerson's eyes. This surprised me, for my husband rarely exhibited any unpleasant emotion. He seemed to be a man who had so disciplined his heart that it beat only when he wished.

That spring Waldo—whom we'd begun to affectionately call Wallie—
was christened by Dr. Ripley, along with two other children of the village. I
dressed him in his uncle Charles's christening gown, which Mother Emerson
had stored away in a garret trunk. During the ceremony, I watched Elizabeth,
waiting for her to raise her eyes and return my glance. But she kept her head
bent and her eyes on the floor, as if finding some great wisdom in the worn
wooden boards. Though she had not spoken of it since her outburst the day
after Waldo was born, I saw that she was still hurt and betrayed by my husband's choice of name.

In the middle of Dr. Ripley's long prayer, I stole a glance at Mr. Emerson.
I was suddenly glad he'd stood his ground. His tenacity felt to me—briefly—
like a great protecting wing of love.

IT WAS AT THIS TIME that Margaret Fuller entered our lives. She'd been
repeatedly recommended to Mr. Emerson as the most remarkable woman in
Boston and he fell immediately under her spell. How can I describe the
woman who became both my friend and rival? She was striking, though less in
appearance than personality. She had thick, red-blond hair that often escaped
the confines of her combs. Her gray eyes blinked with unnerving frequency
and she was always on the verge of laughter. She had an odd habit of drawing
her lips back when she talked so that her teeth were exposed. She was young—
seven years my husband's junior—but age matters little when it comes to
friendship. The house fairly crackled with the electricity of her presence.

Mr. Emerson was entirely bewitched by her. He sat all evening in the parlor, his eyes following the movement of her hands as he listened to her talk. I
was bewitched myself, but not by Margaret. It was my son who enchanted
me—his small face and tiny hands continually beguiled my heart. He was a
miracle of perfection. I carried him about the house, not wanting to be
parted from him for even a moment. I wrote letters while he was nestled in
the cradle of my arm. I mended clothes by the parlor fire with one foot on his
cradle's sturdy rocker. I took him outside daily, convinced of the benefits of
fresh air, pushing him all the way to the Mill Dam and back in the wicker
perambulator I'd purchased.

Lucy, who came from Plymouth to help after Wallie's birth for a few
weeks, admonished me for my devotion, and warned that I was inducing an
unwise dependency in my son. She had taken great pains, she reminded me,

not to spoil Sophia and Frank. I assured her that I'd try harder to restrain myself. But one look into Wallie's dark and serious eyes, one brush of his satin curls against my fingertips, and all my resolve evaporated. I had not imagined that motherhood could so utterly bind me. Where my son was concerned, I was hopeless, a slave to inclination and impulse. A captive of love.

When Wallie was nearly nine months old, Mr. Emerson began to complain that I spent too much time with the baby. "It's time you weaned him," he said. It was a rainy morning in early August; I sat in the rocking chair by the east window of our bedroom, my dressing gown open to expose my breasts, for I was nursing Wallie. It was raining hard and the wind was blowing so that the rain smacked the glass and ran down in watery undulations. Wallie lay suckling contentedly with his head propped on my left arm, his left hand raised to my face, which he occasionally patted, his baby fingers light as down feathers on my skin. He gazed at me, his dark blue eyes serene. As usual, I could not pull my own gaze from his, and answered my husband without looking at him.

"He's an infant," I said, my tone more strident than I'd intended, for the thought of weaning Wallie was so abhorrent that I could not contemplate it without alarm. "Not yet a year old. He still needs my milk. And will for some time." What I did not say was that nursing my baby was the sweetest pleasure I'd ever known. It was more than the comfort of holding his small body against mine several times each day, more than the innocent intimacy between us. There was a bliss in nursing him that was entirely physical; a heightened sensitivity of my skin, a sensation that my blood had been infused with the rarest liquor. With his innocence and need, my son had redeemed my body from my father's touch.

"He absorbs you so," Mr. Emerson's voice was low, a thick rumble in his chest. "Sometimes I think you've forgotten you are a wife."

I felt the weight of his tightly harnessed anger pressing against me from across the room. And I felt my own anger rise in response, climb through my pelvis and chest and lodge at the base of my throat, where I knew I could not hold it long.

"I have not forgotten. How *could* I forget?" Finally, I tore my gaze from Wallie and looked at my husband. "I've been in exile from my home for two years now."

A look of pained surprise leaped into his face, but I continued.

"Our son is my chief duty, and he needs me. And I won't pollute his milk by enjoying marital intimacy before he's weaned. Nor will I wean him early."

"Lidian—"

"You don't need to lecture me on my duty as your wife. I know my duty and will perform it when the time comes."

"You mistake me. When have I ever spoken of duty?" He moved to the bed and slowly lowered himself so that he was sitting, facing me. His hands hung between his knees; the slight smile that usually graced his face was gone. "Is that what the marital act is to you? A *duty*? Another obligation?"

I stared at him. Suddenly, I wanted to take the words back. My terrible words. For he was right—he had never spoken of duty. He had always advocated complete honesty and self-reliance. *I* was the one who navigated duty's fearful waters. I looked down at Wallie again. How could I find words to tell my husband that, while I enjoyed the pleasures of the marital act, it paled in comparison to the profound pleasure of cradling my son?

"Because if my caresses are unwelcome, I will not press them on you." He paused. "I have other options."

I winced. The hiring of women was a common male vice—one that not only degraded the husband but also shamed the wife. It was not a subject Mr. Emerson and I had ever discussed, and it was hard for me to imagine a man of his integrity paying a woman for her favors. Yet it was not the thought of a nameless prostitute that caused my wave of nausea, but the image of Margaret Fuller.

I looked at my husband again and almost said her name out loud. My head was so full of thoughts of Margaret that for a moment I could not form any other words. Margaret, whose first visit to Bush had lasted six long weeks, who spent hours privately discussing philosophy with my husband behind the closed doors of his study. Margaret, who came and went from our home with the capricious fervor of a spring wind, who taught my husband the rudiments of German—a language I did not know—and who threw lively German phrases to him across the dinner table. Margaret, who always commanded any conversation in which she participated, who created a flurry of excitement each time she entered a room. Installed in the Red Room, she had made an evening habit of visiting my husband's study. Often I'd heard her laughter issuing from behind those closed doors after I retired for the night.

"Options," I said dully, unable to erase the pictures of Margaret from my mind.

He pressed his palms together, then separated them and splayed them on his knees. "It's not intended as a threat," he said quietly. "I would free you of obligation."

I slid the tip of my little finger into the corner of Wallie's mouth, releasing my nipple. He whimpered, but I lifted him quickly to my shoulder as I closed my robe, and the patterns of rain on the glass soon distracted him. "I'll wean him shortly," I said, stroking his back as I rose. I glanced out the north-facing window, which offered a view of the road where a carriage was passing, its wheels throwing a great cushion of water into our front yard. "I'll go to Plymouth for a week or two and leave Wallie here with you. When I return, he'll have forgotten the taste of my milk."

Mr. Emerson rose from the bed and reached out to brush the top of Wallie's head with his fingers. His blessed smile had returned.

That evening, Mother Emerson, Louisa, Nancy, and I gathered as usual in the parlor before retiring. Mother Emerson's knees were grieving her, as they always did in wet weather, so I helped her into the chair nearest the door and took my place on the couch. Mr. Emerson sat in his rocking chair, gazing down at his Bible, which lay closed on his lap. The rain had stopped and the sky cleared at dusk, but water still dripped from the eaves. I was about to suggest that Mr. Emerson read a passage from Genesis, but before I had the opportunity, he placed the Bible on the floor beside him, rocked back, and announced that he no longer felt called to lead family worship. It seemed to him a barren formality left from another age, devoid of meaning and purpose. One in which he could no longer in good conscience participate. He then dismissed the servants and left the room.

I looked at Mother Emerson and saw my own shock registered in her expression. As the stairs creaked beneath my husband's tread, her eyes grew watery and I saw tears slide down her cheek. For the first time, I felt sympathy for her, pity for this woman who had trained my husband to be a follower of Christ.

"It's all right," I said, taking her hand—which was always cold—to warm in mine. "I'm sure it's just a passing whim."

She shook her head. "I've seen this day coming for years," she said. "It was only a matter of time."

Again I sought to reassure her. "He's always followed the requirements of his own logic," I said. "His mind is perfectly sound."

But Mother Emerson's tears continued to fall; one dropped onto my own hand as it clasped hers. "I hope you're right." She searched for her handkerchief, which she always kept tucked in her sleeve, but it was not there. When I offered mine, she accepted it, wiped her eyes, and looked at me. "There are things you don't know, Lidian. I fear for him."

I felt the skin across my shoulders tighten. I couldn't imagine what Mr. Emerson had done to concern her so. I did not *want* to imagine. Yet, having heard her words, I could not refrain from asking.

"What things?"

She closed her eyes. She continued to hold my handkerchief, but her hand slipped from mine. "After Ellen died . . ." She stopped and blinked. She dabbed at her eyes and took a slow, deep breath as if to steady herself for an onerous task. "Months after she died, my son went to her family crypt and pried open the coffin."

I swallowed wet air. "I cannot imagine Mr. Emerson doing such a thing." My voice was scratched and feeble, like a small bird the barn cat has caught and played with. "Why would he look on Ellen's corrupted body? It must have turned his heart to stone."

Mother Emerson turned her gaze on me. "It was my suggestion," she said. "He mourned her too acutely. He was *sunk* in his mourning, like a boat submerged in a stagnant swamp. She was an obsession. He could think of nothing but her beauty, of his love for her. He imagined her still living, escaped somehow to some sunny clime. He wanted to follow." She braced her knobby right elbow against the chair's curved arm. "I feared for his sanity. For his safety." This last came out as a slippery hiss—the sizzle of a teakettle just before it boils.

"He would not—" I hesitated, searching for words. "Mr. Emerson would never do himself harm. He is a Christian."

"I don't know what my son is. But I fear he's no longer Christian." She dabbed at her eyes once more. "And I think what he said tonight has proven that."

I felt my face freeze, as if an arctic wind had torn through the August night and filled the room. I helped Mother Emerson up the stairs to her bed, but her words stayed with me. The image of my husband prying open Ellen's tomb months after her death and finding—what? A desiccated and rotting corpse? A scrap of gown he recognized? A handful of black curls? The image was profoundly disturbing. Yet what was far more alarming to me than his violation of a tomb was the possibility that my husband might have entirely deserted his faith.

12

Accommodations

> I have urged on women independence of man, not
> that I do not think the sexes mutually needed by one
> another, but because in woman this face has led to an
> excessive devotion, which has cooled love, degraded
> marriage, and prevented either sex from being what it
> should be to itself or the other.
>
> —MARGARET FULLER

In October of 1837, the Grimké sisters visited Concord. These two plain, devout Quakers from South Carolina had been touring the nation, publicly advocating the abolition of slavery. Mr. Emerson and I attended their lecture and I afterward invited them to tea. I had never met such pure, compassionate souls. They radiated sweetness and simplicity, despite their strident words. They told of women subjected to murderous lashings for crimes no worse than accidentally breaking a vase, and of men chained to stakes and whipped because they refused to work themselves to exhaustion. They described the kidnapping of blacks in Africa, the manner in which they were shackled—more cruelly than any animal—and forced into the holds of ships, where they were stacked like kindling. They suffered and died the most extreme deaths. I could not bear to contemplate the frightful savagery inflicted on those innocent souls.

That evening, as we readied ourselves for bed, I declared to Mr. Emerson,

"I can no longer sit by and do nothing." I was brushing out my hair with more vigor than usual. "The cause of the Negro will be my compass from now on."

Mr. Emerson stood by the fire with his back to me, unbuttoning his shirt. "You distress yourself unnecessarily. The Negro race is coarse and obtuse by nature. It knows nothing of life's refinements." He slid his arm from his left sleeve and turned to look at me. "They don't suffer the way you would, Lidian. Your imagination tries to put you in their shoes, but they will not fit."

"But they're human!" I cried, throwing down my brush. "They feel grief and experience pain!"

He shook his head. "As a dog feels it, not as you or I."

"I cannot agree." I picked up my brush and went to my bureau, where I took longer than usual plaiting my hair.

It confounded me that he could think that some people felt no tenderness simply because their skin was dark, or because they'd been reared in a land of cannibals. Were we not all bound as one family in the sight of God? I had begun to learn that my husband avoided all difficult and painful thoughts, unless they struck a chord in his mind. I suspected that this irksome habit was the means by which he steeled himself against the blows life dealt him.

THAT FALL MARKED a change in our marriage. A chill descended like a cloak of dark clouds. At first I did not notice. I was too caught up in caring for the baby and the endless stream of visitors. I did not mind our lack of physical intimacy since it was for Wallie's protection—it was well-known that milk would sour and curdle if new mothers indulged carnal passions. But the transformation was plain—an acidity that haunted Mr. Emerson's voice when he teased me, an inexplicable bitterness that had not been present before. He no longer delighted in watching me put the baby to breast. He no longer asked after my health. Nor did he any longer make a point of inviting me to join our weekly conversations.

One afternoon Henry Thoreau came upon me in the garden. I was on my hands and knees, weeding my roses, unaware of his presence until he spoke.

"You make a lovely picture." His voice was deep and musical.

I looked up at him, wiping my hands on my apron.

He smiled. "I could not resist the temptation to observe more closely." It was the kind of comment that would have seemed brazen coming from anyone else. But Henry carried such an air of innocence and honesty that I understood at once that he meant exactly what he said.

He asked me about the variety of roses I'd planted and then examined each plant with great interest. Soon he was kneeling beside me, pulling weeds from the soil. We fell into an easy conversation, the words and subjects flowing as naturally between us as if we'd been longtime friends. I found myself talking of Plymouth. As I spoke, a terrible, raw longing welled up in me. I stopped and sank both hands into the cool earth, as if I could locate solace there. Henry Thoreau sat back on his heels so that his back was shaped like a question mark. When I glanced up I saw in his face, not the pity I'd expected, but a startled recognition.

"What is it?" I managed to utter.

"I was thinking," he said, in a voice as hoarse as my own, "of the time I lived in Maine. Away from Concord. I could not—" He stopped and shook his head. "I could not *endure* it." And then he leaned forward, so close that his gray-eyed gaze was all I could see of him. "You do not feel at home in Concord, do you?" I confess I stared into his eyes a moment too long. My heart beat in my chest like a trapped moth.

"I don't know," I gasped, and it was a gasp, for I could hardly breathe. Suddenly the sun was pressing down on my head and face; my eyelids fluttered in defense. I got to my feet. "I have to go inside. There are things to be done."

I left him, kneeling there in the garden, as I swiftly crossed the yard to the house. My back was as straight as a plank.

I BEGAN to yearn more desperately for Plymouth, for the company of friends and relatives. Concord was a socially barren place—a country town where entertaining friends usually meant a raucous evening of drink and tavern music, where a lowly blacksmith and a brilliant solicitor were likely to be found at the same party. Where those who took an interest in philosophy and reform were so rare as to be invisible. Concord was a place where the world was out-of-kilter and unrefined.

One evening, I interrupted my husband's reading to ask if we might plan a trip to the Old Colony.

"I haven't traveled there since Wallie was born," I said, knowing my tone was too plaintive, that it risked irritating him. But I could not swallow away the sorrow in my throat.

He was absorbed in a small volume of Montaigne's essays, but he looked up, placing his finger carefully in the page to hold his place. "What can you be thinking, Queenie?" he said, and there was no warmth in his tone, despite the pet name. "You know I can't spare the time from my work. I have a lecture series to prepare."

"You could work in Plymouth. I know my uncle would happily make his study available."

"Lidian." He sighed. "Why don't you make arrangements to go yourself? Leave Wallie here with me. Surely even you must admit that the time has come to wean him. You could stay as long as you like."

A chill rolled over me, in a long, slow wave, like the ocean in April. I remembered the beach in Plymouth, in winter: desolate, hard, the wind tearing at my hair and cloak, snapping the hem of my skirts against my ankles until they were sore.

I smiled at my husband, a tight smile, icy as the frozen beach. "Thank you, Mr. Emerson." I turned, twisting on my heel in a swirl of gray serge, to leave the room.

The next afternoon was cold, with a bitter wind that swept over the low fields and swirled about the house and barn. When Henry Thoreau knocked at the front door, I invited him in. He stood awkwardly in the hall, his ill-fitting clothes hanging on him as if on a hook. The sleeves of his coat were too long. His hair was unruly and wind-tossed, flying off in all directions. He wore a lumpy hat, shapeless with age.

I smiled. "Welcome, Henry."

A slight flush suffused his face. "I've come to collect Mr. Emerson for a walk."

"On this cold day?" I glanced past Henry through the half-open door. The wind was thrashing on the far side of the Cambridge Turnpike. "I fear my husband's been suffering from a cough lately. Perhaps—" But I was not able to finish my sentence, for Mr. Emerson emerged from his study at that moment to assure me that he felt quite well and had not coughed more than once since rising that morning.

Henry waited in the entryway while Mr. Emerson got his coat. He said nothing, but I had the sharp sensation that his eyes saw past my concern to something even I was not aware of. At the door, I reached to adjust my husband's collar, but his scowl was so disconcerting that I stopped short as if my hand had touched fire.

Henry opened the door and made an odd little bow in my direction.

"Do not tire yourself, Mr. Emerson," I said.

"My wife frets needlessly," I heard Mr. Emerson say to Henry as they descended the steps. "The mother instinct has fairly conquered wisdom of late." There was a fine edge of humor in his voice, but Henry made no response.

THE NEXT DAY I began to prepare for a visit to Plymouth. I felt the most painful mix of emotions—a desperate homesickness for the Old Colony and a terrible dread at the thought of leaving Wallie. It had to be done, though. Lucy had convinced me that it was past time when my son must be weaned. Mr. Emerson was not wrong in his complaint that I'd delayed overlong.

From the moment of my arrival in Plymouth, I felt a rejuvenation of spirits that I'd not thought possible. My interest in society miraculously revived, though I'd considered it buried for good. Nearly every evening I enjoyed the company of old friends and relatives. Their conversations brought me to life once again. I enjoyed tea several times at the home of Aunt Priscilla, where she'd prepared pastries of every sort: tiny lemon cakes flecked with sugar; muffins filled with all sorts of fruits; wee sausages in a sweet sauce; fresh buttered scones; delicate tartlets. And the tea itself, of course, which was the finest money could buy, direct from the Orient.

Many in Plymouth commented on how motherhood became me. They told me I no longer had the gaunt, haunted look of the years before Wallie's birth, but now radiated a deep contentment. My face was fuller and my cheeks pinker. I filled out my gowns so they no longer hung like sacks from my shoulders, and my arms no longer looked like bones.

I thought often of Wallie, yet at times it seemed as if the past two years had been lived in a dream. At times I was nearly persuaded that I had never married, nor borne a child. At other times, I could barely endure the separation from my son. My breasts cried out for him, and I wondered if he cried for them.

I opened the windows and inhaled the cold salt wind that swept past the curtains in restless gusts. In Plymouth, I had no need to concern myself with Mr. Emerson's aversion to cold. I listened all night to the sea roll up the beach in its old familiar lullaby.

When I returned to Concord after two weeks, Mr. Emerson greeted me warmly and took me to bed as soon as it was possible without offending decency. In his arms, I recollected all the reasons I'd agreed to be his wife, and my melancholy at leaving Plymouth vanished in our embrace. My joy was multiplied tenfold the next day when I held my son and listened to him babble.

SPRING FINALLY CAME and the grass grew luminously green. My daffodils raised their yellow heads and my tulips came up in red and gold profusion. Robins bounced everywhere, spading the soil with their questing bills, their breasts so red it looked as if some spectral fire had bathed them.

I soon discovered that I was carrying another child. Mornings, I lay in an impotent stupor, watching my husband through heavy-lidded eyes as he moved quietly around the room. He was considerate and pleased. He confessed that when I was carrying Wallie, he'd truly believed I would die before I was brought to term. He considered Wallie a miracle. As, indeed, he was.

That spring I woke often in the middle of the night and could not return to the solace of sleep without checking on Wallie. I tiptoed into the nursery by moonlight and stood over him as he slept in his trundle bed. There was a rosy flush on his cheeks and his breath scented the air like a delicate flower. He was so lovely I could never prevent myself from kissing him, though Mother Emerson had warned me that I risked spoiling him with too much affection. Sometimes his eyes would fly open, and he would start up in bed as if about to cry out in terror. The next moment he'd recognize me and smile.

WHEN WALLIE'S SECOND BIRTHDAY ARRIVED, I held a soirée in his honor, inviting the best of Concord to attend. I taxed Nancy's patience mightily by fretting over the menu. And I reduced Louisa to tears when I asked her to polish the brass andirons yet again. I was determined that the gathering would be worthy of Mr. Emerson's position in the community. And in the world. I had married a great man. A man of letters whose mind was so radiant that, though he was not handsome, every head rotated immediately toward him when he entered a room.

The soirée was a triumph. All who were invited came, and there were many exclamations over the simplicity and arrangement of the furnishings. The house was filled with laughter. Many commented on the beauty of the new parlor, where my husband regaled our guests with his wisdom and wit.

Only after everyone had left and Mr. Emerson and I had extinguished the lamps and climbed the stairs to our chamber, did I discover that he'd hated every moment of the festivity. He did not need to say it—I knew his expressions well by then. His brooding forehead and the particular jut of his chin when he was troubled immediately proclaimed his vexation. When I pressed him, he shook his head and waved his hand, as if to shoo away an annoying insect and muttered, "Misdemeanors."

That night I dreamed that Mr. Emerson and I were walking in heaven, talking pleasantly together, when we suddenly came upon an immense tree blooming with small pink flowers. Ellen Tucker was sitting under it in her green rocking chair. She rose as we approached, and Mr. Emerson went to her at once. I watched them embrace and understood in that moment that she would always be his true wife, whereupon I turned away and left.

When I related my dream to Mr. Emerson, he listened more attentively than usual, and when I was finished, he caressed my cheek and said, "Your nobility extends even to your dreams." I know he meant it as a tribute, but my heart was aware only of the words he had not spoken.

I began to understand that I would never replace Ellen in his affections. They'd been married only eighteen months; she was not his intellectual match; she never gave him a child. Yet his heart was forever entombed with hers.

I conceived a plan I confessed to no one. It came to me one February afternoon as I sat in the dining room, sewing a linen bonnet for the baby and reflecting on a conversation I'd had with Mr. Emerson the evening before. We'd retired to our chamber earlier than usual that night—for once we'd not entertained guests. Mr. Emerson was in a contemplative mood, and when I inquired, he confessed that his thoughts had been with Ellen Tucker all day.

The uncharacteristic tremble in his voice made my heart go out to him. "Do you have so many sad memories?" I asked.

"On the contrary," he said. "Whenever I think of Ellen, all I remember is happiness." He then told me how the sight of her always filled him with such joy, such hope of delight. He told me how good she was, that she was the source of all gaiety in their marriage. Yet he had many regrets and still rebuked himself for his cold, impersonal demeanor toward her. Because of it, he said, remorse ran through his life like a river through a long valley.

He sat on the edge of our bed as he spoke, staring into the fire, and all I could see was his silhouette against the shimmer of flame. It was as if all the dark sorrow that was inside him came out and crouched upon his back.

I didn't know what to say. How does a woman console her husband for the loss of the woman he loves? Yet I sensed that he wanted some response from me, and I struggled to find words to convey a measure of the comfort he sought.

"I think you are too severe," I said. "It's clear that you loved Ellen well. Your devotion to her memory testifies to that." I stroked his hand where it lay on the coverlet. I felt, in that moment, that we'd never been closer. There was such rare affection in this conversation that it surpassed even the intimacy of our physical union.

"If only I'd been less self-centered." His voice scratched in his throat. "Perhaps her life might have been lengthened. Perhaps we might have enjoyed the fullness of our love." He was staring hard into the fire. He didn't seem to notice when I withdrew my hand. My one thought—the only thought my mind could encompass at that moment—was that, if Ellen had lived, Mr. Emerson would not be my husband.

Yet I was aware—how could I not be?—that he was begging me for absolution. That he wanted to be forgiven for his imagined coldness and neglect of Ellen.

"She knows your feelings," I whispered. "She attends you. You know that. Deny that you can feel her presence." My hand stole to the back of his neck and touched the smooth curls there.

He bowed his head into his hands and, though he did not weep, his shoulders shook as if with sobs.

I sat all the next afternoon, sewing in the green rocker that had belonged to Ellen. It was a comfortable chair, and afforded me a strange solace, for I'd come to believe her spirit hovered near. When I sat in it, I sensed the magnitude of her love for my husband. It seemed to me that it not only endured, but daily grew stronger. Her devotion encompassed our union, and therefore me. The idea came to me slowly, as a rose slowly unfurls its petals, but by evening my mind was set. If our new child were born a girl I would name her after my husband's first wife.

MY LABOR BEGAN just before ten o'clock on the twenty-third of February. The pains were hard from the first, and as soon as Mr. Emerson was notified, he sent for Cynthia Thoreau, who attended me throughout the night.

The birth was fierce and swift. At eight o'clock the next morning, my daughter lay in my arms. When Mr. Emerson came into the chamber shortly afterward, I looked at him and solemnly announced, "I've already named her. She is Ellen Tucker Emerson."

He said nothing, but the blood drained from his face, and he gave me such a haunted look that I momentarily regretted my decision. Then he broke into an angelic smile and kissed me. My heart lifted. I knew that he understood the nature of my gift. And that he would always feel indebted.

Ellen was a fine, healthy infant with fair skin and dark hair. She suckled well from the start. That afternoon, while the family and our friends enjoyed tea in the dining room downstairs, I wrapped her in an eiderdown and placed her near the fire. The ensuing hour was one of the holiest peace. I lay on my pillows, watching her and listening to her baby murmurs. Now there was a new Ellen in my husband's life, one who would take the place of the angel he adored.

Whenever Henry visited he asked to see the baby and always expressed wonder at her beauty. He was unlike other men—he expressed no disdain for the rituals of a woman's life, but rather seemed to find all events of equal interest. Whenever I consented to let him dandle Ellen, his delight was so apparent that I said he should find himself a wife at once, so that he might have a child of his own.

He gave me an odd look, but said nothing.

By the end of April that year, Margaret Fuller was with us again. She came and went like a spring wind, always stirring things up, exciting the air, making everyone in the household alert. I loved to hear her talk, for her mind was filled with noble thoughts and great ideas. She was the queen of conversations, engrossed in all the latest philosophies. Whenever she arrived, she immediately captured Mr. Emerson in the net of her eyes. She had no child to distract her, no household to run, no horde of guests to entertain.

Though she claimed to admire the baby, Margaret was oddly reluctant to hold her and never played with either of the children. Instead she took long afternoon walks with Mr. Emerson. They returned so deeply engaged in conversation that neither of them heard my questions, nor did they notice Wallie tugging on his father's sleeve for attention. Margaret's face was often flushed and her hair tumbled by the wind. Her eyes darted around the parlor like bright dragonflies, seeking a place to light. But there was no face save my husband's where they settled for long. His mind was the only perfume that attracted her for more than a moment.

I felt plain and uninteresting in contrast. I was consigned to the background of household life, caught up in a thousand menial tasks. The management of Bush and the care of the children consumed me. I ceased keeping a journal, for I no longer had time nor clarity of thought to devote to it. When evening finally came, with its opportunity for stimulating conversation, I was drained to the point of silence. I often sat in a daze, watching Margaret and Mr. Emerson discuss great thoughts and principles. Yet, tired as I was, the waves of excitement that passed between them did not escape my notice.

The thought occurred to me that Mr. Emerson might have proposed to Margaret if he'd met her before me. I knew that it was my mind that had most attracted him. Margaret's genius was that her body *was* her mind—the two were indistinguishably fused.

I was well aware of the power my husband wielded over young females, for I'd been influenced by that magnetism myself. I bore Miss Fuller no ill-will despite her flirtatious nature. In fact, I admired her, for no other woman I knew was so independent a genius. When she encouraged me to talk openly with her, I willingly shared my thoughts and feelings. One warm afternoon we walked along a wooded path on the long ridge of land north of the house, discussing the nature of love. I remarked that love and duty were two sides of the same coin.

"Yet love must always triumph over duty," she said, her eyes shining.

"A truly noble person will see no distinction between them," I insisted.

Margaret stopped and faced me and I felt her radiance flow over me—a phenomenon I was certain she controlled in some way—a glow that she cast, the way witches were said to cast spells. "If God himself is love, then what is nobler than obeying the instinct of love? Did not Christ command us to leave all and follow Him?"

I was bathed in an unpleasant warmth. "But he did not command us to follow our whims and instincts! Following Christ is not indulgence, but sacrifice."

"You burden yourself with unnecessary suffering, Lidian. God does not require humiliation but joy." She made an odd, dipping motion with her hand and resumed walking.

"There's little joy in a marriage without warmth," I said.

"You speak of your own situation." She stooped to pluck a wood anemone from a sunlit tuft of grass. Her movements were quick and often awkward—but what she lacked in grace was compensated by her vitality. "I don't envy your position as Mr. Emerson's wife," she said, twirling the small white flower in her fingers. "It can't be easy to sit in the shadow of his brilliance."

"I never thought to sit in his shadow," I said. "Our marriage was to be a partnership of ideas."

She gave me a long glance and then, blinking rapidly, surprised me by tucking the flower over my ear at the temple. "You're a brave woman. I doubt I'd have the courage to marry such a gift to the world."

I did not reply. Despite her words, I believed she secretly thought she would have made a better wife to Mr. Emerson. A light breeze came up and stirred the ribbons on my cap. Margaret wore no cap—a convention that she insisted humiliated women, though I pointed out that it well-served its dual purpose of keeping a woman's hair tidy while preventing dirt from begriming it.

She bent for another flower, which she settled into her own thick hair. "You must allow Waldo his eccentricities, Lidian. In the name of the great wisdom he shares with the world, if for no other reason."

I turned away and commenced walking, for I could not at that moment meet her gaze. The slope we climbed grew steeper, and I began to feel the strain in my legs. "You believe you could accustom yourself to his indifference if you were in my place then?"

"He's a genius," Margaret said, quickly catching up and walking beside me. She held her hands before her as she spoke, her fingers exciting the warm air. "A great deal can be sacrificed for the sake of genius."

I knew she did not believe that he would ever ignore her. She was as innocent as I once had been and mistook intellectual fervor for passion. Yet I had hoped for more from her. She spoke so eloquently and with such great understanding of the lot of women! She knew how much we bore of men's vicissitudes—she upheld the brave banner of sisterhood for us all. It saddened me to discover that her own life was as muddled as the next woman's. It appeared that she too yearned for the solace of a man's love.

We walked in silence for a time, watching the nesting birds and chipmunks skittering in the leaf mold. The sun was high and filtered by pines and hemlocks along the path. Pebbles of light fell at our feet and I took deep breaths, drawing in the clean, sweet spring air. Then I felt a pulse of urgency in my breasts as they filled with milk beneath my bodice.

"I've enjoyed our walk," I said, "but I must head back to Bush. Ellen will soon want to be fed."

Margaret nodded. It seemed that everything suited her that afternoon. "I've meant to ask you," she said as we made our way back down the path, "why did you consent to the name Ellen? I would never have allowed it."

"I named her," I said. "It was my idea."

"*Your* idea? But how can you so plainly incorporate Waldo's first wife into your marriage? Surely it must grieve you."

"Time will break the potency of that bond," I said. "The dead are fixed. But my child"—and I pictured my daughter sleeping, her skin rosy with life against the pillow—"she will grow plump and sweet and smile at him and wrap her arms around his neck. And soon the name Ellen will mean only his daughter."

"I hope for your sake you are right," Margaret said. "It could prove a terrible blunder if her name has the opposite effect."

PART II

April 1841 – July 1844

Transcendental Times

Look at the sunset when you are distant half a mile from the village, and I fear you will forget your engagement to the tea-party.

—RALPH WALDO EMERSON

13

Dependence

I delight much in my young friend who seems to have
as free and erect a mind as any I have ever met.
—RALPH WALDO EMERSON

On the April morning in 1841 when Mr. Emerson informed me that he'd invited Henry Thoreau to live with
us, I'd been about to tell him I was with child a third time. He announced the
arrangement as he bent over the washstand, wearing only his trousers and
braces, which hung in black loops past his knees. His skin was waxen in the dim
morning light as he splashed handfuls of icy water onto his face. He straightened and pressed his face into a towel, then turned to look at me where I lay on
my side beneath the counterpane.

"It's not like you to have no response, Asia." He'd called me Asia after
Wallie was born. I didn't like the name, and yet he insisted it suited me, as it
reflected my emotional nature.

"What would you have me say?" I sat up, pushed the counterpane away,
and swung my legs over the side of the bed. "I know you enjoy Henry's

company and seek to encourage his writing. It's generous of you to offer him shelter here."

"I thought you might object to the extra burden. You've told me often how our guests encumber you."

Indeed, I had frequently protested under the strain of our friends' visits. Just a month before Margaret Fuller and Anna Barker had descended upon Bush and stayed nearly two weeks. As always, with Margaret present, the house was filled with callers, and it was left to me to order sufficient food and make sleeping arrangements, to plan my days around what would bring comfort and happiness to our guests.

He dropped the towel on the washstand, took his shirt from its hook on the door, and pushed his arms into the long sleeves. "Henry's a poet. He needs a situation where poetry is appreciated. His mother's boardinghouse is hardly the place. It's noisy and crowded, filled with unromantic souls."

"I'm familiar with Cynthia's establishment." My voice was crisp. "You forget that I regularly frequent her parlor."

"I did not forget." He turned away from me to button his shirt. There existed a peculiar modesty between us despite six years of marriage. Mr. Emerson's studied reserve was present even in our most intimate encounters. "Then you have no objection?"

"I think it's a noble idea." I sat very still, my hands grasping the edge of the mattress, the balls of my feet brushing the floor. The truth was, this was an arrangement I had contrived to bring about for nearly two years. I'd suggested many times that Henry needed a place to work suited to poets, a place where his writing would be understood and appreciated. Now Mr. Emerson was presenting the idea to me as if it were his own.

He moved to his bureau without glancing in my direction. I heard the clink of cufflinks as he sorted through his box of jewelry. "He seemed pleased by the proposal." He raised his left hand to expose the inside of his wrist and the holes in his cuffs. He pushed his cufflink through, and fastened it. "Since he and his brother closed their school, he's been at loose ends. Rather than rush off to teach in some frontier town, I convinced him to try developing his talent here. I believe it will be an agreeable situation for all of us. I know how often you've depended on him."

Depended. It was not the word I would have chosen, for it seemed too limited to encompass my relationship with Henry. The truth was that I'd come to rely on him in all manner of things—his skill with hammer and saw, his proficiency in the garden, his ability to charm and entertain the children, and—most significantly—his companionship. It was the most unlikely of ties—this strange affinity with a man fifteen years my junior. Yet the hours we spent in conversation had been both exhilarating and sweetly satisfying. Henry had interjected himself into our family so tidily that I could no longer imagine my days without him.

My husband fastened his other cufflink into its slot and looked at me. "Surely your silence has some significance."

I shook my head. "None but happiness. I'm sure Henry's occupancy will be a blessing." I slid off the bed and busied myself with making it. "Is it to be a permanent arrangement?"

"We agreed upon a year."

I slapped the pillows, flipped them, and drew the counterpane over them. "A year." I imagined Henry every morning at breakfast, pictured sitting each evening with him in the parlor, saw myself washing his clothes, sweeping out his room. "Have you given any thought to where he should stay? We don't have an extra room at present, except the garret." Our son and daughter now occupied the room that had been Lucy's—it had become a nursery shortly after Wallie's birth. And the room over the kitchen that was once Charles's apartment had been the servant's quarters for four years now. "Perhaps we should install him in the Red Room."

Mr. Emerson frowned as he put on his jacket. "That would preclude other visitors." I knew from the way his face softened that he was thinking of Margaret. "What about the room at the top of the front stairs?"

"It's more passageway than chamber." The room he suggested was a dark corridor off the front-stairs landing. Opened as a hallway five years before, to access Charles and Elizabeth's bedroom, it had been abandoned, unfinished like the chamber itself.

"Still, it would afford him the privacy he requires."

I pictured Henry in that raw, dusky space, his desk lit only by one small window. I knew how he treasured light and nature. He ought not to be in such a room.

"We'll let him decide between that and the garret," I said.

"The garret's too far removed from my study," Mr. Emerson said. "He's not seeking a life of seclusion, you know." He gave me a slight smile. "He's agreed to perform the duties of a handyman while he's here. There are always things that want repair. As you're ever reminding me, dear wife." He smiled again, more broadly this time.

Was my husband so preoccupied with his studies that he didn't notice when things were fixed, repairs made? Had he forgotten that Henry had been doing handyman chores at Bush for nearly three years, practically from the moment he first stepped across the threshold? First there had been the barn door I'd been after Mr. Emerson to repair for months—a door that hung on one hinge and squealed unmercifully when opened. Henry had come to the house one morning and fixed it unbidden. I discovered it when I went to the barn for my rake to work in the garden. Instinctively bracing myself against the door's shriek and wobble, I pulled the latch. But there was no scrape; the door swung silent and balanced on its doubled hinge. Later Nancy informed me that Mr. Thoreau had come by early with a satchel of tools and spent an hour out at the barn. When Henry came to collect Mr. Emerson for their walk later that afternoon, I met him at the door, embarrassing him with my enthusiastic gratitude.

In public he was shy with me, more deferential than with other women in our circle. He possessed a special affinity for Lucy during the months she boarded with his mother, and had corresponded with her when she visited Plymouth. But the warmth of that association had not extended immediately to me. My relation with Henry had found its own slow path to friendship, mediated by a mutual passion for abolition and a shared pleasure in the daily activities of my children.

Now there would be a third child to delight and exhaust me. A child who would be born while Henry was in residence. A child whose existence I had not yet revealed to my husband. I heard the low murmurs of our son and daughter from the nursery—Wallie and Ellen had wakened and I must go to tend them.

"Mr. Emerson," I said, wrapping my dressing gown around me and moving to where he stood before his bureau adjusting his collar, "there's something I must tell you."

He looked at me, and something in his face told me that he knew what I was about to say. Knew and did not want to know. I put my hand on his arm, on the hard muscle just below the crook of his elbow, as if to steady myself with his strength, and I told him. The words fell from my lips in an odd monotone as if I'd memorized and spoken them a hundred times before. He listened, the grave expression on his face unchanging. He knew how severely my pregnancies drained and tortured me. Yet how I welcomed them! Each child was a gift from God's abundant hand.

He was—as always—gracious in his congratulations. He kissed me and assured me he was pleased. Yet I detected a weariness in him that matched my own, a recognition that a child was as much burden as joy, that the new life growing within me shackled him yet more certainly to the encumbrances of love.

HENRY HAD JOINED our circle of friends upon his graduation from Harvard, soon after Lucy left Plymouth and returned to Concord, where she installed herself in an upstairs apartment at Cynthia Thoreau's boarding-house. She had placed both Frank and Sophia in schools. Concerned that she might grow lonely, I had visited her daily, and grew familiar not only with her chamber, but with the Thoreau parlor. Many afternoons I sat conversing with Lucy and the Thoreaus' youngest daughter, Sophia, a woman whose plain looks were compensated by a lively intelligence and sweet disposition. On one occasion when we discussed a recent lecture of my husband's, Sophia declared that Henry had written a letter to her in the very words Mr. Emerson had spoken. She was so struck by this that she fetched the letter and read it aloud. The correspondence of thought was remarkable. At first I was troubled by this similitude, for I considered Mr. Emerson's a singular and unmatched intellect. But Lucy persuaded me to bring Henry to Mr. Emerson's attention.

"You know how he likes to discover young people of genius. And Henry's similarity of thought will flatter him."

I was not given to flattering my husband, but I recognized the truth in Lucy's words. Mr. Emerson had a penchant for taking an interest in particular men and women, drawing them into his circle, and making them disciples of his metaphysics. Often these people were many years younger than he, but Mr. Emerson was not a man given to antiquated hierarchies. He claimed he judged a man solely on what he said and did. There were no other reasonable standards.

When I spoke to Mr. Emerson about Henry, he insisted on inviting him to one of our evening conversations. Henry did not at first appear to be a valuable addition, for he had little to say, and his appearance was common.

Less than common—there was an extreme disorder in his rumpled clothes and his dark hair was always in turmoil. He looked as if he gave no care whatsoever to his appearance. It was not until the third evening that he spoke more than a few words—I recall how well his voice and words matched, for they were both startling in their sharpness. In response to a remark of my husband's on the value of book learning, Henry referred to a professor's lecture on electricity and asserted that on that subject colleges were blind to the fact that a twinge in the elbow was worth all the books and lectures on the subject. A comment that made my husband laugh and astonished me with its wit and insight.

Thereafter, Mr. Emerson pursued Henry with the zeal of a lover, wooing him with the brilliance of his mind, bent on cementing their friendship. One of my husband's most notable traits was his proclivity for taking thoughts propounded by others and incorporating them into his own work. He harvested ideas like a farmer and refined them to use in his lectures. This harvesting was so characteristic that I did not question it. Mr. Emerson believed adamantly in the universality of thought—that ideas were the property of no one. His gift lay less in his own creative insights than in his ability to glean and blend and polish the thoughts of others.

It was natural that Henry should be deeply flattered by Mr. Emerson's attentions. He was freshly graduated, still searching for his place in the world, still eager to taste all of life's intellectual delights. He enthusiastically shared his insights with my husband, divulging the treasures of his mind the way a small boy proudly displays the stones in his pockets to a friend.

Unlike so many of Mr. Emerson's followers and friends, Henry was a native of Concord. I believe that my husband secretly envied him that distinction, an envy that expressed itself in a periodic vexation with Henry's thoughts and actions. Yet he often referred to Henry as his friend and they took long afternoon walks together, dissecting the issues of the day and the great philosophies of history. They sat in Mr. Emerson's study for hours, discussing poetry and the importance of meter. Henry emerged from these conversations with eyes glowing and cheeks flushed with excitement. At first occasionally, and then with increasing frequency, he sought me out later to talk about what they had discussed. He said he found that my thoughts balanced Mr. Emerson's and brought his own reflections a greater clarity.

"Your perspective *distills* your husband's," he said and though I was not entirely sure of his meaning, the penetration of his eyes silenced me. When he looked at me I felt as if I were being seen for the first time, a circumstance I found both exhilarating and unsettling.

His intelligence was marred by an exquisite sensitivity. When he spoke there was sometimes a tremor in his voice, as if he could barely contain his emotions. Yet when he shared his thoughts during our evening conversations, his words were as caustic and barbed as my own. More than once I heard him speak the very words I was thinking.

Henry moved into Bush on the twenty-sixth of April, carrying his satchel up the front stairs and through the narrow door on the landing into the room I'd prepared. I'd made the chamber as comfortable as I could, furnishing it with a cot and bookshelf, a small writing desk and chair. Because it lacked an adequate window, I installed an extra lamp and supplied two candlesticks besides. That morning I placed a small jar of flowers on his desk—mayflowers and dogtooth violets I'd found in the woods—their pink and yellow petals lending a small dash of cheer to the otherwise dreary room.

I lit the lamp and stood in the doorway, watching him take in the room. He kept glancing at me, as if to assure himself that I accepted his occupancy. He seemed unusually shy, awkward in a way he had not been for more than a year.

"I don't want my presence to add to your burden," he said, placing his satchel on the bed. "I'll wash my own clothes and keep this room clean. Of course it's understood that I'll make whatever repairs are needed about the place. Just tell me what's to be done." He smiled, then looked away.

"I'm glad you're here." Something in my chest trembled as I spoke, a vibration that was part elation, part warning.

He looked straight at me then, directly into my eyes, as if to assure himself that I spoke truly, and his look jarred me. It was a look of deference and esteem, a look that approached veneration, but what shook me was the *recognition* in it. He alone was able to penetrate my carefully acquired refinements and see clearly who I was.

He turned abruptly to the tiny window overlooking the road to the Mill Dam. Turned as if something in my face had alarmed him.

It was his expression that caused me to remember the poem he'd presented to me the previous January. He had spent a morning at our house repairing one of our dining-room chairs that had threatened to collapse due to a loosened rung. When he finished he refused my invitation to dinner but instead took my hand and pressed a folded paper into it without speaking.

The paper contained eight lines written in Henry's jagged hand—his *t*'s and *l*'s made me think of needles—a poem that made my heart pulse in my throat.

> *We two that planets erst had been*
> *Are now a double star,*
> *And in the heavens may be seen,*
> *Where that we fixed are.*
>
> *Yet whirled with subtle power along,*
> *Into new space we enter,*
> *And evermore with spheral song*
> *Revolve about one centre.*

I'd told him that he must show the poem to Mr. Emerson. I did not acknowledge the thump of recognition in my chest, nor did I admit that the poem perfectly described the triad nature of my affiliation with Henry and my husband. I remember my hands dampening, my thumb leaving a feathery gray blot upon the paper. I remember handing the poem back to him even as its words engraved themselves in my heart.

He stood, holding the paper pressed against his chest, and I realized his eyes had never left my face. They were still filled with the expectation of praise, and with good reason, for when had I not commended him on the excellence and delicacy of his words? He had made a habit of showing his poems to me before offering them to my husband. On several occasions I'd taken it upon myself to show them to Mr. Emerson with the hope that he might publish them in his new journal, *The Dial.*

But this one had been different. This was about *us*. With it, Henry had crossed a line into a realm of friendship that touched on intimacy.

Now Henry stood in shadow, his back to me, outlined against the tiny window, in the room I'd prepared for him.

"The children are delighted you're living with us," I said. "Wallie made me promise to allow him a walk with you this afternoon."

He swiveled back to me, and he was smiling again, his hair wind-tossed, as always, every strand pitched in a different direction. "I'm delighted too. To be here," he said, his voice slow and quiet, like a man waking from a pleasant dream. "I feel as if things have finally come right."

"Yes," I said, smiling—I could not help myself—and I sensed something unfolding within me. It was too soon for the new baby to quicken. This sensation was something else, a state of extreme awareness, a rare unity of mind and body. I pictured my heart opening and stretching, like a plant in sunlight.

Then Wallie called out for me from the nursery.

14

Friendship

> It must be rare, indeed, that we meet with one to
> whom we are prepared to be quite ideally related, as
> she to us. We should have no reserve; we should give
> the whole of ourselves to that society; we should have
> no duty aside from that.
>
> —HENRY DAVID THOREAU

Near the end of June, a young cousin of mine came to Bush on an extended visit to help tend the children. Mary, who had been a zealous member of my Bible class in Plymouth, had grown into a beautiful young woman, whose shining eyes reflected her deep interest in spiritual principles.

Soon after her arrival Mr. Emerson began to engage her in long conversations. More than once I came upon them in the parlor—she, sitting on the floor at his feet, gazing up at him with an adoring expression, her skirts swirled around her with the grace of flower petals—he, elaborating quietly on some philosophical point while bestowing his beneficent smile. Her rapture reminded me of how my first glimpse of Mr. Emerson had moved me in a similar manner.

Mary captured his interest only by the compliment of her flattery, and not—as Margaret Fuller did—through the force of her personality and intellect. Yet I did not resent Margaret, but strove to be her friend. Friendship was our constant credo in those days—it was nearly a religion with us. We believed people were drawn together by their natures, and that no relationship should be defined or constrained by traditions of gender and culture. We allowed ourselves many liberties in the name of that virtue. Perhaps too many. I did not believe that Mr. Emerson was subject to the corruptions of the flesh. Nor, I told myself, was I.

Henry's presence under our roof was a special delight. We'd grown close through long and frequent kitchen conversations while we waited for Mr. Emerson to emerge from his study. With Henry, I had the pleasure of being able to fully assert my opinions, for he enjoyed a hearty debate as well as I. Yet I began to sense that Henry felt a certain discomfort in our home. He was forever wandering off alone in the evenings for a moonlit sail on the river or a walk to Walden Pond.

Mr. Emerson professed great satisfaction in knowing that Henry was on hand to help me with the children and the household burdens. My husband traveled often on lecture trips and when he was home he always kept closest company with his books. Ours was a strange household, where each inhabitant went about his daily business alone, like a planet in its private orbit.

I complained, often and loudly. One morning late in June, when my third pregnancy had drained both strength and wisdom from me and Mary had taken the children for a walk, I invaded my husband's study and demanded his attention.

"Surely you could put your papers aside for one hour and give me the benefit of your regard."

He sighed and did not look up from his book.

I yanked at my skirts. "Mr. Emerson, there are times when I believe you would prefer me as a decoration upon our mantel. Perhaps you should have my portrait painted on the wall, so I could come and go to Plymouth as I please. I believe you would be perfectly content."

He finally removed his gaze from his book, and frowned up at me. "You disappoint me. Are you truly suggesting I'm not a proper husband?"

My hands knotted into fists, which I struggled to keep hidden in my skirts. "I'm suggesting that this marriage is not as I had imagined it would be."

He blinked. "That seems to be the nature of marriage. Perhaps if you were less preoccupied with our children—"

"But the children are my one consolation!" I cried.

"You cannot view both sides of the same coin at once." His tone was infuriatingly moderate. "You appear to always prefer motherhood over conversation."

"I'm talking with you now, aren't I?"

"This is hardly a conversation. You're overwrought. Nothing is to be gained by argument." He gazed at me calmly, as if to imply that he alone could perceive the truth. "Now, please, leave me so that I may finish my work. We'll talk later."

I stalked from the room and ran directly up the stairs to my chamber, where I fell into a fit of despondency that lasted the rest of the day. The next morning, I woke with a fever.

As spring progressed and the garden prospered under Henry's management, my husband prospered as well. His winter-weakened lungs grew strong and his face and arms bronzed in the sun. For two months he was constant in his daily attentions to the vegetables he had planted. He seemed to regard their germination and growth with the same wonder one might witness a miracle. But when June came and my roses bloomed he ceased his watchfulness, and began to neglect the garden for his study. The vegetables were not ignored, of course, for Henry's commitment to them never flagged. And Wallie retained his interest in the garden throughout the summer. Whenever I could not locate my son, I always looked first in the garden, where I usually found him on his knees, weeding or pruning the tender plants, performing these chores exactly as Henry had taught him.

It had long been my habit to spend what free time I had in the garden, caring for my flowers. I took special pride in my roses, for many in Concord had remarked on their beauty and fragrance. One afternoon in early July, while Ellen napped and Mr. Emerson conversed with Mary, I found Henry and Wallie weeding the bean plants with such concentrated pleasure that I abandoned my roses to join them.

Wallie welcomed me by holding out his soiled hands as if they were medals of honor for which he should be rightfully praised, whereupon Henry did the same, making me laugh and compliment them both.

We spent an hour there with our hands in the earth, while our conversation ranged from the toughness of weeds to Henry's reminiscence of a river trip he'd made with his older brother John. Soon Wallie wandered off to collect pebbles, and our discourse became more intimate. Henry confessed that he and John had had a brief falling out over a young woman. "That was more than a year ago." He bent over the weeds so I could not see his face. "We had a few disagreeable weeks, but the rift is long since healed." There was a curious entreaty in his tone that invited me to pursue the subject. I wondered at first if I had imagined this, if my curiosity had simply overruled my sense of propriety. But no, he slid a glance in my direction and knocked the soil from the roots of a weed he had pulled.

"Her name was Ellen." He smiled and sat back on his heels. "Ellen Sewall. She's sister to young Edmund, one of the boys enrolled in our school."

I nodded. The private school had been popular, and John and Henry Thoreau had quickly become known for their enthusiastic and progressive educational methods, but John's frail lungs had forced its closure.

"She came to Concord to visit her aunt who boards with us. John and I both enjoyed her company. We went boating, walking, picnicking . . ." His voice trailed off as I detected a distinct reddening of his cheeks.

"It's all right," I said. "It's natural for young men to find pleasure in the company of young ladies."

He raised his head. "Perhaps you recall a conversation you and I had at that time. It was a fall morning and I'd come to repair the kitchen door latch." His words seemed to gather momentum as he spoke, and his last sentence came out in a long rush. "We spoke of love and you said—I recall this very clearly—you said that the only cure for love is to love more. Do you remember?"

"I do," I said. "But it was not intended in a particular sense. Nor was it directed at you. I was thinking of my own situation."

"But it's quite true. When love becomes an illness the cure is not to stop loving—an impossibility, after all—the only remedy is to turn it in a new direction. A sort of homeopathy of love." He smiled, yet I sensed he intended far more than he said—and that he expected me to fully apprehend his meaning.

I got to my feet and clapped my hands against my skirts to remove the layer of soil. "I'm gratified if I said something you found useful. Though I'm not clear what it has to do with your brother or Miss Sewall."

Instantly he was on his own feet beside me. "Don't you see? I was able to control my heart, to turn it toward Ellen, and away from"—he stopped abruptly and looked down at his knees, then back at me—"from its unsuitable desire."

"Unsuitable desire?" I straightened to brush off my sleeves.

"Yes." He was staring into my eyes, holding my gaze with his and in that instant I was certain he referred to me.

"Henry," I said, slapping again at my skirts, despite the fact that all the dirt likely to come loose had already fallen, "infatuations are altogether common for a young man your age. You must not take them seriously." I managed to look at him, though it violated my inclination.

"That's what I told myself." His eyes suddenly seemed unbearably sad. I longed to embrace him.

"So," I said, forcing a false heartiness into my voice, "what happened to Miss Sewall? Did she return to her family?"

"John proposed marriage." He was no longer looking at me, but toward the trees beyond the brook. His voice was dull. "She rejected him. Her family sent her to northern New York to stay with relatives. Then we had our conversation. You and I." He took a long breath and let it out. "And I wrote to her. I asked her to marry me."

"You *proposed*? Henry, why didn't you tell us?" Too late, I knew the answer. I inwardly castigated my too-impulsive tongue. "She said no."

He nodded and his voice dropped. "I had no reason to expect her to accept. But my mother and aunts"—again, he paused—"they all seemed bent on making Ellen part of our family. And I thought I might come to love her enough."

"Oh, Henry!"

"No," he said quietly. "I was—quite honestly—relieved." He turned his gaze on me once again and I saw in his eyes all the answers to the questions I had not asked. Would never ask.

MY GARDEN CONVERSATION with Henry distressed me. Less because of his interest in me than because of my own unseemly response to that interest. I was fonder of him than I had any right to be. My affection went beyond the natural attractions of friendship. I buried my unease in attentions to my children and the cares of the house, cares that increased whenever my husband traveled. His lecturing schedule required him to go sometimes as far as Pennsylvania, and whenever I protested his absence, he reminded me that his lectures and books were the chief source of our income and that I must not begrudge him the capacity to support his family.

"I begrudge you nothing," I said. "I merely ask that occasionally you are

mindful of my needs." It was a Sunday night and we had retired late to our
chamber after an evening conversation with Bronson, Elizabeth, Mary, and
Henry on the subject of duty and love. The night was oppressively warm;
I had flung open the windows. Now, as I stood next to one in my chemise,
hoping to catch a trace of cooling breeze upon my skin, I wondered if I ought
to close them, for it appeared we were about to quarrel.

"Mindful of your needs." He stood before the carved chestnut wardrobe,
the light from the mantel candle wavering across his face and neck as he removed his collar. I had the sense that he'd deliberately turned away from
me, that he did not care to look in my direction. "I observe every marital
courtesy that was ever contrived by woman. What more do you ask?"

"I ask that you honor me with your thoughts, in the same measure that
you honor Mary and Henry."

He stepped back, receding into the shadows. I heard him sigh. "So now
you're jealous of our young guests. Though you have access to me day and
night—"

"Access to *you?*" My voice rose and my fingers clutched the thin fabric of
my chemise. "Access when you are away in Boston or Philadelphia or New York
three weeks each month? When you lock yourself in your study every morning
and take walks with your friends every afternoon? I hardly know you!"

He came into the pool of candlelight. He had put on his nightshirt and it
clung to his chest and arms, attesting to the evening's damp and close atmosphere. A tiny breeze rippled the curtains. I felt it stroke my bare arms and instinctively leaned closer to the window.

"I've never attempted to hide my defects."

"But you no longer love me." Even as I spoke the words I knew how rue-
ful and bitter they sounded. I had not intended that but, spoken, they could
not be taken back.

"Love." He sighed again. "Love is not a tide to flood and ebb. I told you
before we were married that I loved you in a new and higher way. That has
not changed. I know I'm sometimes cold and arid. I don't possess your emotional elasticity. But I don't think you have just cause to complain." He went
to the mantel and blew out the candle. "Now we'd best get some sleep. The
hour is late."

I stood at the window, for I couldn't bear the thought of lying down beside
him. My fingers released the fabric of my skirt and slid together. The emotions that raged through me threatened to shake me to pieces. I left the room,

still in my chemise, and went downstairs, where I paced through the warm, silent rooms, wringing my hands and trying to pray, waiting for my outrage to diminish so that I might rest. I don't know how long I was in that state—it may have been hours, for I was dimly conscious of moonlight growing in long spears across the floor—but eventually I calmed sufficiently to become aware of the sounds beyond my own rapid breathing. I heard the scuttling of mice in the walls, the occasional creak of joists and floors, and finally the chant of crickets, which drew me outside.

I sat on the steps of the east entrance and gazed out across the moonlit fields. There was a haze in the air common to summer nights, and it had drawn itself around the moon like a veil so that a rich amber shimmer fell on the meadow grasses. A few stars pricked through the mist, but most of the sky was vacant and blank. *Like my heart,* I thought, and then censured myself for the sin of self-pity. I had much to be thankful for—my station and comfort in life, and particularly my children. As I bent my head and lifted my plait from my neck, where damp tendrils clung to my skin, I became aware of another sound I'd not yet perceived. It seemed to me, as I raised my head to search for its source, that it had been there all along—in the same way that the song of a common bird serves as background for one's daily round. The melody was sweet and lilting yet it seemed in some way infinitely sad. Someone was playing a flute.

I rose and, mindful of my unclothed state, started back inside. Yet before I crossed the threshold, the music ceased abruptly, ending on a high note that shivered in the air and raised gooseflesh on my bare arms. I turned in the doorway, sensing a presence, but my eyes searched the shadowy yard in vain. Then I heard my name—spoken in so low a murmur that at first I thought it was the wind. It reminded me of the time I'd sat on the hill behind my aunt's house and heard my mother's voice in my ear. That had been the voice of a ghost—for it happened ten years after Mother's death—and this sounded so similar that I shivered despite the heat. Yet this voice was not my mother's, but a man's.

"Henry?" My word trembled just beyond a whisper.

"Here." I heard the rustle of grass to my right and saw a dim flash of reflected moonlight. Then he stepped out of the shadows and stood before me at the bottom of the steps. His shirtsleeves were rolled to his elbows and the braces of his trousers made parallel black stripes from his waist to his shoulders. He clasped his flute in his left hand while with his right he swept his hair from his forehead. Even though he was only a few feet away, his features were indistinct because of the hazy darkness.

He said my name again in a whisper that I realized I was not meant to hear, hushed as the susurration of the horse-chestnut tree leaves above us. The skin between my shoulder blades tingled. I was acutely aware that only a thin cotton chemise lay between his eyes and my skin. I crossed my arms over my breasts, but knew at once that the gesture only emphasized my near-nakedness.

"I couldn't sleep," I said.

"Nor could I."

"Your music is lovely."

He gave a brief, abstracted nod. "Lidian, I couldn't help but hear."

"Hear?" Something dropped into the well of my stomach.

"Your quarrel with Waldo. I was out here, not far from your window."

I shook my head, my heart suddenly racing. I prayed that my flushed cheeks were not visible. "It's not something I can discuss, Henry."

"I just want to help you. If there's anything I can do—"

"No. Please don't talk to me now." And, filled with shame, I rushed through the doorway and up the stairs to my chamber, where I crawled into bed beside my sleeping husband.

HENRY WAS NOT at the breakfast table the next morning, and I supposed that he'd slept late, as was sometimes his habit when he'd been out walking at night. Yet Wallie informed me that he'd looked out the nursery window and observed Mr. Thoreau crossing the field, heading for the woods.

Mary brought Ellen downstairs, still rosy and damp from her night's sleep. I took my daughter and nuzzled her warm cheek. "Shall we take a walk with the children after breakfast? A stroll beside the river would be nice in this heat."

"Oh." Mary glanced toward the window, frowned, and then looked back at me. "I'm sorry. I promised Mr. Emerson I would transcribe one of his essays onto fresh paper. Perhaps we could walk tomorrow?"

"Tomorrow." I felt my smile drain away.

"Or this afternoon if I'm finished with my work?"

"Your work," I said slowly. "I thought it was understood that you would help me with the children this summer. If you can't see your way clear to abiding by our agreement perhaps it is time you went home to Plymouth."

"Surely you can spare her for an hour this morning before your walk, Asia." Mr. Emerson spoke from the door to the dining room. I turned to face him. I wondered how long he had been standing in the hall.

"I've spared her for the past five mornings," I said. "And most afternoons as well. Perhaps Elizabeth could transcribe for you today. Or Henry."

He did not reply, but simply stared at me. This had become his habit in recent months—he refused to engage in a disagreement when others were present. It gave him the appearance of superiority, as if my words and thoughts were so slight as to be undeserving of a response.

I turned my back on him and faced Mary, who looked wretched, as if she were on the verge of tears. "Take the children up to the nursery and feed them there," I said, handing Ellen back to her. "And then get them dressed for an outing." She did my bidding without a word, but I caught the glance she cast toward Mr. Emerson before she left the room.

I faced my husband. "Do you have any idea what you're doing to that poor child?"

"Doing? No. What am I doing?"

"Feeding her infatuation. You spend hours sharing your new ideas and they are magic to her. She's completely under your spell."

"Since when did you object to opening a woman's mind to new ideas?"

I would have answered had not the outside door suddenly opened. Henry stepped into the kitchen, carrying a spray of yellow and white wildflowers nearly as wide as his chest.

"Henry!" Mr. Emerson face broke into a broad smile. "I was afraid you'd deserted us this morning. But I see you've been enjoying the outdoors. And brought some of nature's glories back with you." He reached for the bouquet.

Henry's glance flicked from my husband's face to mine and back again. "They're for Lidian." He stepped past Mr. Emerson and pushed the blossoms into my arms.

My husband watched me. I knew he felt rebuffed; I also knew that he would quickly forgive and forget Henry's slights. Henry amused him, especially when he showed his pugnacious side. As if he had read my thoughts, Mr. Emerson laughed and clapped Henry on the shoulder. "And so they should be, my friend. Who can better appreciate a flower's charms than my good wife?"

"No one." Henry was standing so close that I could feel the warmth of his arm through my sleeve, and the sensation brought with it the memory of the previous night's encounter. I recalled the dark air lying damp and cool against my skin as I sat on the step and heard the sound of Henry's flute. I remembered Henry stepping out of the shadows and whispering my name.

I turned from both men and went to the pantry to locate a vase for the flowers.

IN THE MIDST of breakfast that morning, as we partook of our mutton broth and corn cake, Henry put down his spoon and asked if he might take me and the children for a walk.

"It's a fine, bright day. And I recently discovered a new variety of swamp rose that you must see."

"That's kind of you, Henry," Mr. Emerson buttered a piece of corn cake. "Very kind. Lidian and the children have been eager for a constitutional." He turned to me. "You see, my dear? Things arrange themselves quite nicely when we allow people to follow their own inclinations." And he smiled at all of us like a king pleased with his court.

We left the house an hour later. Ellen insisted on riding atop Henry's shoulders while Wallie ran ahead and soon disappeared in the low brush that choked the path up Bristor's Hill. I fretted that he might lose his way or fall and hurt himself, but Henry assured me that four-year-old boys were the most surefooted creatures on earth, and that Wallie's sense of direction was unerring.

Henry led us to a small cove on Walden Pond where we rested under a pine tree. Light glimmered off the water and touched the soft undersides of oaks along the shore. Hemlock branches swung above our heads, blocking the harshest rays of the sun and offering a pleasant green shade that soothed my eyes and cooled my face. Birds called from the trees and large black dragonflies darted back and forth, fascinating Ellen, who tried in vain to catch one. Later, she fell asleep on my shoulder, while Wallie busied himself building a castle by the water's edge. Henry leaned comfortably back against the tree, gazing out at the pond. The only sounds I heard were Ellen's gentle breathing, the lapping of the water against the shore, and the singing birds.

"It's quite peaceful," I said.

"I come here often." Henry picked up a stone and turned it over in his palm. "At night sometimes I take my boat out on the pond and play my flute."

I thought of our encounter the night before.

"Did you know that music charms the fish?" He turned to face me. I kept my eyes on Ellen's head, where my hand caressed her fine baby hair. "They come up to the top of the water when they hear it and swarm all around the boat."

I didn't know whether or not to believe him. It seemed an odd, unlikely truth, the sort of story he might tell the children.

"I wish you could see it, Lidian. Let me take you out some night and show you. It's an astonishing sight." He tossed the stone up and caught it without looking, his gaze fixed on the pond. "No one would know."

I imagined gliding beneath the stars with Henry. I could picture him gazing at me as he rowed—his eyes filled with that blaze of admiration that I'd lately begun to prize.

"Someone would know," I said. "Such an adventure does not go undiscovered."

He shook his head. "I know the habits of everyone in the house, even the servants. I've observed and catalogued them all in my mind. I know when I may safely come and go unseen."

I felt a small shock at this confession—a tingle of electricity that purled up my spine. "I can't, Henry," I said. "Surely you know that."

He didn't reply, nor did he look at me.

"Which is not to say that I don't want to." My voice was no louder than the riffle of water against the shore.

He continued to toss the stone for a while. Then, abruptly, he stood up, threw it into the pond, and brushed off his trousers. "I think it's time we headed home," he said. And without looking at me, he scooped Ellen up and settled her, still sleeping, against his shoulder, then whistled for Wallie, who came running as if he liked nothing better in the world than to be summoned by Henry Thoreau.

15

Recognition

How much virtue there is in simply seeing!
—HENRY DAVID THOREAU

The Reverend Ripley died that fall, on a day the cruel north wind stripped bright leaves from the trees. Though I protested, Mr. Emerson took Wallie to view the body, insisting that the sooner the boy learned to face death, the better. When they returned, my son was visibly shaken, and though he did not weep, he refused to describe what he had seen. I read fairy tales to him in the nursery for nearly an hour to distract his mind before he complained of fatigue and fell asleep.

I went downstairs and entered my husband's study without knocking.

"You should not have done such a thing," I said.

Mr. Emerson, who was, as usual, seated in his rocker, raised his head and regarded me with astonishment. "What 'thing' are you referring to?"

"Requiring Wallie to look upon Reverend Ripley's corpse! The boy's distraught!"

"He's my son. He must be trained to understand all of life." He took his pen from the inkwell. "Now please leave me to do my work."

I fairly screamed at him. "*Your* son? What of *me*? Am I nothing but an attendant now? A nursemaid to my own children?"

"Lidian, you are hysterical. Go and lie down until you are in control." He turned to his papers, and began to write.

"I will not be dismissed in this manner!" I hissed. "I am your *wife!* If nothing else, you owe me the courtesy of your attention."

"I won't discuss the matter until you've calmed yourself." He did not look up. Short of flying at him in an unseemly rage, there was nothing I could do. I left; the only available satisfaction being the hard slam of the door behind me.

The truth was, of course, that he owed me nothing. As a wife, I had no rights whatsoever—not to my children, my property, or even my own body. Least of all, a right to his attention.

I went back upstairs and shut myself in my chamber for the duration of the morning.

WALLIE'S FIFTH BIRTHDAY was a grand, cold day. An October wind had shredded the leaves from the trees and they lay heaped in bright piles in the yard. Wallie liked nothing better than to hurl himself into them. Ellen watched these proceedings with serious expectation, as if memorizing each leap he took. When she tried to duplicate his efforts she tumbled headfirst into the leaves but, undaunted, pushed herself to her feet and repeated her endeavors.

That week, a traveling daguerreotypist came to town and set up a temporary studio in a tavern on the Mill Dam. Mr. Emory was a tall man with darting black eyes and limbs as thin as sticks. On shelves rigged from loose bricks and lumber, he arranged a display of forty daguerreotypes that quickly became a great sensation. Every man, woman, and child in Concord wanted to have a portrait taken. On a Monday afternoon, Mr. Emerson, Elizabeth, and I all went and sat solemnly while Mr. Emory pointed his remarkable lens at us. The experience was disagreeable, for it simulated sitting motionless in blinding sunlight. The next afternoon, Henry and I took Wallie to the studio for his portrait but, though I pleaded with him earnestly, he could not be persuaded to sit still.

When we finally left the studio, all three of us were peevish and illtempered. As we walked back to Bush we encountered Henry's brother heading home from Hosmer's orchard, where he'd spent the day picking apples. He carried a sack of them, which he lowered to the ground when we stopped to talk. John Thoreau's geniality often made Henry appear dour by contrast. Whenever he and John were together I was struck by their dissimilarity.

John bent and tousled Wallie's hair. "You look very handsome, young man. You haven't had your portrait taken by any chance, have you?"

Wallie poked out his lower lip and hung his head.

"He's feeling restless today," Henry said, watching Wallie.

"Well, maybe some apple picking is in order," John said. "It will discharge the vitality."

Wallie looked up at John, his eyes filled with hope. "Can we go today?"

"That depends on your mother, doesn't it?" John said, unfolding himself and winking at me. He was taller than Henry, and his face was the kind that young women considered handsome, a fact to which he seemed oblivious. "Tell you what. Maybe, if you're very good for the rest of the day, my brother will take you to the orchard tomorrow. With your mother's permission, of course. What do you say, Henry?"

Henry glanced at me and smiled. "I'd like nothing better."

The next afternoon, Henry and Wallie left immediately after dinner. When they returned at dusk, Wallie's cheeks were as red as the apples Henry carried in his sack.

A WEEK LATER, John Thoreau appeared on the doorstep after breakfast. Assuming he'd come to collect Henry, I informed him that his brother had left an hour before for Flint's Pond. "If you hurry, you may be able catch up with him. He often stops to make observations along the way."

John shook his head. "I didn't come for Henry. I have something for you." From under his coat he drew a flat, rectangular package covered in brown paper and wrapped with string. This he handed to me with a small flourish of his wrist. "Open it." He smiled broadly.

"Only if you come in and share a cup of coffee with me."

As he stepped into the kitchen, I caught the scent of apples on his coat. He scooped off his hat and looked around the kitchen. "Where's Wallie?"

"In the nursery." I gestured toward the door to the dining room. "Come in and sit down, John, while I pour the coffee."

John sat in Henry's chair and sipped his coffee from a white china cup while I unwrapped the package. My eyes widened when I saw what it was—a daguerreotype of Wallie gazing pensively into the distance. I turned to John in wonder.

"Where did you get this? When was it taken?"

"Last week, when Henry took him apple picking. On their way to the orchard I leaped from behind a tree like a bandit and spirited Wallie away to the daguerreotypist's shop where I ransomed his freedom for a portrait." His eyes flashed. "It was a grand adventure and ended happily, as you can see. Wallie had his trip to the orchard and you have a portrait of your son."

"But he said nothing about this! How did you manage to keep it a secret?"

John's smile was contagious, igniting my own. "Oh, I swore him to secrecy, of course. He was quite philosophical about it. He's very much his father's son."

Laughing, I again studied the portrait. "It captures his likeness so well I want to kiss the glass. How will I ever thank you?"

"With another cup of your good coffee," John said happily. "I consider it a privilege to be acquainted with such a fine young man—and his family."

Flattery was a nicety we avoided at Bush, seeking, as we did, to always be entirely honest in our words and deeds. Yet it was a pleasure to have John in the house, though there was something ordinary about him, a sort of run-of-the-mill good cheer that was not at all like Henry's earnest generosity.

We sat and drank coffee and conversed about John's plans for the future. He told me that, since his health had improved, he was seeking a position as a schoolmaster in neighboring towns. I asked why he and Henry didn't start up their school again, but he shook his head and said that Henry had had enough of teaching.

"He's better suited to poetry and philosophy. Which is why he's living here instead of at home. And"—he smiled and set his cup on its saucer—"there's the added advantage that our mother doesn't plague him morning, noon, and night about the need to find a job to suit his education."

I heard Wallie's footsteps on the back stairs and went to greet him. I made a great fuss about the portrait, which prompted him to insist that we show it at once to his papa. So it was that John, Wallie, and I all invaded Mr. Emerson's study; Wallie carrying the daguerreotype before him like a prize.

Mr. Emerson was suitably impressed, and insisted the portrait must take up immediate residence on the parlor mantel. We stood side by side, admiring it. "It's a remarkably good likeness," he declared. "But what else would one expect, since the sun itself is the painter?"

MY THIRD CONFINEMENT came at the end of November, the pains commencing two hours after Mr. Emerson's departure for Boston. It was Henry who helped me to my bed and sent Nancy to fetch his mother to serve as midwife. Even before she arrived, he paced the downstairs hall like a father, his footsteps keeping time with my labored breaths. Cynthia kept up a soothing chatter throughout the long afternoon, until I was finally delivered of a girl just after sundown. The baby gave a lusty cry, which was answered by Henry's hearty cheer from below.

An hour later, I begged Cynthia to allow Henry entrance so that he might see the baby. He came in shyly, knowing that the territory he invaded was sacred to women, but too charmed and curious to refuse the invitation. He gazed at my new daughter with a wonder on his face that made it clear he considered her the most profound of miracles.

The sound of the coach rumbling to a stop in front of the house brought us all to the alert. "It's Mr. Emerson!" I cried. "Where are the children?" Henry went to find them, while I urged Cynthia to quickly make the baby presentable.

"Part and comb her hair before Mr. Emerson comes in," I said, anxiously brushing my own tangled mass.

"There's none to part," she said.

And indeed there was not. Her head was nearly bald, covered only with a fuzz of light brown hair. Yet she was the fairest of all my babes, a small pink-and-white rose of rare beauty. Mr. Emerson was suitably impressed, though he expressed no regret at having been away during the birth.

We could not agree on a name. The only one we both liked was Ruth, and Mother Emerson would not allow it. She had never liked her Christian name. The day after her birth, as he took tea with me in our chamber, Mr. Emerson suggested that the child should bear the name Asia.

"No," I said. "It's too peculiar. I don't wish my daughter to be burdened with its implications."

He gave me a startled look. "I didn't realize you felt that way." He poured more tea into his cup and held it between his hands in a meekly sorrowful way, like a talisman of regret.

"You did not ask."

"I meant no offense. It was an affectionate name."

I did not reply. He never again referred to me as Asia.

AS CUSTOM DECREED, I was confined to my chamber for a week after the birth. I lay upstairs in my chamber, nursing my nameless daughter, eating the poor food brought to me by the servants, and listening to the opening and closing of doors below. The evening conversations in the parlor were muffled by the walls and floor, but still sufficiently audible that I could recognize my husband's rising inflections and Henry's explosive, barking laugh.

During that long week, Henry visited me daily, bringing me news of the world and lengthy reports of conversations. He described Bronson's long-winded and poetic diversions and Elizabeth's sweet platitudes in explicit detail. He always took time to admire the baby in her cradle and expressed sincere gratitude when I allowed him to hold her. He never forgot to look in on Wallie and Ellen; he gave them daily piggyback rides and on good days took them on backyard excursions. At the end of the week, he surprised me by announcing that he was leaving Bush.

I let out a cry of dismay. "But why? Hasn't Mr. Emerson given you a sufficient measure of his time?"

He smiled and shook his head. "Waldo's been both fair and generous. And I'm not leaving permanently—I'll be back within a month."

"So long?"

"I mean to write a book on the English poets. There are books I require that I don't have the funds to buy. So I'm going to establish residence in Cambridge with Stearns Wheeler which will allow me access to Harvard's library."

"I thought you were writing poems, not books about poets."

"Waldo doesn't see my future there," he said. "He thinks my poetry inconsistent."

I frowned. "I wasn't aware that Mr. Emerson had changed his opinion of your work."

"I believe he's right, Lidian. He hasn't told me out of malice, but from concern."

"I don't know his reasons," I cried. "But he's wrong! And I mean to tell him so!"

"You may tell him what you wish, but he's only speaking as my friend.

You must not plague yourself with my concerns, Lidian. You must take care of yourself and the children."

I looked down at the baby whose head lay in the crook of my arm. As I watched, she smiled in her sleep, and her sweet expression calmed my agitated spirit.

"Then in return you must promise me not to give up poetry," I said. "And I must have a full report on the English poets when you return."

"You know I'll always give you a report. You are my chief counselor and confidante." He went to the doorway where he stood looking at me, about to leave and yet not leaving. I read his reluctance in the sag of his shoulders and the limp way his arms hung at his sides. And, sinner that I was, his reluctance made me glad, for it promised his return.

THE NEXT DAY I left my room for the first time since the baby's birth. As I stepped into the upper front hall my eyes fell on a trail of dead flies along the baseboard. It was obvious that the servants had taken advantage of my confinement and neglected their cleaning. I was certain that the entire house was in disrepair. I felt so ashamed I moaned out loud.

I heard the sound of voices below me and recognized Elizabeth's gentle inflections. She came to the bottom of the stairs and called up to me. When I didn't answer, she came up and found me bent over the baluster rail. She led me back to bed and I lay with my eyes closed, listening to her soothing voice. After some time, I was able to master myself and rise above my tears.

Yet something had shifted within, and I no longer had a clear perspective on my life. I was profoundly bewildered by the position in which I found myself. I'd maintained from the first that I was ill-suited to be a housewife. The cares and duties confounded me and I responded by concentrating on the tiniest detail—as if a rapt attention to the minutiae of housekeeping might shield me from the terrible realization that I was trapped in a cell of my own making.

HENRY RETURNED TO Bush on the tenth of December in fine spirits, having obtained a letter from the president of Harvard permitting him to use the college library. His satchel was stuffed with books, which he laid out on the dining-room table so I could examine them—volumes and volumes of Scottish poetry and the entire works of Sir Walter Raleigh.

"I believe the only true education I've received comes from books and my own observations," he said. "I'm still determined to be a poet." He settled in again at Bush as if he'd never left. He came and went with a guileless frequency, often disappearing over the fields for hours or closeting himself in his room to read his books and write his poetry. Occasionally he took afternoon walks with Mr. Emerson or Bronson Alcott. Sometimes he spent the entire day in his boat on the river or exploring one of Concord's many ponds. Yet it was not the constancy of his presence that comforted me; it was the dependability of his good cheer. He imparted a rare energy to the house when in residence. We always found some time each day to converse. The disparity in our ideas stimulated and challenged us. We liked nothing better than to test out thoughts against the granite of each other's opinion.

One evening, as he popped corn for the children in a warming pan over the parlor fire, Henry told me that he was thinking of building a small house by the shore of a pond and living there alone. The kernels cracked and burst in the pan, and Wallie and Ellen laughed and then began to squeal with excitement as the exploded corn lifted the cover off the pan, causing several fat white pieces of corn to jump out onto the carpet.

"To what purpose?" I asked, rocking the baby's cradle with my foot as I mended a frayed seam in my husband's shirt. "Why would you wish to separate yourself from society?"

"Society agrees with me less and less." Henry gave the pan another shake and drew it from the fire. "I'm determined to make an experiment. To see how well a man can live without the accoutrements of civilization."

"But what profit would you draw from such an experiment?" The baby stirred in her cradle and I increased the pace of my foot.

"Doesn't every effort profit a man to the degree in which he invests himself in it?" He sat on the floor with Ellen leaning on one arm and Wallie on the other. When he glanced over his shoulder at me, I caught the shadow of a frown. "Don't touch!" he warned Ellen, who was reaching for the pan. And then, gently, "The corn isn't ready yet. But you'll have some very soon." He looked again at me. "Haven't you said as much yourself?"

"Perhaps so." I had to smile. Henry had a flair for pointing a discussion in a direction that took the conversational wind out of my sails. "But, on a practical level, I wonder what you'll do all day living by a pond?"

"Watching the progress of my garden and recording the advancement of my mind will be sufficient activity."

"For many it would be more than sufficient," I said, returning his smile. "But your mind is uncommonly active, and I think it wants accomplishment as well as self-reflection."

He laughed aloud and a corresponding wave of fondness filled my breast, a nearly overwhelming affection for this young man who sat at my feet with my two oldest children. The sight of the three heads bent together over the pan affected me so acutely that tears stung my eyes. I quickly turned my attention back to my mending. Some things did not bear protracted thought.

IN MID-DECEMBER Lucy came to Concord and brought Sophia. As soon as she stepped in the door, Sophia ran upstairs to see the baby. She scooped her up and rocked her in the crook of her arm. She smiled and cooed and sang a little song. The baby gazed at her in that calm and thoughtful way that wide-awake infants have, as if she had the capacity to comprehend all the puzzles of the universe but no way to explain them.

"You poor little nameless dear!" Sophia cried, planting a kiss on the smooth round forehead.

"You must give her a name," I said. "She's been waiting weeks for someone to bestow her true name on her."

"Me?" Sophia looked at me. She'd grown into a poised young woman, with her mother's thick, dark hair and her father's blue eyes.

"You're a young lady now," I said. "And a strong-minded one from what your mother tells me in her letters. She mentioned that two young men in Plymouth have asked for your hand, but that you've rejected both."

"She wants to be like you," Lucy said.

"You mean she must wait to marry until she's thirty-three?" I laughed and patted Sophia's shoulder. "I have only one piece of advice, my dear. And that is never to *settle* for a man."

She gave me an odd look before turning her attention back to the baby. "Edith," she said suddenly. "It means 'joyous.' The baby's name is Edith!"

I saw at once that she had hit upon the perfect name. My new daughter had merely been waiting for someone to come along who recognized who she truly was.

16

Sorrows

The brook into the stream runs on;
But the deep-eyed boy is gone.
—RALPH WALDO EMERSON

On the second Sunday of the New Year it snowed all day. At twilight I lit the lamps, musing on the way the light pooled at the base of the lamps and fell onto the surfaces in the rooms, like water overspilling a glass. An urgent knock at the east entrance startled me from my reverie.

I didn't recognize the boy who stood shivering on the stoop, but he looked so forlorn in his thin coat that I invited him in at once. Disregarding the clots of snow that fell from his boots onto my green carpet, I hurried him into the dining room to warm himself before the fire. He looked about ten or eleven. Stiff black hair poked from beneath his brown cap. His coat sleeve was torn at the shoulder, exposing a dirty gray shirt.

"I've come to fetch Mr. Thoreau. He's here, ain't he, ma'am?" His young voice was so thick with Irish brogue that it took me a moment to understand.

"He is," I said. "But he's not to be disturbed." Henry had retreated to his room at four after spending most of the afternoon outside observing the storm.

"I've a message for him." The boy's hands were bright red and severely chapped. "'Tis urgent, ma'am. Mrs. Thoreau told me so herself." He was still shivering.

An odd, instinctual reluctance made me hesitate. I did not like the thought of the boy ascending our front stairs and entering Henry's room. More truthfully, I feared what this visit might portend.

But duty must always trump fear, so I went upstairs and informed Henry of the young messenger. He gave my hand a light pat as he moved past me to the stairs, his fingertips callused and warm and all too briefly on my skin. I did not follow immediately but gave him a moment of privacy with the boy while I scouted up a pair of mittens for the boy, which I easily found in the nursery closet. Mother Emerson was forever knitting socks and mittens and hats and we had plenty to spare. When I returned to the dining room, Henry had already put on his coat and was knotting a brown scarf around his neck. His face was gray.

"It's John," he said, speaking in such a low tone that I would not have heard him, had my ears not been particularly tuned to his voice. "He has lockjaw and Mother is greatly alarmed. They need me home."

He left at once and I stood at the window, staring out at the white, snow-covered fields, fearing the worst. Word came the next morning that Dr. Bartlett had given up all hope for John's survival. I spent the day in a state of high alarm, constantly distracted by thoughts of Henry. I feared this trial might be too much for him, for I knew how deeply he loved his brother.

On Tuesday evening Henry appeared at our front door. Both Mr. Emerson and I hurried to greet him.

"He left us this afternoon." Henry stepped into the hall, looking stunned and pale, speaking in a voice choked with tears. "He was calm to the last."

"Oh, Henry!" I was about to embrace him when Mr. Emerson laid his arm on Henry's shoulder, guided him into his study, and closed the door. When Henry left Bush an hour later, I was in my chamber, nursing Edith.

I plied Mr. Emerson with questions—what had Henry told him of John's death? How was Henry bearing up?—but short of his assurance that John had faced his last hours with a manly and noble resolve, he could tell me nothing. I was left to pray alone, begging God to be merciful to the Thoreaus and particularly to Henry.

Henry came again late the next morning to collect his clothes. Mr. Emerson was locked in his study with the usual orders not to be disturbed, so I attended Henry alone. He seemed oddly calm; his face and gestures betrayed no weakness of spirit. Yet I knew his heart must be crushed. How I longed to embrace him, to show him the comfort of a friend and companion! Instead, I accompanied him to his room and helped him fold the clothes to fit his satchel. I took my time in accomplishing the task, for the moment seemed to me one of rare gravity and thus doubly precious. There was something about the small, ill-lit room that created a heightened intimacy, and I found myself able to offer my sympathy without any degree of awkwardness.

"We're indebted to him for Wallie's picture," I said. "John had a remarkable facility for interesting children. He must have been a good teacher."

"An exceptional one." Henry stood at his desk, piling up his books and notebooks, wiping off his pen.

"I know you're suffering." I had laid out a shirt on the bed and was folding the sleeves down over the front, running my hand across the fabric an extra time, as if to press out sorrow as well as wrinkles. "But you must believe that when John left this world a pure soul was translated to heaven."

Henry pulled open the second drawer of his small bureau. "He was in great pain, you know. Lockjaw is a terrible way to die." He paused and I heard him swallow. "He spasmed so hard I had to lie down on top of him to prevent him from throwing himself onto the floor."

My breath caught in my throat and my own tears welled up. I was glad I was not facing him for I knew he must be struggling to maintain his composure.

"Yet the last conscious thing he did was to smile at me. He died in my arms."

"I had not heard," I whispered and then turned for I could no longer bear to present my back to him. "You brought him comfort. And reassurance. I'm sure of it. He was fortunate to have you for a brother."

"No. *I* was the fortunate one." His voice broke on the last two words, and he sank onto the room's single chair.

I could think of nothing to say that would not break the fragile moment. In an extremity of compassion, I laid my hand on his shoulder so lightly I was not even sure he felt it. Yet when I started to draw it away he covered it with his hand and held it there. I don't know how long we remained in that posture, but after some time his hand slid away and I went back to folding his shirts and trousers. My task was quickly finished. Too soon no shirts or trousers remained to fold.

I turned and studied him, struck suddenly by his youth. It was a quality I'd not recently considered, for his thoughts had always made him seem wise beyond his years. Sometimes I believed him even older than me. He sat sideways, his elbow propped on the chair rail, his head lying on his arm. He stared at a spot on the floor in front of his shoes. His hair appeared as if a gale wind had arranged it.

"Henry, you must let me know how I can help you."

He nodded without glancing at me. And then quite suddenly he emerged from his reverie, straightened his back, and looked at me. "I don't know when I'll be able to return. My family may need me for some time."

"Of course. You must take as long as required." I took a deep breath, for it was the only way in which I could keep from saying the command that waited behind my tongue: *And then you must come back, for you belong here—with me.*

I attended John's funeral, sitting by Mr. Emerson's side. Wallie accompanied us, for he had asked particularly to be included, and I could not refuse him. Reverend Barzillai Frost, who had become minister of the First Parish Church after Reverend Ripley's death, gave a gracious and moving funeral oration. Every pew was filled, and sobs were audible throughout the service. I watched the Thoreau family follow the coffin down the aisle. Henry looked straight ahead and appeared entirely composed, yet his face was paler than I had ever seen it, and his eyes appeared dull and colorless. A light had gone out of him. I feared it would never return.

JANUARY UNROLLED its long white carpet and the fires roared in the hearths. Mother Emerson no longer haunted the shadows of the rooms but drew her chair close to the fire. My hands roughened and grew coarse, and Mr. Emerson abandoned his cold-water baths. Edith thrived on my milk and I delighted in her—she was the most beautiful of my infants, a pink rose that brought instant cheer to all who beheld her. I wrote Sophia, thanking her for the name, although by then it was unthinkable that Edith should have any other.

My only discontent was that I no longer saw Henry. The house seemed empty without him; it was as if a great melancholy emanated from the plaster and the walls themselves mourned his absence. The children missed him acutely. Every morning Wallie asked plaintively if Mr. Thoreau had returned in the night, and every morning I sadly confessed that he had not.

MR. EMERSON'S LECTURE engagements had grown in number, requiring him to travel more frequently. While he was away I tried to manage things, but the demands of the household fell upon me with double weight. I had little time to devote to concerns outside our family. So it was with surprise and alarm that I heard the news a week after John's death that Henry was gravely ill, struck down by the same malady that killed his brother. It was Nancy who reported this, having heard it from the Thoreau family cook, whom she'd encountered in the butcher's shop on a frigid Saturday morning. Mr. Emerson, who would have called upon the Thoreaus immediately to determine the truth of the matter, was away and would not return for three days. So I hastened there myself, leaving the children in the care of Nancy and Mother Emerson. The day was bitterly cold, yet I relished the stinging wind upon my face. A few years before the family had moved from their home on the Mill Dam into the old Parkman house on the other side of the Concord village. The house was a handsome structure, situated on the triangle of land between Main Street and Sudbury Road. It was a fifteen-minute walk at a brisk pace.

Cynthia answered the door and invited me into the kitchen since the parlor was crowded with boarders drinking coffee and discussing the weather. She apologized for the state of her kitchen, which was indeed a confusion of dirty pots and pans, and sat me down at the table. She offered me a cup of coffee, which I accepted but was reluctant to drink once I'd tasted its bitter strength.

"What brings you out, Lidian?" She did not sit with me but busied herself at the sink while she spoke. "And how is your babe faring?"

"Edith is fine," I said. "I came to ask after Henry. I'm told he's ailing."

"Yes." I watched her back. Her shoulders rose and tightened with each breath.

"But what is wrong?" I took one last sip of coffee and placed the nearly full cup on its saucer. "Does he have a fever?"

She shook her head. "Dr. Bartlett can't explain it. But he exhibits all the symptoms of lockjaw." Her normally strident voice trembled. "I believe he may not live."

"Cynthia! No!" I was on my feet at once, folding her in an embrace that was born as much from my own need as from Christian charity. She briefly dropped her head upon my shoulder then pulled away and went back to her washing. "I must busy myself to keep from thinking of it. This has been the most frightful month of my life."

"I cannot imagine anything more painful than losing one's child," I said.

"That's right—you cannot imagine. No one can. To lose one's child is devastating. And now to lose two—" Her voice broke and she could not continue.

"May I speak with him?" I said, then wished I hadn't, for when Cynthia looked over her shoulder at me I was shocked to find her eyes blazing with animosity.

"I fear he's too ill for visitors. You'd best go home and tend your own babes." And she dismissed me by turning her back again, begrudging me the simple courtesy of showing me to the door.

For the next two days I spent many hours in prayer, pleading with God to spare Henry's life. When Mr. Emerson returned from his journey I told him what I'd learned and watched the alarm spring into his face. He went immediately to call on the Thoreaus and came home several hours later with the encouraging news that Henry had turned the corner and was beginning to improve.

"They believe he'll fully recover." Mr. Emerson touched my shoulder as he spoke, as if he sensed that I required steadying. We were standing in the hallway between the Red Room and his study. "Yet I fail to understand how he could contract lockjaw." He shook his head in puzzlement.

Nor did I understand God's purpose in striking Henry. Yet when Mr. Emerson closed himself in his study a few moments later, I went immediately to my chamber and knelt to offer thanksgiving.

ON SUNDAY MORNING Mr. Emerson took Wallie to worship service, though it was against my wishes for it was a cold, wet morning and church the dampest of places. The next day Wallie awoke with a cough, and by Tuesday he had contracted a fever. His skin was red and hot and he complained of nausea. I felt his forehead and neck; his pulse was racing. I put him to bed and dosed him with tea and honey, and that afternoon, because his condition had worsened, I gave him castor oil. Later that day a rash broke out. He slept fitfully, moaning and crying in his bed. I rocked him as often as I could, but it did not calm him.

"My throat hurts!" he moaned, clutching at his neck. When I gently pulled his hands away, I felt the dry heat pour from his skin. Edith began to cry, and I left Wallie to tend her. When his fever continued to rise that evening, I sent for Dr. Bartlett.

"It's scarlet fever," he said after examining him. "The rash is proof." He ran his hand over Wallie's chest where tiny scarlet blisters winked their dark blue points. "His pulse is full and hard. I must bleed him."

I watched him take his knife and cup out of his black satchel. Yet I could not make myself look when he bent over Wallie's arm and made the necessary incisions. It took only few moments and when he finished, I could see that it had an immediate and satisfactory result. Wallie had fallen into a light sleep and was no longer moaning and thrashing about.

When I showed the doctor to the door, he advised me to keep Ellen away from her brother. "There are those who suspect it's contagious," he said. "Try not to expose Ellen or the baby."

"How long will it last?" I remembered lying for weeks in my garret bed at Aunt Priscilla's house when I was nineteen and ill with the disease.

"We should see improvement in a day or two." The doctor closed his satchel and put on the coat I held for him. "I'll come back in the morning to check on him."

That night, Wallie's fever continued to climb and, between applying cold compresses to his neck and chest and nursing Edith, I was not able to sleep. Ellen began to cough in the middle of the night and by dawn her fever was also rising. Wallie thrashed on his bed and was no longer calmed by my touch. He soon entered a delirium, neither awake nor asleep, but murmuring nonsense in a hoarse and rapid voice. Mr. Emerson abandoned his study and sat by Wallie's bedside, stroking his hand. I put Ellen in our bed and ceaselessly traveled the short hallway between our chamber and the nursery. Finally, exhaustion overtook me and I was forced to lie down. But I was not allowed to sleep, for Wallie—apparently sensing my absence despite his hallucinations— kept calling out for me over and over in a piteous voice and could not be persuaded to stop.

When I went to him, he did not recognize me and the first note of terror rang in my heart. I rocked him against my breasts and spoke gently to him and the sound of my voice seemed to quiet him.

I was frantic with worry and fatigue. Mr. Emerson tried to calm me. "The fever's about to break," he said. "He'll soon be well and running about the house again."

"Get the doctor." I buttoned and then unbuttoned Wallie's nightshirt. "Go and find him and bring him here at once."

My husband left without a word, as overcome with anxiety as I.

When Dr. Bartlett came, he entered the house without knocking and dashed up the stairs. I stood watching, my fingers clenched in the folds of my skirt as he examined Wallie.

He straightened slowly and his arms fell away from my son. He turned, shaking his bowed head. I looked into his face to discover what hope was written there, but he had closed his eyes.

I sank onto the bed beside my son, whose shallow breaths were accompanied by faint moans. His closed eyes were sunken in their small sockets and his body—when I slid my arms under him and gathered him into my lap— was limp. The extremity of heat had left his skin and the hectic flush on his face was gone. He had slipped into insensibility and I found only a tiny measure of comfort in the knowledge that he was beyond pain.

I don't know how long I held him. Time had slipped far beyond my awareness, though I felt my senses to be singularly acute. I was aware of the drape of the blanket from the bed to the floor, the flat, sour scent rising from his skin, the rasp of his small, rapid breaths, and the echo of footsteps in the hallway below. Mr. Emerson came and went from the room with numbing regularity. Tending to things, I assumed—I did not realize until later that he was treating his own heartache by pacing between the nursery and our chamber. Once, when he came into the nursery, he placed his hand on my head and very gently stroked my hair. A few moments later, Wallie shuddered and made a little choking sound deep in his throat. He then let out a long sigh and breathed no more.

Mr. Emerson bent his head. "My boy!" he whispered, again and again.

It was just after eight o'clock in the evening. Outside, the air was so cold it formed crystal ferns on the window glass.

SOMETIME AFTER Wallie died I loosed my arms from his stiffening body and released him, laying him gently on the bed and covering him with the blanket, though I could not bring myself to shroud his face. Mr. Emerson stood beside me, his hand on my waist. He said nothing, but led me down the stairs and settled me in a chair by the parlor fire. Mrs. Emerson was there, her pale face softer at the edges than normal, as if grief had melted the ice in her jaw.

We sat in silence for a time, and then began to speak of the day's events, going over them with a peculiar calmness. I heard my own voice as if from a great distance. It seemed as if some stranger spoke of the death of her son, and my heart went out to her. Firelight flickered on the walls and on our faces. Mr. Emerson took the poker and rolled the log on its andirons. The fire snapped and blazed, sending up a sudden fountain of sparks. We stared as if the embers contained answers to questions we could not bear to ask.

I recalled the death of my two-year-old brother, John, and how I'd watched my mother wash the little black-and-red dress he'd worn the night he died. She'd lowered it into the washtub with such tender care she might have been bathing John himself. Then she spread it on a stool before the fire and took up her scissors. Tears raced down her cheeks as she cut a square of material from the hem. I wondered why I did not weep now. How I longed for the release of tears! But they refused to come. I felt as if my heart had shriveled and dried so that it now resembled a small, bloodless stone.

We separated just after midnight. I went alone to my chamber where, because of her fever, Ellen slept in my husband's place while he retired to the Red Room. I checked on Edith in her cradle and unbuttoned my dress. I undid my hair and put on my nightgown. I sat on the bed and brushed out my hair. I knelt and briefly prayed, then rose to blow out the candle. The corporeality of the routine was a comfort. I climbed into bed and drew the blankets over me, dimly aware of Ellen's great heat as I lay down beside her. I stroked her cheek. She lay drowned in fever and sleep, submerged in her immobility.

I lay in the darkness thinking of Wallie's silent, still form on his bed in the nursery only a few steps away. A thousand memories assailed me—I recalled the way he liked to climb into my lap and take my face between his hands and kiss me. I recalled his thoughtful observation of the flight of birds and his desire to include Ellen in everything he did. It was then that grief overwhelmed me, and I choked on a great flood of sorrow. I rolled onto my stomach and wept into the pillows until Ellen stirred and cried out in her sleep and then woke thrashing, requiring me to tend her. I covered her in cool wet cloths and gathered her against me. The heat of her body burned through my nightgown. I prayed—or tried to—for God's pity, begging him to spare my daughter. I felt as if I were a swimmer washed out to sea by a merciless rip-tide, battling rising waves, dragged farther and farther from the shore.

I dozed in the rare moments when Ellen was still. I longed for the oblivion of sleep, but it was the most fleeting of consolations.

Later Edith woke me to nurse, and I sat with her in my arms by the dying fire. There was a sweet, blind solace in the warmth of her infant flesh. Just holding her bestowed a small measure of comfort. I became slowly aware that she was moving restlessly, stretching around to smile at something behind her head. Yet when I looked I saw nothing there but shadows.

A sudden comprehension invaded my mind. In her innocence, Edith was able to perceive what I could not—her brother's spirit. And then I became certain that he was standing in the room just a few feet from me.

I reached out to my son and whispered his name, but there was no answer.

17

Endurance

Oh, that boy! That boy!
—RALPH WALDO EMERSON

The morning after Wallie died, I buttoned myself into mourning clothes while Mr. Emerson closed himself in his study and wrote letters—death announcements—to our friends and family. When he emerged at noon he climbed the stairs to our chamber, looking as if he'd been struck by lightning. His hair rose at acute angles and his eyes appeared singed; his arms hung flaccidly from his shoulders and he hunched forward over his chest.

"How is Ellen?" His voice was as dull and lifeless as his eyes.

I was seated by the window, rocking Edith while Ellen slept. My eyes were sore. "She passed the crisis. I believe she'll recover." I did not add that I had believed the same of Wallie.

That night, Mr. Emerson returned to our bed. We did not speak or touch as we lay down. The darkness that girdled us was more than the absence of physical light. I fell slowly into sleep to the sound of his breathing.

I woke at three, wondering what had disturbed me. The windows were suffused with pale light. The moon had risen and so had my husband. I saw him standing at the window.

"What is it?" I asked.

"Every cock in town is shrilling," he said. "Why? Why now? I can make no sense of it." He did not turn from the window.

"It's the moon," I said. "They've mistaken it for the sun."

He turned then and came to the bed. He was stooped, bowed down by the weight of his grief. He lay down and surprised me by reaching for me and pulling my body against his. He held me for a long time and when he spoke I barely heard him; his voice seemed lost in the weirdly lit room.

"The wisest man knows nothing," he whispered. His head lay beside mine, yet it seemed at an infinite distance. "Sorrow makes us all children." He continued to hold me through what remained of the night until he finally lapsed into a shallow sleep. I lay awake, my arms cradling him as if he were a feverish child.

BY THE DAY of Wallie's funeral, Ellen was able to sit up in bed. She played with a basket of clothespins and asked to play with Wallie. I had to sit down—my legs would not hold me—and I told her that he'd gone to heaven to be with God. He was very happy there I said, for the angels were bringing him flowers.

"Red flowers?" she asked.

I fondled the ringlets that fell across her forehead. "Red and purple and yellow. Hundreds of flowers—all the colors of the rainbow."

She burst into tears. "I want to go too!" she cried. She was inconsolable.

Edith had not sickened nor did she show any signs of weakness. Dr. Bartlett told me that my milk had protected her. That I had saved one of my children was my sole comfort in those desolate days.

I could not comprehend God's purpose in taking Wallie so soon. He'd been a strong and healthy boy, clearly destined for great things. His death was so monstrous that it bent the very backbone of my faith. What I felt was a great numbness, as if I'd suddenly been struck deaf, dumb, and blind all at once. I believe my outward appearance suggested that I felt a true Christian resignation, but inside I was screaming, shrieking like a madwoman, sunk in a grief so deep I knew nothing but darkness and pain. Even the hope that

Wallie was with God brought no comfort. It was like bright sunshine falling on a scorched body.

Nor could I turn to my husband, for when I looked into his face, I saw an anguish there as raw as my own. For him there was no consolation to be had, since he no longer believed in heaven. He withdrew into a grim and constant solitude. Even in the presence of others, he was alone. He claimed that the responsibility of work kept him from society. I knew it was not work, but grief. When I begged him for one comforting embrace three days after the funeral, he turned away.

We were utterly unable to succor each other. The collision of our private sorrows had wounded us beyond striving. Though I recognized that our son's death had driven Mr. Emerson yet farther from Christ, I could do nothing to repair the breach.

While I spiraled downward into a melancholy so profound it hurt to breathe, he planned a lecture trip to Philadelphia. I lay in bed for days with the curtains drawn, staring at the ceiling. I nursed Edith and kissed Ellen good morning and good night. Yet when Mrs. Emerson came with her Bible and tried to comfort me by opening the curtains and reading my favorite Psalms, I rolled away and faced the table where I'd set my homeopathic powders. The small bottles winked in the afternoon light.

Elizabeth came and sat by my bedside, stroking my forehead and praying for God's mercy. A fever raged in me—a fire so hot I imagined it might scald her gentle hand. It did not abate for weeks, for the fever was caused not by illness, but by grief.

After a month, Lucy declared that I could no longer afford the luxury of illness. I had two children to care for. I closed my eyes and turned away from her as well.

On the first warm day of March, Henry came to see me, still weak from his own illness. The snow had crystallized into crumbly undulations in the field, and icicles dropped beads of water from the roof, creating the narrowest of moats in the snow. We had let all but the kitchen fire go out and I was lying beneath a blanket on the chaise in the parlor, reading—or trying to— though my sense of desolation kept obscuring the words. He entered the room so quietly that I did not at first know he was there. I happened to glance up for a moment and saw what appeared to be a shadow. I started and nearly dropped the book. Henry looked utterly stricken. *Heartsick* is the only word that suited his appearance that afternoon. I put out my hand to him, the way a drowning woman might extend hers above the waves.

"Henry!" I said. "What a welcome sight you are!"

He tried to smile. I recognized the slight upturn at the corners of his mouth. Yet his attempt failed miserably, and all I could be certain of was the grave solemnity of his eyes.

"Sit down. Please." I closed my book and smoothed the blanket across my lap. "I'm glad you've recovered. And very grateful that you've come."

He closed his eyes and turned his head away, as if he could not bear to see what showed on my face. Yet his hand finally reached out and met mine. I was struck by the cool relief that came from his touch.

"I'm sorry it's taken me so long." He withdrew his hand and lowered himself carefully onto the straight chair next to the window. The way he moved gave an impression of extreme fragility, as if his bones lay directly beneath the surface of his skin and were in danger of shattering should he jar them with any sudden motion. His hair was uncharacteristically neat, evenly combed and slicked down, and its conformation to his skull made his ears appear to stick out. But what had changed most were his eyes. They appeared faded and colorless, like broken shells upon a beach. I looked at them, and then away, for I could not bear the pain I saw. My glance then fell upon the daguerreotype of Wallie on the fireplace mantel and my throat knotted as I recalled the morning John Thoreau had presented it to me.

I glanced back at Henry and discovered that he'd followed my gaze. "We owe so much solace to John," I said. "I cannot believe they are both gone."

He bowed his head.

We sat for some time in silence. I heard the water dripping from the eaves, and the clamorous conversation of crows in the trees beyond the garden. Sunlight dappled the screen of young hemlocks outside the west-facing windows. I became aware of a profound camaraderie in our silence, an easeful goodness that rose from our proximity. I thought how rare and blessed it was to be in another's presence without speaking, to sit comfortably in utter stillness. And I noted something else, as well—a faint pulse of vitality had been restored to me when I saw Henry. I no longer felt wholly dead.

After some time, Henry raised his head. "How are you faring, Lidian? Tell me, is your faith sufficient consolation?"

We had argued over Christianity many times, and Henry was often disposed to make light of my orthodoxy. Yet I sensed in his question a solemn and sincere concern for my welfare; his usual disdain was entirely lacking.

"There is no consolation," I said. "I sometimes picture him enjoying heaven and that brings a small measure of comfort. What's most difficult is the way the world goes on without him. I could not have imagined that it would even exist—I *cannot* imagine it—and yet it does."

"It's not the same world," he said softly. He was leaning forward, his head turned at an odd angle so that he watched me as if from behind some obstacle. His hands, spread on his knees, closed into fists and opened again. "Everything—*everything*—has changed. I feel that I must learn to walk and talk—to *breathe*—all over again."

"Oh," I murmured, and my eyes filled with tears, as I felt the truth in his words. I had thought and experienced them all myself. I rose, the blanket rolled to the floor, and I grasped Henry's hand and sank to my knees in front of him. "Oh, my dear friend," I whispered. "You know! You understand!"

He did not move as I placed my forehead on his knee, still clinging to his hand. After a moment I felt his free hand graze the top of my head—the softest of blessings—and then move to my shoulder.

"Stand up, Lidian," he said. "Please get up."

It was not until that moment that I realized my gesture caused him a profound discomfort. I rose, and though it took me only a matter of seconds, the motion felt exceedingly awkward and seemed to last a very long time. When finally I stood before him, he rose too and said he'd promised to return home before dark.

He moved to free his hand from mine, but I would not release it. "You must tell me when you're coming back to live with us," I said. "You *are* coming back, aren't you?"

He gazed at me with his haunted, pale eyes and I saw in them a yearning as strong as my own, a hunger so fierce it frightened me. "Yes," he said, squeezing my hand. "Yes, of course I am. As soon as I can make arrangements."

WHEN HENRY CAME THROUGH the front door the next afternoon, I was trimming the parlor lamps. I hurried to greet him, and found him at the open doorway of my husband's study frowning in at the empty room.

"Is Waldo out?" His brown satchel sagged from his shoulder. "I'd hoped to speak with him."

"He left for New York this morning. Another lecture tour. He won't be back before the eighteenth." I found myself brushing at my apron an inordinate number of times. "I didn't expect you so soon, Henry. But it's good to have you home." I could not stop myself from touching his arm as I led him up the stairs to his room. There I made up the narrow bed while he unpacked his clothes.

I was just plumping up the pillows when Ellen peeked around the door-frame. She threw herself at Henry, wrapping her small arms around his knees so that he swayed and I feared he might crash to the ground. He did not lose his balance but instead, hooked his hands beneath her arms and swung her high into the air where she squealed with delight.

When he put her down, Ellen begged for more, but I told her to hush and reminded her that Mr. Thoreau had been sick. She looked up at him solemnly. "Wallie was sick, too," she said. "He's gone to heaven now."

Hearing my daughter speak these words in Henry's presence struck me with a strange new pain, and I made a small sound that he must have taken for a gasp. He brushed my arm with his hand—the briefest gesture of reassurance—and then squatted in front of Ellen, so that their heads were at the same height.

"But I haven't gone to heaven, as you see. I'm not yet good enough for the company of angels."

Ellen poked out her lower lip. "I wish the angels would let Wallie come down and play with me. Just for a day."

"I think the angels must love Wallie so much they can't spare him. And besides"—he touched a small curl in front of her ear. I noticed that his finger had a long scratch running the length of it—"my brother is there too, and he'd be lonely if Wallie left."

Ellen regarded him thoughtfully for a long moment. Then she nodded and reached up to touch his face—a simple, babyish gesture, though she was no longer an infant. "Will you pop corn tonight?"

Henry laughed. "That's up to your mother. But I'd certainly like to."

I thought of all the fall evenings when Henry had popped corn for Wallie and Ellen, recalled the firelight flickering on their joyful faces, the shine of their hair. The memory rose up and enfolded me in its sweetness.

"Of course we'll pop corn tonight," I said. "In celebration of Mr. Thoreau's return."

That evening, as I watched the white puffs of corn fly out of the old warming pan, I laughed for the first time since Wallie died.

I slept easily that night, for I felt myself wrapped in a warm, embracing peace. Edith lay close by me in her cradle where I could tend her. Ellen slept in the nursery, and Henry was back in the chamber at the head of the stairs. Grief and desolation had been banished from the house.

In the middle of the night I sat up in bed so suddenly I nearly cracked my head upon the post. I reached for the cradle and was reassured when my hand struck the familiar smooth wood. Edith was fast asleep. I wondered what had wakened me. Then I heard the plaintive notes of a flute. I sat listening in the darkness. The melody was sweet and yet somehow unspeakably sad, as if Henry had taken all the tender, poignant music in the world and combined it into this single strain. I let my head fall back against the pillows and allowed the music to rock me as the sea had rocked my father's ships, as my mother's arms had rocked me as a child.

18

Tribulation

As for Waldo, he died as the mist rises from the brook,
which the sun will soon dart his rays through
—HENRY DAVID THOREAU

I did not believe that my roses would bloom again after
my son died. Yet that June, as always, the damasks raised
their tight pink fists to the sky, and the sun peeled them open, petal by fragile petal. Thus did God slowly strip me of every illusion—even the conceit of
despair.

That June, Henry planted a garden in the dooryard of the Manse for
Nathaniel Hawthorne and his new bride, Sophia. At my husband's suggestion, the Hawthornes had rented the house Reverend Ripley left vacant when
he died. Mr. Emerson was successfully fulfilling his dream of creating a community of intellects and writers. Henry spent much of the summer working
the soil. I understood, as others did not, that this unique gift was born of
Henry's grief. Like me, he instinctively knew that only direct contact with the
earth could ease an anguished heart.

In the midst of that summer of sorrow, Margaret Fuller came again to

Concord and took up her customary residence in the Red Room. Her presence erased the deepest lines of grief from my husband's face. She brought a new vitality and cheer into the house.

I was glad for him. I yearned to enjoy Margaret's company and wit as much as he. Yet the very day she arrived I was confined to my bed with a tooth abscess. I listened to her bell-like voice from my chamber, my jaw throbbing, dazed with pain and laudanum. In my stupor I imagined my husband welcomed Margaret not just into his study, but into his arms.

It was almost a week before Margaret finally visited me in my chamber. She brought flowers—bright yellow roses. Filled with remorse that she'd neglected me for so long, she stroked my hand with the tips of her fingers, murmuring her sympathy.

"Do forgive me, Lidian," she said. "I'm mortified that I disregarded you so! Truly, I didn't realize you were home. I assumed you were in Plymouth visiting relatives."

I looked at her and tried to summon some Christian forgiveness. Yet all I could find was the realization that Mr. Emerson had not mentioned me or my illness.

"I'm heartsick over Wallie's death," she continued. "He was the most extraordinary boy! I feel as if I've lost my own son."

I withdrew my hand. The pain in my jaw made it impossible to speak, so I did not tell her what was in my heart—that she had not the faintest glimmer of understanding. Margaret knew nothing of motherhood and could not begin to perceive the depth of my mourning.

Again that afternoon, I heard her laughter below in the hall outside my husband's study, as they prepared to embark on a walk. I pictured her arranging a bright scarf over her curls, smiling up at him, her eyes shining like stars.

Throughout her stay, Margaret was constantly by Mr. Emerson's side. Every day they took long walks in Walden Woods and Sleepy Hollow. They bantered over the dinner table. They enjoyed late-night conversations in his study and in her chamber.

Meanwhile, I spent day after day lying in shuttered darkness, my head fierce with pain. Dr. Bartlett bled me and applied a ginger poultice to my jaw. My fever subsided but my morbid suspicion did not. I longed to confront my husband. Yet I feared becoming a shrew. Had he not expounded the priceless worth of friendship in his lectures? Had I not fully agreed with him?

One Sunday I spent the evening pacing in my chamber, while Margaret,

Henry, Bronson, and my husband sat in the parlor and discussed the importance of the great German philosophers. Back and forth, back and forth I went, my heart hammering in my chest. I pulled at my fingers and feverishly stroked the backs of my hands. My eyes leapt from the window to the far wall and back again. I tugged at my hair, pulling it from its combs until it fell in unruly turmoil down my back. I had a sudden, vivid memory of the sea during a severe winter storm in Plymouth twelve years before. The ocean had churned and gnashed, rolling six-foot waves up the beach and sucking them back down again into its dark mouth. I had an ocean storm within me, one barely contained by my flesh.

I heard Bronson and Henry leave. My husband and Margaret remained in the parlor, continuing their conversation. I imagined Mr. Emerson looking into Margaret's eyes, perhaps touching her arm, or holding her hand as he spoke. The sound of her nasal laughter pierced the walls and ceiling. My husband's voice rose and subsided. I thought of bubbles frothing at the base of a waterfall. I recognized a tone I had only heard him use during our marital intimacies. Jealousy assaulted me with a ferocity that scalded my neck.

If I'd allowed myself to weep, I would have covered the floor with my tears. When at last I heard the door of the Red Room close and my husband's footfall on the stairs, I retreated to the nursery and crawled into bed beside Ellen, letting her warm flesh and gentle breathing soothe my trembling body.

When, three days later, Dr. Bartlett declared me well enough to resume my duties, I discovered that Henry had grown angry during my indisposition. He glowed with a transparent fury as he came and went about the house and yard. When questioned, he would not speak of his reasons, yet one afternoon I found him in the barn, repairing a broken chair rung. I insisted that he reveal the source of his vexation.

"If you must know, it's Miss Fuller," he said. "Or rather, Waldo's absorption with her." He picked up his hammer and pounded the new rung into place.

"You've told me yourself that Mr. Emerson is a sun that naturally attracts planets," I reminded him.

"Yes, I've made that comparison." His voice was bitter. "Yet the sun does not cast an excess of light on just one of its planets, but on all of them equally."

I turned away, for I could not bear to look into his eyes and see my own sorrow reflected there.

The next morning Henry and I, drawn together by our mutual sadness, lingered over breakfast, probing the nature of love and death. The following morning we did the same, and the next, and many more after that. We created our own society of two. Neither of us mentioned Mr. Emerson, though he stood between us like a sentinel, measuring the significance of all things.

Gradually, Henry's antagonism toward Margaret infected mine. I found myself growing bitter and jealous. Finally, on a humid morning in August, I knocked on Mr. Emerson's study door and, when granted entrance, asked him to reveal exactly what he discussed during his late-night conversations with Margaret.

He had been writing. Papers were spread all over his table. The vase of roses I had placed there the day before had been set on the floor. He put down his pen and looked up at me.

"We speak of philosophy," he said. "It wouldn't interest you."

"That's absurd!" I said. "You know I've always been attracted to the study of philosophy!"

"You relish debate more than investigation, Lidian. Your Christianity constricts your understanding."

"You dare say such a thing?" My pulse pounded in my neck and my hands thrashed in the folds of my skirt. "Make an accusation of my faith? You *know* that's not true! Christ is the lens of my understanding." I paced back and forth, whirling in front of him, my fists beating at my waist, as if their frenzy might contain my rage. "Margaret has poisoned your mind against me!" I gasped. "I should not have allowed so much freedom in my house. Had I known—"

"Calm yourself!" he said, his voice sharp as acid—a tone I'd rarely heard him use. "We cannot have a conversation if you behave like a child in the midst of a tantrum. Sit down." He turned, gesturing to the settee.

I managed with some difficulty to settle myself on its hard red cushion, though I was inwardly raging. I took a deep breath, and tried to begin again.

"I don't begrudge your friendships, but I wish to be included. You told me when you proposed marriage that you considered me your dearest friend and that you wished to regard me thus for the rest of my life." I placed my hands in my lap but they would not obey me—they kept tearing at my skirts. "Yet now you turn away from me toward others whose minds you imagine to be brighter. As if our physical intimacy has bred in you a disrespect for *my* mind."

"That's not true, Lidian. You're needlessly overwrought. Think of how many times I came to you for advice on something I wrote. Think of the countless times we've discussed slavery and the rights of women."

"I think of them often. Would it surprise you to know that I feel more used than nourished after those sessions? I fear I'm less your counselor than your servant."

He stared as if my face had suddenly become unfamiliar to him. "What would you have us do? Turn our guest out into the street and be known all over Boston for our lack of hospitality?"

His words had their intended effect, for I felt an immediate sympathy for Margaret. Despite my jealousy, I admired her and could not bear the thought that she—or anyone—should perceive me as inhospitable. "Of course not! Margaret shall stay as long as she likes."

He nodded gravely. "Then it's settled. And now, I must ask you to leave, for I have a lecture to write."

I rose stiffly. Despite the heat, my body was bathed in a strange, damp chill, and I left the room without another word to my husband. As I closed the door quietly behind me, Margaret came out of the Red Room across the hall. She wore a black-and-turquoise day gown that did nothing for her wide hips.

I made myself smile. "Good morning. I hope I didn't disturb you."

"Oh, not at all!" She smiled and fluttered her hands about. "I'm desperate for some company. Sometimes I think your house is simply *too* quiet. It can't be healthy." She blinked her large eyes and laughed—that explosive, horselike laugh that both repelled me for its coarseness and intrigued me because of its open sensuality. I did not understand Margaret Fuller, and even less my reaction to her. She was dazzling in her intellect and I thrilled to her lectures. During the winter of 1840 I'd made a weekly journey to Boston with Elizabeth Hoar and Mary Brooks to participate in her conversation series. I rarely found myself in full agreement with her, yet I deeply admired her conviction that women were the equals of men. Her passion for that ideal had already caused my husband to modify his views.

"Mr. Emerson believes that poets and philosophers require solitude in order to produce their work," I said.

"Oh, I'm aware of Waldo's beliefs." Margaret wrinkled her nose and her eyelids flickered. "He's always trying to convince me it is what *I* ought to believe as well." She laughed again. "Come, Lidian, we'll take a morning walk and cast away our cares beneath the trees by the river."

I looked into her smile and was tempted—more tempted than I wanted to admit. I longed to forget my children and husband, hungered to neglect my household duties and escape to some pleasant, shady spot. I imagined spending not only the morning, but the entire afternoon as well, sharing confidences and philosophies with this carefree woman. Yet, as quickly as I imagined it, I rejected the possibility as the most deceptive sort of nonsense. I had obligations entrusted to me by God, duties I ignored to my peril.

"I've a great many things to do today, Margaret. Such leisure is not possible for me." And I hurried away, leaving her standing alone in front of Mr. Emerson's study door.

Two DAYS AFTER our conversation, Mr. Emerson came into the dining room where I was nursing Edith in Ellen Tucker's rocker. It was mid-morning, a time when he was customarily at work in his study. Without greeting me, he went to the window and stared out in silence for a long time. I said nothing, for I was immersed in the pleasant serenity granted the mother of a suckling babe.

Finally, he spoke. "I'm no longer convinced of the value of permanent marriage," he said quietly. He did not look at me.

For a moment his words did not register. "Are you referring to *us?*" My hand went numb on Edith's tiny chest. "Or is this some new philosophy of yours?"

"A philosophy divorced from life is of no use to anyone," he said. "I've given it a great deal of thought. You shouldn't imagine this is an impulse. It seems to me that marriage is, by nature, a temporary relationship, with its own birth, climax, and death."

"Then you're suggesting that we break the vows we made before God?" I shifted Edith higher against me, lengthening my arm beneath her tiny torso. She was sleeping peacefully, heedless of the emotional storm gathering around her.

At last he turned to face me. "I bear you no ill will, Lidian. But I think it's plain to both of us that we're no longer united."

"That's because you've turned away from God! How can you expect a marriage to thrive if it's not bound to Christ?"

He sighed and closed his eyes. "You know that I cannot resign myself to religious conventions any more than worldly ones. I've always sought my own direction."

"Yes," I hissed, "and where has it brought you? To a cold and lonely place, separated from your wife and children by this bold new principle of self-reliance. You would usurp God's power for the sake of your pride!"

He stared, as if startled by my ferocity. After a moment he spoke quietly. "Pride has nothing to do with it. You know me better than that. It's honesty, Lidian. I've always striven to be honest."

Edith stirred in her sleep and I moved her carefully to my shoulder. "Then you are saying that honesty provokes you to abandon this marriage? To apply for divorce? What of your promise to *me*? What of your children?"

He stared at me, his expression impassive, almost bored, as if he were listening to the drone of some tedious lecturer, not his wife.

It was then that I asked the question that had been plaguing me for months—the question that all women ask in the midst of their pain. "Is it someone else? Have you found a new love?"

He did not answer.

I stroked Edith's back. Beneath my fingertips was the soft cotton of her little dress, warmed by her body. "It's Margaret, isn't it?"

"No," he said. "It's not anyone else, Lidian. It is *us*." Whereupon he took his hat from its peg and left the house.

I WALKED at night, for I could not sleep. I paced the house and the yard, strolled outside under the stars, hoping to find a solace that did not exist. I walked often to the churchyard to kneel by Wallie's grave.

One evening Margaret offered to accompany me. We walked under moon-streaked clouds, the dim light welcome to my sore eyes, for since Wallie's death I'd come to prefer night to day. A light breeze tugged at my veil and the hem of my skirts. I felt akin to a spirit born of shadows, as if I had no substance but darkness.

When we reached the graveyard I opened the gate and led Margaret straight to Wallie's stone. I could hear the rattle of the river a few yards away, and the thrum of crickets in the grass. I fell on my knees and pressed my forehead against the cold slate. Margaret stood nearby, her head bowed. She may have been praying—I did not know. We both remained in our distinct postures for a long time. When I finally rose, the moonlight had shifted, casting Wallie's marker into blackness so the words could no longer be read.

Margaret took my arm and guided me away, pointing out the odd shape of a cloud that hung directly above us. I looked at it dispassionately and made some remark about its color, though it had none. As we started back to Bush, Margaret turned to me.

"You ought not to lock your sentiments away, Lidian. They will scald your heart."

The truth of her words struck me—it was as if they opened the lock in a canal and suddenly my ship of grief could sail forth. I began to talk of how Wallie continued to grow in my heart. I spoke of what an extraordinary child he was, of how wise he'd been, how unlike other children—more patient, tender, and in possession of a Christian compassion that few adults exhibited. I felt compelled to tell Margaret everything. I was aware that she was uncharacteristically silent, but in my need to speak of Wallie, I attributed her silence to interest and compassion. When I finally retired to my bed that night, it seemed as if a small portion of great sorrow had been lifted from me and my burden was easier to bear.

19

Arrangements

The life of woman must be outwardly a well-intentioned, cheerful dissimulation of her real life.
—MARGARET FULLER

Margaret's visit had lasted a month when Mr. Emerson informed me that he'd invited her to live with us permanently. We were readying ourselves for bed. I stopped in the midst of unbuttoning my skirt and stared at him.

"Why did you not tell me this before she came?"

"She thought it best not to inform you until she'd decided one way or the other. She wished to make a trial stay first." He didn't turn to look at me as he spoke, but busied himself in front of his bureau by slowly removing his collar.

"*She* thought? Am I no longer mistress of this house?" My fingers froze on a button, numb now as if I'd plunged them into a drift of snow.

"Of course. But you've not been well. And since Wallie's death, I've not wanted to add to your distress."

"Distress!" I said. "Is it not distressing to discover that my husband has been making household arrangements without my knowledge?"

He turned quickly then, spun on his heel like a marionette snapped on the end of a string. Despite the dim light, I could see that he was scowling. "She's your friend as well as mine. You yourself declared that our house must be open to all our friends, a port of safety for philosophers in an unwelcoming world."

"That was years ago. Before Wallie was born!" I yanked the skirt off and hurled it to the floor, popping the button and sending it flying across the room. It hit a window and pinged onto the floor. One of my cats—the charcoal tom—pounced upon it from behind the rocker.

"No, Flavius!" I lunged across the room to scoop the cat into my arms, and then retrieved the errant button.

"Has motherhood now hardened your heart against your friends?"

"Of course not!" My voice rose; I heard the annoying shrill in it, but could not control its timbre. The cat lay briefly still in my arms, then leaped away in one long, elegant arc, landing on his feet in the center of our bed. "I mean that, ill or not, I ought to be consulted on such matters. Margaret herself has argued that a woman is no less wise or intelligent than a man. So should I not have equal say with my husband about who lives in our house?"

Mr. Emerson was silent. He stared at me without moving. As usual, when he refused to debate, my ire quickly dissipated. "I apologize for losing my temper," I said. "Of course Margaret is welcome."

He nodded, but continued to watch me. It was a gaze I recognized—a dispassionate, unforgiving look—not dissimilar to the one I saw each day in the mirror.

The next afternoon at dinner, as I passed the platter of sliced veal to Margaret, I asked her to join me on an afternoon stroll. "I'd like to talk with you about our new arrangement," I said.

Margaret glanced at Mr. Emerson. "Oh dear," she said, "I've promised to walk with Waldo."

Henry, who sat beside me, made a small rude sound in the back of his throat.

My tears erupted without warning. I had not cried in weeks and they felt hot and unfamiliar. They burned my eyes; scored ridges in my cheeks. I pressed my hands to my face. "Then you must go with him," I said. "I would not wish you to break your engagement." I heard the bitterness in my voice and regretted it, yet the truth was I had carried this venom in my heart for so many weeks that I could no longer prevent its expression.

Margaret coughed into her napkin and looked again at my husband, but he didn't return her glance. He continued to study his plate with apparent disinterest as he chewed his veal. Henry put down his fork.

Margaret reached across the table and touched my arm. "Dear Lidian. I'm so sorry. Of course I'll walk with you. My little excursion with Waldo can easily be postponed to another time." Again she looked at him.

"No!" I whipped my hands from my face and rubbed my eyes fiercely with my napkin. "You must walk with him. It's what he wishes."

My husband's expression was utterly blank, as if his ears had become deaf to human speech.

Margaret shook her head and rose. Her entire demeanor was filled with apology and regret. She repeated that her walk with Mr. Emerson could be postponed. Yet I did not look at her. I could not, at that point, accept her pitying reversal.

Throughout the horrible scene, my husband continued to stare silently at his plate. After a moment, Henry rose and excused himself. I saw that he had left his food untouched. Mother Emerson asked me to pass the potatoes and commented on the weather, which threatened rain.

After the meal, Margaret persisted in her efforts and finally persuaded me to take a short walk with her. We headed across the low, swampy flats past Edmund Hosmer's large house and the dilapidated Fletcher farm. Margaret was at her most understanding. It did not take her long to draw out my feelings. I'd experienced a sympathetic woman's ear too rarely since coming to Concord. I willingly shared my frustrations concerning Mr. Emerson. If nothing else, I hoped to disabuse her of the notion that he had a warm and compassionate nature.

"He's become so stubborn and implacable lately," I told Margaret. "But what hurts me most is his lack of affection."

Margaret murmured her understanding. She agreed that Mr. Emerson was difficult, that he had not given me the love I had reason to expect. Then she stopped in the road, put her hands upon my shoulders, and turned me toward her.

"Yet you must know that I regard you as the most fortunate woman in the universe! Surely the honor of being Waldo's wife makes the faults of genius bearable!"

I stared at her. "If you were married to him you'd not find yourself so fortunate as you believe."

"Oh, Lidian!" Margaret's eyes were filled with the pity I abhorred.

THAT EVENING Henry joined me in the parlor, while my husband strolled outside with Margaret. I was seated on the couch with the ever-present mending piled in my lap when he came into the room and sat beside me. He said nothing at first—he had a way of looking at me that surpassed speech. Just the weight of his gaze could cause my throat to knot.

"Henry," I said, not knowing what I wished to say, but feeling that some word must be spoken. I recalled how he had sat at the dinner table during my outburst, staring at my silent husband with an expression of disbelief and disdain. I knew he neither understood nor approved of Mr. Emerson's silence. I'd heard the scorn in his voice on more than one occasion and wondered if Mr. Emerson detected it as well. But my husband no longer shared his confidences with me. He had younger, more malleable minds to mold.

After saying Henry's name, my thoughts returned me to a silence so deep that I started when he placed his hand over mine. "Don't break your heart on the rock of his indifference," he said quietly.

I closed my eyes. "He is my husband."

"A husband who does not love you." The words shocked me, less for their boldness—it was characteristic of Henry to state his thoughts with supreme confidence—than because they so exactly echoed the doubts in my own heart.

I slid my hand from beneath Henry's and picked up my mending. I meant to go back to it, to bury my suffering in the tedious monotony of stitching, but I made the mistake of looking at him. His eyes—usually filled with gray and blue light—appeared nearly black, for he sat beyond the range of lamplight, and was engulfed in shadow. Yet I felt them searching my face and drawing my own eyes more deeply toward his until we were locked in a mutual gaze so intense I felt a scorching heat burn the length of my back.

"He loves me as he can," I said weakly. "Genius must follow its own inclination."

"Some would incline differently," Henry whispered. And though I knew he'd returned his hand to his own knee, I had such a powerful sensation that it still covered mine that I had to look twice at my lap to assure myself that my hands had both dutifully returned to the task of mending Mr. Emerson's Sunday shirt.

THAT NIGHT in our chamber, I lay beside Mr. Emerson thinking of Margaret. If she knew my husband's true nature, would she pursue him so earnestly? Would she allow him to pursue *her*? I wished I had the courage to confront Mr. Emerson directly—to ask if he had ever loved me at all. But he slept peacefully beside me, and I did not try to wake him.

I did not know him when I agreed to marry him. Nor did I know him now, seven years after we were wed. There was something in him so cold it was beyond knowing.

I could not sleep. I rose and put on my robe and paced the downstairs rooms all night in the moonlight, wondering whether my husband had been physically intimate with Margaret. In my wild, sorrowing state, I did not perceive that neither Margaret nor Mr. Emerson was the true cause of my anguish, but that its root burrowed deep into my heart.

THE NEXT MORNING at breakfast, Margaret announced that she must soon end her visit. She claimed she had family matters to attend—her mother was unwell. She hoped she might find her own residence in Concord at a later time.

I wondered what had prompted this change of heart. Had Mr. Emerson asked her to leave? I glanced across the table at him, but his look was impassive as he sat thoughtfully chewing upon one of the day-old biscuits.

On Saturday evening I gave a tea in Margaret's honor, inviting all her Concord friends. Margaret seemed pleased with my efforts, though I heard later that she complained to her sister that it was "too much a mob" for her taste. At the end of the evening, when Margaret declared she'd accompany Sophia Hawthorne and her mother back to the Manse in their chaise, my husband volunteered to go with her. For safety's sake, he said. I stood in the dining room holding a plate of cake crumbs, knowing—as did everyone present—that this would require Margaret and my husband to walk the long way back to Bush by moonlight. Yet I could not object without seeming jealous and common. I had to watch, unprotesting, as they left the house.

They did not return for three hours. Though I retired to my chamber,

I could not sleep. Eventually, I heard the front door open and close and then my husband's low voice and Margaret's muffled laugh. A short time later, his tread sounded on the stairs. I did not speak to him when he entered the room.

The next day Margaret sought me out in the kitchen as I measured the breakfast coffee. She thanked me for hosting such a grand farewell and then confessed that her walk with my husband had been the most memorable of her entire visit. "Waldo and I were more truly together than usual." Her pewter eyes were soft with the memory.

Fury sparked at the base of my spine and surged upward through my body. "Do you mean to take my husband from me?" The words were out before I could stop them.

Margaret's eyes widened. "Lidian! How can you think such a thing?"

But I was deaf to her shock. "You imagine him capable of an intimacy of which he has no comprehension. His warmth—his tenderness—is all on the surface. Your belief in his attachment to you is the surest warranty that you do not know his heart." I was fairly spitting my rage. Margaret took a step backward; her right hand rose to her throat.

"Oh no, Lidian, you're wrong! Waldo is kindness itself!" She swallowed audibly and her fingers fell from her throat to her collar, where they restlessly twisted the white lace into knotted beads as she spoke. "If he seems remote it's because of his grief at the loss of your son! Surely you perceive that!" She reached toward me, withdrew, took another step back. "He's poured out his soul to me so eagerly! All he wants is a listening ear, an attentive heart. If he's not turned to you it's not because he has grown cold, but because you're so deeply mired in your own grief you've no compassion to spare!"

"I invited you into my home as a friend," I hissed. "Not to berate and betray me."

"I *am* your friend! More truly than you realize. If my words seem harsh, it's out of concern for you. Have we not pledged from the start that we would be honest with each other?" She lurched toward me again and this time took my hand between hers. "I offer this only out of love for you. Perhaps if you scolded Waldo a little less you'd find him more tender."

Her touch had an odd effect upon me. I suddenly found myself clutching her, not merely her hand, but her arms, and then her shoulders until I finally clasped her to my bosom. My words rushed out of their own accord and tangled themselves in her hair, which fell in thick, soft loops from her temples so I could not know if she heard me or if her sweet and compassionate response was merely a reaction to my excess of emotion. I felt her hands on my back, patting me, reassuring me, then her soothing voice in my ear.

"You poor dear. You must not do this to yourself! He loves you in his own way! You know that!"

I shook my head violently. "If I've scolded, he's driven me to it! You have no idea, Margaret, what it is to be married to Mr. Emerson! A man the world perceives as a sage and a saint—flawless, noble, without sin. Some regard him with an awe that ought to be reserved for Christ."

I became aware that she was trying to pull away from me, murmuring protests as she twisted in my arms. I released her but continued to speak.

"If you win him from me you'll regret it for the rest of your life. He'll take the gift of your intellect and drain every ounce of brilliance from you."

She stared at me. Her face was unnaturally flushed and her breath came in rapid bursts. "I've no desire to win him from you! Lidian, I'm his friend and philosophical companion! Nothing more."

I was silent for a moment and when I spoke each word fell from my lips with a solemnity and slowness as if I were the voice of doom itself.

"For him, that is everything."

Margaret covered her face with her hands. As I watched her, I felt the anger go out of me all at once. All I knew was compassion, for I saw that she was a woman exactly like me in her passions and principles. I took her hands and pulled them from her face and saw her tears. And in that instant I forgave her everything.

20

Collisions

The lot of woman is sad. She is constituted to expect
and need a happiness that cannot exist on earth.
—Margaret Fuller

The duty of a wife is to her husband and although I strove
to comply, submission was not in my nature. Every day I
endeavored to discharge my responsibility to Mr. Emerson, and every night
I sank into sleep, bruised from the continual collision of temperament and
obligation.

What can a woman do when she's sacrificed her life to a man's conceit?
When she's given all in the false hope that virtue will be rewarded with love
and appreciation? When she's subdued her nature at great cost—all for nothing? What hope is there for such a woman?

Were it not for Henry, I would have flown into hourly rages, and perhaps
deserted Mr. Emerson entirely. But Henry cautioned me to remember what
I already knew—that only when I addressed Mr. Emerson with reason and
composure would he listen to my thoughts and accord them his respect.
I strove to calm myself, forcing the rage deep into a hidden closet of my heart

where it could not be detected. Few knew the ice that limned Mr. Emerson's soul. How many times I asked—*begged*—him to discuss the insufficiency of love in our union! Yet while he would discuss love and marriage in the abstract, he could not—or would not—speak of it in a personal way. I had long ago seen that by his philosophy Mr. Emerson could describe the earth but could not work with it; he could expound on truth but could not share his heart. Nearly everyone was deceived by his eloquence, the warmth of his smile, and the brilliance of his thought. Even those who did not admire him would have thought me a fool for forsaking the great fortune of being Mr. Emerson's wife.

There was only one person in Concord who understood. Only one who saw the depth of my suffering and stood by me through it all.

How strange that the love of another man was the very glue that bound me to my husband.

NOT LONG AFTER Wallie's birthday, I received a letter from Lucy informing me that Sophia was gravely ill. "She's been unwell for some time," she wrote, "though I'd not realized it for she was determined to hide the fact from me and go about her daily rounds. I fear her stubbornness has been her undoing. She asks for you often and I tell her that you will come when you are able."

I arranged at once to make the journey to Plymouth. Since Edith was still a nursing babe and Mr. Emerson was lecturing out of town, I had to take both children with me, though I feared for their safety in bringing them into what I suspected was a house of fever. Henry, who had been away on a walking excursion along the Merrimack River, returned to find me overwrought, and offered to stay at Bush and care for Ellen. But I could not bear the thought of being parted from either of my two living children. So, on a cold November morning when hoarfrost had etched each dying leaf and blade of grass, Henry helped the three of us board the public coach and we rattled off down the long road to Plymouth.

Despite the unhappy occasion, I was elated to be in Plymouth again. The sea air was bright with salt; a soft gray sky overarched the harbor where seven four-masted ships swayed on the dark tide. I walked down North Street with the children, my shoes clicking on the cobblestones amid the chime of horses' hooves, the scent of baking bread emanating from the two bakeries we passed.

Lucy greeted us at the front door of the house where she boarded and led us up a dark, narrow staircase, to the two small rooms she and Sophia occupied. It was nothing like the spacious chambers of Winslow House, but I was so glad to be reunited with her that I made no comment, but simply laid a sleeping Edith on the bed, sat Ellen in a chair, and heartily embraced my sister. I reflected, as I felt the sweet comfort of her cheek against mine, on how altered I felt in Plymouth. The very scent of the air seemed to restore my spirits and deliver my true self back to me.

"How is Sophia?" I asked, removing my gloves and bonnet and laying them near Edith on the bed. "Your letter alarmed me."

Lucy nodded. "I'm sorry for that, but her condition was alarming." She lifted Edith to cradle her against her bosom. "Thankfully, she's improved. The doctor came and bled her this morning and it seems to have done her good." She glanced sideways at me and I detected something odd—an unspoken and painful burden—in her look.

"There's something you haven't told me, isn't there?" Ellen was swinging her legs, kicking the rung of the chair. I picked her up, sat down, and placed her on my lap. My encircling arms seemed to calm her and she laid her head on my shoulder. I looked at Lucy again. "Confess it. I've not come all this way to be kept in the dark."

Lucy sagged onto the bed, still holding Edith. As she gazed down at my babe's sleeping face, I noted with dismay that there were tears in her eyes. "I don't know how I can tell you," she said.

"Why ever not? I thought we have always confided in each other." I was growing impatient. I wished I could kick the chair rung as Ellen had.

"It's mortifying," Lucy said. She was silent a moment, staring down at Edith. Finally she turned to face me. "She has miscarried a child," she whispered.

"A child?"

Lucy nodded and closed her eyes.

My mind was a storm of questions, none of which my sister's expression permitted me to ask. I took a deep breath and clasped Ellen more tightly. I felt that if I did not hold her fast, I'd begin trembling. I recalled Sophia's beguiling smiles and the gay coquetry of her manner with Henry and the oldest Hosmer boy on the recent occasions when she'd visited. I recalled a long conversation we'd had on the nature of love and marriage. She'd told me that she had no intention of marrying, since men so rarely kept their promises. I said I'd felt the same when I was young, but that she should not forget that marriage was the road to motherhood, which was the most satisfying of a woman's duties. She'd looked at me thoughtfully, her head tilted, and announced that it was satisfying only because it was the one opportunity in which women could exercise power and influence. Stunned at the wisdom of her insight, I was unable to contradict her.

"The father?" I inquired.

"She will not tell me."

"Oh, Lucy!" I murmured. Yet I could think of nothing to say that would grant my sister the solace she required.

Lucy raised her head as if it contained a terrible weight. "She went to visit Frank at Brook Farm last summer. She came back changed. I did not think at the time—" She stopped, choking on the words. "I believe the father was one of the community members. But she will concede nothing. She just looks at me with the most sorrowful expression and begins weeping."

"What an ordeal for you!" I could no longer remain seated, but rose and went to stand by my sister, still carrying Ellen who had fallen asleep. "Your son hiding himself in that community and Sophia brought so low! Didn't Frank offer to leave the farm?"

When she shook her head, I sighed loudly. "I'm grieved that you bore it so long alone. Take Ellen and I'll go and speak to my niece."

Lucy did not protest. She seemed very faraway when I lowered Ellen onto her lap, sunk deep in her own anguish.

Sophia lay propped high on pillows, her oval face nearly as white as the casings. Her chestnut hair had lost its sheen and her eyes were so deep in their sockets they gave the appearance of having shrunk. As I entered the room, she turned her head and gave me a feeble smile.

"Aunt Lydia." Even her voice had been drained of strength; it was no louder than the wind in a hemlock grove. She started to raise her hand toward me, but the effort was too much for her. I noted a small bloodstain on her arm—a relic of the doctor's morning physic.

A narrow chair was drawn up beside the bed and near it was a small table, cluttered with vials of potions, the stub of a candle, and a worn Bible. I recognized the Bible, for I'd given it to her on the occasion of her twentieth birthday.

I sat in the chair and took her hand. Her fingers were cold, though her palm was warm with fever. These symptoms alarmed me, for I'd seen them before—when death was near.

"Dear Sophia," I said, in as calm a voice as I could manage. "Oh, my dear niece, I cannot bear to see you like this."

Her eyes filled instantly with tears. "Mother's told you?"

I nodded. "Are you in great pain?"

"No more than I deserve." She moved her fingers against my palm. "Thank you for coming."

"I blame myself for this. I've stirred you to love liberty but have not sufficiently influenced you toward Christ."

Her eyes closed and her hand seemed to shrink in mine. "I know what I did"—she paused, opened her eyes and took a shuddering breath—"was unforgivable."

"Nothing is unforgivable," I said. "God's mercy is infinite."

She sighed and seemed to wait while gathering strength to speak. "I've offended everyone I love. Beginning with God."

I leaned closer to hear her better, for her voice was dissolving into silence.

"I went to Mrs. Ruedel on Leyman Street." She spoke slowly, pausing between each word. "She gave me a potion. She told me I'd be quickly freed of my burden. But it took three days." She stopped and sank deeper into her pillows. The room's silence spread around her in waves, like the ripples caused by a stone cast into water. It lapped against me and washed into my mind, where it rolled in shadowed undulations. I don't know if Sophia's breathing grew louder or if it was simply the effect of the silence upon my ears, but it seemed to me that her inhalations became desolate moans. I took both her hands in mine in a futile effort to warm them. At last she spoke again, though I had to strain to make out her words.

"You'll take care of Mother, won't you, Aunt Lydia? She needs someone to comfort and provide for her. I've only brought her shame."

Though barely audible, these were the last words I heard Sophia say. Two hours later she slipped into a coma and the next afternoon she died.

I did what I could to console Lucy, but my own heart was breaking as I made arrangements for my niece's funeral and burial. I washed her body and laid her out in the cramped room. The next day Uncle Thomas came with a coffin and took Sophia to his house, where the funeral was held. Frank traveled from Brook Farm, in the company of two young men. One, a tall man with wide shoulders and straw-colored hair, seemed particularly moved by the simple service. I could not help but wonder if he might be the father of Sophia's child, and the author of her death as well. He seemed bowed very low with grief. When I greeted Frank he kissed my cheek but quickly turned away, and avoided me throughout the day. I insisted that Lucy return to Concord with me and she offered no resistance.

Lucy cried continually on the long ride, desolate over her loss. Yet she thanked me again and again for my kindness and several times reached across the space between us to lay her hand on my arm and remind me that now we were bonded not only as sisters but as mothers in mourning. I hardly needed to be reminded of this, for Sophia's death renewed my own anguish in the most piercing way. And I also mourned Sophia, for I'd been the most doting of aunts before my marriage, and continued our intimacy afterward by writing to her often and inviting her for numerous visits.

I reflected, as we jounced along the turnpike with its wind-whipped leaves and rutted track, that 1842 had been the most terrible of years. Only two good things came from it—it brought my sister back to Concord, and it bound me in a profound friendship with Henry Thoreau.

When we finally reached Bush and pulled up before the front door, the twilight sky was a clear indigo, punctured by two brightening stars. Mr. Emerson emerged from the house to hand us down from the coach. I placed the sleeping Ellen in his arms, and Lucy carried Edith. So I had no one to hold as I advanced up the walk and entered the overly warm house. It was evident that Mr. Emerson had stoked the fires himself and in the process probably used up a great deal of firewood. When the door swung shut behind me, I wanted to fling it open again at once.

"Shall I carry her up to bed?" Mr. Emerson looked at me over Ellen's head, which lay on his shoulder.

I nodded and reached to take Edith from Lucy. There were times when I felt my children were the only nourishment for the hunger of spirit I felt at Bush.

I put Lucy in the Red Room and went through the east entryway into the dining room, still cradling Edith, for I did not want to let her go. I heard my husband's footfall as he moved above me through our chamber to the nursery. I thought of Sophia's shame and wondered how much of her plight could be attributed to the way I'd spoken to her of marriage. I'd urged her not to settle and warned her of the dangers and constraints that a bad match presented for women. Perhaps she'd heeded me too well.

I did not tell Mr. Emerson. On the evening I returned, when he asked the details and cause of Sophia's death, I told him it was a fever and that I was convinced she'd died in a state of grace. He did not pursue the question.

Lucy stayed with us only a few weeks, quickly making arrangements to board elsewhere in town. She did not consider the Thoreau establishment, for she had been wounded by Cynthia's tactlessness, and Lucy had a hard, unforgiving side much like our father. Instead, she found lodging at the home of a neighbor. Before she was settled a month, Mr. Emerson arranged to buy a small house for her on Lexington Road, within sight of our front gate. The house was in poor condition and required extensive remodeling, but he assured me he had the necessary funds and that it would be worth the expense to abolish my endless worry about Lucy's health and happiness. Once she was settled only yards away from my doorstep, I could reassure myself hourly, if need be.

There were times when I believed my husband the most generous and considerate of men.

ON THE FIRST ANNIVERSARY of Wallie's death, Mr. Emerson was in Philadelphia, and I could not relieve myself of the thought that he had fled there to be far away from the site of mourning. I lay in bed most of the morning, rising only to dress the children and wander through the rooms, adjusting the placement of vases and books. I sent Nancy to the market without instructions, not caring about the kind or quality of meat for dinner. When she brought back a gristle-laden cut of beef, I did not admonish her. At dinner, I had no appetite and did not touch my food, though Mother Emerson chided me for not keeping up my strength. When Nancy carried the pudding in from the kitchen, Henry, who'd been silent throughout the meal, put down his fork and rose.

"You and I are going to take a long walk," he said. "Right now." He would not listen to my protests. He helped me dress the children and bundle Edith into the perambulator. It was a mild January afternoon. The snow melted in tiny rivers beside the road. I complained that my gown would be quickly muddied, but he paid no heed to what was underfoot, but pointed out every chickadee and squirrel. He demanded that I note the clarity of the sky and the intriguing shapes of the clouds.

"I am not so old that I'm already blind," I told him.

"No, indeed. You'll never be old in my eyes, Lidian. For the heart sees with perfect clarity." He was staring at me with an expression of such plain and open affection that I felt a jolt of alarm.

"You must not say such things," I said quickly, easing the perambulator over a large rock in the middle of the road. Yet my admonishment was not born of virtue, for even as I spoke I blushed with pleasure.

"And why not?" He stopped beneath a large chestnut tree whose branches formed a black lacework against the gray January sky. "I determined several years ago I'd adhere to the truth of things and give no heed to the voices of those who limit freedom."

"I admire your convictions, but they don't pertain here. You know the reason."

"Because you're married."

"Yes."

He folded his arms. "In name only."

My breath locked in my throat. "That is not for you to judge."

I saw his upper lip twitch and thought he was going to say more, but instead he took Ellen's hand and turned his attention back to the road. "I'd like to walk out to Walden Pond and look at the ice," he said.

His sudden abandonment of our argument took me by surprise. It was unlike him and left me wondering whether or not he accepted my prohibition. I half wanted to continue the dispute.

"Is it too far?" He wasn't looking at me, but loomed over the perambulator, watching Edith, who was peacefully asleep.

"Not at all." I realized then that his words and the admiration in his gaze had so invigorated me that I was eager to walk those two miles and more—all at Henry's brisk pace.

And of course we talked. For when did Henry and I not converse? Our bond was rooted in our conversations, for it was in the exchange of thoughts and ideals that we both became most completely ourselves. Our most intellectual exchanges always had the greatest emotional effect upon me, for I had discovered long before that heart and mind were not two separate units, but connected by the most indestructible filaments.

On this occasion we fell into a discussion of the relationship between love and hate, Henry asserting that the two were inextricably entwined.

"The person toward whom I feel love is the same who commands my hate," he said.

"No!" I replied, laughing at the absurdity of the declaration. "Love and hate are opposites. They cannot exist within the same heart. Not, at least, at the same time."

"But think on it, Lidian!" He stopped in the middle of the path and released Ellen, who ran off to gather pinecones. The bough of a young pine hung above his head, scattering the sunlight into yellow droplets that splashed across his face. "We do not hate those whom we do not know or care for! The Chinaman on the far side of the world is not my enemy for I know nothing of his life. I have no feeling for him at all! Even the Irishman in his hut down by Flint Pond is only an acquaintance, toward whom I hold the mildest sentiment. It's those closest to me, the ones I most love—my sister, my parents, my most intimate friends—who arouse the greatest anger. Which is the same as hatred, is it not? It's only those whom we hold dear who can break our hearts."

I was frowning throughout this speech, for my mind did not want to admit the truth of his words. "I hate the slaveholder," I said, "though I do not know him. I hate the man who abuses his livestock, no matter where he lives in the world."

"Ah, but antipathy is not the same as *hate*. There's a natural—a noble—aversion to injustice. But hatred is something else. It comes from the very depths of the heart."

Ellen returned and begged to be carried, so Henry lifted her to his shoulders, where she sat, happily surveying the world as we continued walking.

"Then are you suggesting that our friendship is based in hate?"

"No!" He spun in a full circle and Ellen giggled. "It's based in what is most real—most alive—which is both love *and* hate. Don't you see?"

I did not, but could not think how to refute him. The idea struck me as so alien that it would take me years to comprehend it. Meanwhile, we had reached the pond.

The sun was halfway down the sky, chasing tree shadows out over the ice. Edith was still asleep in the perambulator. We stood beside the road looking down at the pond—for I could not easily make my way down the steep hill to the shore with the carriage. Henry pointed out the way the ice was cracking in long perpendicular lines along the shore.

"I've wondered about that phenomenon—it seems curious to me that the ice should break so uniformly."

I studied the blue lines in the snow-covered ice. They were remarkably straight, as if carved there by some mammoth skater. "Perhaps the ice cutters began their job but couldn't complete it."

He shook his head. "I considered that, but I've examined them closely and those marks are natural."

"Look!" cried Ellen, pointing eagerly at a group of skaters emerging from a cove near the far shore. "I want to skate too, Mama!"

"When the ice is stronger you will," Henry said, without awaiting my answer. "I promise that you and I will skate out to the very center of the pond. And perhaps your mother will come with us too."

"Oh, no, Henry," I said. "I couldn't."

"Why not? Have you never skated?"

"Yes, as a girl. But that was many years ago, and I'm sure I've lost the knack."

"It'll come back to you." He spoke with such boyish assurance and enthusiasm that I laughed.

"I'm quite serious," he said. "I wish I had a pair of skates with me to prove it to you."

"I'm very glad you do not." I looked at him and was instantly unnerved by the challenge in his eyes, for it was not a challenge simply to skate, but to cast away my cautious vigilance.

Part of me longed to accept. At that moment, I wanted nothing more than to fling away all my restraint and self-discipline and dance across the ice at his side. The ice of the pond was solid, but the ice of my despair had cracked under Henry's joy.

Then, as if in warning, Edith stirred in her perambulator and I quickly bent to attend her.

THAT NIGHT as I lay alone in my bed, I listened to Henry moving about his room. There was but a wall between us, a few plastered lathes, a layer of wallpaper, and air. After a time I heard his bed frame creak and I pictured him reclining beneath his blankets, the weight of his head indenting the pillow I'd stitched from sacking and filled with the feathers of my hens. I imagined the rhythm of his breathing and wondered if he were sleeping. Or was he was lying awake in bed, staring at the ceiling as I was, unable to sleep?

WHEN I WOKE snow was falling beyond our curtains in its own thick drapery. Dawn had grayed the windowpanes, and a small ridge of snow lay on the floor beneath the sash, for as always I'd opened the window to the night air. The house was so cold the floorboards snapped when I stood.

I went into the nursery and checked on the children, who were still sleeping deeply. I wondered if Henry had risen before dawn, as was his custom, and gone abroad before breakfast. But when I went downstairs I found him stoking the dining-room fire. The cap of snow melting from his hair declared that he'd already been out.

"Just to the barn for wood," he said, when I commented on his appearance. "There's two feet of fresh snow out there. Not the best conditions for walking." He stood and brushed briefly at his knees, then rubbed his hands together. "Did you sleep well last night?"

"Better than usual," I said. "And you?"

He nodded. "Very well, thank you. Outdoor activity is the best tonic. You should dispose of your pills and powders and partake of the air more often."

It was the sort of raillery he frequently adopted in our conversations, and I rarely allowed it to go unchallenged.

"My pills and powders mystify you," I said. "Perhaps if you learned to bottle the outdoors I'd partake of it more regularly."

He laughed. "But it's impossible to contain such wealth. Though I mean to share some related thoughts with you after breakfast. If you'll allow me." He gestured to the table where lay a small leather-covered book. "My journal."

That morning, and many mornings after, he read to me from its pages. Our habit was to retire to the parlor as soon as the breakfast plates were cleared and settle ourselves into the two rocking chairs before the fire. He didn't read chronologically but selected pages by some unexpressed logic of his own. There were descriptions of the weather and plants he'd discovered, observations of birds and animals, narrations of events he'd witnessed, and philosophical musings. He chose plain, direct sentences to make his points; there was no pretense in his language. Each morning, I found myself more eager than the last to hear new passages he read.

On the day Mr. Emerson was to return from Philadelphia, Henry read longer than usual. I listened, enraptured, to his account of a midnight sail upon the Concord River.

He smiled as he closed the book. "You inspire confidence just in the act of *listening*," he said. "All that is good and admirable in me is due to the fact that you're my friend."

I was about to refuse his compliment, when he pulled his chair closer to mine and reached across the space between us to take my hand. Instantly a vivid happiness blossomed within, and I felt myself yielding to and returning the ardor I saw in his gaze.

"If I inspire you, it's only because your companionship sustains me," I said. "I could not have endured this past year had it not been for your kindness."

He drew my hand to his mouth and kissed it tenderly. A stab of pleasure went through me. Then, just as quickly as it had bloomed, my happiness withered, and I was flooded with a sensation of guilt. I withdrew my hand and lurched to my feet. I did not look at Henry as I hurried from the room, murmuring that I must tend to the children.

I was disturbed that on the very day I was to be reunited with my husband, I'd found such pleasure in another man's touch. I fled not to the nursery, but to my chamber, where I fell on my knees and prayed for God's mercy. Yet I was so wretched in my sin that I found no relief even after an hour's prayer. Finally I rose and opened my Bible for guidance—a practice that I was given to in times of distress—and my eyes fell on the text of Galatians V:16–17: "This I say then, walk in the Spirit, and ye shall not fulfill the lust of the flesh. For the flesh lusteth against the Spirit, and the Spirit against the flesh: and these are contrary the one to the other."

The message was clear—though I'd willfully fallen from God's grace I might yet repent and live a pure life in the Spirit. In fact, it was what God commanded me to do, the direction in which He'd pointed me when He brought me into Mr. Emerson's sphere. He had brought Henry into our mutual sphere that Mr. Emerson and I might direct him toward His purposes. I resolved to strive more earnestly for obedience, and disabuse Henry of any romantic thoughts. What God had brought together, and I had almost abandoned, with His help I might restore. I spent what remained of the day in single-minded devotion to housekeeping chores.

Mr. Emerson returned on the late-afternoon coach. He was visibly tired as he carried his satchel into the house. I greeted him with a warmth I'd not exhibited since before Wallie's birth, yet his response was to ask what mail had come for him. He did not remark on my change in manner, nor apparently notice that I was more subdued than usual that evening. When he inquired after Henry, I reported that he'd gone to the Alcott home for an evening conversation. He retired to our chamber shortly after, where I joined him as soon as I'd settled the children for the night.

I expected to find him asleep, but instead he sat by the fire, going through a small stack of letters that lay on his lap. His expression was one of contentment; the exhaustion I'd detected earlier and the grief that had lived in his eyes ever since Wallie died was gone.

I stood in front of my dresser and began to take down my hair. I could see his form in the mirror, and I felt a rush of unexpected tenderness. "Letters from your admirers?"

He glanced up. "These are Ellen's letters."

My hands began to shake; one of my fingernails caught on a hairpin and the pin clinked to the floor.

"I keep them in my satchel and read them from time to time." He leaned his head back against the chair and sighed. "They restore my spirits. And coming home"—he paused and I saw his reflected shoulders rise in a shrug—"this house is a place of such sadness." His voice trailed off.

I pulled out another pin and placed it carefully upon the bureau. I thought of Henry's hand curled around mine, of the warm brush of his lips upon my fingertips. I turned to face my husband. "If her letters sustain you then I'm glad. Perhaps you'd read a passage to me?"

He studied me thoughtfully. "Sometimes your nobility humbles me." He looked again at the page in his hand, opened his mouth to read, then swallowed, cleared his throat, and tried again. " 'Few, let them love ever so ardently and purely, have the happiness to lie down in the earth together—the hand of death when it destroys one, merely numbs the other as warning or as a comfort . . .' " He stopped, cleared his throat again, and then folded the letter carefully and slid it into its envelope. "I apologize." His voice was broken and raw. "I thought I'd be able to, but I cannot. Someday you must read them for yourself." He looked up at me finally. "I wish you'd known her, Lidian. She was as pure and bright a soul as ever walked the earth. When she left this world, I knew it would never see her like again."

My hair was all down by then, flowing past my waist. My arms felt stiff and leaden as I removed my dress and chemise and pulled my nightgown over my head.

"I've taken pains to assure that this second marriage will not be a betrayal of my love for her."

I must have looked stricken for he half-rose out of the chair, spilling the letters onto the floor. He bent to retrieve them and though I felt an impulse to help, I did not move but stood paralyzed, watching him tenderly collect the envelopes and cradle them against his chest.

At last he straightened and looked at me. "I've always held you in the highest regard. You must not think I regret our marriage. I'm devoted to you and our children."

But I was not comforted. Devotion is not the same as love.

21

Reputation

Public opinion is a weak tyrant compared with our
private opinion. What a man thinks of himself that is
which determines, or rather, indicates, his fate.
                                    —HENRY DAVID THOREAU

Though mutual grief often binds a couple together, my
husband and I withdrew into separate worlds after Wal-
lie's death, and the rift between us widened each day. Mr. Emerson dwelt in
the cell of his study while I chained myself to the care of the children and
house and fell into a fretful and distressing invalidism. I was beset by
headaches and vague pains in my heart. I no longer rose early, but lay abed in
a somnolent drowse. I contracted low, persistent fevers, strange debilities of
my arms and legs, and a dyspepsia for which the doctor could find no cause
or cure.

Yet daily I grew closer to Henry. He came to my chamber when I was ill
and read to me. He read the newspaper and his poems and passages from his
journal. He listened patiently to my symptoms and encouraged me to walk
outside when I felt strong enough.

"There's no remedy more potent than nature," he said.

He encouraged me to speak of Wallie. Despite his religious doubts, he didn't scoff at my assurance that my son was well and safe in heaven, that I'd see him once again. And we talked also of John, who'd been not only Henry's brother but his dearest friend.

Yet Henry and I had little need of conversation, for there was an understanding between us that ran deep and pure as an underground river. We were linked at a subterranean level by an attachment that went beyond understanding. How many times the same words sprang from our lips! How often we reacted with the same shudder of excitement to the wind! Or found ourselves swaying to a musical tune with the same delight. Our lives were knit together with no visible seam.

My feelings for Henry were more complex than the fascination I'd felt for Mr. Emerson during our courtship. They evoked the same ferocity as my feelings for my children, though I never thought of him as a child, despite the difference in our ages.

Yet I still loved Mr. Emerson. He was a generous and tolerant man, a tender father to my daughters, one of those rare men able to see through the superficial trappings of wealth and fashion and perceive the true value of others. There was not one ounce of dishonesty in him; he was incapable of dissembling. Above all, he was a man who valued ideas, who knew and honored the highest principles. It was as necessary and certain that I love him as it was for the sun to rise each morning.

How was it possible for me to love two men without feeling that my affections were divided? That was a mystery I begged God to open to me. More, I prayed for the obliteration of my love for Henry, for surely it could not be God's will that I love them both. Henry's presence must have its purpose, which I'd not yet discerned.

My feelings persisted and strengthened as the weeks passed. I knew—though I could scarcely bear to admit it to myself—that my attraction to Henry would soon reach a point where I could not continue to be in his presence daily without risking my virtue—and his.

ONE WINTER DAY when Mr. Emerson was in New York lecturing, snow flew from dawn to dusk. Henry spent the morning writing and in the afternoon he shoveled a path to the barn and one to the road—two white corridors that drew Ellen outside without my knowledge—I happened to glance out the dining-room window to find her dancing along like a snow sprite. My alarm was mollified when I saw Henry following her. A few moments later he carried her through the east entrance like a trophy, set her down, and squatted to gently brush the snow from her hair and cloak.

His cheeks were ruddy and his hair—which he'd neglected to cover with a hat—was more wind-tossed than usual. As he straightened and bade Ellen warm herself by the fire, I circled his waist with my arm and he instantly responded by circling mine with his. It was as natural and intimate a gesture as a brother and sister who've known each other all their lives. I looked straight into his eyes and found my own desire gazing back at me. We turned toward each other, my free arm half-raised as if to caress his cheek, and as we turned, my breast grazed his chest—the slightest contact, almost imperceptible. I felt an electrical heat course through my body, and I believe he felt the same, for we instantly dropped our arms and took a step back.

It was only then that I became aware that Mother Emerson was not in her chamber as I'd assumed, but was sitting in a chair close by the dining-room windows. Nearly obscured by the curtain shadows, she stared at me with hard, black eyes.

My hands felt as cold as the stones beneath the snow.

The day after his return from New York, my husband began to voice dissatisfaction with Henry. He attacked him vigorously in conversation, and made disparaging remarks about his abilities as a poet. He remarked on his lack of ambition.

"Henry's presence has caused a certain inconvenience," Mr. Emerson told me one night in our chamber.

"Inconvenience?" My hand froze in the midst of brushing my hair.

"He takes up too much of your time. Just this morning you spent over two hours with him in the kitchen."

"We were discussing my cats."

"Cats," he said. "He ought to be attending his own affairs." There was a new repugnance in his look that chilled me.

I knew that Mother Emerson had told my husband what she'd witnessed that snowy day, and that he was offended by my conduct. I also knew that he would not accuse me of impropriety. How could he when he'd both propounded and demonstrated a new understanding of friendship between men and women? Yet I knew the incident rankled him, for a scandal could ruin his reputation as a moral philosopher. I prayed fervently for guidance, daily begging God to strengthen me so that I might resist the temptation of Henry's presence. But each day when I greeted Henry at breakfast, I was persuaded anew that I could not tolerate an existence without him. His sympathy and encouragement—his cheerful intellect—nourished my soul in ways I could not live without. I began to believe that God had brought Henry into my life for this encouragement—this daily ration of joy.

I woke in the middle of the night, haunted by the fear that Mr. Emerson would declare Henry no longer welcome at Bush. Yet I could not bring myself to speak to anyone of these matters. I should not have been so foolish as to think I could hide my thoughts and feelings from Henry. I doubt there was ever a man born whose skill at observation equaled his. He was always studying his surroundings, noting details others missed. So it should not have surprised me when he addressed me in the barn one snowy February afternoon after I had fed my chickens. He'd been repairing the leg of a kitchen chair by the gray light of a window, but when I came out of the chicken coop, he set down his tools and approached me.

"There's something troubling you," he said. "You've hardly spoken to me in days."

I glanced at him then looked at the window where snow was painting white ruffles on the glass. "I've not been feeling quite myself," I murmured. "A touch of the grippe."

He shook his head. "I ask nothing more of you than honesty."

I looked into his eyes, fearing the direction this conversation was about to take. My apron pocket still had a handful of grain in it, and I curled my fingers around the kernels. They were warm and silky, oddly soothing. I took a deep breath.

"Mr. Emerson has suggested that you ought to look to your career." It was all I could do to choke out the words. They felt as dry as the grain dust that coated my apron.

"Career?" He gave me a startled frown. "I thought it was clear that I want to be a poet. I nurture no other ambition."

"I know." I closed my eyes and turned away, though I did not separate myself by any further movement.

He didn't speak for some time, and when he did his words came slowly, each one carefully measured for meaning and effect. "Perhaps there's some wisdom in considering other options. Our arrangement was for one year's residence. I've stayed nearly two."

I whirled back to face him. "No. Henry! Your presence has been a blessing—to both of us. You surely know that."

"I know you've been more than generous. I fear that in my contentment I've allowed my occupancy to inconvenience your family."

His choice of the word *inconvenience* distressed me. Yet it was the same term my husband had used. Did he and Henry perceive even the most subtle nuances of their association in the same way? I took my hand from my pocket, cradling a few grains in my palm. "It's not—it has never been—an inconvenience."

"But I believe it has to Waldo."

I looked at him and my resolve evaporated and, as the feed grains scattered like snow, I stepped forward and drew him toward me.

"Don't leave!" I murmured. "Please, I beg you!"

I heard him make a sound halfway between a gasp and a groan and then his arms circled me. He turned his face to my neck and I felt his breath—warm and sweet as fresh milk—stir the hair at my temples. I felt his fingertips and palms on my back, radiating heat through my shirt. The embrace lasted no more than an instant, for Henry quickly drew away. Yet that instant felt as if it had fallen outside time and was not part of the ordinary world.

I felt a throb of deprivation and loss. Then I looked into Henry's face and saw that he was as shocked as I by the gravity of the situation. He picked up his hammer and went back to the chair, while I plunged through the door and ran to the house. As I shook out my snowy skirts under the portico of the east entrance, I recalled Mr. Emerson's embrace on our wedding night. It had been an expected and even proper gesture—courteous and considerate. He'd held me and stroked my hair with the utmost gentility, and I'd felt honored and queenly. At the time I'd believed it to be everything I ever wanted in a man's touch. But Henry's embrace contained a hint of fire—a dangerous and unseemly passion I had never before experienced, and it frightened me profoundly.

AT DINNER two weeks later, Mr. Emerson announced that Henry was to travel to New York on the first of May. He would serve as escort to Mother Emerson who wished to visit William, and he'd remain there as tutor to William's young sons. I looked at Henry, who was smiling, though his pallor was gray.

"How long?" I felt an unsettling weakness in the base of my stomach.

"A few months at least," Henry said, scooping a wedge of boiled potato onto his fork. "Long enough to give me an opportunity to explore the publishing world. I hope to find an editor for my poems."

"I wondered when your ambition would assert itself," said Mother Emerson.

I gave her a cold look, noting that she'd not touched the mutton on her plate. "Is ambition now to be the hallmark of a well-lived life?"

"Certainly not." The wrinkles around her mouth deepened. "Yet I'm certain Henry's family would not want his education to go for naught."

"A poet's education is hardly for naught," I said, my voice sharper than I'd intended.

Mr. Emerson turned to Henry. "We wish you well."

"Yes," I said, "my prayers will go with you."

I don't know if Mr. Emerson heard the ardor in my tone or detected the sudden flush in Henry's face, but I perceived that the room's atmosphere had grown intimate. Nonetheless, I dared another declaration.

"I shall miss you terribly, you know." I let my gaze meet his. "I cannot think how we'll manage at Bush without you."

His eyes darkened and I immediately regretted my words, for it was plain I'd caused him embarrassment.

"Yet it will be good for your career, Henry." Mr. Emerson took another slice of mutton from the platter. "And we'd never want it said that the Emersons placed their own convenience over their friend's welfare. Would we, Lidian?"

I did not answer.

"Lidian?"

"No, the Emersons would never want that," I said. I bore down on my knife to cut a prong of meat.

Mr. Emerson nodded solemnly, "It seems we're all in agreement that Henry has sojourned with us long enough."

ALL THAT MARCH and April my time with Henry poured away like milk from an overturned pail. Some days I felt this to be another death, one I did not think I could bear. Yet I said nothing to Henry but locked my anguish away and smiled.

Two mornings before he left, when we retired to the parlor after break-fast, Henry read me a poem from his journal.

"I wrote it the night before last," he told me. "Did you see the moon?"

I nodded. I'd not been able to sleep that night and was tempted to venture outside for a walk in my garden. Now I was glad I had not, for encountering Henry would have undone me. Instead I'd stood at the east window of our chamber and watched the moonlight pour across the fields.

"It was bright enough to write by. I sat in your garden and these lines just came to me. As if I'd charmed the muse herself." He glanced up at me with a smile so penetrating that I felt a blush climb my neck.

"Please read it," I said.

He turned back to his journal. " 'Cans't thou love with thy mind,' " he read. " 'And reason with thy heart? Cans't thou be kind, And from thy dar-ling part?' "

"Oh, no. Henry—"

He held up a silencing hand and continued. " 'Cans't thou range earth, sea, and air, and so meet me everywhere? Through all events I will pursue thee; through all persons I will woo thee.' "

I'd been holding my breath throughout his reading, as if I feared my ex-halation would distort his words. The boldness of the poem shocked me, even as its sentiment echoed powerfully in my heart. It was sorrow and reas-surance mixed together, the promise that our bond would remain unbroken by distance, as well as a sad confirmation of the fact that neither of us could be whole without the presence of the other. The recklessness of this declara-tion overwhelmed me. I knew my cheeks were flushed hot with the force of my agitation.

"Waldo has already seen it," Henry said. "He pronounced it well-crafted." He lifted his head as if a breeze had just caressed his face. And then he smiled straight into my eyes.

22

Passions

You must know that you represent to me woman,
for I have not traveled very far or wide.
—HENRY DAVID THOREAU

The first of May dawned rainy and cold. Henry and Mother Emerson were supposed to leave on the morning coach, but flooding had rendered the road from Fitchburg impassable, so the coach did not arrive until late afternoon. By then I was both exhausted and distracted by the drawn-out grief of Henry's departure. When the coach finally pulled up at our east entrance, a wave of panicked sorrow seized me. Despite everyone's protests, I insisted on going out in the rain to bid Henry good-bye at the coach door. There I dutifully embraced Mother Emerson and pressed a small package into Henry's hands—it contained a cloth pouch I'd made in which I imagined he might keep his flute.

"Open it when you reach New York," I said, my eyes saying what I could not say aloud—*and think of me.*

"Thank you," he said. "Now go back into the house. I'll not have you catch a fever on my account."

I glanced over my shoulder at the house, where Mr. Emerson watched from beneath the shelter of the portico. "I'll miss you," I said and extended my hand. But instead of taking it, he withdrew into the coach.

"Go," he said quietly. "Your husband's waiting." He closed the door.

I turned and fled back into the house, past my husband and up the stairs to my chamber, where I fell on the bed. I heard the coach pull away from the east entrance and rattle across the yard to the road, and though I wanted to, I could not make myself rise and watch his departure from the window.

After a time, I heard Mr. Emerson come into the room, but I did not turn to him. Let him think what he would of me, I no longer cared.

How empty the house was without Henry! I wandered from room to room, as if I might find him reading by some sunny window. I insisted the Prophet's Chamber remain his room, and told Nancy I'd see to the cleaning myself. I found a particular peace in that room, with its simple desk and chair and cot, the one small window. Its intimacy moved me to pray, and I began to use it as my private chapel. Mr. Emerson had his study in which to exercise his intellect. I now had Henry's room for devotion. If Mr. Emerson noticed, he said nothing.

My body slowly collapsed around my loneliness. I fell ill with a fever that drained my vitality and confined me to my bed. On the days when I was strong enough I immersed myself in my children and garden.

My husband began to express impatience with my illness. Infirmity and disease, he claimed, were tests of will and courage. During our evening conversations, he discoursed on how willfulness and spiritual hubris could become the sources of illness.

Yet I knew his first wife had been ill all the time he knew her. He certainly did not disdain her weakness. Instead, it was her path to sainthood.

A week after Henry's departure, I wrote to him, sunk in a despondency so low that I feared I would not rise. In all the months of our friendship, I'd had no occasion to write, and my words were unnaturally formal, but I trusted that he would understand their import.

I did not write of Mr. Emerson or the children, but only of my own sickness and despair. I felt myself sinking fast. I wrote of how a permanent darkness had descended upon me, that I was fated now to live in the shadows. My eyes could scarcely bear the sunlight. Though my garden thrived, I did not. I informed him of my attempts to find someone to replace him as handyman and gardener. I described my interview with Hugh Wheelan, a garrulous man whom I hesitated to engage, knowing that neither he, nor any man, could replace Henry's efficiency and usefulness, not to mention his companionship.

I received Henry's letter two weeks later. Like mine, it was stilted—it did not convey the nuances that I understood so easily when we talked. Yet, it was alive with warmth and concern. He tried to persuade me out of the dark place where my soul had hidden. He encouraged me to hire Hugh, and pointed out the advantages it would bring to my garden. He told me of a tree that was popular there—a tulip tree—and promised me a sapling for my garden. Beneath his words, I sensed his homesickness for Concord. One sentence in particular cut to my heart: "I have hardly begun to live on Staten Island yet; but like the man who, when forbidden to tread on English ground, carried Scottish soil around in his boots, I carry Concord ground in my boots and in my hat, and am I not made of Concord dust?" I heard his stress on the word *forbidden,* and my heart ached.

I wrote a very long reply. I told him of my confidence in his talent and my certainty that he would one day be known as a great writer. I reassured him that the trial he was undergoing in New York would strengthen and test him for the grand future for which he was destined. I described a dream I had the night after he left Concord, wherein a great crowd of people sat at his feet waiting for him to speak. I wrote to him of how certain I'd been, upon waking, that it was a sign of his coming greatness, and that he must not abandon that bright promise, but hold it high, like a torch, to light his way. I tried to make my letter inspiring and cheerful, as his letter had been to me.

His answer arrived in the last week of June. It was a cloudy, gray morning, promising rain. As I rocked Edith to sleep in my chamber, I looked out the window where men were baling hay in the fields, hurrying to bring it in before the storm. I saw a woman enter our gate from the direction of town, yet only when she was halfway up the walk did I recognize Cynthia Thoreau. I settled Edith in her cradle and went quickly downstairs, thinking she might have news of Henry.

Mr. Emerson was already at the door. He was in unusually good spirits, for he invited Cynthia inside, though he usually had little toleration for inter-ruptions.

"What brings you to our door?" he inquired, smiling.

Cynthia slipped her hand inside the pocket of her skirt and took out an envelope. "I was at the post office and Mr. Keyes told me that Henry had written Mrs. Emerson." She gave me a long look. "I offered to bring the letter directly."

"How kind of you," Mr. Emerson said.

I took the envelope.

"I'm sure my wife is eager to share it. Come, read it aloud, Lidian." He headed for the parlor. "I'm hungry for word from our brave young Henry."

I stared after him. He could have no idea what might be in the privately addressed letter. Why did he press me to read it when he'd never before indi-cated an interest in letters addressed to me? Was he trying to embarrass me in front of Henry's mother? My lips pressed tightly against each other. Let him hear which what he might—it would only serve justice if Henry expressed anger over his banishment. I sat on the couch and tore open the envelope while Cynthia settled in a rocker by the fire. My husband stood with his arm on the mantel, watching me. I unfolded the letter. My eyes quickly ran down the page and my heart leaped in alarm.

It was a love letter.

I put my hand to my head. "I fear it makes little sense," I said, "except as poetry." It was the wrong thing to say. I knew it as soon as I spoke the words.

"You know how fond I am of poetry," my husband said. "Please read it, Lidian."

And so I read the letter aloud. It was one of the most difficult things I had done in my life. "'My Very Dear Friend,—I have only read a page of your letter, and have come out to the top of the hill at sunset, where I can see the ocean, to prepare to read the rest. It is fitter that it should hear it than the walls of my chamber. The very crickets here seem to chirp around me as they did not before.'"

I stopped and smiled. "A fine image," I said. But Mr. Emerson did not re-turn my smile. Nor did he even look at me. His eyes were focused on the wall above Cynthia's head.

"Keep reading," he said.

I did, though every nerve in my body protested. "'It was very noble in you to write me so trustful an answer. The thought of you will constantly elevate my life; it will be something always above the horizon to behold, as when I look up at the evening star. I think I know your thoughts without seeing you, and as well here as in Concord. You are not at all strange to me.' "

I closed my eyes. The room was ponderous with silence.

"Is that all?" Mr. Emerson asked.

"No," I whispered.

"Then please continue."

I bent my head over the page, as if the words might fly off the paper into the room and be lost forever. " 'I cannot tell you the joy your letter gives me, which will not quite cease till the latest time. Let me accompany your finest thoughts.' "

I paused and looked at my husband. I did not want to read the final words. There seemed no need to wound my husband with Henry's probing wit. "There's nothing more, save that he sends his love to you," I said.

"Does he indeed? And how does he turn that phrase?"

I hesitated, then quickly read the words: " 'I send my love to my other friend and brother, whose nobleness I slowly recognize.' "

Mr. Emerson surprised me by laughing.

I folded the letter and fumbled it back into its envelope. I was aware of Cynthia's gaze on me and forced myself to return it. "I don't deserve such flattery," I said. "He sets me higher than I am."

"Well," Cynthia said crisply, "Henry was always tolerant." She was flushed, and I knew it was not from the walking.

Mr. Emerson rose. "I daresay he's recovered his low spirits." He gave me a blank smile, which in all my married years, I never learned how to read.

The existence and contents of the letter quickly became known throughout Concord. I was sickened by the thought of the gossip's tongues desecrating Henry's words. Mr. Emerson said nothing further about it, perhaps thinking that the wound Cynthia had dealt me was sufficient.

When I wrote again to Henry, I confessed what had happened, and begged him to keep in mind that everyone in Concord was eager for word of him. No letter of his could be considered private. It was many months before I again received such a warm letter from him. Indeed, his correspondence turned immediately cold and distant. I could tell only from certain private and familiar terms that he meant me to understand that his feelings for me had not changed.

I was surprised, but relieved that Mr. Emerson had no private reaction to

Henry's letter other than mild amusement. Except for one curious thing. The night after the letter arrived, my husband, who had not touched me since Edith's birth, asserted his marital rights in a most vigorous and insistent manner.

THE NEXT LETTER from Henry was carefully addressed to Mr. Emerson and contained nothing of a personal nature. In fact, he made no mention of me at all, save in a brief addendum expressing polite concern for my health. His salutation was a simple *Friends*—a plain-enough signal that he'd received my message. And there was an alarming farewell tone in his words, as if he were settling his earthly estate. One section, in particular, struck me: "But know, my friends, that I a good deal hate you all in my most private thoughts, as the substratum of the little love I bear you. Though you are a rare band and do not make half use enough of one another."

I could almost hear the pique in Henry's voice as I read the words. He had many times commented that my husband did not sufficiently appreciate the contributions of my intellect and loyalty. It was like Henry to veil his words in such a way that the reader would find them perplexing and be forced to work at them like a puzzle to extract their meaning. I do not think Mr. Emerson ever understood Henry's intent.

"I sent Henry to New York to further his career," he complained one day. "But he shows next to no ambition. What does he do in his free time? Walk on the beach?"

I listened in silence for I could neither contradict him nor explain. The truth was that Henry was never at ease in New York. In every letter, in every report of him I heard, he made it plain that he wished to return to Concord. How I wished for the freedom to write to him and openly tell him how desperately I missed him! I wanted him to return at once, but knew I couldn't risk the chance that my letter might be discovered by William Emerson or his wife.

IN EARLY NOVEMBER, after a long Sunday morning service, Cynthia Thoreau happily informed me that she was expecting Henry for Thanksgiving. "He'll only stay a few days," she said, her bonnet strings flapping in the cold wind.

"Well, I trust he will pay his respects to us at Bush." It was all I could do to contain my hands within their gloves. "My husband will wish to know how he fares."

"No doubt he'll stop in." Cynthia gave me a cold smile. "He's well aware how much he owes Mr. Emerson—in both currency and kindness. Yet he has other obligations, you know. He's scheduled to lecture at the Lyceum on the ancient poets."

"A lecture! I did not realize." I smiled broadly. "When is it to be? I'll make a point of attending."

"Wednesday the twenty-ninth." Cynthia gave me a slight bow and turned to give her attention to Mary Brooks. But my excitement was too high to be dampened by bad manners.

For the next two weeks I went about the house singing. My daily toil felt effortless, and tending the children no longer wearied me. Mr. Emerson commented on my changed demeanor and though he did not ask its cause, it seemed to light some dormant fire in him, for he again claimed his role of husband in our bed. On the fifteenth, Nancy came back from the market with the news that Henry had returned.

"He came in the coach late last night," she said, as we chopped sausage for a pie. "Flora—she's Mrs. Thoreau's new kitchen girl—Flora says he looks fit enough. Don't sound like the city's harmed him one whit."

The flutter in the pit of my stomach reminded me of a quickening child. I kept my eyes on the bits of pink sausage beneath the blade of my knife.

"Though he complains about it enough," Nancy went on. "So I hear. All he talks about is how dreadful 'tis, Flora says. He calls all those fine city museums 'catacombs of nature.' What do you make of that? Can't see why he went in the first place if he feels that way. Now *I'd* trade places with him in a minute. What I wouldn't give for a chance in a big city like New York."

The early afternoon light was coming in through the southern window, lying in a long sword across the table. I felt something deeply sorrowful in that light. Perhaps it was the effect of the bare trees, or the ivory quality the sunlight had in November—I wasn't certain of its cause. It struck me as odd that I would notice, for it was in such direct contrast to my joy.

I could hardly restrain myself from running to the Thoreau boarding-house that very instant and seeing Henry. When I answered the knock at the east entrance late that afternoon and found him standing there, I began to tremble so violently that I had to grasp the doorframe for support. I croaked his name and stood gazing at him, believing that I'd never looked upon a fairer smile or nobler visage. In truth, he was pale and fatigued, weary from his journey, and harried by his many weeks in the city. Yet my spirits rose so to see him that I overlooked the strain on his face, and drank in the sight of him—to me it was as water to a man dying of thirst.

"Lidian!" He smiled.

"Henry, how are you?"

"Well enough, now that I'm back in Concord. May I come in?"

"Of course!" I flushed. "Come in, come in!" And I backed away from the doorway to allow him entry, though I wanted to draw close against him.

"I brought the tulip tree I promised you from Staten Island." He stepped into the entry and stood looking about. "I just finished planting it in your garden." For a moment I did not comprehend his meaning, but then I recalled his mention of a tree by that name.

"The tulip tree! I'd forgotten!" I said.

A pleasant satisfaction played on his face and I was no longer able to check my joy. I took his hand in mine.

"Thank you! It's so good to welcome you home again! How I've missed you!"

He smiled and I could have drowned in his gray eyes, for they seemed to draw me into their depths almost against my will. His head bent slowly to me as if to inhale the air from my lungs.

Suddenly he straightened and stepped back, withdrawing his hand. I turned to find my husband framed in the doorway to the Red Room. He was looking at Henry, his mouth holding the implacable smile I had come to mistrust.

"Henry!" he said. "How good to see you, my boy! New York has served you well by the look of you!"

This was patently untrue. Henry's color was gone; he hardly seemed the same man. New York had aged him by several years. Yet I did not contradict my husband—nor would he likely have heard me if I had, as he clapped Henry on the shoulder and drew him into the parlor.

There they talked for the rest of the afternoon. I went in and out, offering tea and cake, in the midst of tending my household tasks. I hoped my husband would invite me to sit with them, but his annoyed expression made it all too plain that he regarded each entry as an intrusion. I stood in the hall outside the parlor, my eyes closed, listening as Henry related his New York adventures to my husband. Life there, he said, was superficial and hectic.

"The atmosphere of the apartments—there are no spirits in them and only the echoes of real voices. Even the children cry with less inwardness and depth than in a Concord cottage. William's sons are only average scholars. They cannot hold a candle to their cousin Ellen's brilliance." He announced he did not think he was made to be a tutor, but must find some other occupation that better suited his nature.

I could no longer restrain myself. "The only occupation that truly suits you," I said, stepping boldly into the room, "is poet and philosopher. You are a true observer of nature. Are you not happiest when you're tramping through someone's field or strolling in Walden Woods?"

He did not laugh, as I expected—he didn't even smile. He glanced at me quickly, then looked away.

"Lidian," Mr. Emerson said, "Henry needs peace rather than advice for now."

I left the room without complaint—how well I held my tongue that afternoon!—but not happily. I retired to my chamber and opened my Bible, trying to find some means of mastering my anger, but though I read psalm after psalm, not one offered relief. In fact, their repeated references to persecutions merely reminded me of my situation and increased my rancor. I tried to pray, but my words were hollow shells in my mouth. Finally I rose and paced back and forth in an attempt to subdue my emotions, but it was no use. The injustice of my situation overwhelmed me. My husband had denied me—and apparently meant to continue denying me—what I valued most in the world— conversation with my dearest friend.

In a fury, I dashed off a note. "I need to meet with you alone," I wrote. "I long for your company! I'll go tonight to the low place by the riverbank where we used to take the children to play. Mr. Emerson has claimed your afternoon. Let me claim your evening." When I heard the study door open, I swept downstairs and slipped the note to Henry as he passed on his way out.

That evening, as a pale moon rose over Concord's harvested fields, and a light frost touched the sheaves of corn bundled for winter storage, I complained of a headache and excused myself from the overheated parlor to get some fresh air. Mr. Emerson, who was elaborating his thoughts on the nature of experience to Ellery Channing and Elizabeth Hoar, merely nodded in response to my declaration, and as I wrapped up in my warmest shawl, I reflected that his lack of feeling did much to spare me from a proper guilt.

I glided out the kitchen door and into my garden, where I quickly followed the path down to the river. The thickets and brambles bordering the path caught at my dress and tore my petticoat. Yet I hurried along, for only rapid movement could govern my agitation.

As I approached our rendezvous spot, my fear grew that Henry would not be there, that either his family obligations or his own judgment would keep him from leaving home that night. Then very softly, and at first, almost inaudibly, the notes of a flute were borne to me on the wind.

PERHAPS IT WAS the cover of the darkness, or the soft mystery with which the moon illuminated the familiar landscape, but what occurred that night between Henry and me seemed to take place in a realm not of this world. It was as if I'd stepped across an invisible boundary between earth and heaven into a place where the old laws no longer applied.

As I approached the riverbank, Henry, who'd had been seated on a rock, rose, put away his flute, and extended his hands. In an instinctive and most natural gesture, I clasped them and drew him close.

"I have missed you so!" I whispered. "I could hardly bear it this afternoon—to see you and yet not be able to talk with you!"

"It was the same for me." He put his arms around me, pressing me to him.

A sensation of absolute peace flowed through me. I felt in that moment as if I had finally come home after wandering for years. My head perfectly fitted the hollow of his shoulder and my breasts conformed to the contours of his chest. The scent of dry leaves poured over me. I breathed his name.

"You're shivering!" he said, and indeed, I was trembling lightly but not from cold. He insisted on leading me back up the path and into the barn, where we climbed into the loft and arranged ourselves amid the heaps of warm straw by spreading out one of the horse blankets piled there.

We sat for some time, simply talking, with a deep and abiding joy in each other's presence. Then, as the moon rose higher and disappeared from the small window that overlooked the nest we had made, a kind of darkness overtook us, and we fell into a profound silence.

I do not believe I intended our encounter to lead where it did. Sitting with Henry in the darkness of the barn loft, enfolded in the sweet hay, warmed by the proximity of our bodies, having discovered anew the supreme satisfaction of our conversation, I was chiefly aware that the grief that had overwhelmed me for months was gone. My pleasure—my rising delight—stemmed as much from pure relief as from any animal attraction.

Perhaps it was the same for him. When we leaned close to each other at the same moment, it seemed both wondrous and inevitable. I opened my arms eagerly and moved against him.

He kissed the top of my head; his hand stroked the length of my back and found its way to my neck. I caught my breath; he murmured my name. Then, in a fluid motion that seemed as inevitable as sunrise, he covered me with his body.

For one timeless and inexpressible moment, I was flooded with joy. I felt supremely, astonishingly cherished. I had not imagined that a man's body could elicit such a powerful sensation. For the first time in my life I understood that in sanctioning intimacy between man and woman, God had ordained joy.

It was only later, when we lay side by side in darkness, Henry dozing with his head on my breast, that I woke to the full burden of what I had done.

23

Transgressions

Love is the profoundest of secrets.
—HENRY DAVID THOREAU

I slid my arm from beneath Henry's head and reached for my clothes. I still felt his warmth and weight along the length of my body, as if his skin had left an indelible impression, a memorial to our passion. Yet as soon as I began to rise the pleasure faded—too frail to withstand even the trivial reality of buttoning my bodice and skirts around me. I recognized a third presence beside us there in the hayloft, a presence no more substantial than a word, but as real as a guest I had invited—*adulteress.*

The word spoke over and over in my heart as I gathered my hair, pushed the pins back into it, and tucked it into my cap. The straw that had been beneath our blanket only moments before now stabbed my arms and legs. A wintry wind had invaded the loft during our embrace, a cold that I would normally have welcomed but that now turned my skin hard and coarse. I pulled my shawl around me but its extra weight did not warm me.

Henry lay naked on his back, one leg crooked out and bent at the knee, his arms angled as well, curved upward beside his head. He looked appallingly young.

I closed my eyes and bent my face into the darkness of my hands. Not only had I betrayed my husband, I had corrupted a man who I was certain had lived a life of virtue and chastity until that evening. A man whose soul was purer than any I'd encountered. I had deliberately seduced him—had arranged our meeting, accompanied him into the loft, and leaned into his body as eagerly as a harlot. I had erred wantonly and knowingly and God would not offer pardon to such a sinner.

I covered Henry with one of the heavy horse blankets. I did not know how long he might sleep, but if he were like Mr. Emerson in his intimate habits, he would slumber soundly for some time. I thought it strange that the act of passion so completely exhausted a man. I found myself invigorated, profoundly awake.

I longed to wake Henry, to again press my face into the hollow of his shoulder, to obtain from him the relief of affection, if not absolution. But I swallowed my impulse, knowing that doing so would only compound my guilt. I was solitary in my sin, utterly alone as I'd been the night my mother died.

I relived the confusion I had felt at sixteen when I woke to find sunlight leaking in the curtained windows, my aunts moving quickly about the room, speaking in hushed tones across my mother's still form. I remembered my terrible guilt, my certainty that I'd betrayed her. All because I could not resist the impulse to sleep.

Now impulse had led me into a darker sin. I had dishonored my husband and, like Judas, had broken faith with God as well. And for what? For nothing as tangible as thirty pieces of silver. For passion and the solace of a tender embrace.

Stooping beneath the barn rafters, I made my way to the loft ladder and climbed down. My legs felt shaky and ineffectual, my head feverish. I paused a moment at the bottom to steady myself and listened to the sound of Henry's breathing. Behind me, the horse stamped and blew in his stall, then settled into silence. I turned and ran to the house.

In the east entry I stood for a moment, letting the warm house air enfold and steady me. I pressed my hand to my chest, as if it might still my racing heart. I wished suddenly that I'd wakened Henry and we had talked.

The parlor was dark, but a soft glow came from under the door of the study. I started toward the stairs, then hesitated and put my hand on the door latch, suddenly overwhelmed by a compulsion to confess my sin. Mr. Emerson seemed to sense my presence, or perhaps I rattled the latch, for I heard him speak my name as a question.

I entered the study, and instantly regretted it. He sat at the circular table he favored, regarding me with a kindly smile, his writing papers spread before him. "I have disturbed you," I said, wanting to retreat. "I'm sorry."

"Never mind." He raised one hand to dismiss my apology. "You look unusually well this evening. Why didn't you join our conversation?"

I stood in the doorway, a profound confusion preventing me from proceeding into the room. I couldn't possibly look well. I stood there covered with shame. Was this the absolution I sought? The lamp on the table illuminated the familiar contours of Mr. Emerson's face in golden light, and I felt a rush of affection for him, a sensation I'd not experienced in months. It was a most untimely occurrence, but it drew me across the threshold and to the brink of disclosure.

"You know how the heat of the fire fatigues me and the fresh air revives," I said. My voice sounded surprisingly normal. Where was the repentance I had planned? "I'm glad your conversation was a good one. Is Elizabeth feeling better?" She had been ailing with a slow fever for several days.

"She lacks her usual strength, but fortunately her ailment has not diminished her eloquence." The fondness in Mr. Emerson's voice was always present when he spoke of Elizabeth.

I nodded. "I'm glad she's recovered. When I called on her a few days ago, I suggested she take an hourly infusion of tansy, but I suspect she did not."

"Elizabeth is of an independent mind."

I looked down at the paper where his hand still lay, his pen stylus resting in the open V between his thumb and forefinger. "Isn't it late to be writing a lecture?"

"Indeed." He nodded affably. "But this is a more agreeable task—a letter to Margaret."

"Oh." Her name snuffed out my flicker of tenderness. I wished suddenly—fiercely—that I had not left Henry. "Then I shall leave you to your writing. Please give her my regards." And I turned and swept from the room, feeling the oddest mixture of righteous fury and reprieve.

I climbed the stairs to the nursery, where I looked in on the children and opened the windows to permit the circulation of cold air. I lingered there, gazing out into the blackness, my eyes fixed on the spot where I knew the barn to be. I pictured Henry asleep in the straw, and my mind flooded with a renewed tenderness so sweet it temporarily washed away every drop of guilt.

That night I slept fitfully. Henry came and went through my dreams. In one, he danced with me beneath tall trees while Wallie and Ellen picked flowers at the edge of a long field. I heard the sound of a bell, and when I turned I saw it was not a church bell, but a tarnished silver bell hung on the neck of a cow.

I woke when Mr. Emerson entered the room. I watched him place his candle on the mantel. He stood gazing at it, as if it held some strange fascination. His face held the unreadable smile that he so often wore. I closed my eyes and rolled onto my side away from my husband and back into my dream.

I HOPED and expected to see Henry the next day, for I was certain his need for association after our encounter would be as fierce as my own. I was occupied with preparations for Thanksgiving, only four days away. I rolled out piecrusts for twenty pies, peeled onions and apples, pounded cinnamon sticks and cloves, and crushed an unusually large sugar loaf until my arms ached. I boiled cranberries and squashes, cracked eggs and melted butter, chopped citron and cut slices of candied lemon for a marrow pudding, and all the while my eyes kept stealing to the window, hoping for a glimpse of Henry's familiar form coming across the fields. In the afternoon, a cold wind rose and twisted drifts of dry leaves into the air, spinning them like tops and dropping them suddenly. The clouds darkened and it looked as if it might soon snow. I set Ellen and Edith up at the kitchen table with a small bowl of flour and water and a handful of raisins and they happily tried to imitate me while I worked on steadily. I hoped that the reward for so much housewifely diligence would be a glimpse of Henry. But he did not come.

I no longer entertained the thought of confessing to my husband. That impulse was entirely gone, swept from my mind as thoroughly as my broom swept our gritty floors in preparation for the holiday. My sin was no worse than his—his affection for Margaret was surely only the surface of a greater darkness. At the very least, his ardor canceled mine.

The evening before Thanksgiving I cut branches from the hemlocks on the west side of our house and decorated the fireplace mantels and windowsills. I laid holly branches atop the window casings and arranged a vase of dried leaves and flowers for the table. I still expected Henry to appear at any moment, but Thanksgiving morning came without even a glimpse of him. As usual, we entertained a large number of people. Besides our immediate family, we welcomed George Bancroft, Ellen and Ellery Channing, and the entire Alcott family. Bronson and Abba had come with their children for a brief respite from Fruitlands, their utopian community—an experiment my husband had proclaimed a perpetual picnic. Bronson's four daughters were a boisterous lot, particularly Louisa, of whom I was especially fond. She had recently slipped into my life like an autumn leaf blowing through an open door, so young I did not immediately recognize our kinship. In some ways we were opposites—she dark-complexioned and wild, I ghost-pale and known for my precise manners. Yet our hearts beat at the same furious cadence, and we both chafed at the restrictions of womanhood. Before I was fully aware of it, she had replaced Sophia in my affections, and I was determined to nurture her in every possible way.

The Alcott girls ate with a zeal that betrayed their hunger, and even Abba and Bronson loaded their plates with several helpings of squash pie and applesauce. The dinner conversation centered, as it had so often of late, on the slavery question. Though all present agreed it was an abomination, there were different opinions on what action must be taken. Bronson spoke of the need to transform men's hearts. "Abolition can only be accomplished through constant lecturing and philosophizing."

"If men's hearts could be transformed through speech," Mr. Emerson said, "I doubt we'd require any philosophy."

"Perhaps men ought to look to women for such transformation," I ventured.

Abba Alcott nodded as she helped herself to another slice of green currant pie. "I agree with Lidian. Transformation is a spiritual matter rooted in the influence of women." Her right hand lay exposed on the linen tablecloth and I could not help noticing how blistered it was by cold and hard work.

I felt a sincere compassion for Abba, especially since she'd moved to Fruitlands. The experience, I knew, had been a hard one, especially since the community did not permit themselves the use of any products of slave or animal labor. They regarded it as a form of slavery. Even leather was banned, and they wore only linen slippers, refusing the use of both cotton and wool in their clothing.

I leaned toward Abba to address her privately. "How is the experiment proceeding?" I asked. "Are you well prepared for winter?"

"I daresay we're well-prepared philosophically," she said. "And the girls and I have put by some food, but our crops were very poor and our harvest disappointing."

I murmured my sympathy and glanced again at the girls. They all looked too thin, especially Lizzie, the quiet third daughter. I wondered how much longer the experiment would continue. I knew Abba to be a fierce mother—she would surely leave Fruitlands before she allowed her daughters to starve. Yet I could see that lack of proper nourishment had taken its toll on her as well. I hoped it had not affected her mind. I felt a pang of guilt. I'd often advocated a meager diet for physical and spiritual health, yet it was clear that one could go too far when experimenting with simplicity. I was pondering how best to voice my thoughts on the matter, when the conversation suddenly turned to Henry.

"I saw him walking just this morning," Bronson said, addressing my husband. "He told me you had asked him to introduce the speaker at last week's Lyceum lecture. I regret I wasn't able to attend."

The piece of cheese I'd been swallowing thickened in my throat.

Mr. Emerson wiped his mouth with his napkin. "I was unwell for a few days. My lungs"—he returned the napkin to his lap—"they complain at this time of year."

"Perhaps they long for Italy," Ellery said, evoking a general laughter that I did not join.

"When were you unwell?" I asked.

He turned his imperturbable gaze on me. "The better part of these past two weeks. Hasn't my cough sufficiently annoyed you?" He smiled.

"I wish you'd brought it to my notice," I said. "I purchased some new powders recently. They might have helped."

He shook his head. "I've decided to foreswear homeopathic cures for the present. They don't agree with me as they do you. Usually the mere prospect of ingesting your remedy is ample cure."

There was more laughter, and this time I joined in, though it was at my expense. Yet I planned to remind him later of the many times my poultices and powders had effected a near-miraculous cure on him and our children.

It was a conversation we did not have, for just after twilight that evening, as Mr. Emerson and I sat with the Channings continuing our dinner conversation, Henry walked through the east entrance and into our parlor. He sat on a low stool near the fire, rubbed his hands between his knees to warm them, and looked at everyone in the room but me.

"You're looking exceedingly well, my friend." My husband leaned out of his chair to welcome Henry with a handclasp. "Thanksgiving must have been a hearty feast at the Thoreau home."

"The food was hearty and more than sufficient," Henry said. "But it's the music we play after dinner that sustains me."

"Ah, music! I think we could benefit from some." Mr. Emerson looked at me. "Lidian tells me that it improves the digestion. Is there any chance you've brought your flute with you?"

I knew—and I was certain my husband did as well—that Henry carried his flute everywhere. "I trust you're not weary of playing, Henry? We would all be grateful if you'd offer us a tune," I said.

Since I'd addressed him, Henry could no longer avoid looking at me. When his gaze met mine, I felt an electric charge throughout my limbs.

"You flatter me, ma'am," he said. "I'm a poor player compared to my father." His smile had vanished, leaving a strange expression that seemed to be a mixture of tenderness and grief.

"It's *your* music that we've missed," I said, and immediately perceived a responsive flash in his eyes, a flicker of longing that told me he'd heard the meaning beneath my words. What I did not say—what I wanted to say and what I hoped he heard—was: *There's no music in this house without you.*

Henry bent his head briefly and then drew from his jacket pocket the cloth pouch I'd made for him and took out his flute. He had once told me it was carved of fruitwood, which made its music particularly sweet and fluid. He blew lightly into the end twice, and then placed his fingers with quick precision on the metal stops.

He played my favorite tune—a sweet waltz called "The Garland of Love." I saw the toes of Ellen Channing's right foot lifting the hem of her skirts to the tune, and my own feet itched to join hers. Ellery had closed his eyes and dropped his head back, his face blissful with appreciation.

I recalled that my French dancing master had once—as a reward for my mastery of a particularly difficult dance sequence—played his mandolin to accompany my steps. I had felt my legs and feet grow buoyant as I glided over the floor's worn surface as lightly as an insect skims the water. I twirled past a window and through a spray of sunshine, followed my arms into a deep bend and pointed my toes, then pivoted back into the light.

As I listened to Henry, the longing to dance overcame me so that I nearly rose from my chair. Only Mr. Emerson's cool gaze pinned me to my seat.

Henry finished his song and lowered the flute. As I joined the flutter of applause, my gaze was drawn to his hands. I was entranced by the way he held the flute, as if it were a young animal that required particular tenderness. I recalled those hands upon my skin, the way heat had collected under his fingertips and left loops of fire on my breasts and around my navel.

I became aware again that my husband was watching me. I recalled my aborted determination to confess my sin to him. A dark fire of shame crawled up my neck and into my face. I put my hands to my cheeks, and it was at that moment that Henry also looked at me. The expression in his eyes was a naked mixture of adoration and anguish. I perceived that he'd been as undone by our encounter as I, and that his absence since that evening was caused not by his indifference, but by the conflict in his heart.

It was Mr. Emerson who drew Henry's gaze from me. "I've looked forward to your Lyceum lecture for weeks now," he said. "I'm hoping to detect the changes New York has wrought."

Ellery chuckled and Henry swiveled on his stool to face my husband. "I fear you'll find my city experience has only made me more contentious," he said. "And more fixed in my opinion that Concord is the most agreeable place on earth."

I rose and excused myself to the kitchen, where I took my time fetching the tea. Nancy had been given the evening off, so I was alone in the kitchen, taking the cups from their hooks inside the cupboard, when the door opened. Startled, I spun.

"Can I help you?" Henry said.

"Oh, Henry!" I whispered and then, in shame, turned back to the cups, setting them one by one on the shelf on the shelf beneath the cupboard. Suddenly I hit one with my elbow. It spun into the air and seemed to hang there for a moment, in what could only have been an illusion, before smashing to the floor.

I cried out and knelt at once to pick up the pieces. Instantly, Henry was beside me, scooping the shards into his palm. "No matter," he said, his voice strong and quiet in my ear. "It's only a cup."

"It was my mother's china," I said and burst into tears. I don't know why I wept, for I'd never before felt an attachment to my mother's effects. Yet the broken cup struck me as of immense significance.

"Lidian, don't!" Henry's voice was pleading, urgent. "I can't bear it," he whispered.

He touched my hands, pulled them from my face, and I saw that he'd cut the finger of his right hand. I started to rise to find a towel to bandage his wound, but he pulled me back beside him and would not release me.

"This is my fault," he said in a low voice. "I've betrayed you. And Mr. Emerson." Though his eyes were wild with remorse, he looked directly at me as he spoke. "Yet I can't bring myself to regret what we did."

I stared at him, barely able to speak. "Nor can I," I croaked, finally. "But the blame is mine." My knees no longer held me, and I collapsed against him, sobbing. "Oh, Henry, what will we do? What will happen to us?"

"I don't know." His voice was just shy of a sob. He kissed the top of my head, just in front of my cap. I felt the warmth of his lips against my scalp. I heard the youth in his voice, and the terrible vulnerability of his innocence. I realized at that moment that I had to be the strong one. Much as I longed to seek comfort from him, to depend upon his gentle strength to untangle our situation, I knew that he needed my strength even more.

I raised my head and drew my hand from his. "We'll put it behind us," I said with an assurance I did not feel. "We'll go on just as before. Nothing will change."

I got to my feet, took my handkerchief from my skirt pocket, and dried my tears. He was still kneeling on the floor, staring at me in bewilderment.

I took a clean towel from the basket by the pie safe. "Let me tend your wound," I said. "I can't have you bleeding all over my floor." And I gave him a smile, to encourage one from him.

He rose, holding the broken cup shards. I gestured to the table, and he opened his hands and tipped out the pieces. They lay there shining in the lamplight—a dozen small white daggers.

After I bandaged his hand, we set the tea things on a tray and Henry carried it into the parlor. As I poured out five cups of tea and passed them around, Mr. Emerson inquired—in a tone of both concern and curiosity—about Henry's hand.

"Ah Waldo, I believe it's your fault," Henry said, his eyes sparkling. "Being in your company again has infected me with the notorious Emerson clumsiness. I dropped a cup while taking it from the shelf and complicated the gaucherie by stabbing myself with its remains."

There was a round of laughter and more banter on my husband's renowned ungainliness. I found myself sipping my tea and gazing past Henry into the fire, wondering how either of us could pretend that our tryst had not permanently fissured the landscape of our lives.

I DID NOT SEE Henry again until the evening he lectured at the Lyceum. Mr. Emerson and I sat with the Hoars, the Minotts, and the Channings; together we took up an entire row of seats. The night was cold; there was frost on the church windows. The vestry was well lit and we sat far forward, so I easily detected the strain in Henry's face as he took his place behind the podium. He arranged his papers and looked up at the audience. In that instant, our eyes met. He seemed momentarily to forget himself, then his shoulders gave a little jerk, and he looked down again at his papers.

"I've entitled tonight's discourse 'Ancient Poets,'" he said in a voice that was unnaturally thin. "These great men—Homer, Ossian, and Chaucer—are the first teachers of the poetic form, and any modern poet must examine and heed their practices."

He glanced up at the audience. It was fortunate that he was the only speaker that evening, for I could not wrench my gaze from his face. While he did not have Mr. Emerson's skill in delivery, the words he spoke rang with earnest authority. I sat, mesmerized, by the music of his language. I leaned forward, my back taut as a harp string. His voice did not wash over and soothe me as Mr. Emerson's had when I first heard him lecture, but instead filled me with a fiery excitement that was not unlike the agitation I experienced in conversation with Henry. When the lecture ended, I was the first to applaud.

I wanted to speak with him. I stood and took some time arranging my shawl, hoping the group of men and women surrounding Henry would quickly adjourn. I caught a brief glimpse of his head between the shoulders of two men. He was turned in profile to me, listening intently to a woman's question. I was struck by his resemblance to Mr. Emerson. It was not the first time I'd noted this likeness, but it had never before disturbed me. Now I felt oddly deceived, as if he had in some manner disguised himself.

"Come, Lidian," Mr. Emerson said, taking my elbow. "The hour grows late."

I looked at him in surprise. "I thought you'd want to congratulate Henry on his performance." I said.

"I'll speak with him tomorrow. Tonight is Concord's chance." He smiled and, with a small movement of his hand, turned me toward the door and swept me cleanly from the room.

Henry returned to New York early the next morning. His coach must have rumbled past my chamber window while I slept, for I did not wake until the sun was high in the sky and the children had long since tumbled cheerfully from their beds.

A strange lassitude overcame me that day, a deep fatigue that rest or sleep did not alleviate, and that continued unabated for many days. By the time three weeks had passed, I knew the reason.

I had embarked on my fourth pregnancy.

24

Quandaries

In love and friendship the imagination is as much
exercised as the heart.
　　　　　　　　—HENRY DAVID THOREAU

I had not imagined I would bear another child after Edith.
Not only had I passed the age of forty, but relations with
my husband had cooled so that it seemed most unlikely. Yet the signs were
unmistakable—my breasts were sore and heavy; I was dyspeptic and weak
with lethargy. And I had missed my regular menses.

Still, for several weeks I tried to convince myself that my symptoms were
due to illness. I felt tired all the time and so depleted that I thought only of
my craving for sleep. Then one night I dreamed that I was walking by the
river and met Henry carrying a basket. I stooped to look into the basket and
saw a sleeping babe. I awoke in a wash of perspiration. Gray light formed a
spiral on the ceiling. I stared at it, overwhelmed by a drowning sensation that
began in my chest and fell rapidly through my torso. I was not sick at all.
I was expecting a child—a child that might be Henry's.

I placed my hand on my stomach, as if it could warm the sudden chill that settled there. I had foolishly never considered the possibility that my sin-gle tryst with Henry might bear such fruit. My shame warred with my feel-ings of protection and love for the unborn child. I thought of the way my niece, Sophia, had dealt with her condition, and wondered—briefly—if I should do the same. I rejected the repulsive thought.

TWO WEEKS AFTER Henry's Lyceum lecture my husband informed me that Henry was returning to Concord. It was a cold December morning, just past ten o'clock, and I'd been driven from the kitchen to the parlor couch by the odor of roasting ham, which sickened me and made my head spin, as did all food odors before early afternoon.

"He's on his way back from New York this very day." Mr. Emerson dropped into his rocking chair by the fire, and began to rock back and forth. The sight, combined with the spinning, increased my nausea to such a degree that I was forced to close my eyes.

"He's returning? Now?" I fought off the whirling sensation and opened my eyes. "Is he unwell?"

"Somewhat." He gave me his smile. "But I believe he'll recover quickly once he's living again in Concord."

I felt a bubble of joy. "I'll ready his chamber tomorrow."

"There's no need. He plans to live with his parents." There was a darkness in his tone, a warning that I ought to have heeded. But the room had begun to spin again, and it was all I could do to remain upright.

"This is a better place for him to write," I said. "And we're always in need of his repair skills."

"There are other considerations than his convenience and our comfort." He began to rock more vigorously. "In any case, it is not your concern." His eyes had turned flinty. "Right now I must return to my labors." He rose. "I'm sorry you're feeling unwell again, Lidian."

I had not yet told him I was with child. "I believe I will soon mend." I said.

He had already turned his back and walked away.

The time would come when I would have to tell him. I wondered what I would say—and how he would accept the news. Would he be pleased at the prospect of being a father again? Would he bless me with his smile the way he had when I told him the first time I had conceived?

Within a few weeks this new pregnancy would be obvious; the child would announce itself to the world if I did not. I had to tell my husband before people started gossiping. There were women in Concord who watched me—watched everyone—with savage scrutiny.

First, I would tell Lucy. That would be easy—she'd be happy for me, gracious and sisterly. She would see the new child as a blessing, a means of healing my grief. And perhaps her own. She would buoy me up and give me the strength to tell Mr. Emerson.

And then—somehow—I would find a way to tell Henry.

EARLY THAT JANUARY, Bronson Alcott and his family abandoned Fruitlands and returned to Concord. Matthew Lovejoy kindly offered them lodging in his big farmhouse east of town. Rumor had it that Abba had threatened to leave him, for the children were on the verge of starvation and she was exhausted from shouldering all of the domestic labor for the group.

I was gratified to have Bronson back in Concord, for he was one of my few admirers. I compared his mind to a magic carpet on which he carried all his friends, though his theories often led him to more exotic thoughts than I could endorse. Yet when he left Fruitlands, he was uncommonly despondent. When I learned that he had taken to his bed and lay there day after day refusing to accept food, I hurried to call on him, bringing with me a loaf of bread and a crock of hearty soup to nourish the girls. His daughter, Louisa, met me at the door and informed me that her mother was out.

I kissed her and inquired after the health of her sisters. They were all quite well, she told me, as she led me upstairs to the chamber where her father lay. It was clear from her expression and the lightness in her step that she was overjoyed to be back in Concord.

Bronson lay prone on the bed, covered by a thick layer of quilts. He was a tall man, even taller than Mr. Emerson, and the bed did not fit him well. It made for a comic effect, as his feet created a small tent on the footboard of the bed.

"Lidian," he said, pushing himself to a sitting position. "Welcome. I thought never to see you again." He was silent a moment and then said, "Our endeavor failed."

"It does not matter." I found a wooden chair in the corner of the room and dragged it close to the bed. "You did the best that you could."

He sighed. "I think we would not have failed had Henry joined us. I nearly had him convinced on one occasion." I had not heard this news, nor was I certain I believed it. Bronson made a habit of jumping to unwarranted conclusions.

"Henry's just returned from New York," I said. "No doubt he would have preferred many places to the noisy streets of that city." Bronson's long head, graced with its abundant fair hair, lay weakly against the wall. "What will you do now, my friend?"

He was silent a moment. "I'd thought your husband might make some financial arrangement. . . ."

"Arrangement?"

"I've spoken with him about the possibility of purchasing a house for us, a place where we might live free of rent and landlords." He smiled yet again, that benevolent, blessing smile, the smile of a saint. "He seemed amenable."

"Did he promise you this?"

"Not yet, but I have hopes. He's been generous in the past."

My back tightened in a spasm of resentment. Mr. Emerson was ever chafing at me for my lavish spending habits. Though I admired my husband's generosity, I did not understand how he imagined that we might support not only our own growing family but Bronson's larger one as well. Yet I knew he felt beholden to Bronson for his many profound insights, which had deeply influenced Mr. Emerson's own philosophy. He believed Bronson Alcott to be the most philosophical man in New England.

I became slowly aware that Louisa had been standing for some time in the doorway, her dark eyes taking in the scene.

"Well," I said quickly, smoothing my skirts and rising, "I have other errands. I'm glad to see you looking better than I'd imagined. I hope you will soon be up and about."

"No doubt I will," he said. "With the good care of neighbors like you I'll be philosophizing again in no time."

I turned to Louisa. "Give my best to your mother," I told her. "And come and visit us. Mr. Emerson has an entire library of books for you to read."

A light leaped into Louisa's face and she bounced on her toes. "I'll come this very afternoon!" she cried.

"You are welcome anytime," I said. And I could not resist placing my hand briefly beneath her chin, in the same reassuring gesture my aunts had used when I was a young girl.

BY FEBRUARY I had to loosen my skirt waists and move the buttons on my bodices. I knew I could no longer keep my condition from Lucy and so, one snowy afternoon while the children napped, I picked my way across Lexington Road to my sister's house.

She greeted me at her back door, her hands dusty with flour and her apron speckled with oil spots. The kitchen was permeated with the sweet, heavy odor of frying doughnuts, which instantly took me back to my childhood and the time when our mother had taught me how to roll the sticky dough into circles and lower it carefully into the black iron kettle filled with simmering fat. I recalled watching the circle of dough fall and hang suspended amid the translucent bubbles, then bounce suddenly to the surface.

"What's the occasion?" I asked, gesturing to the stove. I knew that Lucy rarely spent a penny except for necessities. "You appear to be planning a celebration."

She shrugged. "February's a hard month. It wants festivity. Help yourself." She pointed to the row of cooling doughnuts on the table, scrutinizing me as if she had not seen me in weeks, though we'd spent the afternoon together only three days before. "You look uncommonly well, Liddy. I believe you're putting on some weight."

"That's what I've come to tell you," I said, seating myself on one of the chairs and picking up a doughnut. The outside was crusted a deep brown. I took a small bite. It was still warm and the spicy sweetness filled my mouth.

"That you're gaining weight?" Lucy peered into the kettle. "I agree, it's an occasion. Everyone who loves you has been after you for years to put some meat on your bones." She glanced over her shoulder at me. "You've always been much too thin, Liddy."

"Not the weight itself," I said. "But the reason for it."

"Reason?" Lucy straightened and placed her hands on the back of her hips, stretching tall to her ease her back. "No!" She stopped abruptly in midstretch. "You're jesting. Surely, you're jesting."

I put down the doughnut and placed my hand on my abdomen. "It's not a jesting matter," I said.

"Oh, Liddy!" Her hands fell to her sides. "Are you glad, then? How long have you known?"

"I've suspected since before the start of the new year."

Lucy crossed the room and sank heavily into the chair beside mine. "So the child will come in summer?"

"In August," I said, though the truth was I did not know. "I haven't told Mr. Emerson yet."

Lucy smiled. "I'm surprised he hasn't noticed. He'll be pleased, I'm sure."

"Pleased?" I felt oddly sleepy.

"Perhaps another son?" Lucy leaned toward me and took my hands from her lap. "You look so well, I never would have thought—"

"This child is unlike the others," I said. "There's a calmness—a completeness—about it I didn't feel before. Not even with Wallie."

"The child will be a blessing. A healing," Lucy said softly, looking into my eyes, forcing me to acknowledge her words. "I'm sure of it."

I found myself on the verge of tears—though a common condition in many pregnant women, it was rare for me—and I squeezed Lucy's hands tightly. My tongue was unable to formulate any words, but my heart filled with a resounding *Yes!*

The next afternoon, determined to tell Mr. Emerson of my condition, I found him in the dining room, fretting about the upcoming edition of *The Dial.* He had all the pages spread out on the table where he was shifting them from place to place, determining the best position for each article.

"This will likely be our final edition," he told me, moving a poem to the far end of the table. "It was all too short a venture."

"Final edition? What do you mean?" I knew how dearly he prized the magazine. It had become for him a community in print. And it had the added appeal of linking him to Margaret Fuller in a way that was both seductive and gratifying.

"I mean we no longer have sufficient funds to carry on. Our sponsors are limited in means, and so it follows that we shall be, too."

"I had no idea. I thought you and Margaret—"

"We've decided the time has come to furl the sails of our literary ship." He frowned down at a page that was densely covered in writing, picked it up, scrutinized the words, then set it back where it had been.

If *The Dial* were a ship, it was one they had launched eagerly from the harbor of their affectionate alliance. I wondered what Margaret would do

with her time without the magazine to fume about. Would the friendship between her and my husband continue, though they now had less occasion to
write? Or would lack of occasion make no difference? I suspected that their
association had less to do with the magazine than Mr. Emerson believed.

I wondered suddenly—did a secret part of me wish them intimate, imagining that it would justify my intimacy with Henry?

I watched my husband move to the far side of the table, pick up three papers and place them in the table's center. "I abhor dragging you from your
work, but I have something I must tell you," I said.

He took another sheet and regarded me over the top of it. "The servants
again?" I saw that he was not focusing on me but through me, as if I were so
transparent he could study the painting on the wall behind my head. "Has
Nancy been insolent?"

"It's not the servants."

"Good." He frowned at the paper.

I no longer recalled the words I had planned for my announcement. I
fumbled with my pocket, which was empty, though I was certain I'd tucked
a thimble in it just an hour before. "It's about me. Us."

He picked up another sheet and held the two side by side. "I wish Thomas
had limited his remarks to the three pages I asked."

"Mr. Emerson," I said, "kindly put those papers down and listen to me."

He looked startled and lowered the pages. "Tell me quickly," he said. "I
have a great deal to do."

I took a deep breath. "It seems I am again with child."

"With child?" I saw not merely surprise but anger in his cold gaze.

"I know it is unexpected—"

He rounded the table and came toward me. "You're carrying my child?"

"Of course it's your child." The words dropped from my mouth like coins
from a torn pocket. I realized, as soon as I spoke that I'd misapprehended
him. He'd not stressed the word *my*, but was only trying to grasp the import
of my announcement. He searched my face, as if he might discover there the
key to my reaction. I told myself that I *had* spoken the truth as I knew and
believed it. As I *wanted* it to be.

"Well," he said finally, "I shall welcome this one as I have the others."

Which meant what exactly? Despite his warm affection for our daughters,
he'd not spent much time with them since Wallie's death. He dandled them
briefly after dinner, but within a few minutes was always impatient to set out

on his daily walk. Where Wallie had been permitted unhindered entrance to his father's study, the girls were allowed inside only if the door had been left ajar. I wondered if that would change if the new baby were a boy.

"The child will be born this summer," I said. "Perhaps you could keep your lecture schedule clear for a few months. So that you will not miss this birth as you did the last."

He sighed and returned to the other side of the table. "Unfortunately, several dates have already been set, and we're hardly in a financial position to forego the income. Especially with a new child coming." He studied my waist, as if trying to determine the character of the infant beneath the layers of cloth and skin.

"Then I will pray to deliver this child on one of those rare days when you are at home." I took a step backward, edging away from the dining table and its glut of papers.

He braced his hand on the table. "Bitterness does not become you, Lidian," he said quietly, and returned to his work.

He was right. Bitterness did not benefit anyone, neither its object nor its carrier. Yet I did not take criticism easily, even when it was well-intentioned, and I did not believe that Mr. Emerson's was. I watched him shuffle his papers and thought again of the confession I had never made, the revelation of my encounter with Henry. How close I'd come to telling what had happened! And how abruptly my resolve had vanished in the face of the reminder of his relationship with Margaret! Since that evening, I had not once considered divulging the truth. It had remained buried in me like a boulder in a field, to be unearthed only by some future tilling—a tilling that I now believed would surely break the plow.

I did not tell Henry of my condition. I did not have to, for within a few weeks the town gossip reached his ears. He came to me one afternoon while the children were napping and I was reading in the parlor after a morning of baking.

He did not sit near me as was his habit, but took a seat across the room beside the window. For several moments he did not speak, but fumbled with his jacket cuff, which I could see needed mending. "I've heard you are soon to be the mother of another child," he said finally. "I wanted to know—to ask—" He faltered, stopped, cast a pleading look in my direction as if I might help him, but I said nothing except to confirm the news with a nod.

"I've been wondering—" Again he stopped and his right hand rose to pull briefly at his ear. "Considering what happened—the events—" He heaved a great sigh. "I cannot help but wonder"—and here his voice dropped to a whisper—"if the child is mine."

I closed my book and set it carefully on the table next to me. "The child is Mr. Emerson's," I said. "I'm certain of it."

His relief was palpable. The burden rose from his shoulders, a smile flooded his face and eyes—and I felt a responsive pleasure in having bestowed this gift. Yet I also detected a flicker of mute disappointment that flashed across his pupils as briefly as a falling star—a sorrow I did not wish to consider at that moment. The lie of my certainty was so easily given, so readily received, it seemed to have a weight of its own. And because it sprang from love, it seemed to me to be true. Truth, I suddenly realized, was more malleable than I had imagined. At times the truth of love could have such gravity that it made the truth of mere fact weigh almost nothing.

25

Peculiarities

Everything in the Universe goes by indirection.
There are no straight lines.
                          —RALPH WALDO EMERSON

From the moment I assured Henry that Mr. Emerson was the father of my unborn child, I endeavored to believe it. It became a kind of creed for me, a warranty of virtue. I rose each morning and fastened myself into my determination as routinely as I bound my hair with combs and pins beneath my cap. I reminded myself that a single encounter in a chilly hayloft was unlikely to beget a babe, especially for a woman my age. The child was almost certainly my husband's. I recalled the many weeks it had taken to conceive Wallie—all the nights I had submitted to Mr. Emerson's intimate touches and long, damp shudders as he lay upon me, with no fertile result. Children did not generate instantly in my womb—they had to be coaxed into life. If I believed with sufficient resolution, it would be true.

I greeted Mr. Emerson with a cheerful smile no matter his mood, and refrained from complaining of the dyspepsia of pregnancy. On those occasions when he asked after my condition, I assured him that his child was growing well.

Yet I was unable to dismiss the possibility that Henry might be the father. And our ongoing association did nothing to eliminate the thought. Henry frequented Bush daily and often took meals with us. He was forever borrowing books from Mr. Emerson's library. There were many afternoons when I looked into Mr. Emerson's study to find Henry standing before the wall of books, his head bent over a volume. Once, something in the innocent cast of his face moved me so deeply that I stepped into the room and spoke his name. He closed the book, as if I'd startled him in some nefarious act, and his eyes slid away from me in a manner that was almost shy. I felt a wave of tenderness that was both protective and passionate and reached to clasp his hand. He flinched as if burned. I recalled how he'd commented, that night when he held me in the hayloft, on the unusual heat of my skin. He insisted that he always knew by touching a latch whether or not I had recently opened a door. It was something I'd not been aware of until he told me. Neither my husband nor Lucy had mentioned such a phenomenon, but Henry's senses were keener than others. Perhaps he alone could detect my strange heat.

He took a step back and gave me an apologetic smile. "You startled me," he said, but his voice was strained.

"I'm sorry." I turned and left the study, and it seemed to me that I left an awkward silence in my wake that was amplified by the hiss of my slippers on the carpet. A few moments later, from the sanctuary of the parlor couch, I heard Henry quietly open the front door and go out.

On certain other occasions a similar tension rose between us, when the air became unexpectedly charged. But mostly Henry came and went as before, making repairs, displaying his woodland treasures, engaging Mr. Emerson in long discussions of poetry and philosophy, and taking the children for afternoon rambles through the fields.

The one change so conspicuous that even Mr. Emerson noticed was that both Henry and I avoided the barn. I stopped collecting the eggs, but set Nancy to that task. Henry no longer carried broken tables and chairs to the barn, but repaired them in the yard or in the storage room above the parlor. When, over a dinner of beef and biscuits one February afternoon, Mr. Emerson remarked that I no longer appeared to derive pleasure from my chickens, I replied that their location was inconvenient. "A small chicken house near the back door would be much better." I cut a slice of beef so thin it slipped between the tines of my fork. I did not look at Mr. Emerson nor at Henry, who was sitting to my left. "A low structure like Sarah Bartlett's that will not dissipate the heat. It takes the comfort of the hens into account, and she assured me they reward her by laying eggs of a remarkable size and quality."

Mr. Emerson chuckled. "I fear you have more concern for your hens' comfort than for your husband's time. What lecture do you propose I cancel so that I might build this fine chicken palace?"

"The hens' comfort provides your own, Mr. Emerson," I snapped. "Or would you wish to serve our guests flat cake and eggless puddings from now on?"

"I'll build it, Waldo." Henry reached across the table for a platter and took a third biscuit. "It's a simple enough task for me, and the world ought not to be deprived of your wisdom on a flock of hens' account."

Mr. Emerson and I looked to perceive if he spoke in jest. But he was busy buttering his biscuit and the telltale prankster glint was missing from his eyes.

"Thank you, my friend," Mr. Emerson said, putting down his fork. "I believe you have rescued my marriage once again."

Within the week Henry had constructed a fine shed for the chickens by the kitchen door—three feet high and ten feet long, with tiny windows and an ingeniously contrived roof that folded back on its hinges for ease in collecting the eggs. Mother Emerson—usually the last to applaud Henry's efforts—praised its advantages. The hens took to their new quarters immediately, as if grateful to be free of the cavernous barn.

The barn, of course, still loomed behind the house, casting its shadow over my garden. And over me, for each time I ventured outside I could not prevent my gaze from flying up like a swallow to the window that provided the hayloft with its only light. By the end of February I could bear it no longer. At breakfast I begged Mr. Emerson to walk outside with me a moment before closing himself in his study.

"Is this some new health practice?" he asked as he followed me out the east entrance. "Are cold baths no longer sufficient?"

"It's the barn," I said, indicating its large shadow. "Look how it blocks the light. I want to tear it down and build another over there." I pointed to the far end of the yard.

Mr. Emerson straightened from inspecting the twigs on a lilac bush and, clasping his hands behind him, frowned at me. "Surely you know we cannot afford such a project, Lidian. Just a few weeks ago you acquired a new chicken house and yesterday you informed me we need a new parlor carpet. Now you desire a new barn? It would be easier to move the garden." He turned to look about him. "Besides, I thought when you laid out the garden you took the barn's shadow into account."

I could not deny this, and in other circumstances I would have relinquished the contest, yet in this case I was desperate to change his mind. "Since you are so concerned with economy, Mr. Emerson, I would think you'd at least consider what an unfortunate waste of space the loft represents. There's nothing but moldering straw up there."

"What do you suggest?"

I remembered the Wheelers' upstairs hall in Plymouth, where I had spent so many festive evenings. "It could be made into an excellent dance hall."

"A dance hall!" Mr. Emerson's lips creased with distaste. "I cannot dance a step as you well know. What would I want with a dance hall?"

"There's the pleasure of our guests to consider," I said, aware of the sharpness in my voice, but unable to bridle it. "Not everyone likes to spend all their waking hours in conversation."

"Our guests come from great distances to participate in our conversations. There are dance halls all over New England, if that's the wisdom they seek."

I took a moment to subdue my temper before I replied. "Surely you can't deny that the loft could be put to better use than it is now."

He shrugged, but I sensed he was considering my words. He walked away from me, then turned at the bottom of the garden, and came back. "Perhaps a meeting hall or a schoolroom." He looked at the barn. "We could engage a teacher for the girls and invite other children to join them." He faced me again, nodding. "I rather like that. It would give them an opportunity to study the classics, learn Latin and Greek."

"It's a fine idea."

"Fine?" He smiled. "You surrender your dance hall so easily?"

"It's not an unmerited surrender. Your idea was the better one."

He raised his eyebrows. "Then there will be no more argument from you? No suggestions for improvement?"

I raised my chin. "An argument is only necessary when you think wrongly, Mr. Emerson."

And he laughed, as I had known he would.

———

THOUGH I FELT a keen relief in knowing that the hayloft would be transformed, I also experienced an unexpected sadness. Was there a part of me that wanted to sustain—or even repeat—my sin? I prayed earnestly that God would cleanse me. But my prayers were not answered. They seemed to fall like flecks of chimney soot, crusting on the blackened grate, defiling the hearth of my soul.

Soon after our discussion in the garden, my husband asked Henry to undertake the renovation of the hayloft, but Henry demurred, claiming engagement in his father's pencil-making business. So two carpenters from town were hired and for a month the sound of hammerblows accompanied the birdsong from the trees. At the end of four weeks, Mr. Emerson insisted that I inspect the room. "A preventative," he said. "So you'll have no cause to quarrel with the work when it's done."

I was more than four months gone in my pregnancy, and not eager to climb the narrow stairs built against the barn's west wall, but one Sunday afternoon I complied with my husband's wish. I climbed the stairs slowly, my heart racing, not because of the effort but because of the trepidation I felt. At the top, I steadied myself by clasping a beam and waited for a wave of vertigo to pass.

The straw had all been cleared away and new floorboards laid. A small stove stood against the east wall. The beams and lath were still exposed, for the walls and ceiling had not yet been plastered. The lath made light crosses of wood against the outer wall. My gaze moved slowly, almost reluctantly, to the circular window. Beneath it, in the spot where I had lain with Henry, stood a small wooden chest. I stared at it in horror, for it resembled a child's coffin. I stood frozen, my hands pressed to my belly where my unborn child waited in darkness.

All the rest of that day I was filled with a nervous unease. The vision of the child's coffin was a terrible omen, and I feared not even prayer would safeguard my coming babe. Instinctively, I sought comfort from my husband, and when I heard his buggy pull into the yard that evening, I went to the door to wait for him while he bedded the horse. The clouds of the day had drifted away late in the afternoon, and the sky was clear. A full moon had risen and no doubt it reflected off my white nightgown, presenting a ghostly image. As Mr. Emerson came out of the barn, he stopped in midstride and stared at me, his arms loose at his sides.

"Lidian?" I heard the worry in his tone, but it did not occur to me that I'd alarmed him until he began to run. He had a trundling gait when he ran, a way of throwing his arms from side to side as his legs moved forward, resulting in an appearance of recklessness, a clumsy disregard for his own safety.

"Are the children ill? Is Mother unwell?" He stood below me on the bottom step. "Has something happened to Elizabeth?"

I shook my head. "No, everyone's fine. We're all quite well."

"Thank goodness! You frightened me. You look"—he stopped, and rubbed his chin with his fingers—"Your appearance—something in your posture— reminded me of the day Charles died. When I came back from that lecture in Salem, you were waiting at the gate with Mother's note."

He looked at my hands, and my eyes followed his, as if we both expected to find a letter clutched in my fingers. "No," I murmured. "It's nothing like that."

He came up the steps and stepped past me into the entry. "What is it then? Something's amiss or you would not greet me this way." He took off his hat and hung it on its peg.

"You can't believe it's from concern for you?"

"I'd first require a reason for the change." He smiled—not at me, but at the doorway to the dining room, as if some appreciative audience crowded the darkness there.

His words stung and the impulse to confess my fears vanished in that instant. He watched me a moment, as if waiting for a response, but when I volunteered nothing, he moved past me and started up the stairs. "It's late. I must go to bed."

The small lamp on the table against the wall cast a flickering, yellow light on the ceiling and banister. It made my husband's face appear sickly and drawn. The creases at the corners of his mouth looked lined in charcoal.

He'd started up the stairs but he stopped on the third step and turned. "Are you coming, *wife*?" He emphasized the last word, as if leaning on it, and I felt a dark, watery swirl of guilt twist behind my forehead and with it came a vision of Henry lying naked on moonlit straw. I squeezed my eyes shut to erase the picture. Would I never be free of that image?

My husband resumed his climb—his tread on the stairs was heavier than usual, as if he bore a terrible weight. I opened my eyes and looked up. His back and shoulders sagged wearily; I saw the deep fatigue in his slow ascent.

A wave of pity bowed my head. The sad compromises of our marriage, I realized, had cost him as dearly as they had me. I took the lamp and followed him up the narrow stairs to our chamber.

MORE AND MORE my fear was that the child in me would be stillborn or delivered sickly and fail to thrive. Or worse still—be born a monster. I'd heard of infants whose limbs were twisted into useless shapes or whose lips were so deformed that they could not suck.

Lucy reminded me that I'd tormented myself over these things before. All women did. It was as natural as birth itself. The child would be fine, she assured me. In fact, my excessive anxiety presented the greatest danger to the babe's well-being. She added sternly that I ought to look to my nourishment— she'd noticed that I'd been eating poorly again, and it would not do. I must eat for the child's sake if not my own.

Mr. Emerson chided me as well. Though I tried, I could not conceal my worries from him. I fretted, moving about the house in a frenzy of activity that I hoped would distract me from all memory.

"You must stop this!" he said, as I passed him once in the hallway. He grasped my shoulders and pressed me firmly into a chair in his study. "Your imagination is too active, Lidian. You must seek to control its excesses."

Only I knew that my fears were not excessive. I could not convince Lucy or my husband of their merit, for they knew nothing of the guilty reason for my dread.

And what of Henry? Did he perceive the demon that possessed me that spring as I swelled like a ripening pumpkin? Did he observe me with his uncommon scrutiny and guess my foreboding?

If so, he didn't make his thoughts known to me. That spring he seemed infected by a particularly cheerful spirit and filled his conversation with plans for mountain travels.

"I'm going on a walking trip through the Catskills," he announced one April afternoon when he stopped by to return a book of Mr. Emerson's. "Ellery Channing will be my companion."

"Ellery!" I grimaced. I'd not liked the man from the first and Henry knew it. "Why not Edward Hoar or one of your more amiable friends?"

"More amiable than Ellery?" His gray eyes glinted merrily. "Surely you know I don't choose my friends for their amiability. Else how would I have chosen you?" And he surprised me by leaning close—his face moving so near mine I could smell his breath. I had only to incline my head slightly toward him and our lips would meet. I felt faint. I reached out to steady myself and his arm went around me instantly. I gratefully leaned against him as he guided me into the Red Room, where he settled me on the long sofa there.

"You're ill!" He squatted before me like a boy, and the sight of his earnest and innocent face was yet another forceful reminder of his youth.

"No. No, it's my condition. A momentary faintness." I gestured for him to rise. Prayed that he would rise, for I did not think I could bear the combination of his posture and proximity. I longed to tell him everything—all the thoughts and feelings that had passed through me during the past five months. At the very least I yearned to confess that I'd lied to him—that I did not truly know if the child I carried was my husband's. The urge was so powerful I had to press my hand to my lips to keep from speaking.

Henry continued to study me for some time.

"I'm fine now," I said, unnerved by his scrutiny. Apparently this satisfied his concern, for he rose and resumed telling me of his trip plans. I tried to attend to his words, but my sensibility seemed perversely determined to focus on his body—on the particular slope of his left shoulder and the arc of his arm through the air as he described the Catskill Mountains, at the small cleft in his chin, and the way his neck rose so eagerly from his collar, as if it longed to escape its starched confines. Oh, I was depraved! I could no more guide myself back to virtue and self-discipline than I could have climbed the highest peak in the Catskills.

I absorbed very little of what Henry told me that day. I recall an unfamiliar relief when he finally returned Mr. Emerson's book to its shelf and left. I went immediately to my chamber, where I fell on my knees and prayed for God's forgiveness. I begged Him to show me what I must do to be healed of my desire. I knew if I could not curb it I would sin again.

26

Complications

> The intercourse of the sexes, I have dreamed, is incredibly beautiful, too fair to be remembered.
>
> —HENRY DAVID THOREAU

It was an unusually dry spring, for the snow had melted early and the long rainy days that were so typical of April never manifested themselves. Instead we had day after day of clear skies and bright sun. The trees budded early and the roadside ditches filled with cowslip and dogbane. Mayflowers and bunchberries crowded the woods. Yet the stream at the bottom of the garden was narrow enough to step across, and the shores of the rivers and ponds widened daily. Ryegrass lay stunted and brown in the fields and the sweet spring soon dried up. I began to worry that our well might run dry and no longer insisted that the entire family take a cold bath each morning. Mr. Emerson expressed a jovial satisfaction at this change in routine, for he'd complained from the first at the shock of cold water on his person. Yet he surprised me by resuming the custom later that summer. It was my first indication that, despite his protestations, he actually prided himself on practicing some of the healthful habits I introduced.

April ended as dry as August. In the middle of the afternoon on the last day of that month, young Louisa Alcott burst into our kitchen and announced in a wild voice that a fire raged in the woods south of town.

It was laundry day and Elizabeth Hoar had taken the children for the afternoon so that I might scrub the stains out of their dresses unimpeded. I was grateful for the opportunity to unbend from the washtub, wipe my hands on my apron, and massage the ache in the small of my back.

"A fire?" I said. "I didn't hear the bell." It was the custom in Concord when a fire was discovered for a general alarm to be raised by the strident ringing of church bells. At that signal, all able-bodied men filled their fire buckets and hurried at once to the scene. Mr. Emerson's two leather buckets hung ready beneath the stairwell in the east entrance.

I saw that Louisa was trembling. "Where's Mr. Emerson? Marmee bade me come and tell him." She stood with both hands on her small bosom, her words punctuated with hiccups of panic.

"At the town meeting. Surely your father's there, too."

She shook her head. "He went to visit the Shakers today."

At that moment, the alarm began to ring—first the low, solemn First Parish bell, then the livelier one of the Trinitarian Church. Louisa ran outside and I followed.

"There!" Louisa pointed to a low ridge of trees beyond the poorhouse. I had to squint to detect the braid of gray smoke unraveling on the horizon.

The sound of hooves made me turn to see Edmund Hosmer bearing down on us with his big plow horse and wagon. The wagon bed was filled with water buckets and three of his sons. One of them waved happily, but Edmund, who sat on the high wagon seat, set his face grimly on the road ahead, barely nodding as he passed.

"Oh, if *only* I were a boy and could go!" Louisa ran a few steps after the wagon. The yearning in her narrow shoulders was plain. The sight made me recall the crisp autumn day in 1828 when my brother left for Paris to study medicine—how I'd longed to accompany him! I stood on the wharf for more than an hour, watching the cold wind fill the ship's huge sails and drive it slowly out of Plymouth Harbor. Despite Lucy's earnest pleas that I would catch my death, I'd not moved until the last sail disappeared from sight. I'd thought then—and since—how well the sea represented the great chasm between the lives of men and women. No matter how many books I read, no matter how fiercely I debated the newest philosophies, I could never become a doctor or a lawyer. My sex was more constricting than any corset.

I looked at the barn, at the wide, dark door below the schoolroom window. It had been left open to allow the horse and cow stalls to freshen in the spring air. "Louisa," I said. "I'm going to hitch up Mr. Emerson's buggy and ride out to Fair Haven and observe the situation myself. Would you like to come?"

She spun and stared up at me. Though she said nothing, her eyes grew round and wide.

"It would be a sort of adventure," I said. "Just the two of us. The kind of thing I used to do when I was your age. One night I took my papa's mare for a long ride on the beach. There was a full moon out and I could see everything so clearly. I must have been thirteen or fourteen. I didn't bridle her. I can't abide the practice." For a moment, I felt again the salt wind in my face and my loosened hair streaming out behind me as I raced along the beach. The mare's great hooves thudding beneath me, the suck and hiss of the tide, and the moon rising like a silver plate above the water—it all came back to me in a wash of memory.

"You?" Louisa took two sharp breaths, and a pucker appeared in her right cheek. "I can't picture you galloping about on an unbridled horse." But the pucker had deepened to a dimple and she was looking at me with an expression that mixed confusion and hope. I smiled and reached for her hands. "There's much that people in Concord don't know about me," I said. "I've changed since I was your age. At least, outwardly. But"—I moved my hand to her shoulder and smiled so broadly I felt my own dimple begin to reveal itself—"we must hurry if we're going to reach Fair Haven before the excitement's over."

Though it had been years since I hitched a horse to a buggy—my mother and aunts had often cautioned me against such unladylike ways—Louisa was familiar with the task, and in a surprisingly short time we managed to back Sable into the traces and harness her to the buggy. It was when I climbed clumsily aboard that Louisa—who had already scrambled up to perch on the high driver's seat—gave a soft cry.

"I forgot your condition!" She had half-covered her mouth with her hand and was gazing at my abdomen. "You can't drive on the Fair Haven Road! There are too many ruts! What about the baby?"

"Nonsense!" I said, losing my own uncertainty in the face of her distress. "Babies are sturdy creatures, well protected within. Any jarring we're subjected to will be mere rocking to the child." I sat beside her and picked up the reins. "Besides, Mrs. Child recommends exercise in the open air while carrying a child. In her book she claims it's very beneficial."

"Mrs. Lydia Child?"

"Yes, your mother's friend. Perhaps she's discussed such things during one of her visits."

"No," Louisa shook her head. "Or perhaps she has, but I haven't paid attention since I don't plan to marry."

I almost laughed at the childish satisfaction in her voice. "When I was your age I had no plans to marry, either." I flicked the reins and urged Sable onto the road. "But God has a way of reformulating our plans for His own purposes."

"Well, if someone like Mr. Emerson proposed to me, I'd accept." Her voice had softened.

I glanced at her. A fine blush had darkened her olive-toned skin. I'd known for some months that she harbored an infatuation for my husband, as had so many girls before her. I had even spied her singing a love song outside his study window one warm summer evening.

I felt a sudden rush of affection for her. "See? You make my point! We must not erect obstacles to God's will, but be always open to His calling."

"Well, I hope He calls me to be an authoress like Mrs. Child." She sighed and folded her arms across her breast. I saw that the blush had not yet left her cheeks. I smiled, for her reveries made me remember my own girlish dreams. I'd once imagined writing a book—a philosophical tome, heavy with ideas. A book that would so impress the deans at Harvard College that they would allow me to attend classes there.

Sable trotted along easily, without urging or direction. The fields were beginning to green but the trees had not yet put out their leaves so there was no shade to shield us from the sun. My eyes began to water and I was forced to pull my bonnet forward, screening my face. As we turned onto Sudbury Road, two men on horseback rode past at a gallop, fire buckets attached to their saddles. I recognized John Wilder, the Trinitarian minister, and George Minott, our neighbor across the way. Louisa waved cheerfully and I nodded my regards. Smoke burdened the air as we neared its source, and soon we both began to cough. I pulled my handkerchief from my sleeve and urged her to hold it across her mouth and nose as protection from the noxious fumes. A rabbit bolted suddenly across the road in front of us and I pulled hard on the reins, slowing Sable to a walk. My heart ached at this proof that the fire was driving animals from their dens.

"Whoever set this fire is a monster!" I cried, letting impulse rule my tongue.

Louisa looked at me solemnly. "Maybe it was an accident. No one would set fire to the woods on purpose."

"Carelessness does not render one unaccountable!" I reminded her.

We rode on in silence for a time, holding our thoughts in private. Smoke billowed around us, like a great gray cape blown in the wind. Fair Haven Hill rose up ahead, a massive dark mound, reminding me of the back of the whale I'd once seen surface and roll out of the dark water beyond my father's ships in Plymouth Harbor. There was a powerful smell of burning wood and the acrid stench of wet ashes. Through the trees, I could see flames at the height of my head, blistering the trunks. Then I caught sight of a man walking toward us through the smoke, his shoulders hunched forward and his head bowed low. I slowed the buggy, and was turning Sable toward the right ditch when Louisa cried out, "It's Mr. Thoreau!" and tumbled from the buggy in a commotion of limbs and ringlets. She ran pell-mell toward the figure while I peered through the soot-filled air, quickly satisfying myself that she was right—it was indeed Henry who walked so dejectedly toward town. I would have climbed down from the buggy myself had not the stench so overpowered me at that moment that I was forced to bend forward and inhale deeply to keep from vomiting.

By the time I straightened, Louisa had clasped Henry's arm and drawn him near the buggy.

"Henry!" I cried, barely able to speak as my own weakness poured into sympathy for him. I knew how he prized the woods surrounding Concord, and was certain their destruction cut him to the quick. Supposing him weary from battling the blaze, I urged him to climb into the buggy. "Let us carry you home! You're exhausted!"

He raised his head and looked at me. His eyes were sunken and the skin of his cheeks pouched sadly. "It's my fault." His voice scratched the air, a dark abrasion in the smoky gloom.

"Your fault?" I gaped at him, wondering if the smoke had made him go out of his head. "Nonsense! Climb into the buggy and we'll get you out of this horrid smoke."

But he shook his head and made a sweeping gesture toward the flames that, I saw with alarm, were advancing toward us through the trees. "I started it—a fool's idiocy—I was bent on cooking up a chowder—" He stopped and coughed.

"Spare your voice," I said. "You can tell your story later. For now it's urgent that we leave this place."

But he shook his head again, and backed away, shaking off Louisa's hands as well as my words. His eyes momentarily met mine and I felt the shock of his despair. He turned away and walked quickly into the woods. Though I knew black moods sometimes assailed him, I'd never seen Henry so melancholy.

As quickly as I could, I climbed down from the buggy and together Louisa and I attempted to follow, but the smoky conditions and the thickness of the undergrowth made the task impossible. Nor did I have sufficient heart for it, knowing that Henry was bent on resisting any attempt to secure his safety. I prayed he would return home safely and that I would subsequently learn the truth of the matter.

Mr. Emerson met us at the front gate of Bush, fire buckets in hand. He greeted Louisa as he always did—with a paternal smile—and helped her down from the buggy. "Go home, child," he said, patting her shoulder. "See to your mother and sisters. There's a fire in the woods south of town."

"We saw it!" Louisa exclaimed, fairly dancing around him in her excitement. "That's where we were!"

Mr. Emerson frowned up at me. "Is this so?"

"I'm fine," I said. "We drove out toward Fair Haven, but smoke overcame us and we turned back." I set the reins in their hitch and climbed down. "I don't think you ought to go, though, Mr. Emerson. Your lungs weren't strong this winter and smoke would damage them further."

"I won't put myself in needless danger," he said. "I'm sure every man in Concord is fighting the fire at this moment. My absence would be noted."

"Then go if you must." I knew there was little point in arguing with Mr. Emerson when public opinion was in the mix. My husband's concern for his reputation had grown with his fame. I turned to Louisa, who seemed about to speak. Intuition told me she was on the verge of telling my husband about our encounter with Henry.

"Go home, as Mr. Emerson told you," I said quickly. "Your poor mother is probably sick with worry."

I watched Louisa run through our small orchard to Lexington Road, while Mr. Emerson climbed into the buggy. I handed up his fire buckets.

"I'm glad Henry's on an excursion today," he said. "This would be very hard for him to bear. Though I suppose it will be just as hard when he returns."

I said nothing, holding my silence and patting Sable's flanks as he turned her toward the road. But if I hoped by my silence to protect Henry's reputation, it was a futile effort. By the time the sun rose the next morning over the haze-rimmed trees, the entire village knew that he and young Edward Hoar—Elizabeth's brother—were responsible for the conflagration. They had been rowing a boat up the Sudbury River and stopped near the Fair Haven cliffs, where they had cooked their cache of fish in a hollow stump. Sparks from the fire ignited the undergrowth. Henry and Edward battled the flames for more than an hour, but their efforts were in vain. I learned later that after our encounter on the road, Henry climbed to the top of the cliffs and sat in a daze, watching the fire for hours.

I did not see him until three days later, when he walked into our dining room where I was repairing the torn hem of a bedsheet.

"Henry!" His appearance was quite normal, in remarkable contrast to what it had been the day of the fire. Indeed, he looked as if he'd just come fresh from a country ramble, for his hair was disheveled and his cheeks a wind-stung red. I thought I detected the odor of soot upon him, but it could have been my imagination, so completely had my thoughts remained with him in the fiery woods. "You look surprisingly well," I said.

He smiled with his customary cheer. "And why shouldn't I? I've just come from a long morning tramp on the Old Marlborough Road."

"I thought you might have confined yourself to your chamber after . . ." I could not complete my sentence.

"After what?" His eyebrows folded softly together. "Why would I confine myself to my chamber on such a fine day?"

I wondered if he had truly put the fire out of his mind, or if he were playing some prank. His fine sense of humor blended with a skill at playacting that had often deceived his family and friends. He had several times bested my husband in this way, for Mr. Emerson, despite his intellect, was ill-equipped to see through a prankster's deceit.

"I thought perhaps you were still melancholy because of the fire." I felt awkward and coarse, my body bulging beneath my skirts. My hands frittered at a woolen pleat.

He nodded and his eyes went sad. "It's a loss to everyone in Concord. Particularly the birds and animals that nested among those trees. There are few woodlots as it is, and the destruction of one impoverishes us all."

I searched his face for some trace of the guilt I knew he must feel. The entire village was talking about his part in starting the conflagration, but he appeared innocent of any culpability.

"Henry?" I said. "Don't you remember our encounter on the afternoon of the fire? In the woodlot on the road north of the cliffs?"

"Encounter?" His face went soft with confusion.

"Yes, on the road to Fair Haven, in the smoke." I reached for him; my fingers grasped his coat sleeves and drew him toward me so that I could command his gaze and force him to see that I knew what had happened. I longed to assure him that he did not need to hide the truth from me.

"I'm sorry," he said. "I don't recall meeting you that day."

His gaze was so lacking in guile that I believed him at once, yet the fact that he could lock the event away in his mind troubled me. I wanted to take him by his shoulders and shake the memory back into him. What did it signify that a mind as sharp and penetrating as Henry's could shut away an entire afternoon's ordeal in some compartment of his brain? How could a man put any event of his life at such a vast remove from his knowing self?

And then a new thought chilled me. Had he forgotten not only the fire he set in the woods, but also the fire he'd set in me? Was it possible that he'd also locked away our love for each other in some never-to-be-opened partition of his mind?

The thought left me feeling an odd blend of sorrow and relief. Perhaps Henry's recent remoteness did not hide the guilt and remorse I'd imagined, but a willing renunciation of memory. He'd turned back the clock to before our tryst, and had locked the recollection away deep inside himself. Yet even as he willfully turned away from it, our secret was within me, readying itself to greet the world.

After the fire, word spread throughout Concord and neighboring towns that Henry Thoreau was a shiftless, irresponsible young man, careless to the point of danger. Some suggested he should be arrested and tried. He seemed oblivious to the rumors, yet over the course of the summer I noted another change—one so subtle that many did not perceive it. I believe he began to accept and even appreciate the ways in which he had been misunderstood. He started to wrap himself in his eccentricities as if they were a grand cloak.

I mentioned my concerns to Mr. Emerson. "People are beginning to regard Henry as either offensive or ridiculous," I said one warm August day after dinner as we lingered over Nancy's sweet apple cobbler. "He's become a sort of clown. Perhaps you should let him know that this posturing is having a disagreeable effect."

"He's not a clown but an antagonist." Mr. Emerson pierced a spicy brown slice of apple with his fork and lifted it to his lips. "It's his habit of contradiction. He substitutes the word everyone expects with its exact opposite. He praises wild forests for their domesticity, ice for its warmth, woodchoppers for their urbanity. Channing finds this habit charming." He opened his mouth and ate the apple slice, watching me as he did so.

"And you?" I demanded. "Do you also find his contradictions amusing?"

He put down his fork. "We must allow Henry to be Henry." He wiped his mouth with his napkin. "Now if you'll excuse me, I have letters to write." He rose and left the dining room, leaving me to ponder the matter alone.

One fact was undeniable—Henry was growing into a peculiarity not unlike my own—one that set him apart from the world and condemned him to set a private moral compass. Thus, though we were separated in our situations, we grew more alike in our strangeness, as if the very forces that sought to isolate us rebounded to draw us closer together.

MY LABOR PAINS BEGAN on July ninth, while I was in the midst of the day's chores. I'd rolled up my sleeves in the sultry afternoon, but rivers of perspiration ran down my arms and back and legs. By evening, when it became apparent that my labor was in earnest, I sought out Mr. Emerson in his study.

"My time has come," I said and watched him rise from his chair, his face flooding with alarm, his arms reaching to support me even before he'd crossed the room. In that moment I felt an affection I'd not felt toward him in years. I leaned upon him readily and allowed him to guide me across the hallway into the Red Room, which we'd agreed would make a worthy birthing chamber. His hands, as they helped me remove my gown and assist me into bed, were strong and steady, unusually capable, as if he'd acquired an uncommon grace for that circumstance alone.

In the throes of labor all my resistance to Mr. Emerson vanished. I lay in my shift while he stroked my hands and forehead. I closed my eyes and concentrated on the sound of crickets grating through the open window. The humid air amplified their rasping so that it reminded me of a woman's despondent cries.

"You'd best get the midwife," I gasped, during an especially strong pain.

He nodded. "Have you arranged for Cynthia Thoreau again?"

"No. No, not Cynthia. Lucy. I want only Lucy." My pain subsided. "Send Nancy for her."

"I will." He squeezed my hand. He seemed oddly reluctant to leave me.

"Quickly," I said, gasping as another pain began to grip my lower back. "Tell her to hurry."

He ran from the room. I heard his feet thumping down the hall to the kitchen, where Nancy was likely sitting on the back stoop, trying to catch what breeze she could. I was alone for only a few moments when Mr. Emerson returned. He drew a chair close to my bedside and began to talk quietly of simple, homely things, avoiding any topics that might upset me. Several times he touched my arm and stroked it. From the frequency with which he shifted in the chair, I knew he was uneasy in his role, that he wished as fervently as I that my travail would soon be over.

"Are the pains very bad?"

I turned my head and saw a compassion in his eyes that I'd never noticed. At that moment I believed him the most devoted husband in the world. I pushed myself up, braced my back against the headboard, and pulled him to me. It was a gesture I'd not made since the early days of our marriage and I was shocked at my own boldness. Yet he did not draw away, but put his arms around me, supporting and enfolding me. I breathed in the soap-and-salt scent of his shirt and his warm skin beneath. I listened to the steady, strong cadence of his heart. I felt another pain begin to mount. Instead of releasing him, I clung more tightly. When it was over, my arms dropped away and he lowered me gently onto the pillows.

"It grieves me that I can't be of some service." His voice sounded cracked and old.

"You are." I smiled. His mouth was drawn tightly against his teeth, as if he, too, experienced my ordeal. In that moment, my heart flooded equally with love and guilt. I prayed that this noble man who was my husband was also my child's father. I reached up and pressed my hand to Mr. Emerson's cheek.

A moment later Lucy came in, ordered Nancy to bring water and a supply of clean cloths, and abruptly banished my husband from the room. She then opened all the windows and drew back the curtains to allow what cool air there was into the room. She rubbed my feet and applied cold compresses to my forehead and arms. And when I wept from exhaustion, she wiped my face with her handkerchief and whispered encouragement.

In the middle of the night, I woke from a swoon to find Lucy's hand covering my mouth. I looked up at her—my mind abruptly, briefly, clear, as if a wind had swept everything away except a shared unspoken knowledge—and knew that I had spoken Henry's name aloud. I felt horror rise, but it was overtaken by a crushing pain, and I fell back into the confounded state of a woman seized by labor. Yet there lingered in me a certainty that I'd made a terrible confession and that Lucy now knew what had transpired in the hayloft between Henry and me.

My second son was born a few hours before dawn. I lay back on the pillows, dazed, watching Lucy wipe the blood and mucus from his tiny body.

"Is he healthy?" He had cried only once, a weak fluttery cry. I pushed myself to a sitting position and reached for him. "Give him to me!"

"Be patient, Liddy. You've waited nine months. You can wait a moment more." Lucy turned her back so I could no longer see the child. A crazed panic seized me and I was certain the babe was not well—that he was deformed. Or perhaps—and the thought caused me to sit up straight despite my soreness and exhaustion—the child was Henry's after all, born a month too soon.

"Lucy!" I snatched ineffectually at her dress. Finally she faced me and placed the babe on the foot of the bed, where she swaddled him tightly in a blanket and slid him into my arms. I stared down into a red face with slited eyes and a delicate rose mouth. One hand came loose from the swaddling and opened and closed near his left cheek.

"Something's wrong," I whispered, convinced that Lucy's reaction signaled some calamity, though I could not yet perceive it.

Lucy made a soothing sound. "I think he's fine. Nice and pink and healthy." She touched the tip of her finger to my son's palm. "Just a quiet one."

I gazed down at my new son who had begun to root for my breast. Was he Mr. Emerson's child—a full-term baby? Or was he the child of my shame, born early and weak? I couldn't tell. I drew back the blanket and studied his body for some sign of unsoundness but found none. I searched for some indication of his paternity, yet he looked as my other babes had—dark hair and pale skin, the round chin and button nose of all infants. He appeared completely normal. It occurred to me that Dr. Bartlett would know if the babe was full term or not. Yet I realized if I pressed the issue—if I asked too many questions—he would want to know the reason. And sooner or later he'd guess my secret.

In that moment, I realized I would never know the true identity of my son's father.

I bared my breast and offered him my nipple. His lips opened but he did not grip it properly. I slid my finger inside his mouth and brushed his palate and his mouth closed around my finger. I worked with him patiently while Lucy hovered until finally he took my breast. Moments later he was suckling with steadily increasing vigor. I smiled in relief. It was a good sign. I did not know if he was an early babe, but he was well-formed and would thrive.

I looked up at Lucy. "Please go and tell Mr. Emerson that he has a son."

"I DID NOT THINK it would be a boy," my husband said, his voice heavy. He sat in the same chair as before, though it was now in its original position by the window, where Lucy had moved it before the turmoil of delivery. His hands were planted on his knees, reminding me of the time I'd questioned him after his proposal. The "closed-eye interrogation" is how he teasingly referred to it, thus setting aside the seriousness and solemnity of my inquiry. Yet I perceived now—as I had not then—that his posture was constrained and stiff—controlled by some discomfort or inadequacy.

Earlier he'd entered the room carrying Edith and Ellen, whom he'd awakened to inform them of their new brother's arrival. Lucy had allowed each girl one peek into the blanket's folds. Ellen took a long, hard look, then frowned up at Lucy. "When Papa said brother, I thought it was my *real* brother." Her voice was high and sweet. "Where's Wallie?" Lucy immediately swept her from the room, leaving Mr. Emerson and me staring at each other.

Now my husband shook his head sadly. "I always wanted my son to bear my name. But I don't have the heart to call this new one Waldo."

"Nor do I," I whispered.

Wallie seemed suddenly present in the room—a phantasm of light and shadow that I longed to grasp and draw to myself. "He's here!" I whispered, my gaze sliding from one corner of the room to the other, as if I might by this restless seeking light upon some trace of my eldest son.

"Who?" My husband's word sounded as if it had been wrenched from his mouth.

"Wallie," I said. "He's with us right now! I'm sure of it! Can't you feel him?"

"No, I'm afraid I can't." He rose and came to stand by the bed, looking down at the babe in my arms. "I've sometimes wished I had your spiritual sensibilities, Lidian. But more often I think they must be a great trial to you. A burden of discernment I'm happier without." He did not say so, but I knew that he believed that I, too, would be better off without them.

I looked down at the babe. "I think we must name him tonight, Mr. Emerson," I said. "I don't want him to go nameless for weeks as Edith did."

"Where's the harm?"

"I just *don't*." My voice was sharper than I'd intended. I tried to think of a suitable name, and *Henry* flared in my mind—a small, bright flame that I immediately extinguished.

"How about William, then?" He slid his hands down into his pockets, then pulled them out again and took a step back. "Or Thomas, after your uncle."

"What about Charles?"

He shook his head sharply. "No. Not Charles." He went to the window and looked out, as if he might be able to discern something in the darkness. It was an unfriendly posture, his back presented in that way; it felt repudiating. "He doesn't look much like the others, does he?" he asked after a while, twisting to look at me over his shoulder. My back knotted and I inadvertently jostled the baby, who fretted as I straightened on my pillows. I did not know if Mr. Emerson was earnestly asking this question or if it was yet another token of his bereavement. And what did it mean—what did it portend?

"Of course he does," I said. "He looks exactly as Ellen did when she was born."

He seemed to draw some comfort from my assurance, for he turned full around then and said, "We could call him Edward."

"Edward?" I had never met my husband's older brother, who had perished in Puerto Rico, nor did he often speak of him.

"There's a pleasant symmetry in having all our children's names begin with the same letter." He smiled—yet it was his lecture smile, the smile he used to charm the crowds who revered him. It was not the smile he gave to his friends. "We could use Waldo as his middle name."

I felt as if some opiate had suddenly filled my brain and I could no longer distinguish pain from pleasure—as if it were all one. "Edward is a good name," I said, through lips that felt numb and stiff. "Edward Waldo Emerson."

As I spoke the name, my husband returned to my side. "Yes, I think that will do very well." He sounded relieved, as though he'd just wakened from a troubling dream. He reached down and touched the baby's cheek—Edward's cheek—with his forefinger, and held it there, as if imprinting a seal on the soft pink skin. His fingernail glinted in the lamplight.

HENRY WAS NOT in Concord when Edward was born, for he had gone off to the Catskill Mountains on his postponed walking tour. These excursions became more frequent after our encounter in the barn. Although he never said a word to indicate there was a connection between our intimacy and his wilderness explorations, I was convinced they were related.

I could not fairly consider his absence at the time of Edward's birth to be anything but coincidence. Yet his unavailability during my hour of travail—especially after he'd been present when I labored with Edith—seemed to signify his desire to withdraw from the new child. I knew this notion was nonsense, that my thoughts were irrational and founded in ignoblity, yet they persisted. When Henry finally presented himself at my chamber door ten days after the birth, a bouquet of wildflowers in his hand and a smile on his face, I refused him my usual warm welcome.

"Where have you been? The child is ten days old!" I fumed at my skirts and snapped the folds of my cap behind my ears. I had just tucked Edward into his cradle and seated myself by the window, where a faint breeze stirred the curtains. I'd reached the stage of my confinement where I felt incarcerated, and yearned for escape.

Henry took a step back and his hand, which had been about to proffer the flowers, fell to his side. "I came as soon as I was able. I've been away."

"I *know* you've been away. The whole town knows you've been away." I saw from his face that I'd wounded him, yet I could not still my tongue. "Not that you gave me any notice. If you told Mr. Emerson, he neglected to inform me."

"I'm here to offer my congratulations," he said quietly. He stepped back again, so that he now stood in the doorway. "Perhaps another time would be better."

"I would think you'd want to see the child before you leave." I looked directly at him. He returned my gaze, but showed no comprehension of the significance of my words. Did he truly believe he could not be the child's father? Had I convinced him of what I had not been able to convince myself?

"Yes," he said, "I'd like that, of course. But only at your convenience." His face was faintly damp with perspiration. I perceived his vulnerability, the fatigue that lay in the muscles of his cheeks, less like a sleeping cat than a stalking one. I felt a wave of pity. My anger folded upon itself and wilted, a blossom shriveling in the snow.

I rose and extended both hands. "Forgive me. I'm nearly frantic from lack of activity. Who decreed that a woman must be restricted so long to her chamber after giving birth?"

He blinked and came toward me, pressing the bouquet into my outstretched hands. "I know nothing of women's mysteries. But it seems to me that rest is so rarely available to you, Lidian, that you ought to make use of it while you can."

I brought the bouquet to my face and pressed my nose into a yellow lily.

"Thank you," I said, raising my face. "I appreciate your concern." I drew closer and touched his arm, then—to my own surprise as well as his—leaned forward and kissed his cheek. His eyes flashed, and I saw that I'd embarrassed him, for the tips of his ears reddened noticeably.

"Come and see the babe," I said, turning quickly away. I laid the flowers on the bed and crossed the room to the cradle, wondering at myself. The kiss that seemed so natural—so *necessary*—at the moment of impulse, now struck me as a sign of my abiding iniquity.

I bent and picked up Edward. His eyes, which had already turned from the newborn's slate-gray to a clear, dark blue, fluttered open. I handed him to Henry, aware of the possibility that I might, at that moment, be presenting my son to his father.

Henry cradled Edward's head in the crook of his left elbow, and stared down at him for some time in silence. I wondered if he studied him—as I had—for a telling family likeness, some defining hint of his paternity. Yet he made no remark on his appearance, but merely asked the child's name.

"Edward," I said.

He nodded. "Edward. I like that. I believe it suits him."

I stepped closer, for I had not heard the baby stir into full wakefulness and wanted to assure myself he slept peacefully. Death—though I was loath to give it recognition—made me inordinately vigilant with my children. Yet when I looked at Edward I saw, with surprise, that he was wide-awake, his eyes gazing straight into Henry's. There was a solemnity in his expression—a look I'd often observed in newborns—that caused me to reflect on the great, unspoken wisdom they bring into the world, a wisdom beyond the ability of an adult to comprehend.

I glanced again at Henry and saw on his face a look of reverence and astonishment. I felt at that moment that I hardly knew him. He looked as if he were about to weep. Then, abruptly, his face resumed its normal cast and he was no longer a stranger.

"He's quite perfect," he declared, smiling. "A philosopher, I think. Or a poet."

I knew there could be no higher compliment from Henry, since his own aspiration was to be a philosopher-poet like my husband. He looked back at Edward, whose gaze locked again on Henry's. I sensed that something profound was taking place between them—something I both did and did not want to disturb. But no—it was more than that—what I saw was a mutual *recognition* in their eyes. Their tiny circle excluded me as surely as a stockade.

I swiftly took Edward from Henry's arms. "He will be whatever God in His wisdom desires." I held him close to my breasts, desperate to reacquaint myself with his weight and form and smell. Yet, even as I embraced him, I had the uneasy feeling that I had not broken that circle. Some intimacy bound them to each other. I stepped back, away from Henry, clutching Edward tightly. Unwilling to return him to his cradle, I paced back and forth as if he required soothing. Henry watched me.

"He's quite wonderful, Lidian," he said.

"Yes," I said. "Entirely wonderful."

As I walked my son, clasping him securely to my bosom, I had the odd sensation that he and Henry were very faraway, as if Henry had carried him to some new country where the language, the laws—everything—was different. And I was left alone to watch them on the further shore.

PART III

July 1847 – April 1882

The World on Fire

She remembered them that were in bonds as bound with them

—FROM THE GRAVESTONE OF
LIDIAN JACKSON EMERSON

27

Transitions

I left the woods for as good a reason as I went there.
—HENRY DAVID THOREAU

For nearly eight years Henry had been my companion and friend. I had come to believe his presence was the one ingredient that made my life bearable. When he declared his intention to build a cabin on the shores of Walden Pond and live a simplified life there, I encouraged him. I had imagined he would live there for a few months and return to the Thoreau family home by winter. But when he stayed on I championed his efforts, though I saw him less frequently and sorely missed our walks and conversations. Two years had passed and our friendship had dwindled—partly through reduced association—but also because it became increasingly clear that the weight of his attention was no longer focused on me. Henry—whose passion for life was reflected in a wide net of attachments—now concentrated his energies on nature.

I wanted Henry back. In the end, it was that simple.

Circumstance and desire rarely contrive a solution as easily as they did on that occasion. When Mr. Emerson announced later that summer that he intended to make an extended European tour, I was at first stunned, then infuriated. He had been to Europe before we met and seen all the famous places he cared to. Or so I imagined. More significantly, our children were young and our funds limited. When I protested, he invited me to accompany him, knowing that I would certainly refuse. Both my maternal responsibilities and my natural inclination forbade such a journey. I'd been ripped from my Plymouth home by marriage. I would not now be ripped from American shores by my husband's conceit.

For three weeks I fretted. I would manage household chores and my husband's business contacts—I'd done so regularly when he was away on his lecture tours. But how would I contact him if I had sudden need? What if his mother became ill or—and I could hardly bear to entertain the thought, yet how could I not think it?—one of the remaining children sickened and died? I raged. I wept. I told him his trip would be my undoing. He turned a deaf ear and concentrated on his plans. Whatever affection he had once had for me was gone.

One night near the end of August I dreamed I was walking along a country path and suddenly came upon Henry. He was standing at the edge of a great river, the sunlight slanting in such a way as to make his hair look like golden fire. When he saw me, he turned around and came toward me, his arms outstretched.

"You are the star by which I set my compass," he said.

I woke, my face wet with tears.

At breakfast I confronted my husband. "If you are set on going to Europe, then I want Henry here to take care of the house and land." I'd not yet taken a bite of my pie, nor had I the slightest appetite for the coffee that filled my cup. I sat with my hands in my lap, my back as straight as if laced into a corset. "You cannot expect me to run this household without a man. I insist on Henry's presence."

Mr. Emerson frowned and put down his fork. "Henry is not yours to command. He's committed to his experiment at Walden Pond."

"I believe you could persuade him," I said. "He is, after all, living on your land."

His mouth drooped at the corners—an expression I'd rarely seen. "I have no intention of curtailing his freedom. You may speak to him if you like."

"I want you to do it. It's my condition for your trip."

"Condition?" His shoulders jerked, as if some object had physically struck him in the chest. "You're my wife. It's not your place to offer conditions."

I drew in a slow breath. "A wife is not a slave, Mr. Emerson, no matter that she is often treated as such."

He pushed back his chair with such a violent motion that a tongue of coffee sloshed out of my cup and onto the tablecloth. "I have never treated you as a slave!" I'd never heard his voice so animated by rage. "You are my *wife*. We are one flesh!"

"No one owns me but Christ!" I cried, rising to my feet, for I could no longer remain seated. "And if you are to leave me, I want Henry here!"

His eyes burned in the cold iron of his face. "There will be gossip," he said.

"Are you now afraid to be defended by the truth?" I looked at him, meeting his penetrating gaze with my own for a long moment before I resumed my seat. "I assure you I will do nothing to dishonor you," I said, full knowing that I would constantly struggle with my desire for Henry.

"I have been a good husband to you. I have given you a home and a family. I have put food on your table. I have not beaten you." His voice was low and deliberate—if I had known him less, I would have imagined that he was calm. His face was as stony as our granite doorstep.

"More than common courtesy is required to make a marriage," I said.

He sighed. "What is required of us is that we follow the prompting of the Spirit within."

"Which is why I insist that you persuade Henry." I was surprised to hear tears in my voice, for my eyes were dry.

"Very well," he said. "I'll try to persuade. But I will not coerce. If he comes, it must be of his own free will." He picked up his fork again and studied me over the tines. "But I doubt he will agree, Lidian. He's grown very jealous of his solitude."

"Tell him it is my request," I said. "He will come."

My heart was less certain than my words, but they proved true. Henry left his cabin at the pond without a backward glance. On the sixth of September, a month before Mr. Emerson sailed for Europe, he moved back into the chamber at the top of the front stairs.

It was heaven to have Henry under our roof again, so near to hand and heart. I felt as if the world had finally righted itself. If he experienced any regret at leaving the pond, he did not tell me, but plunged into our domestic round with a grace and enthusiasm that captivated the children and me. Mr. Emerson alone appeared unaffected. He remained immersed in his studies, apparently oblivious to my new happiness and the immensity of my relief.

Henry was as kind and considerate as ever, and I was gratified to detect a familiar luster in his eyes when he looked at me. I contrived ways to be in his company, hoping I might steal a few moments alone with him. I planned outings for the children, asked for his advice on writing poetry, and requested his thoughts on the new philosophers. I insisted that I needed his help on my shopping rounds on the Mill Dam so that my purchases might be safely carried home. I inquired about the details of his life at the pond. I drew him into discussions of gardening and philosophy, the sort we had previously enjoyed. He seemed as happy as ever to turn his mind down those familiar paths.

Yet sometimes I sensed a hesitancy, a subtle diminution of attention when he listened to me, as if he were hearkening to a distant voice. I wondered if he were reliving his experiences in the woods—if his time there had transformed him in some enduring way.

September was the loveliest of seasons in Concord—it combined the ripeness of late summer with the piquant tang of early fall. I found myself going outdoors often, even on days when household duties burdened me. I worked in my garden and took walks across the fields as Henry did, often stopping at Edmund Hosmer's farm to share a cup of coffee with his wife and discuss our children's constitutions.

I BEGAN to wonder where Henry's long afternoon rambles took him. I imagined that he might be on a round of appointments in the woodlots surrounding Concord—secretive meetings with shadowy figures. Then something happened that confirmed my suspicions.

It was an afternoon in the last week of September, and I'd gone upstairs after dinner to rest while the children took their naps. It was warm and the sun had rolled across a hazy sky to the far side of the house, so my chamber was in shadows. The birds were always silent at this time of day, but as I lay there, I could hear the bristly murmur of bees at my window and the blows of Henry's hammer. He had been repairing the house clapboards all morning. I thought of his callused fingertips and work-smoothed palms. I felt a wave of desire as I recalled how they had felt on my skin that November night in the barn four years before. I'd called him away from Walden Pond and he had come. This gave me a perverse and shameful comfort. I experienced the full gravity of womanly power.

I heard the east door open and Mr. Emerson call Henry's name. Then the sound of footsteps—my husband's.

"The summer house looks handsome enough in the shade of that chestnut," Mr. Emerson said. His voice was quite clear—I realized he must be standing directly below my window. "As long as one is not too near." He referred to the strange structure Bronson Alcott was building in the field east of the house. Mr. Emerson had wished for a simple shelter where he might sit and meditate in the gentle breezes of a warm afternoon. But Bronson was as fanciful in design as he was in conversation. The building was an arrangement of curving gables and beams, and appeared to always be on the verge of collapse.

I heard Henry's chuckle. "Today it cants east. Yesterday to the west. Who knows where it will lean tomorrow? Perhaps it will decide to walk to Boston."

Mr. Emerson laughed and then his voice turned somber. "You must keep me informed while I'm in Europe."

"Of course."

"I'm depending on you to watch over my property and children. I know—" Mr. Emerson paused. "I must be candid with you, Henry."

"I hope you're always candid with me."

"There's the matter of Lidian."

I sat up abruptly and the left side of my cap twisted loose from its hairpin and hung askew. I fixed it quickly, and sat forward to get a clear view. The field was in shadow, but I could see the summer house roof—light brown against the darker land.

"Yes, I'm aware of that," Henry said.

I saw my husband in my mind's eye, his hands pushed down into his pockets, a trait he manifested when ill at ease. "As you know, it was her wish that you stay here while I'm gone. I myself didn't think it the wisest course."

Henry was silent. My husband cleared his throat. "My station in life requires that I not look like a fool. Or that my wife appear to be a woman of low reputation."

"Lidian is not—"

"No, hear me out. She's an overly sensitive woman. She doesn't master her passions well. You must watch out for her in many ways." He paused. "Do you take my meaning?"

There was another silence and then Henry said, in a cold voice, "I believe I do."

I touched my cap again, though it did not require further straightening. A cold sickness spread through my body.

"Nor do I want her involved in this transport business of yours. I believe your cause is just, but it's dangerous. If Lidian gets wind of your activity, you know as well as I do she'll not stay out of it," my husband said. "She's like a snapping turtle—when she latches onto something she will not easily let go."

"I believe her tenacity could prove an asset to you," Henry said, "if you'd allow her more influence."

"She influences me quite enough." My husband's tone was crisp. "What I would like is your word on this, Henry. Do I have that?"

There was a short silence before Henry said, "Of course."

"Good. Now we'll have no more of this conversation, my friend. I am content."

I lowered myself back onto the bed and stared up at a crack in the ceiling plaster that formed a V over Mr. Emerson's pillow.

MR. EMERSON LEFT for Europe on the fifth of October. It was a dark day, promising rain. As my husband boarded the packet ship *Washington Irving*, I stood beside Henry on the dock, our clothes whipping about us in the strong sea wind. I heard the slap of the tidewater as it sloshed against the pilings; the cries of seagulls sounded in my ears. My shawl sounded like a log crackling in the fire as it snapped repeatedly against the length of my back. The ship was a long, low vessel, painted black above the waterline, with cream molding along the plank sheer.

Henry stared straight ahead, his left elbow lightly brushing my right. I knew he was as aware of me as I of him, for he shaped the motions of his body to mine, as if we were engaged in the patterns of a dance. A new burst of wind came off the water, carrying with it the stench of rotting fish. It swirled about me and lifted my hem like a fractious kitten so that I was forced to bend and soothe it.

Mr. Emerson appeared on deck and leaned over the rail. I lifted my hand and waved; Henry did the same. After a moment, Mr. Emerson waved back. Then the anchor was weighed, and a noisy steam tug pushed the ship out of Boston Harbor without a sail being raised. I watched the packet grow small and black in the distance, until I could no longer be sure it was the ship I saw against the horizon or an errant wave. Not until long after it had disappeared did I turn away.

WE FORMED a family—Henry and the children and I—not a common family but an ideal one, for there was a lively affinity and pleasant association whenever we were all together. Henry and I were true companions—united in a kinship that was rare even among married couples.

Mother Emerson traveled to New York to stay with William's family during my husband's absence, and a new and happy ease entered my household routines. Henry assumed the role of father as if born to it. He was attentive, playful, and patient with the children. He was also demanding when the occasion warranted, and they obeyed him instantly if a certain tone came into his voice. I often watched him as he frolicked with Edward across the parlor carpet, and yearned to declare him Eddy's proper father. Yet I curbed my tongue and contented myself with the pleasures of daily intimacy.

One snowy winter evening Henry insisted we go coasting on Bristor's Hill. He would allow no dissenters but bundled the children in their warmest coats and scarves, and insisted I do the same. He piled Ellen and Edith aboard our biggest sled while I drew Eddy on the small one, and we merrily set off. The moon was nearly full—it cast silver light everywhere, transforming the familiar trees and houses into fantastic fairyland castles.

We coasted for nearly two hours, going up and down the broad white hill again and again while the moon climbed the sky and the stars glittered silently above our heads. It was not until Eddy's spirits began to flag that I declared it was time to go home.

When the children were safely tucked in bed, I went down to the kitchen, where I found Henry warming a pan of milk.

"A good-night tonic," he said, turning to smile at me over his shoulder. "You look as pink-cheeked as a schoolgirl!"

He poured the milk into two bowls and we sat beside each other at the table and slowly drank it. The sweet milk warmed and calmed me, and a wave of sleepiness swept through me, so profound that I could not stifle a yawn. Henry chuckled as I set down my bowl and then startled me by covering my right hand with his. I looked at him and found him gazing back at me with a worshipful expression. In that moment, all the months of estrangement and uncertainty were swept away. I moved toward him at the same moment that he reached for me. He rose and gathered me into his arms in an embrace that was infinitely sweeter than I remembered. For several moments I was aware only of his scent and his strong hands moving over my back. Then virtue overtook me and I broke away. He blinked as a man does who steps suddenly from darkness into sunlight. I turned and fled to my chamber. My breath came in little gasps, my chest heaved, but whether it was from shame or bliss, I could not tell.

THE NEXT AFTERNOON, Henry and Eddy built a snow cave in the garden. I watched from the window as first the children and then Henry crawled in and out. At twilight, I put on my shawl and went out to join them. My lamp cast petals of light onto the snow. I was entranced by the fantastical patterns.

"The snow defuses the light!" Henry cried, suddenly beside me. His face was radiant. He took the lamp, got down on his hands and knees, and scrambled into the cave. The snow seemed to swallow the light at first and then softly disperse it. It made me think of a rose opening for the first time.

I laughed when Henry emerged, for snow scalloped his shoulders and matted his hair into the shape of a skewed halo. He wanted to see if, by sealing up the cave as tightly as possible, the lamp could be put out, or at least diminished, the way the sound of voices was inside the cave. Yet the wick burned as brightly as ever, no matter how tightly the cave was sealed, which seemed to utterly delight Henry.

Later, as I knelt in front of the kitchen stove, chaffing Eddy's hands, Henry came and knelt beside me.

"You see, don't you?" he said quietly. "The flame is not put out. Neither cold nor isolation can quench it. Even winter has no dominion over light."

THAT SPRING I became ill with a jaundice that so weakened me that I could no longer stand. I spent day after day in my chamber, drapes closed against the sunlight, while my skin assumed an alarming yellow pallor. Lucy did what she could and Elizabeth Hoar came often to lend her quick and gentle hand. But Henry was my chief comfort. He minded the children with care and affection; he oversaw the housekeeping, and attended to the guests who continued to visit Bush despite Mr. Emerson's absence. In the late afternoons, he read to me—long, elegant books on Greek and Roman history, poems from the great English masters, and his own journal entries describing the beauties of the natural world. He denied me the newspaper, insisting that the sad business of the nation would only worsen my health.

"When you're well again, you may immerse yourself in that sorrow if you wish," he said gently. "But now you must concentrate your attention on happiness."

He brought me wildflowers, Indian arrowheads, and small, smooth stones of many colors. He wrote to my husband, informing him of my illness, and reporting on various household matters. I wrote when I could, though for many weeks I did not have the energy to lift my pen.

It was some time before I heard from Mr. Emerson. This saddened but did not surprise me. He had long since ceased to write to me except in the most perfunctory way. Henry, however, expressed indignation at my husband's lapse of kindness.

"You're ill and I've informed him of the seriousness of your situation! There's no reason why he could not promptly express his concern." He refused to write to Mr. Emerson for many weeks, claiming that no matter how eminent a personage, a husband had an obligation to show some regard for his wife's health and comfort.

Henry's anger affected me in a strange way. Though I was ashamed for my husband, and begged him to write more often, the infrequency of his letters helped to draw Henry back to me; his previous remoteness vanished. And so— sinner that I was—I encouraged Henry. I showed him my letters before I sent them, imploring him to discover what inadvertent phrase might offend my husband. In one I pleaded with Mr. Emerson to address me more intimately, more as a husband ought. His cool response was that such a course would be unwise, since I made a habit of sharing his letters with my friends and family.

Angrily, Henry marched up and down the parlor, flinging his arms about like a marionette that had lost its strings and was no longer controlled by the puppeteer.

"But you cannot deny the truth of his words." I went to him and tried to still his arms with my hands. "Sharing is our common practice."

"Exactly!" Henry squeezed his eyes shut and pressed the heels of his palms against them. "He writes such words to silence you." He dropped his hands and opened his eyes.

"No!" I clung to Henry's arm. "He writes to explain his actions. So that I might understand."

"Lidian." Henry turned to face me. "You cannot deny that he neglects you. There is a cold indifference about him. He's taken this tour with no thought for your convenience. He shows no proper sympathy when you're ill. And he continues to pursue Margaret Fuller in Europe."

My hand fell from his arm. "What?" I said. "How do you know this?"

He looked down at the floor. "I'm sorry. I should not have told you."

"Indeed you should if it is true!" My voice was on the verge of breaking. "I knew Margaret was in Rome, but I thought she was embroiled in some political situation. I did not imagine they might arrange an assignation!" Despite my weakness, I began to pace the room.

Henry caught me by the shoulders and pressed me into a chair. "Calm yourself! You're alarming the cat." He gestured to the windowsill, where the gray tomcat, which had been sunning himself a few moments before, was crouched with his back to the curtain, his tail flicking angrily in and out of a beam of sunlight. I felt immediate regret and tried to rise from my chair to allay the creature's anxiety, but Henry's grip remained firm on my shoulders, so I could not move.

It occurred to me that he was playing the part of my husband. That he was, quite consciously, doing what he would do and say had we been man and wife. I inclined my head so that my cheek rested briefly upon his arm.

"Tell me," I said, knowing even as I spoke how hypocritical it was of me to fret over my husband's infidelities when I had been unfaithful myself. "I can bear it."

He closed his eyes. "My mother heard from one of her boarders that he's to rendezvous with Margaret in Paris. He means to entreat her to return to America and live with you."

"Live with us?"

"Oh, Lidian!" Henry eyes opened; his face was charged with compassion.

"I ought to have guessed," I said as my anger drained. "He has never promised to give her up. Yet from something he said before he left, I believed they no longer felt a strong attachment." My hands dropped into my lap, and I found myself staring at them as they lay there, as if they did not belong to me.

"I don't understand why you stay with him," Henry said. "I truly do not. He has so little regard for your thoughts and none at all for your feelings. You ought to consider leaving him."

I stared at him, wondering if he had lost all sense. "Leave him? How could I do that?"

"Would it be so difficult? You're a grown woman. You have resources, family and friends—"

I cut him off. "Do you imagine for a moment I could desert my children?"

"Of course not. You would take them with you."

"With me?" My shock deepened. Surely Henry knew that children lawfully belonged to their father. "How could I do that? The only place I feel at home is Plymouth; Mr. Emerson would know exactly where to find me."

"There's a whole continent to the west. Land is plentiful. Anonymity is easily obtained."

"You can picture me as a pioneer woman?" I laughed. "You don't know me as well as I thought. It's a rare woman who has the necessary stamina and resolution, and I'm surely not made for the frontier. I'd perish in the first month."

"I was not suggesting you go alone," he said quietly. "We'd go together. I'd gladly take you from your misery and help you find happiness there."

I studied the hem of my right sleeve. The black cloth had begun to fray. If I did not see to it soon, it would disintegrate into tatters. I wondered if my skills with the needle were sufficient to repair it. The meaning of his words finally penetrated my awareness.

"Are you proposing marriage?"

He did not answer at first, and his silence told me more than his words. "I'd not thought we needed that formality," he said finally. "The West is a place of freedom."

"So you would rob me of my reputation—both past and future," I said.

"What do you care for your reputation? That's the concern of vain women, of small-minded souls."

His words scalded me—I was suddenly and bitterly angry. "You do not understand the nature of marriage, Henry. Nor do you comprehend the situation of women. We own nothing *but* our reputations! It's the currency upon which our security depends."

"It's your own lock which you fix to that cage," he said. "I've sworn to take care of you. Have I not proven myself capable?"

Each word was a blow to my heart. "You have proven that you can manage a home and keep it in good repair. You have proven that you are tender with children. But what warranty do I have that you would not turn cold as

Mr. Emerson has once I agreed to your proposal? It's in the nature of men to relish the pursuit. But their ardor quickly wanes once they've achieved their goal." I could hear the fury in my voice, could nearly taste it on my tongue. "What assurance can you give that you will not resent me and my children as obstacles to your career, once you've burdened yourself with us?"

He looked stricken, his sun-weathered face suddenly pale.

"You see?" I went on. "You cannot give me any warranty, for you know the nature of men."

"I am not like other men," he said in a low voice.

"And I did not believe I was like other women, until marriage forced me into this mold. You have no idea—you can't know—what marriage does to a woman. It is a kind of servitude from which there is no emancipation."

He was silent a moment. Too long a moment, I thought. When he spoke, his words were measured and slow, as if he were appraising each for size and shape before he said them.

"There is always emancipation if one is willing to pay its price," he said. "You misjudge me, Lidian. I know better than anyone what you suffer. And not merely for yourself. Your compassion for others is beyond compare. Of all the women I have met, I rate you most courageous. You hold fast to your principles, no matter the cost. You speak your mind and demonstrate your beliefs at great expense to yourself. You are—you have always been—my inspiration."

I shivered under the onslaught of his words. Here, at last, was what I'd yearned for—a man who wanted me not just on the periphery of his life but at its center. A man who knew me through and through and still loved me. I wanted nothing more than to rise and step into his arms, to feel the consolation of my heart beating against his. Yet I did not move. I had spent years disciplining my mind and body to ignore my own desires. Once again I forced myself into the stocks of my determination.

"Your words are kind, Henry. But I don't seek to be anyone's inspiration. I seek only to do God's will."

"I was being candid, not kind. And I know you do not believe that God wills your slavery."

I looked again at my hands, at the chapped skin and chipped nails. His words rang in my heart like the tolling of a great bell. I was unable to summon a reply, and so I sat silent until Henry finally turned and left the room.

————

A TIDE TURNED that afternoon in our relation—there was a new distance between us. Henry and I still saw each other daily. We still sat across the table from each other at breakfast, dinner, and tea. We still frolicked with the children in the evenings, and still took them together on outings. Yet now there was a discomforting caution in the air. Though he was still my chief assistant and companion, I no longer opened my heart to him. Nor was he as candid with me. This unfamiliar wariness produced a curious effect—I became aware of the depth of my lust.

My lust was not carnal. Though I'd enjoyed pleasure with him, it was not his body I desired. I lusted after Henry's soul.

28

Nemesis

In spite of Virtue and the Muse,
Nemesis will have her dues,
And all our struggles and our toils
Tighter wind the giant coils.
—RALPH WALDO EMERSON

One evening in late spring after I'd put the children to bed, I began reading *Narrative of the Life of Frederick Douglass,* which had been published more than two years before. I was soon so absorbed in the description of life on the Lloyd plantation that I did not hear Henry enter the parlor. I chanced to look up as I turned a page and found him standing in the doorway.

"You're reading Frederick's book." He did not smile.

I nodded. "Yes, I can hardly put it down."

He came into the room and sat on the couch. He was hiding something from me. I was sure of it. I thought suddenly of the business of transport my husband had mentioned before he left for Europe.

"Henry, please—tell me—" Here I paused while I tried to compose my thoughts into a sensible order. "I know you're involved in some intrigue. Something that Mr. Emerson asked that you hide from me." I watched his hands slide from his knees, where they had been resting, to the couch. They lay open beside his thighs, as if in supplication. Though he said nothing, I clearly read the dismayed question in his expression.

"I overheard him speak to you that afternoon—when you were repairing the clapboards below my chamber window."

He closed his eyes and his head sank toward his chest. The gesture unnerved me. I dropped my book and went to kneel before him. I took his face between my hands. I meant only to raise his head so that he might look at me and see my tender regard. But he shook his head and his hands covered mine to draw them away.

"Don't," he whispered. "Please."

But I was determined now to know the truth. "Just tell me. I'm more afraid of ignorance than peril."

"Waldo is my friend." His eyes had fastened on mine. "You're asking me to betray him."

"Betray him?" I wanted to push aside the wall of his resistance. I wanted to remind him that together we had perpetrated a far graver betrayal five years ago. Had he truly forgotten our tryst? "Haven't we both betrayed him already?"

He frowned and I saw something flicker in his eyes—a strange and urgent light.

"Mr. Emerson need never know," I said gently, and I waited for him to speak, my palms still clasping his face while his hands covered mine. The silence of the room grew suddenly oppressive. I had an urge to rise and flee— an urge that flooded me—then as swiftly ebbed.

Then I did a strange thing: I rose on my knees, pulled his face close to mine and kissed him full on the mouth. I know I shocked him and, indeed, I shocked myself. Yet I felt him respond—his lips plainly welcomed mine— and my passion rose as the scent and taste of his breath mingled with mine. My hands slid from beneath his, fell to his neck and shoulders. I pressed closer, a movement that drove his knees into my stomach, but I did not care, for I felt his hands on my back.

Suddenly, he broke away and leaned back into the couch cushions. I pressed my hands over my lips. I could not tear my eyes from his face, for I saw there a reflection of the stunned fear that filled my own heart.

"I'm sorry!" I whispered. But he had closed his eyes and perhaps his ears as well. I let my arms fall to my sides. I did not understand how I could have done such a thing. It was proof that there was no goodness left in me. "Oh, Henry!" I reached to place my hand on his knee. His eyes blinked open and he stared at my hand—stared at it as if it were a repulsive insect that he discovered climbing his trousers. He got to his feet and crossed the room to pick up the book. It seemed odd for him to stand across from me in the room, while I sat on the floor.

I stood up. I smoothed my skirts. My numbness—the numbness that I'd felt for weeks—had passed. I felt a rush of relief and then an overwhelming shame. "Henry, please say something."

His back was turned to me, yet I clearly heard each word he spoke. "You asked if I'm involved in an intrigue."

"Yes." I wondered if I should go to him. I studied his back, noting that his shoulders looked less broad from that angle than when he faced me. It was a discomfiting perception—it had the ominous feel of a premonition. "Yes, I would like to know," I said, my voice low, as if I were conspiring with him to perpetrate some abhorrent crime.

He sighed. "For the past three years, I've been doing what I could to help slaves escape their masters."

"Slaves?" I'd heard rumors of an elaborate and secret system of transporting escaped slaves to safety in Canada, but it had not occurred to me that anyone living in Concord might be involved. "How do you do this?" I approached him and, since he did not turn, circled him so that I might observe his expression.

"I transport them. I hide them in safe houses and I succor them. I do whatever I can to assure their freedom." He looked at me then, finally. A flush instantly rose on his skin over each cheekbone.

"I knew that whatever your endeavor was it would be noble," I said. "I would like to help you. Surely there is some way I can be of use in this effort."

He regarded me thoughtfully. His gaze produced in me a most uncomfortable sensation—as if he did not know me. Had he already forgotten our kiss? His flush denied it, yet there was a remoteness in his eyes.

"You can trust me, Henry—I assure you—I want only to relieve their suffering."

"My situation is complicated." He still held the book in his hand. "I've been party to several schemes. Schemes for the purpose of ending slavery. In any way possible." He glanced down at the book and then looked back at me. "By any means," he said softly. "Do you understand what I'm saying?"

I was not certain that I did, yet I nodded. "I'm not afraid, Henry. If I were your wife, you would trust me."

It was an impulsive statement. As soon as I spoke it, I regretted having done so. I pressed my hand over my mouth and stared at Henry, expecting to see my own shock registered on his face. But he was not looking at me. He had turned, and was looking at the doorway into the darkened hall.

I wondered what he saw. The children, I knew, were fast asleep, and the maid had retired to her quarters more than an hour ago. A faint chill crawled up my back, the sort of sensation I'd felt when I attended one of Cynthia Thoreau's seances.

"What's wrong?" I said.

When he did not answer, I moved around him and stepped into the hall. I caught a flicker of something white in the darkness. I hesitated, still bathed in the uncanny chill. *Wallie?* All my faculties were alert to the slightest motion or sound. I took a step toward the stairs and there was an answering flutter and a small thump. I glimpsed a small foot.

"Ellen?" I called, for I knew it must be one of the children, and most likely Ellen, since she was always the leader in their games. I found her, curled on the bottom step in her nightdress. Her head lay against the banister, and her thin arms circled her knees. She looked up at me and, despite the dim light, I could detect great sadness in her face.

"Did you have a nightmare? Did something give you a fright?" I took one of her hands and tried to pull her to her feet, but she would not move. She was nine years old, too big to lift. "Come, you must go back to bed," I said, my tenderness fading in the face of her defiance.

She shook her head and pulled her hand from mine. Her long black hair flickered through the air, slapping her shoulders and partially covering her face.

"Ellen!" My tone grew sharp. "Stop that! I insist that you go upstairs to bed immediately!"

She ceased shaking her head and looked up at me through the snarled tresses. "I saw you," she whispered. Her tone was both urgent and injured. "I saw you with Mr. Thoreau."

"Mr. Thoreau is a friend of your father's and mine, Ellen," I said. "You know that."

Her forehead puckered. She was silent for a moment, then she said, "I saw you *kiss* him, Mama!"

Pain stabbed at the back of my eyes. "Dear God!" I whispered, and low-ered myself to the step beside her. I pressed my palms to my forehead. I wanted with all my heart to tell her that she was mistaken in what she saw, that what had passed between Henry and me was an innocent sign of our friendship. But I could not falsify the truth without damaging myself.

I slowly raised my head. "Ellen, I'm sorry you did not stay in your bed as you were told." I spoke slowly and carefully. The words felt hard as chips of stone pried from frozen ground. "Spying on one's elders is a serious sin. You must pray for forgiveness."

She stared at me.

"Come." I rose and held out my hand. "We'll pray together for God's mercy."

Reluctantly, she took my hand and got to her feet. We climbed the stairs quickly, leaving Henry to bank the fire and extinguish the lights.

However fervently I might wish that Ellen would forget what she'd wit-nessed that night, I knew she would not. From a tender age, Ellen had dis-played a remarkable memory, a fascination with detail and discourse that enabled her to recite entire dinner conversations. She spent hours with Mother Emerson, relating the particulars of her day, and this brought them close. Over time, Mother Emerson drew Ellen into her pattern of thinking, and demonstrated a prim and cautious Christianity. She taught her how to be crit-ical of people's manners and eccentricities. And she encouraged her to always side with Mr. Emerson over me.

The night Ellen saw me embrace Henry I marched her upstairs and tucked her firmly into bed beside Edith. I warned her not to rise again until morning. She did not cry, nor even pout, but gazed at me with large, sorrow-ful eyes—her father's eyes—their piercing blue exactly matched Mr. Emer-son's. I could not erase from her memory what she had seen and heard, but I hoped that by stressing the sinfulness of spying she would not magnify it by the error of gossip. From her doorway, having left her without bestowing my usual kiss, I said softly but firmly, "A person's privacy is a sanctuary, Ellen. It must always be respected."

She nodded, and drew the blanket tightly beneath her chin. I knew she was entertaining thoughts that she would not divulge. In this she was like my husband, who rarely shared his reflections with me.

I remembered the life we had planned together in the days of our courtship—thoughts of a home distinguished by a warm and gracious hospitality, where we would welcome not only our friends, but all seekers after truth. And now the unwelcome seeker was my own child, and I was the one who sought to hide truth.

When I finally descended the stairs, I found the parlor empty.

I DID NOT SEE Henry again for two days, days I spent in wretched bouts of dread that alternated with fury at being so tightly bound by convention and shame that I seemed incapable of advancing my own happiness. When I finally came face-to-face with him, in the afternoon gloom of the downstairs hall, his glance flicked away from me, as an exposed finger jumps away from a flame.

"Be assured it won't happen again," I said, certain that he would grasp my meaning, though the passage of time since Ellen's interruption had shorn it of context.

He sighed. "Lidian—"

"No, hear me out." I was suddenly and fiercely angry—not at Henry but at myself and my foolish desires, which had victimized Henry and done nothing to liberate me. "I want to put all this behind us," I said. "All these unseemly thoughts and feelings."

He nodded slowly, as if weighing the wisdom of my words.

"We cannot continue as we have." I took a step toward him—my skirts floated over the floor. "We must refashion our friendship. To that end, I want to work with you to liberate the slaves."

He gave me a started frown. "You have no idea what you're asking."

"I mean to learn. Emancipation is everyone's work. Or it ought to be." I felt the fury of righteousness. I lashed out in what I now understood was a desperate attempt to save my life. "Don't deny me this, Henry! In the name of God, you must know that I cannot sit by and do nothing while you and others risk your lives fighting this great evil!"

He stood with his arms at his sides, watching me.

"Please, let me help you," I begged, my voice breaking. "Don't leave me to while away my hours in useless domesticity. I could do so much to help! This house has dozens of spaces to shelter fugitives. And so many strangers visit here that no one would suspect more comings and goings."

I stood before him, like a penitent submitting her fate to a judge. "Don't deny me this," I whispered. "If you have any feeling for me at all, you will say yes."

He closed his eyes briefly. For a moment I imagined he might be invoking God's direction, and when he opened his eyes again and gazed directly into mine, I knew that if he had not been asking God's help, God was at least there helping me. "Very well," he said. "There are ways you can be of use."

"That is all I ask."

BY THE END of the month, I was absorbed in what came to be known as the Underground Railroad. Nearly every week I welcomed new fugitives into my home, sequestering them in the garret and spending as much time near to hand as was possible without arousing suspicion. What was most surprising is that I was able to keep my endeavors from my curious children. They were always following me about like so many barn cats, hoping to be fed. Yet Henry contrived to deliver fugitives to my door under the welcome protection of darkness, when the children were long since tucked safely in their bed in the nursery upstairs.

One night after the departure of a young slave who had spent three days at Bush, I was in the garret tidying the area where he'd slept, making it ready for the next fugitive, whoever he might be. After I finished, I wandered among the discarded and stored furniture, my mind churning. By a strange trick of fate, a tall desk set against the wall in the northeast corner drew me, and I found myself standing before it, peering into its cupboards and sliding open the drawers. Most were empty, but I found in one a small packet of letters in blue ribbon. I undid the ribbon and examined the envelopes more closely. The packet was a collection of Ellen Tucker's letters.

I recalled my husband reading her letters, but I'd not seen him do so in recent years. I'd allowed myself to imagine that he had destroyed them, thus freeing himself—and me—of that bond. Instead, he'd hidden them in a secret place. I wondered how often he climbed the stairs to the garret, how many yearning nights he pored over them. I suddenly imagined myself standing before the fire in my chamber and dropping the letters one by one into the open flame. I could feel the liberation this action would bring to my mind and heart. All my married life I'd lived in the shadow of Ellen Tucker's beauty and gaiety. Whenever my husband spoke her name, his voice filled with a tenderness that I craved for myself.

I slid the packet into the pocket of my gown and closed the empty drawer.

I went down the stairs and passed Henry's room. There was a line of light beneath his door. I pictured him at his small desk writing. I had often seen him bent over the page, so absorbed in his work that he didn't hear my approach. Lately he'd been working on a series of essays about his two years living beside Walden Pond. He dreamed of making them into a book—a sequel to his volume of adventures on the Concord and Merrimack rivers. I hesitated, longing to knock and enter, to show him the cache of letters. I believed he would share my despair.

Yet I knew he would not welcome the interruption, for though he was unlike Mr. Emerson in many ways, in their close attention to their work they were the same—both immersed themselves so thoroughly that even the smallest distraction provoked a rebuke. I went past the door and into my own chamber, my skirt hems shushing along the floor, making a sad sound that reminded me of rain.

I placed the lantern on the small table by the bed and knelt in front of the fire. I was gratified that beneath a fine layer of gray ash I found the coals still glowing. I soon had a fire blazing heartily. I slid the packet from my pocket. Oddly, it seemed to have grown heavy and damp, as if each letter had been saturated in tears. When I untied the ribbon, several of the letters slipped from my grasp and fluttered to the floor.

I stooped and picked one up. It had escaped its envelope, and I found myself reading the first two lines.

Dear Waldo, I love you, says Ellen T. I dream about you again night and day.

I opened another envelope and scanned the lines. Ellen's handwriting was exquisitely ornamented—nothing at all like my sharp, open scrawl. And her words—such love, such unaffected adoration!

I collected all the envelopes and carried them to the bed, spilling them there in white profusion. I don't know exactly what was in my mind. Perhaps nothing more than a sudden whim. At that point, I still believed I would burn them, yet my curiosity compelled me to read more.

What I found was poignant courage and a sweet and gentle wit.

Waldo the parting prayer murmured over my pillow is sweetly receiving its answer. . . . I want to tell you that I love you very much and would like to have you love me always, if consistent with your future plans.

No wonder Mr. Emerson could not let her memory die.

I read until dawn, opening one envelope after another. I read until my eyes were sore and my heart ached. Reading her words, holding the very paper where she'd rested her hand, I felt as if she were present in the room, regarding me with her large, enchanting eyes, her perfect lips tilted into a gentle smile. I imagined her as a dear younger sister—gentle and sweet-natured, impossible not to love.

The last envelope was fatter than the others. When I opened it, I discovered that it was not a letter at all, but a sheaf of poems. I read them slowly and with great tenderness. The last one must have been written shortly before her death.

> *And Hope, sweet bird & kind, at last has flown*
> *And of her beauty scarce a trace is found*
> *Save a slight tinge where her last splendour shone*
> *And there a golden feather quivering on the ground—*
> *Just bright enough to cheat the eager eye*
> *Just strong enough temptation for a lie.*

Light was sliding between the curtains when I folded all the letters and poems back into their envelopes. I wept openly, unable to stem my tears.

As I tied the packet together again, I felt a terrible longing to talk to my husband. It occurred to me that Henry was probably awake—he always rose before dawn—and that I could turn to him as I had so often in the past. And yet I hesitated. For though I knew he would be sympathetic to my situation, I believed he would not comprehend the conflicted condition of my heart. As I read Ellen's actual words for the first time and knowing, as I read, how brief her life span was to be, my heart had unfolded and opened like a summer rose. I suddenly understood how completely she had transformed my husband's life—she'd given him his most profound experience of the divine—she had softened his heart, made it pliable and true. Though what I most frequently encountered in him was ice, still I knew that he was capable of fire.

I reflected on the core of great tenderness that lay within my husband. His apparent coolness was not the result of a stony heart, but a protection from a surfeit of suffering. I'd spent years striving in vain to turn his affection toward me. Yet I understood now that it was not because I was unlovable, but because Mr. Emerson was not capable of opening himself so widely to anyone again. Ellen's death had scarred his heart too deeply. And Wallie's passing had dealt a second, near fatal blow.

I heard a cock crow from the direction of the Hosmer farm. Within the hour, I would hear the children begin to stir in the nursery. I'd not slept that night; my eyelids were heavy, yet I knew I could not rest before I had unburdened my heart to my husband.

I carried the lantern to my writing table, and sat in the straight chair. As I picked up my pen and dipped it in the glass inkwell, it occurred to me that I, too, had fallen in love with Ellen Tucker.

29

Fidelity

Love must be as much a light as a flame.
—HENRY DAVID THOREAU

In the second week of May, I received Mr. Emerson's reply to my letter. I'd expected dismay and disapproval, even harsh words, but he wrote that he was deeply moved by my action and observations. Once again, he extolled Ellen's sweetness and virtue, reminding me again of how dearly he had once loved her—and loved her still. His melancholy reminder that I'd not known her was softened by his commendation of my feelings, which he called just and noble. I carried his letter throughout that week, as if it were not mere words but the gentle caress of his hand that I could draw from my pocket at will. One afternoon as I sat reading it yet again in my garden, Henry chanced on me and asked what caused my wistful expression. I handed him the letter and he read it standing silent before me. When he finally raised his eyes to meet mine, he sighed.

"This is typical, isn't it? Ever since I've known him, Waldo's slighted you.

He recognizes your nobility only in light of your admiration for Ellen. He praises you for docility and submission while your true strength and power is lodged in your passion and independence."

My passion and independence. Henry's words had the strange effect of making my heart beat more quickly. I rose slowly.

"I'm not insensible to his slights." I recalled Henry's proposal that I flee with him to the west. He had made it weeks before, yet it seemed to me as if he had suggested it only moments ago—the memory was so fresh in my mind that it seemed to demand an immediate response. "I have thought about your proposition."

His forehead puckered. "Proposition?"

"That the children and I could go west with you."

"My business is here in Concord now," he said. "My situation has changed."

I did not allow any embarrassment to show. I raised my chin and fixed him with a look that was not unlike my husband's penetrating stare. "As has mine," I said. "I was about to tell you that I believe it would best serve the Cause to remain as Mr. Emerson's wife."

Henry studied my face, and his own appeared to redden, though I told myself it was the late afternoon light. "You are right," he said. "Your wisdom is as discerning as ever."

"I wish I were wise enough to compel my husband to listen to me," I said.

"That is not your deficiency," Henry said, handing the letter back to me. His voice had the buoyancy of relief. "It is his."

MR. EMERSON SAILED back to Boston at the end of July. His return was quiet, undisturbed by fanfare or celebration. The coach from Boston simply pulled up in front of our door late one afternoon, and he stepped off and walked into the house. I was in the nursery folding the children's linens, and when I heard the door, I went to the top of the stairs and peered over the rail. When I saw my husband looking up at me, my legs propelled me down the stairs and into his arms. I disregarded his stiffness, and his awkward confusion about what to do with his hands; I embraced him with warmth and thanksgiving. I voiced no recriminations for the infrequency and coldness of his letters. I welcomed him back into our home with simple gratitude that his long journey was over. If Mr. Emerson puzzled over my behavior, he said nothing, but immediately settled into his customary routine.

When Henry came back from his afternoon walk and found Mr. Emerson in residence again, he went up to his room and packed his things. He found me in the kitchen, where I was rolling out a piecrust.

"I'm going home." He stood stiffly in the doorway and it was only when he didn't come into the room and drop into a chair as was his custom that I noticed he carried his satchel.

"Home? But this is your home!"

He shook his head. "No longer. I have other lives to live."

Something in the shape and width of his shoulders made me see in him a strength and a competence I'd not fully comprehended. He was nearly thirty-one years old. It was time for him to draw apart from Mr. Emerson's influence. I had read his book; I knew the life he celebrated in those pages could only be lived by someone unburdened by wife and child. He had become his own man. He was no longer Mr. Emerson's. He was no longer mine.

"You've changed," my husband told me a week after his return as we walked after dinner in the garden. "There's something serene about you—not your usual studied composure, either. This is different. New."

"Thank you." I bent to pick a wilted rose from its stem.

"It is an observation, not a compliment. Did something happen while I was in Europe?"

I looked at him. His eyes were searching me, *seeing* me, in a way they had not for years. He seemed to find me interesting again.

"A great deal happened," I said. "You were gone for ten months."

He sighed.

I plucked another dead blossom. "If your concern is for my reputation, I can assure you it is intact. The people of Concord still view me as the peculiar wife of the great Mr. Emerson."

"Lidian." He put his hand on my arm, but it was his tone more than his gesture that caused me to look at him. "I know our marriage has not been what we desired. What we had reason to expect."

His words so startled me that I could think of no reply. I stared at him.

"But I do not feel that I—that either of us—is much to blame in this. We were beguiled by illusions of love and marriage and easily misled. It's natural.

But there are consolations." His hand slid up my arm to my shoulder. "Our children have brought us both great joy. And there is, I think, a mutual respect between us, a generous compassion, despite the strains and trials. Don't you find it so?"

I looked down at the brown petals in my hand. "I would like to think so, Mr. Emerson. But it is small comfort when compared to my hopes."

He nodded and then surprised me a second time by taking me in his arms. He held me with rare and unexpected tenderness. I closed my eyes and, for a moment, all the anguish of the previous thirteen years dissolved in the perfect silence of the garden.

I wondered, in the days and weeks that followed our encounter, if my husband and I would find the will and determination to renew our marriage. Mr. Emerson was more solicitous of my health than he had been in many years, and he smiled at me more often over his dinner plate. Yet much of the time he sought solitude or the company of his philosopher friends. He no longer walked with Henry, however. A strained antagonism stood between them now, one I feared would continue forever.

IN MAY OF 1850 came news that nearly undid my husband—the brig *Elizabeth,* bound for New York from Italy, had run aground in a storm on the shoals off Fire Island only fifty miles from home. Among those who perished in the cold seas were Margaret Fuller, her husband, and their infant son.

Mr. Emerson spread the paper across the dining-room table and sat, poring over the words for hours, as if to memorize them. Finally he closed the paper and stood up.

"I'm going to New York," he said. His voice was hollow, as if he spoke from the depths of a cave. "I intend to bring her body back here—to Concord."

"Here?" I was shocked. "But her home is in Groton. Her family will want her buried there, surely."

He shook his head violently. I had never seen him so agitated. His hands were clamped into bony fists and his mouth was a dark cleft in his face.

"You don't understand," he said. "I feel responsible. I begged her to come here to live—I have paid for a home for her—" His voice caught; he swallowed, holding up his hand that I might not interrupt him. "I owe a great deal to her, Lidian. So many of her thoughts became my own."

"You owe a great deal to every one of your friends," I said bitterly. "And to me as well."

"You are my wife," he said softly.

"Indeed, as I was while Margaret visited," I said, carefully. "Let Henry go in your place. He can be your ambassador and bring her remains back to Concord if that's agreeable to her family."

Henry's name invoked the briefest flinch. "I doubt that Henry will accommodate me. He tells me I have offended him, though he will not say how."

"Then I'll speak to him," I said.

He was silent a moment. Then he said, "I'd be grateful if you would."

Henry left for Fire Island the next day.

Neither Margaret's body nor her husband's were found. Henry showed us a button he'd torn from a coat belonging to Margaret's husband. It struck me as unutterably tragic that Margaret had died so soon after becoming a mother. There was a fateful symbolism in it, as if history affirmed that a woman could either put her mark upon the world of men or bear a child, but she could not do both.

My husband, as was his habit, buried his grief in his work. He wrote a memoir of Margaret to inform the world of the power of her intellect, and the pure force of her character. He reread every letter she'd written him, every essay and poem she had published. He began a new notebook devoted solely to her life and works. He spoke of Margaret constantly, insisting that when she died, he had lost his chief audience. Her friendship, he announced, had opened his eyes to female possibility and had introduced him to a new level of intimacy.

Margaret's death opened a chasm between my husband and God—a chasm that would not close. He began speaking as if his life had no meaning or center. The world had become for him a welter of confusion, a dark chaos of suffering and death. Though I clung to my faith, it seemed at times that I dangled at the edge of a precipice and that God's mercy alone was the reason I did not fall.

ONE BRIGHT AUTUMN afternoon, as I cut flowers for an arrangement in the parlor, Mr. Emerson joined me in the garden. He greeted me pleasantly and asked the name of the flowers I held.

"Asters." I extended one of the dark pink blossoms out to him. He took it and examined it as if there were some philosophical wisdom to be found beneath its velvet petals.

Something prompted me to watch him rather than return to my labors. "What occasions your company?" I asked finally. "I thought you planned to visit Bronson today."

He looked up from the flower. "I'll go shortly. There's a concern I must discuss with you—about Ellen."

I could not think what this might be. Ellen was his favorite. I did not imagine she could do or say anything that would trouble him.

"What's happened?" I glanced over my shoulder at the house, where the children were rolling their hoops in the dooryard.

"She has a fine imagination, but she needs to learn its proper use. Like an unharnessed river it can destroy as well as nourish."

"What do you mean?"

He fixed me in his hawklike gaze. "She has told me a story that, if spread, could become an ugly rumor. I reprimanded her, but I think you ought to caution her as well, since the story concerns you."

"What story is this?"

He crossed his hands in front of him, grasping his left wrist in his right palm. "She says that you and Henry Thoreau kissed in my absence. I think you ought to persuade her that it's not true. She seems to have confused imagination and reality."

"But it is true," I said quietly. "She's reporting what she saw."

His somber expression twisted toward a smile. "But don't you see? Her limited vocabulary misrepresents your friendship. We must strive more resolutely to make the situation clear to her, lest her words become rumors. These ambiguities try everyone, and are nearly always misunderstood by society."

I absorbed the possibilities in his amiable smile. Here was my chance to dismiss my sin, to put my adultery behind me. My husband was giving me an opportunity to collaborate with him in a gentle lie. There would be no recriminations between us, no unpleasant scenes. I closed my eyes a moment and what rose in my mind was the face of a slave I'd sheltered a few months before—a young woman so weak from hunger she could barely stand—a woman who had nearly lost her life in her quest for freedom. And I knew in that instant that to collude with my husband now would be to make myself forever a slave to falsehood and deceit. My soul was chained—had been chained for years, as surely as any slave's body—to two men. I'd imagined first one, then the other, would make me free. But I had to set myself free.

I took a deep breath. "I believe she accurately interpreted what she saw," I said.

He was silent for a long time, but I did not redirect my gaze. I looked straight at him and waited for my words to penetrate. Finally he frowned and touched the side of his nose. "I know that you and Henry are friends. I never imagined it was more than that."

"It was always more than that." The flowers trembled against my skirts, but I did not drop them.

His face went hard—turned to granite before my eyes. "How many times?"

I frowned at him and at this absurd notion that mathematics mattered.

"How many times were you intimate with him?" His words came out as separate beads of sound.

"Once."

"Once? Do you expect me to believe that?" I read contempt in the line of his mouth and the raised eyebrows.

"It's the truth," I said.

His upper lip twisted oddly. "Your assignation must have been unsatisfying, then, if it was only once."

I shook my head. "No. It was the most joyous moment of my life, Mr. Emerson. I finally learned what love can be."

I saw that I'd reached him, for it was plain that my words struck hard. He winced with each one. He turned away and sat down heavily on the nearby bench. I did not move.

"When was this single tryst?" He spoke without looking at me—his gaze was directed at the ground. "After you kissed him?"

"No. Long before—when he was working on Staten Island and came home for Thanksgiving. The incident in the parlor—" I hesitated. I did not believe there were words to express what I had to say. "I wanted to reawaken his memory of our love."

I could feel the force of my husband's scowl. "Reawaken his memory?"

"He does not acknowledge our tryst," I said. "He never speaks of it. It's as if it never happened."

He made a ticking sound in the back of his throat. "I think it highly unlikely that a man—especially a man like Henry—would forget such an event."

"Then perhaps he remembers but chooses to lock it away from his recollection. It isn't the first time. He did the same with the woodland fire he set with Edmund Hoar. And he never speaks of his brother anymore."

Mr. Emerson made a small sigh, yet I knew he was weighing the truth of my words. "There's an element in Henry that embraces paradox, that loves contradiction."

"Then you do believe me." I said it so definitively that there was no room for argument. Nor did he offer any. Mr. Emerson sat on the bench, his head bowed, his hands on his knees, silent for so long that I had the preposterous thought that his mind had turned to other concerns. Then he spoke into the silence.

"And how widely is this infidelity known in town?"

His question startled me. "I believe no one knows," I said. "Is that all that matters to you? Your reputation?"

"Were you expecting me to exhibit a manly jealousy?"

"Hardly," I said. "But perhaps you might acknowledge the fact that the incident was not only my doing, but yours."

A startled expression flickered briefly on his face before it returned to its customary repose. "*My* doing?"

"Mr. Emerson, whatever has happened in the past, I am now seeking a reason to salvage our marriage. A reason beyond reputation."

"Disillusion is the nature of marriage."

"That's only true in a union where there is no love." I took a deep breath. "I have learned not to seek, nor expect, your affection, Mr. Emerson. Yet I believe I could have experienced a true and loving marriage, had it been with the right person."

His expression turned scornful. "If you imagine that Henry is that person, you're mistaken. Of all the men I have ever met, he's the least suited to marriage."

"There's a great deal about Henry that you don't know."

"No doubt. But I daresay that's true for you as well. For everyone, in fact, who claims him as friend. But where do these facts leave us, after all? Are you asking my forgiveness? Do you seek a divorce?" He straightened and folded his arms across his chest. "Is that it? You are about to leave me? To run off with a young man whom I've welcomed into my house and treated as a son?"

"You have treated Henry as a disciple, not a son," I said coldly. "And I think your condemnation of me ought not to wax too righteous."

"You're thinking of Ellen."

I shook my head. "I could never expect you to stop loving Ellen. She was your wife, after all. I was thinking of other transgressions." He bowed his head and I knew that I'd hit the mark. Yet I found no pleasure in my accuracy, but only a great sadness, which swept through me like the wind that suddenly came up and tossed the branches of the hemlocks behind us. "I cannot forget the moonlight walks you took with Margaret Fuller," I said. "Nor the long hours you spent in her chamber when she lived with us, while I lay upstairs, ill with one fever or another. And there were others besides Margaret—Anna Barker, Caroline Sturgis, Mary Russell."

"They were not the same as Margaret," he said, so softly that I could barely make out his voice above the wind.

"You persuaded her to live with us," I said. "That's why she was returning from Europe—to settle here, so that you could continue your association."

He said nothing, staring down at the bench seat, as if he might wrest some wisdom from the grain of the wood. Finally he looked up at me. I took a deep breath, but said nothing.

"For what it's worth, I could not persuade her. She refused to accommodate me. I believe she loved Count Ossoli very much."

I thought of Henry and my love for him. I thought of how both Mr. Emerson and I had struggled to be faithful to our vows while espousing a new openness in the relations between men and women. Of how we had each failed in our own way. In the fullness of that moment I saw myself for the first time, not as a captive of God's will, but as a woman who had the strength to live the life she was given. As a woman free in the world.

I approached my husband and laid the flowers on the bench beside him. "I haven't left you, Mr. Emerson, because I have not yet chosen to."

He looked up at me. The sun was full on his face as I stood before him and he was forced to squint. "But your words suggest you will."

"I don't know what the future will bring," I said. "I only know that I am free to choose."

He raised his hand to shade his eyes. "What is it that you want of our marriage, Lidian?"

I had no answer. I closed my eyes.

"Perhaps it is not too late to amend it," he said slowly.

His words took a moment to penetrate my thoughts. I looked at him. "Amend it. In what way?"

"By modifying our habits," he said. "We ought not to continue opening our home to everyone." He was no longer looking at me, but off into the distance, the way he often did when he was introducing an unfamiliar idea into a conversation. "We ought to attend less to new philosophers and more to each other."

I knew how he treasured his friendships, how dearly he held the image of himself as a gracious and welcoming host.

"It's a hard thing to remake a marriage when so much suffering has passed between us." I picked up the flowers and sat beside him on the bench. They lay in my lap, downy pink orbs on long stems.

"Perhaps suffering is the very tie that binds."

I thought instantly of Wallie. "In some cases. But not, I think, in ours."

He looked quickly down at the ground.

"What will this new arrangement require of me?" I asked after some time had passed.

"Nothing, except that you stay with me," he said in a low voice.

"Surely you want me to break my attachment to Henry."

"I think that you will do so without my requiring it. Your own nobility will not allow you to do otherwise."

I felt a flash of astonished gratitude. "A forlorn nobility is no substitute for love," I said.

He studied my face thoughtfully. "I often entertained that very thought after Ellen died," he said quietly. "For of course you are right—there is no substitute at all for love. But perhaps we are better suited to each other than we imagined." He surprised me by taking my hand. "Let's begin again. For the sake of our children, if not our vows. Will you not try with me, Lidian?"

I looked into his eyes and saw a glimmer of hope. I thought of the intellect and nobility and honesty that had first caused me to love him.

"I will," I said.

After that night, we no longer invited our friends for prolonged visits. The Prophet's Chamber and the Red Room stood empty except for a rare overnight guest. We lived as two friends who knew each other long and well— side by side, but unfettered. We attended lectures and social events according to our own particular interests. I no longer arranged my life around my husband's schedule, but made plans and traveled on my own. I went often to Plymouth and stayed with my aunts and cousins. I went to New York and visited childhood friends. I went to a water treatment spa in Maine, where Mary Moody Emerson indulged herself in the healing waters.

My life assumed the shape of a nautilus shell—it held many chambers, divided by fragile, translucent walls. I lived separate, discrete lives within these chambers—there was one for each of my children, one for my husband, one for my garden, one for Plymouth, and one for Concord. And one—the smallest and closest to my heart—for Henry.

30

Constancy

I am not wiser for my age,
Nor skilful by my grief;
Life loiters at the book's first page.
Ah! could we turn the leaf.
—RALPH WALDO EMERSON

Despite Mr. Emerson's expectations, I never formally broke with Henry. But after my confession, the quality of urgency left our association. If Henry was relieved or saddened by this change, he never told me. Instead, he honored it by no longer intruding on my solitude. The dwindling of our friendship had a curious effect on him. It seemed to drive him deeper into the exploration of nature, and I gradually became convinced that this was his true calling.

When, in August of 1854, Henry's book, *Walden,* was published, he inscribed a copy to me. I read it slowly and carefully, distilling his rare and original wisdom. Many of the thoughts were familiar to me, for he had spoken them in conversations, and read passages aloud from his manuscript while I mended clothes in the parlor on winter afternoons.

The next spring, we repaired the leaking roof over the back of the house, and finished a large bedchamber above the parlor for Mr. Emerson and myself. Henry's chamber was opened into a hallway, leading from the front-stairs landing to the back of the house. The room Henry had occupied was gone.

THE ABOLITIONIST John Brown came to Concord in January of 1859 seeking funds. He was such a polite and gentle man I could not credit the rumors that circulated of his involvement in the atrocities in Kansas. I regarded him as the trumpet of God, calling the nation to righteousness.

I rejoiced when war came, convinced the beginning that it was a holy struggle and that God ordained its course. When the men who had enlisted left Concord, I was at the railway station to salute them. What courage they displayed! Their sacrifice for the grandest of causes stirred my heart. How much more valuable is a life lived for a noble purpose!

I believe that Henry would have volunteered to join the army had his failing body allowed it, for his hatred of slavery would have permitted him no other choice. But by the time the first shells fell upon Fort Sumter, he was already in the advanced stages of consumption. He still took long walks and frequented my parlor, but one look at his face told me how ill he was. His eyes were sunken and there was an ashen cast to his skin. He coughed incessantly and no longer went abroad in the early mornings. He grew a beard in emulation of John Brown, though I believe it was also an attempt to hide his wasted features. The gray and white tangle of hair gave him the appearance of a sage and, curiously, made him look older than my husband. Something in Henry seemed to soften and settle. He grew less combative, less judgmental of the opinions and actions of others. This was a phenomenon I'd observed before in the very ill. Usually I found it cheering, but in Henry's case, it merely increased my sorrow.

THE LAST TIME I saw Henry was in January of 1862. I was putting linens away upstairs, and when I came down I found him standing quite still at the bottom of the stairs. It was typical for him to come unexpectedly and let himself in the east entrance, and so my only surprise was the advanced debilitation of his features. There was no denying the fact that he was dying. The bones of his wrists looked sharp and abnormally large beneath his thin skin. An incessant rattle came from his lungs, yet his face was remarkably peaceful.

After a moment he seemed to start awake, as if out of a dream, and, glancing up, he saw me. His gaunt features brightened. "Ah, Lidian! You look well."

"And you?" The lace of my cap brushed my cheek. "How are you faring?"

"Let's not talk of that." He smiled. "I was just recalling one of our winter outings with the children, the year Waldo was in Europe. We skated on the river—do you remember? It was Eddy's first—" He broke off to cough into his hand, then pulled a handkerchief from his pocket and pressed it hard against his mouth. My stomach clenched, for the gesture reminded me of my mother in her last months. There was the same hectic flush in his cheeks, the same circle of ashen skin around his mouth. When his seizure subsided, he wiped his mouth carefully. I could see flecks of scarlet on his handkerchief. He caught my glance and stuffed the cloth quickly into his pocket.

"There's no need for alarm. It's as good to be sick as to be well. It makes no difference to my spirits."

I studied him to determine if he were telling the truth, though I knew it was not in Henry to lie. The words he spoke were always sincere, if sometimes paradoxical. It was his silences that held the darkness.

"I assure you, it's true—I enjoy life now, as much as ever, though I have little of it left." He paused and a smile tugged at the corners of his mouth. "So they tell me. But one never knows about these things, does one? I could live to be a hundred. It would not surprise me."

It was a jest, and a dark one, yet I mustered the strength to join in. "Nor I." I returned his smile. "I've always thought you are like one of your venerable and beloved trees—built to endure for generations."

He shook his head. "It would be a curse to endure for more than one. I'm content to have lived where and when I have." His gaze had softened though it still penetrated; his eyes that day were the hue of the sea before a storm. "Yet there are other lives I would willingly have lived," he added quietly.

I sucked in my breath. "As would I," I whispered.

He smiled and I tried to smile back at him, but my mouth would not work properly. Nor would my stinging eyes, for his face rippled and blurred.

"Lidian."

Something broke inside me. I turned and rushed up the stairs, no longer able to bear the sight of his sad expression, knowing as I fled that I would never see him again in this life. Knowing that he did not believe in another.

For the last three months of his life, Henry was confined to his house under the scrutiny of his mother, while his sister Sophia ministered to him as tenderly as a wife. On the afternoon of May sixth, Mr. Emerson came home at midday with the news that Henry had died that morning around nine o'clock. He stood in the hallway with his head bowed—I could not see his eyes. "I called at the house and Sophia met me at the door. She said it was very beautiful." He hesitated and took a long breath. "There were birds at the window, and spring sunshine pouring over him."

I said nothing, but bent my head away from him and shortly retired to my chamber. I stood at the window, staring out at the garden, where the lilacs were budding, though they would not bloom for another three weeks. My hands found their way to my heart and rested there, one on top of the other, as if their weight might still the incessant beating that would not give me rest.

Mr. Emerson insisted that Henry's funeral be held in the First Parish Church. This over my objection and the puzzlement of Henry's friends, who quickly perceived the irony in it. More curiously, Mr. Emerson took charge of all the arrangements. I never learned how my husband wrested that right from Cynthia and Sophia. Perhaps he appealed to Cynthia's vanity. By that time my husband had become so famous that wherever he turned his regard, attention followed.

The funeral was held at three in the afternoon on the ninth of May. The weather was mild and the air redolent with flowers. Birds sang as the church bell tolled once for each of Henry's forty-four years. I leaned on Mr. Emerson's arm as we walked near the head of the long mourning procession. Henry's coffin stood in the church vestibule, covered in wildflowers. I stood a moment, gazing down at it and, without pausing to consider the significance of my gesture, I stepped to the coffin and caressed it. How I longed to raise the lid and look once again on Henry's dear face! But the coffin was closed, as Henry himself had requested. What was death to look upon? he had said. It was *life* one must be about.

The service began with the reading of selected Bible passages, and then the choir sang a hymn written by Ellery Channing. Bronson Alcott read a few passages from Henry's own writings, and my husband delivered a eulogy that moved many to tears. Then Henry's body was carried to the graveyard at the end of Bedford Street. A long procession followed, including hundreds of schoolchildren bearing armfuls of flowers.

The coffin was lowered and more prayers spoken. As the first shovelful of earth dropped into the grave, I let out a small gasp. But that was all. I shed no tears, spoke no memorable words. My body felt as cold as a corpse.

I looked down at the grass by my feet, where early violets were blooming.

As my husband turned away from the grave, he spoke the words I'd so often spoken in private, but with which he had never before concurred, "He had a beautiful soul."

Within days of the funeral, Mr. Emerson had appropriated Henry's letters and journals from Sophia and locked himself away with them in his study. For weeks he pored over the papers, reading them with the concentration of a hunter. What was it that he sought? Was it—as he encouraged his friends to believe—a simple thirst for wisdom? Did he mean to ferret out proof of his influence over Henry? Or—and this was my fear—was he searching for evidence of my intimacy with Henry? If so, he remained unsatisfied, for all mention of me had long since been torn from Henry's journals.

The only record of our affection lay in the small garret room above my bedchamber. There, hidden under a floorboard, resting in a wooden box Henry had given me one Christmas, were the letters he had written me. They were filled with all the tenderness and devotion I'd longed to receive from my husband. I read them over in times of loneliness and despair, climbing the attic steps as one might climb the stairs to heaven, for my heart always lightened, knowing what I would find.

There were sixteen letters, written over the course of nearly twenty years, and I'd read every one so many times I knew them all by heart. Yet my pulse still quickened when I unfolded one and held the yellowed pages, clasping them with as much tenderness as I'd once held my babes. No matter how many years passed, Henry's words never failed to bring both pain and solace. The script had faded on the page, but the words were branded into my heart.

I cannot tell where you leave off and I begin. I love you as I love my own flesh, for I have annexed your soul to mine, as a man annexes a new field and it becomes part of his farm . . . I can love you purely, knowing you will demand of me only my best self. You complete me . . . My heart will always answer to your heart. Your presence enhances my entire life, and makes the flowers bloom and the birds sing with new delight. All the days of the year are fair because of you . . .

Tucked in the folded page of one letter was a sprig of dried andromeda. It was Henry's favorite plant. He admired its delicacy of form, the elegant narrow leaves and pure white blossoms, shaped like tiny bells. For years, he had brought me small bouquets of it from his woodland excursions. Now, one dried ivory floweret was all that remained.

THE YEARS BURST around me, like pods of milkweed in late August, erupting in filaments that sailed past on the wind of time. In 1862, my husband traveled to Washington, met President Lincoln, and delivered a speech urging the immediate emancipation of the slaves. A year later, Mr. Lincoln proclaimed that emancipation and I celebrated that Day of Jubilee as I had no other. When the president was assassinated, I mourned with the rest of the Union. In 1865, Edith married Will Forbes, who had courted her for seven long years. The next year my husband woke me one morning to announce that I was now a grandmother. Edith had given birth to a son. Little Ralph was followed in 1867 by Violet, and eventually by seven others, three of whom died while still children. Life always brings endings as well as beginnings. In 1868, Louisa Alcott published the book that made her famous, while I nursed my sister through her final illness. Lucy went to her rest as quietly as dark shadows leave a room at dawn. In 1871, Edward became engaged to Annie Keyes and my husband traveled to California. Then, one spring afternoon in 1872, Mr. Emerson returned from his walk with soot in his hair and the news that the grove of trees Henry had planted by Walden Pond had burned.

"The pines?" I recalled Henry's bright smile the evening he returned from planting the seedlings.

"Yes," Mr. Emerson said, nodding. "All gone. A few may survive. Three or four. Perhaps half a dozen."

I pictured the low hillside in flames and my stomach twisted. "I cannot bear it," I said aloud.

Mr. Emerson looked at me. "*You* cannot bear it? It's not your land, Lidian. It's mine. When was the last time you even set foot near the pond?"

"There are things you do not know."

"I know you spend weeks at a time in Plymouth. I know you putter in your garden as if the quantity and size of your roses made some difference in the world. I know you fret endlessly for the children's welfare, and not at all for mine." He rose slowly. "I know enough, I think." And then he walked past me and into his study, where he firmly shut the door.

Something in me released when that door shut. It was as if a hidden cyst burst open, expelling years of pain. I followed him and, without knocking, thrust open the door. He was seated in his rocking chair at the table, shuffling papers.

"Care not for *your* welfare!" I stood in the doorway, bracing one hand on each side of the frame. He scowled up at me. "Why do you imagine I have stayed with you all these years if it was not because I care for you?"

He dropped the papers and leaned back in his chair, which rocked gently beneath him. "Why? Because you believe God will punish you if you leave me."

"No," I said. "You are wrong, Mr. Emerson! I no longer worship the chastening God of my childhood. It's because I *love* you that I stay married. Love you despite all the disappointments and deficiencies in our union."

He looked stricken, his countenance unnaturally pale, his mouth open, waiting for words he could not find. For a terrible moment I wondered if he'd fallen into an apoplectic fit. I went to him and reached to touch his face, but he caught my hand and rocked back in his chair, making me lose my balance. I fell against the table and, putting out my free hand to steady myself, caught up a sheaf of papers. I looked at them as I righted myself, and my eyes caught the words: *I have no facility for society or love, nothing but a bleak determination.*

Startled, my gaze flashed to meet my husband's and I perceived what I never had before: Mr. Emerson's lack of confidence, his childlike yearning for approval and admiration. I saw the boy he had been—had never ceased being—beneath the familiar lines of his aging face. I dropped the papers.

"Waldo," I whispered, surprising myself as well as my husband by using the name I'd forsworn. I put my arms around him and pressed his puzzled face to my breast. "Oh, Waldo, how could you not have *known?*"

I heard a sound come from him—a strangled moan—and then his arms went around me and he pulled me down onto his lap. He pressed his face to my breast and I cradled him there as naturally as I would a babe. After some time, he raised his head. I saw that he was as astonished as I by this new and unfamiliar intimacy. His expression was so unguarded—so utterly defenseless—that I could not stop myself from kissing him on the mouth—a liberty I'd not taken in years. He murmured my name and put his hand to my cheek, the tenderest of gestures.

We sat in mutual silence for a long time. Finally I slid off his lap and left him to his papers. I went out to the garden, feeling less encumbered than I had in years.

That night, after Mr. Emerson retired, I burned Henry's letters in the kitchen stove. The little packet, tied with a blue ribbon worn to shreds, recorded Henry's generous love in bold handwriting that marched across the pages as vigorously as he had marched through my life.

One by one, I opened the letters and read them. One by one, I dropped them into the flames.

I was free.

FOR MR. EMERSON, the end came in 1882 with merciful simplicity. On the nineteenth of April, he came home from his afternoon walk drenched by a cold rain. The next morning, as Ellen helped him descend the stairs, he cried out and staggered as if he had been struck a blow. He began to experience pain early on the evening of the twenty-seventh. Edward gave him ether, for nothing else would calm him. I sat beside him and stroked his hand, determined to watch through the night. He died just before nine, with a slow and gentle exhalation, much as Henry had described Wallie's death so many years ago—like mist rising from a pond.

I did not weep. I rose and went down the hall and into the room that had been my bridal chamber, where I stood at the window staring out at the night sky. There were no stars. The church bell began to toll out my husband's death. Seventy-nine long peals, one for each year of his life. The chimes seemed to go on forever in the April darkness.

IT SNOWED during the night. I rose just before dawn and went to the window where I'd stood the night before. Ice crystals frosted the lower pane, forming tiny white ferns. I looked down at the rhodora blossoms, drooping under their burden of snow. How perfectly the snow symbolized God's mercy, falling unnoticed through the darkness, transforming everything.

I touched the frosted glass with the tip of my finger. The edge of a fern instantly dissolved into silver beads of water, and I saw how plainly the lesson was writ—that I could destroy a thing of beauty with thoughtless ease. I was no different from anyone else, despite the many years I'd striven for perfection. The more I strove, the more deeply I'd become mired in sin. My life had been fixed on coupled stars—from my double baptism and two names, and my twofold home of Plymouth and Concord, to the twin constellation of my attraction to Mr. Emerson and Henry Thoreau.

Yet God had set only one North Star to guide the sojourner, fixed a single design at the heart of creation.

I gazed out at the yard where my snow-shrouded garden lay in shadow, waiting. A tongue of pink light licked the horizon and glimmered over Bristor's Hill. Soon the sun would rise and fill the tracks of rabbits and birds with light; the snow would melt and the rhodoras would open their petals. Each day there was this gift of possibility, this emblem of mercy, showing that forgiveness is the North Star of the soul. The only warranty of love.

Lidian Jackson Emerson survived her husband by nearly ten years. She died on November 13, 1892, at the age of ninety, having outlived nearly all the members of her social circle. Although I have included many real events from Lidian's life in the novel, her motivations, perspective, and personality are my invention. History, tethered by fact, cannot probe very far into the dark fissures and bright voids of life. *Mr. Emerson's Wife* explores the "cracks" in the historical record, the places we do not—cannot—know. It tells what "might have been." Like all fiction, it is an attempt to explore not merely the truth of chronology, but the truth of the human condition.

For the factual record of the life of this brilliant and remarkable woman who influenced America's most influential literary figure, the reader should turn to the scholarship of Delores Bird Carpenter and the collected letters of Ellen Tucker Emerson.

Acknowledgments

The life of Lidian Jackson Emerson, shrouded to the point of obscurity in many biographies of Ralph Waldo Emerson, has been made accessible to the public primarily through the scholarship of Delores Bird Carpenter. Her extensive work in editing and commenting on *Lidian Jackson Emerson* by Ellen Tucker Emerson and *The Selected Letters of Lidian Jackson Emerson* has been an indispensable resource in writing this book. I've also drawn from many other sources, including *The Letters of Ellen Tucker Emerson,* edited by Edith E. W. Gregg; Carlos Baker's *Emerson Among the Eccentrics;* Raymond R. Borst's *The Thoreau Log;* Joel Porte's *Emerson in His Journals;* Henry Seidel Canby's biography, *Thoreau;* and the work of Phyllis Cole, including *Mary Moody Emerson and the Origins of Transcendentalism.*

I am particularly indebted to Gary Robertson. His questions first led me to Lidian's doorstep, and his friendship and interest have sustained me through the long research and writing process. My deep appreciation goes to Wallace

Kaufman, for his generous encouragement, penetrating comments, and poetic sensibilities; to Bret Lott, for showing me how to shape a novel from the particulars of history; and to Victoria Redel, for her insights and enthusiasm for Lidian's story. Continued and warm thanks to Susan Ramer, my untiring and understanding agent; to Jennifer Weis, my editor at St. Martin's Press, whose interest in my work has spanned a decade; and to her assistant, Stefanie Lindskog, who so promptly and graciously answered my many questions.

I reserve my deepest gratitude for my husband and children, whose devotion, patience, and love have made this book possible.